7/20/09

P9-CQC-863

Praise for the novels of

EMILIE RICHARDS

"This special book is one of the best women's
contemporary novels you might read this year,
and one that you will recommend to all of your friends."
—*Fresh Fiction* on *Sister's Choice*

"Richards subtly stitches together old and new
characters, nimbly embroidering their tales with
an artful balance of empathy and emotion."
—*Booklist* on *Sister's Choice*

"[Richards] draws these women of different generations
together. Richards should've included a special
pull-out hanky insert, but readers looking for
positive resolutions won't be disappointed."
—*Publishers Weekly* on *Sister's Choice*

"Magically interpreting the emotional resonance
of love and loss, betrayal and redemption through
luminously drawn characters…glows with
transcendent warmth, wisdom, grace, and compassion."
—*Booklist* on *Touching Stars*

"[A] heartwarming, richly layered story."
—*Library Journal,* starred review of *Endless Chain*

"Richards's ability to portray compelling characters
who grapple with challenging family issues is laudable,
and this well-crafted tale should score well
with fans of Luanne Rice and Kristin Hannah."
—*Publishers Weekly* on *Fox River*

EMILIE RICHARDS

happiness key

AR CASS COUNTY PUBLIC LIBRARY
400 E. MECHANIC
HARRISONVILLE, MO 64701

MIRA®

0 0022 0355539 2

If you purchased this book without a cover you should be aware
that this book is stolen property. It was reported as "unsold and
destroyed" to the publisher, and neither the author nor the
publisher has received any payment for this "stripped book."

MIRA

Recycling programs
for this product may
not exist in your area.

ISBN-13: 978-0-7783-2660-1

HAPPINESS KEY

Copyright © 2009 by Emilie Richards McGee.

All rights reserved. Except for use in any review, the reproduction or
utilization of this work in whole or in part in any form by any electronic,
mechanical or other means, now known or hereafter invented, including
xerography, photocopying and recording, or in any information storage or
retrieval system, is forbidden without the written permission of the publisher,
MIRA Books, 225 Duncan Mill Road, Don Mills, Ontario, Canada M3B 3K9.

This is a work of fiction. Names, characters, places and incidents are
either the product of the author's imagination or are used fictitiously, and
any resemblance to actual persons, living or dead, business establishments,
events or locales is entirely coincidental.

MIRA and the Star Colophon are trademarks used under license and registered
in Australia, New Zealand, Philippines, United States Patent and Trademark
Office and in other countries.

www.MIRABooks.com

Printed in U.S.A.

With love and thanks to my aunt, Laura Coleman,
for many happy childhood days
on Pass-A-Grille and Treasure Island.

chapter one

The old man still wasn't answering.

Tracy Deloche made a fist and banged the border of Herb Krause's screen door, wincing when a splinter won the round.

Flipping her fist, she dug out the offending sliver with nails that were seriously in need of the attentions of her favorite manicurist. Unfortunately, sweet-natured Hong Hanh was more than two thousand miles away, filing and polishing for outrageous tips at the Beverly Wilshire hotel, while Tracy banged and shouted and tried to collect Herbert Krause's measly rent payment so she could put something in her refrigerator and gas tank.

"Mr. Krause, are you *there?*" she shouted.

"Well, what's up with that?" she muttered when nobody answered. She could see his ancient Dodge sedan parked behind the house. She'd been sure her timing was perfect. Apparently she was as good at collecting money as she was at everything else these days.

Tracy flopped down on a wooden bench beside three carefully arranged orchids in clay pots. Something green and slimy flashed past her and vanished in the Spanish moss mulch. Florida was like that, teeming with things that darted at you day and night, some with more scrawny legs than a bucket of fast-food chicken.

Happiness Key. She almost laughed.

CJ, her ex-husband, was responsible for the name of the "development" where Herb's cottage and four others stood. In a rare stab at poetry, CJ had called this hole the yin and yang of Florida. On one side, white sand beaches with tall palms swaying in a gentle tropical breeze; on the other, Florida's wildest natural beauty. Mangroves and alligators, exotic migratory birds, and marshes alive with Mother Nature's sweetest music. Who couldn't find happiness here? Particularly CJ, who had expected to expand his considerable fortune wiping out most of that music when he developed the land into a marina and upscale condo complex for Florida's snowbirds.

From the side of Herb's cottage, Tracy heard an air conditioner grinding, and the sound made her teeth hurt. Visiting him was like summering in Antarctica. How long before the ancient window unit ended up in the Sun County landfill, and she was down hundreds of dollars for a replacement? Herb was older than the mangroves that blocked access to the bay, older than the burial mounds at the far end of Palmetto Grove Key, where Florida's first residents had dumped their dead. No surprise his internal temperature control was out of whack. Tracy was just glad the old man paid his own electric bill. Evicting one of the state's senior citizens to save a few bucks would get her just the kind of publicity she didn't need.

She'd already had enough of that in California.

Leaning back against the concrete block wall of the cottage, she folded her arms and closed her eyes. Since rolling out of bed that morning, she hadn't looked at a clock, but she supposed it was almost nine.

The air was beginning to sizzle. May on Florida's Gulf Coast might as well be full summer. Of course, she hadn't yet lived here in full summer, so maybe June was going to be that much worse; maybe June was going to be unbearable. But considering how unbearable her whole life had become since her divorce from CJ, what were a few degrees here and there? Let the humidity condense into something thick enough to eat with a spoon. What did she care? She would take it and make something of it.

That was her new mantra. And she hadn't paid some West Coast guru or his slavish followers to find it for her. She'd found it all by herself. For free.

A door creaked nearby, and for a moment she thought maybe Herb Krause had found his way across the frozen tundra of his living room. Then she heard what sounded like a broom moving back and forth over concrete. She opened her eyes and leaned forward to see Herb's neighbor, Alice Brooks, garbed in a voluminous red-and-white housecoat, sweeping her doorstep. It wasn't the first time. Tracy paid only as much attention to her renters as she absolutely had to, but even she hadn't failed to notice Alice outside with her broom morning, noon and night.

If *her* life ever came down to primly snapped housecoats and a stoop clean enough for surgery, she would wade into the gulf until the water was over her head. Then she would simply make herself at home on the bottom and expire.

Alice looked up from her stoop, and her eyes met Tracy's. She seemed puzzled to find her landlady sitting across the lawn on Herb's bench. For a moment she gazed around in confusion.

Tracy pushed herself to her feet and strolled across the wide expanse that separated the cottages. Alice was next on her list anyway, and since Herb was either avoiding her or out for the morning, she might as well move on. Somebody had to pay rent today or Tracy's checking account was going to be as naked as a Paris Hilton video.

"Good morning, Alice," she said, as she covered the distance. She smiled, although the effort seemed to bead, like perspiration, in the resulting creases. "Never a moment's rest, huh?"

"Sand. And trees." Alice shook her head.

"Uh-huh." Tracy wasn't quite sure what was up with Alice, who always seemed the slightest bit off-kilter. "Well, I just thought I'd pick up everybody's rent checks before the sun gets higher."

Alice nodded, her wide forehead crinkling in confusion. "Today?"

"Right. May fifteenth. Rent day. Remember, I said it would be easier if everybody paid on the same day?"

Alice nodded, but she still looked confused. She wore wire-rimmed glasses that were the silvery-gray of her hair, and little button pearl earrings with old-fashioned screws to hold them in place. Deep lines fanned out from her nose to the corners of her mouth, which always drooped and today looked sadder still. Tracy had a feeling the past years hadn't been filled with happy moments for Alice.

Welcome to the club.

A voice rang out from the house, what sounded like a child's, maybe a girl's, from the high pitch. She had already noted a newish Saab in the driveway beside Alice's ten-year-old Hyundai.

"I'm sorry," Tracy said. "Sounds like you have company. I could come back in a little while if that's better."

"Company?"

"Somebody in your house." Tracy pointed to Alice's screen

door. Alice's cottage, like all the others in the little development, was a cinder-block shoebox with a shabby shingle roof. The outside of Alice's was painted a soft yellow, the shutters and doors a bright coral, the sashes and window grills a deep sea-green. For decoration, three turquoise seahorses descended the wall at a forty-five-degree angle. Tracy thought they might be trying to escape.

Alice glanced behind her. "Granddaughter. My son-in-law. Come to live."

Tracy was surprised. "Here? With you?"

A girl with long hair, most likely the aforementioned grand-child, came to the door and flattened her face against the screen. "Hi. Do you have any kids?" she asked hopefully, lips against the mesh.

Tracy tried to remember the terms of Alice's lease. Could renters really invite *anybody* to come and share these cottages without her permission? With vast plans for the property, the paper trail had been thin when CJ rented them out. With thirty days' notice, rentals could be terminated by either party, and all repairs were at the discretion of the owner—that being Tracy now, since good old CJ was engrossed in landlord problems all his own.

The little girl's face was distorted by the screen, an old-fashioned affair that was rusting in places. It was hard to tell how old she was, or anything else about her, through the mesh, but Tracy guessed she wasn't yet an adolescent. Before Tracy could answer, a man's voice rumbled from the back of the house.

"Olivia…"

"Do you?" the girl repeated in a softer voice. "Somebody to play with?"

Tracy imagined what her life would be like now if she and CJ had added a child to their personal equation.

"Not a one," she said with real gratitude. "Sorry. Not even a parakeet."

"Olivia…" The man's voice sounded friendly enough, but his reminder did the trick. Olivia backed away, becoming a three-dimensional figure. Then she disappeared into the house.

"Lee writes them," Alice said.

Tracy turned back to her. "I'm sorry, what was that?"

"Checks. Lee writes them."

"Your son-in-law?"

Alice looked grateful Tracy understood. "He will."

"Great. Would you like to ask him to do it now? While I'm waiting, I'll just try Herb again. His car's there, but when I knocked earlier, he didn't answer."

"Haven't seen him."

Tracy filed that away. Was Herb gone, or had he moved out? *Without paying.*

"Lee takes care of…things," Alice continued.

Tracy supposed Alice's living arrangements didn't really matter, as long as she paid her rent on time and vacated once she was asked to. For now, Tracy needed to stay on her good side, so she manufactured another smile.

"I'm glad you have family to help. That's important."

Alice wasn't quite a shuffler, but she did drag her slipper-clad feet as she started back inside the house. Before she closed the door, Tracy saw her cast a longing glance at the broom.

As she started back to Herb Krause's cottage, Tracy had to admit that in a pinch, having family *was* important. She knew that from experience, because for all practical purposes, she had no one. She was newly divorced, abandoned by her parents and the majority of her friends. To add insult to injury, she had been transported to a mosquito-ridden swamp and forced to grovel for money to buy groceries.

At least CJ, who was probably sunning himself in the prison yard at Victorville, knew where his next meal was coming from. So what if he breakfasted on powdered eggs, stale toast and watery coffee? No matter what other trouble he ran into in the next twenty years, at least the Feds would make sure his stomach was never empty.

That was something, at least. She hoped CJ was learning to count his blessings. In the decades ahead he would need to focus on every single one.

"Well, here she comes."

Wanda Gray set *The Pirate's Bride* beside her on the lounge chair under the jacaranda tree in her front yard and watched the new landlady trudging up the dirt road toward her cottage.

"Kenny…" She aimed her voice toward the screen door and her husband. "It's that Deloche woman, come for her check. Don't you interfere now. I'm going to handle this."

She thought she heard a grunt, but she wasn't sure. A grunt was as much as she got out of Ken these days. She was sorry she hadn't circled the date of their last conversation on the calendar. No matter. A calendar that old had already been recycled into cheap napkins or some of that nasty-looking stationary no normal person ever wrote a letter on.

"Don't trouble yourself none," she said under her breath. "Why would you start now, seeing as you haven't done a blessed thing around the house since Pluto was a pup?" She probably should have circled *that* date, too.

She had no intention of standing to greet the Deloche woman. She took off her glasses and set them next to her book before she smoothed her sundress over pudgy knees. One hand went to her lacquered red curls, the roots freshly tinted with her favorite copper shimmer. But that was as much primping as she was going to do. So what if Tracy Deloche was as skinny as one of those girls on *Sex in the City?* Wanda Gray was no second fiddle, not even at fifty-six.

What exactly did the young woman have to be snooty about, anyway? Sure, she owned this twenty-five-acre spit of land on Palmetto Grove Key, across the bay from the town of Palmetto Grove, and it was probably worth millions. But exactly what good was it doing her? Ms. Deloche was what they called land-poor, and it served her right for calling a dump like this Happiness Key, and thinking that everybody and his Uncle Jack would come flocking just because of its fancy name.

From what Wanda could tell, the Deloche woman was going to have one heck of a time getting rid of the place, what with the economy the way it was in Florida, plus all those people at Wild Florida screaming because the Army Corps of Engineers had given Ms. Deloche's ex a permit for development, then running the whole thing through the courts. Add the folks who wanted to save every inch of the mangroves, and the ones who thought increasing traffic and widening the road would damage that old Indian mound. Ms. Deloche had one fine mess on her hands, and right now Wanda aimed to add to it.

With enthusiasm.

Today the landlady was dressed in baggy black capris and a matching bikini top, with a gauzy white shirt exposing everything but her shoulders and arms. Her midriff, chest and neck were taut and tan; her dark brown hair fell straight as an arrow on its way to her shoulders. She had one of those smiles money *could* buy, and the kind of unlined skin that was best slathered with sunblock. Wanda hoped she wasn't thinking that far ahead. A line or two would serve her right.

By the time Tracy finally arrived, Wanda was waiting, fingertips steepled, like she had all the time in the world.

"Hi, Wanda," Tracy said, flashing ten-thousand-dollar teeth. "You look cool and comfortable."

Wanda wasn't fooled. Tracy Deloche wouldn't notice if Wanda was writhing in the final throes of a coral snake bite.

"You look cool and comfy yourself." Wanda lifted a brow. "What with you wearing a bathing suit and all."

"Trust me, this top's never seen the water. It would fall apart."

"Now isn't that something? A bathing suit you can't get wet. What'll they think of next?"

Tracy smiled, as if to say the time for chitchat had expired. "I won't keep you from your book." Her gaze flashed down to the cover of Wanda's favorite paperback, then back up again, but she didn't quite conquer a smirk. "I was just stopping by to pick up your rent check."

"I thought maybe that's why you'd come." Wanda didn't move.

"Then it's ready?"

"Nope. Not ready at all, seeing as I got a list of things that got to be done before you get even one penny." Wanda watched with pleasure as Tracy's smirk faded. The second it was gone, she dove in for the kill.

"And before you remind me our lease—if that's what you want to call that scrap of paper Kenny signed—says you don't have to do a thing on the place, I'll just tell *you* I had a chat with some folks over at the courthouse this week and told them all the things that were wrong here."

Wanda paused just long enough to let that sink in. "Of course, I didn't tell them exactly where I lived. Not *yet*. But they were talking about condemning this shack if half the things I said were true. So I figure that you, being a smart woman and well-educated…you'll agree that making a few repairs now and keeping the renters you have will serve a lot better than going through all that rigamarole before you can find new ones."

Tracy was silent. Wanda wondered if she was trying to keep her temper.

"You want that list?" Wanda asked at last.

"Did you ever consider just telling me the problems and seeing if we could resolve them?"

"Honey, people like you don't ask people like me to sign such a stinking old lease unless you're planning to hold it over our heads."

"Honey…" Tracy's eyes narrowed, and the word came out more like boiling cane syrup. "People like *me* know that people like *you* happen to be married to a cop. So even if I was a slumlord, which wasn't ever one of those things I wanted to be when I grew up, I'd have thought twice about ignoring real problems here."

Wanda glanced down at her hot pink nails, noting the tiniest chip on the polish of one. She supposed the chip was due to that platter of grouper she'd carried to table six yesterday. She had known better than to carry all that grouper in one attempt, without a free hand for emergencies, like the swinging door that had raked her fingertips.

She looked up again. "You want the list? I got it right here. 'Course, all you really have to do is look around a little. I'd have guessed you'd do that before now, on account of my Ken being that cop you were talking about."

"Give me a break, okay? I've been here just two weeks. I've spent the whole time mucking out that hovel I'm living in. I haven't exactly had time for house inspections."

"Nope, you been hoping we'd just take that lease at face value. Don't go pretending it's not so."

Wanda lifted an envelope from under her book and held it out. "Stove's throwing out so much gas both those crotons outside my kitchen window keeled over. Roof's leaking in the bathroom. Toilet's got more rust than a battleship. And if I wanted pets, I'd get me a kitty cat, not some flock of palmetto bugs. I already paid for an exterminator and somebody to patch up some of the biggest holes where they were getting in. You can take that off my rent."

"Gosh, no travertine tile? No granite counters?"

Wanda put the envelope on top of her book when Tracy didn't take it. "You just go ahead and be sarcastic. But you think about it. We're not going anywhere while you do. You have any idea how hard it is to evict somebody these days? Especially when the sheriff happens to be friends with a certain member of the Palmetto Grove police force?"

Tracy leaned over and snatched the envelope. "I'll do what I can, but don't expect miracles."

Wanda watched her stalk down the road toward the cottage where those folks from India had taken up residence. Wanda didn't try to stop her, even though she knew they weren't at home because she had seen them leave an hour ago. At least if the landlady ever found them, the dark-skinned young couple at the end of the road spoke English. Wanda had to give them that much. That was one thing about Indians. They usually came knowing English and had good manners. But their presence some fifty yards away was just another sign that this place where Ken had settled her was a world filled with strangers. It was never going to feel like home.

"Happiness Key, my eyelash."

Morosely, she watched Tracy Deloche's tight little butt swing in a determined rhythm until the young woman was finally out of sight. She didn't even yell inside to tell Ken she'd taken care of the problem. Wanda knew what a waste of time sounded like.

chapter two

Rishi ate cereal for breakfast, whatever brand Janya bought him at the grocery store, usually whatever happened to be on sale. Her husband preferred cereal as sweet as candy and as light as a cloud, smothered with milk until it melted into a soggy paste. But perhaps this, like so many things, was her fault. Perhaps Rishi would eat a better breakfast if she made an effort to prepare some of the foods her mother had served in the morning.

Janya dreamed of childhood breakfasts of steaming masala milk and *poha* made with flattened rice, served with a sprinkling of grated coconut. She craved *idli*, the comforting rice dumpling dipped in fiery lentil *sambar*, and their cook's richly spiced omelets, served with an array of breads from the grill or oven. Sometimes she imagined waking to a morning array of fruits. Mangoes and papayas, pomegranates and particularly *chikku*, with its sweet caramel flesh, something she had not seen in stores here in Florida.

But Rishi wasn't used to such foods, so he didn't ache for them. The aunt who had raised him in Massachusetts had rarely prepared such delicacies for her own family, and even more rarely for Rishi. Rishi was her husband's orphaned nephew, and as such, the aunt was required to make him a home. But she was not required to love him, as she had loved her own sons.

Now Rishi was Janya's responsibility, and she, too, was required to make him a home. But she wasn't required to love her new husband as she had once loved the man she had lost. Janya was fulfilling the basics of her marriage contract. She shared Rishi's home, kept it tidy and put meals on the table. She even shared Rishi's bed, but she could never share her heart, nor could she accept his, although she knew that was what he hoped for.

This morning Rishi had left early for work, not pausing to eat his cornflakes or brew himself a cup of coffee. He had risen and left by the time she returned from her sunrise walk on the beach to their quiet little house that smelled like incense and rotting vegetation. Relieved that she would not have to make vacuous conversation, she showered, then dressed in an informal *salwar-kameez*, an embroidered cotton shirt, with pants that narrowed at the ankle. Finally, before she could change her mind, she consulted the bus schedule, locked the door and set off down the road that bisected the peninsula where their house stood.

Janya was glad she didn't have to pass any of her neighbors' houses, although it was doubtful any of them, except perhaps Mr. Krause, would expect her to stop for a conversation. The walk was long and tiring, and by the time she came home, the sun would torment every step. At least the bench at the bus stop was positioned beneath a huge banyan tree.

She waited alone, watching as cars with tops down and radios screaming sailed by. Few people rode the bus in Palmetto Grove, and accordingly, it only came and went infrequently. People did not hang out of doors or jostle fellow passengers, the way they did at home. She always had a seat; she never had strangers leaning against her or small children pulling at her clothes.

If the bus didn't remind her of home, the banyan did. The banyan was India's national tree, and the word itself was Gujarati. She still remembered a part of a Vedic text she had learned in school, although she could no longer recite it in Sanskrit.

Brahma-shaped at the root, Vishnu-shaped in the middle, and Shiva-shaped at the top, we salute you, the king of all trees.

There was a day in June when women could fast and pray to the banyan, and ask that each time they were reborn, they be rewarded with the same husbands. June was not far away, but this was a ritual in which Janya would certainly not participate. Not now or ever.

The banyan had been planted in Florida almost a century ago by the inventor Thomas Edison. Rishi had told Janya this just yesterday, on a sightseeing trip to Fort Myers that had been calculated to make her fall in love with her new country. Her husband was fond of the oddest details, of facts and bits of information he could categorize and store in his computerlike brain. His enthusiasm for the trivial made her head ache.

She told herself not to think about Rishi and their marriage. She wanted to savor these brief moments of independence. At the very least, she wanted to pretend she was like everybody else, only mildly unhappy with her lot.

The bus arrived on time, and as always, this seemed almost miraculous. She climbed aboard quickly, afraid it might leave while she was shaking her head in wonder.

The ride was short. Palmetto Grove was a peaceful city, small and emerald-green, with bursts of tropical color. Cars rarely honked their horns, and pedestrians were perfectly safe as they strolled across the streets. A small city center just blocks from the gulf held shops for renting videos, restaurants with pleasant outdoor seating, and stores that sold hardware, auto parts and wedding cakes. Sidewalks gleamed in the sunshine, and women of all ages, in shorts or sundresses, walked arm in arm with men sporting tans and sunglasses.

Coming to town always made Janya feel so homesick she could hardly bear it. Not because Palmetto Grove was anything like Mulund, the suburb of Mumbai where she had been raised. Because it *wasn't*. Things were so easy here, so sensible, so polite, so utterly different. She had never wanted to leave India. Unlike so many of the educated upper class who had seen their future in other places, she had always seen hers where she was born. Now she wondered if she would ever go home again.

Last night, to keep homesickness at bay, she had made a list of what she would do today when she got off the bus. Take documentation of her address to the small downtown library so she could get books. Visit the specialty grocery store that sold a variety of lentils and spices, along with hummus and fresh pita bread for the town's transplanted Mideasterners, jerk seasoning for the Jamaicans, and plantain chips and Sunchy tropical juices for the Cubans. Check out the recreation center.

As part of his campaign to make her happy, Rishi had told her about the center. There were classes, he said, for anybody who lived in Palmetto Grove. The fees were small, and she would meet others like herself, young women with more time than money. He had insisted it would be good to leave the house and get to know Americans. Someday she would be one, too.

This was an event she did not look forward to. To Janya, all Americans seemed lonely. So much space around them. So little family. Old people like Herbert Krause and Alice Brooks lived alone and took care of their own needs. Where were the children, the grandchildren, the nieces and nephews, to feed and clothe them?

Of course, sometimes family was worse than nothing. She knew this, too.

An hour later Janya had a library card and two books, red and yellow lentils, asafoetida and fenugreek, and six cans of Cuban fruit nectar. After debating whether it was time to head home, she started toward the recreation center for the last stop of the morning.

The Henrietta Claiborne Recreation Center was a gift to the town of Palmetto Grove from an eccentric hamburger heiress whose car had broken down outside of town four years ago, while she was crisscrossing the state, alone and incognito, from her Palm Beach mansion to its twin in Newport, Rhode Island. While she waited in a local café for somebody to drive to Tampa and retrieve a part for her Jaguar—she wasn't *that* incognito—Henrietta had overhead a conversation about how badly the town needed a recreational center so the people who lived there year-round would have a place to socialize, and the town's children and teenagers would have a place for their activities.

Henrietta was so impressed by the courtesy and helpfulness of Palmetto Grove's citizenry that she wrote a check on the spot, and presented it to the mayor just minutes before she and the newly repaired Jaguar cruised out of town again. The treasurer had taken a week to send the check to the bank, believing that the strange old lady was delusional. He, like the mayor, had wanted to give her a head start so nobody would find her if the bank pressed charges.

If Rishi hadn't told Janya this story in excruciating detail, she would have learned it now from the plaque beside the center's front door.

Inside, the building still smelled new. The walls were painted in creamy pastels. Dusty rose for one hallway fanning away from the reception area, aqua for the one on the opposite side. The reception area was flanked by floor-to-ceiling windows, and the walls surrounding these were a buttery-yellow. Once school let out, children and teenagers would be everywhere, but today there were only a few people in sight. A woman with a toddler on her hip reading notices on the bulletin board. A man signing a list to one side of the long entryway counter. The woman seated behind it, who was as plain and starched as one of the nuns who had taught Janya as a girl, smiled a welcome.

"If you know where you're going, ignore me," she told Janya. "But if I can help, let me know."

Janya felt encouraged. "I came to see what classes you offer."

The woman smiled again. "Do you know what you're interested in? We have a few that are still open. Some exercise classes, basic computer skills, conversational Spanish, choosing books for children…"

"Exercise classes?" If Janya was going to come here, she wanted more incentive than a new language—she already spoke three fluently, and could read and be understood in two more. And she had no need of children's books.

"We have a volleyball league that still needs a few people."

Janya shook her head.

"Yoga."

She shook again.

"Belly dancing?"

"No, I don't think so."

"Dance aerobics."

Janya inclined her head in question. "What is that?"

"Dancing to routines that get you in shape. Our teacher's great. I can guarantee you'd love it. I do the evening class."

Despite herself, Janya was interested. She loved to dance, was an unabashed fan of Bollywood extravaganzas, and as a girl had often cavorted and sung to routines she and her cousin Padmini invented and sometimes filmed with Padmini's video camera.

That unfortunate reminder of home sobered her immediately. But the receptionist didn't notice. She had stopped noticing anything else the moment Janya smiled.

The woman got to her feet and came around the desk, checking her watch. "Come with me. They're about halfway through. You can drop in for the rest of the session at no charge. Then you can sign up or just drop in for four dollars a shot whenever you feel like it."

"Oh, no, I couldn't—"

"Sure you can. You don't have to stay a minute longer than you want. You can just watch and see if you like it."

Janya didn't want to make a fuss and refuse, not when the woman was so kind. "Thank you very much."

As they walked down the pink hallway, the receptionist outlined an extensive program. "And then we have all the pool activities. Water aerobics, and lessons for beginners all the way up to lifesaving."

Janya felt particularly strange here. The woman acted as if she belonged, as if it was a normal thing to check out a class she might want to attend. She wanted to explain that this was not her country, that she didn't belong in Florida or here in this center, that she would not feel comfortable dancing with people she didn't know. But they were in the doorway to the gymnasium, and then inside a portion of it walled off by a folding screen, before she could find a way to leave.

A group of about a dozen women were throwing their arms around and sliding their feet to music the Americans called "country." No one paid attention when the door opened except the instructor in the front, a well-proportioned woman in her thirties in pants that were tight and shiny, and a knit shirt held up by tiny straps.

"Feel free to watch or join in," the receptionist told her, voice lowered just enough that Janya could still hear it over the loud music. "But if you don't like this one, we'll find you something else. Let me know." She patted Janya on the shoulder and slipped back out the door.

Janya wondered if there was a back exit to the building so she could sneak out without disappointing anybody.

At that moment the instructor caught her eye and pointed, shouting as she did. "Why don't you get right there, at the end of the back line? Just follow the people in front of you. Nobody's any good at this yet. Have fun."

Now she couldn't leave. Janya was trapped in this as she had been trapped in so many other things. With little choice, she set her groceries awkwardly on the floor by the door and slipped into the back line as three women made room. She had no idea what she was doing, but she began to follow the movements of the slender dark-haired woman in front of her. Only when the dance required everyone to spin around and she didn't, did she realize the woman was Tracy Deloche, her landlord.

The Henrietta Claiborne Recreation Center reminded Tracy of a sprawling public high school, although she'd never attended one of those herself. The slightest noises echoed; the floors were scuffed from too many gym shoes sliding and squeaking; the architect had been less interested in aesthetics than utility. The halls were wide enough to run the Kentucky Derby, and the walls were bare of adornments. She missed her gym at home, where each session began with a personal trainer and ended with a massage. She missed the steam room and sauna, the grotto with its tepid plunge pool and soothing waterfall, the beverage table with fragrant herbal teas and bowls of fresh fruit.

Still, exercise was exercise, and after a frustrating couple of days, swinging her arms and jumping around felt good. She was just surprised to find one of her renters in the line behind her. Sure, it was an equal opportunity kind of place, but the Kapur woman—her first name escaped Tracy—was the last person she would have expected. Of course, she'd never given any thought to the way people in other countries chose to exercise. Maybe India or Pakistan, or wherever the Kapurs were from, had dance classes on every corner. Maybe dancing was a requirement of their religion.

Mrs. Kapur looked to be younger than Tracy. She had a curvy figure with womanly hips instead of the boyish shape that was in fashion. But there was no denying her beauty. Today her long black hair was braided, but one afternoon Tracy had seen it falling halfway down her back. She'd never seen hair so thick, with a natural wave right at home in the Florida humidity. The young woman had been born with skin the color so many of Tracy's friends struggled to perfect in tanning beds. She had black eyes without a fleck of brown, huge and round, and rimmed with thick black lashes under arching brows. She was quite simply exquisite, and probably didn't have to work at it.

Tracy was growing accustomed to finding the world unfair.

The music stopped for the last time, and her renter started toward the door, but Tracy caught up with her.

"Hi. I'm sorry, I can't remember your first name."

The young woman looked more resigned than pleased. "Janya."

"John-ya." Tracy attempted to commit it to memory. "That's pretty."

Janya smiled just enough to reveal strong white teeth, almost perfect, except for one eyetooth that wasn't quite aligned.

Tracy, whose father advertised himself as orthodontist to the stars, recognized a smile that was exactly the way the creator had made it, with no intervention.

Tracy wasted no time getting to the point. "I stopped by your house yesterday, and this morning, too. To collect the rent."

"It was due yesterday, correct? We were gone in the day, but my husband took it to your house last night."

Tracy wondered if stiffing the landlord was a worldwide custom. "I don't think so. It wasn't in my mailbox."

"Rishi said that he did not want to leave it where someone might take it. So he slipped it under your door."

Tracy had left the house by the kitchen door that morning and never thought to look anywhere except in the mailbox beside the road. The check was probably in her living room right now, and she had missed it.

"Oh, well, that explains it." From Janya's expression, she realized more was required. "Thank you, or rather, thank him for me. You're the only renters I didn't have to dun."

"Dun?"

"Harass. Beg. You know, insist."

"I know insist." Janya turned away, but Tracy, who felt a stab of guilt for accusing the woman of something she hadn't done, put her hand on her arm.

"How did you like the class?"

"I think it has been a long time since I have done so much so fast."

"It was pretty strenuous, wasn't it?"

"And now I must hurry to the bus stop or I will miss the next bus."

Janya turned away again, but Tracy stopped her. "You took the bus? If you're just heading home, why don't you come with me? I'll drop you off. It's not out of my way."

"Thank you, but that's not required."

"Well, right, of course it's not. But I'm offering. It's no skin off my nose."

"Skin off your nose?" Janya wrinkled hers.

"It's no trouble. Just another way of saying it." Tracy glanced at her watch. "But I have to leave right now. I can't seem to find Herb Krause, and I'm hoping he'll stop home for lunch. You know how these senior citizens are. They swear Social Security doesn't extend as far as a fast-food hamburger."

She realized she was leaving Janya in the dust. The woman's English was excellent, although with hints of the rounded vowels and distinctive rise and fall in pitch that late-night comedians loved to imitate. But Tracy had been speaking quickly, probably too quickly. She paused.

"So, are you coming?" she asked, after she thought Janya had been given enough time to process everything she'd said.

"Yes, thank you."

"I'm parked out front." Tracy circled her, strode through the door and out into the hallway.

In the reception area, Janya paused, then looked chagrined. "I'm sorry, but I forgot my groceries. I must go back. Please go on without me."

Tracy waved off the suggestion. "I'm not in that much of a hurry."

Janya disappeared the way they had come, leaving Tracy beside the community bulletin board. Tracy tapped her foot, glancing over the notices while she waited. Somebody wanted a job babysitting for the summer. She shook her head at a copy machine photo of a calico cat with a phone number and "Reward" in bold letters beneath it. Business cards littered the board. She took a pad out of her purse and jotted down numbers for a roofer and plumber. She hoped Wanda Gray had been exaggerating the problems at her cottage, but considering the state of Tracy's own, she doubted it.

Half of the board was devoted to official notices, county and city. One, in the most prominent spot, stood out. The heading read "Henrietta Claiborne Recreation Center" and below that "Job Openings."

She scanned the notice, starting at the bottom and working up. The center was looking for weekend maintenance personnel. They needed another swimming instructor for the summer. Keeping a bevy of little kids from drowning was a nightmare. Tracy knew that from experience, having been required to do it in college.

At the top of the notice was the most important job, taking up more than half the space, with "filled" scrawled across it in a felt tip pen. Recreational supervisor. The position was temporary, terminating in the fall when the present supervisor returned from maternity leave. She read the list of duties. She was only halfway through when Janya returned with two plastic bags in hand. But by then she'd figured out that the unfortunate new employee had the task of managing the youth program for the upcoming summer, as well as leading a hefty number of activities. Whoever had taken the position at this late date deserved a CEO's paycheck.

"All set?" Tracy led the way. In the parking lot, she motioned to what was fast becoming a vintage BMW convertible roadster. "Hop in."

Janya stroked the silver paint. "I think you must enjoy driving this."

"I learned to drive in this car."

"It's that old?"

Tracy felt the question to the tips of her toes. "Ancient, and so am I."

Janya smiled. "Neither of you is quite ready for the grave."

Tracy unlocked Janya's door. "My ex thought the car was. When we got married, he wanted me to sell it, but I was sentimentally attached, so we squirreled it away in our garage. My father bought it for me, or I guess I ought to say he was there when I bought it. He took me to the dealer the day I got my learner's permit and told me to pick out anything I wanted, while he sat in his car and talked to his receptionist on the car phone."

She straightened, realizing how that had sounded. She no longer hung out with people who understood that kind of life. To friends at home, this would have been wryly funny, particularly those who knew that dear old Dad and Summer, the receptionist, were now married and raising a second family.

"It's a good thing I hung on to the car," she said, trying for a more self-deprecating tone. "It's too old to be valuable."

She got in the driver's seat and started the engine. They drove in silence, crossing a low bridge, then turning onto the narrow road that led to Happiness Key. Tracy was about to drop Janya at her house, the first of the five in the "development," when she had an idea.

"I hate to ask a favor," she said, although it wasn't really true. "But would you come with me to Mr. Krause's? Just for a moment? If he doesn't answer, I'm going to peek inside and see if he's still living there. If I'm going to unlock his door, I'd like to have you there, you know, as a witness that nothing was disturbed."

"You must have a witness?"

"I think so." Tracy had experienced enough persecution in the days leading up to CJ's arrest and later during his trial. She didn't want a repeat.

In the weeks since she had moved to Happiness Key, the one thing Tracy could say about her new "neighborhood" was that everyone, with the exception of Herb Krause, was obsessed with privacy. She appreciated this, since, of course, she had no desire to socialize with her neighbors, either.

Janya's desire not to get involved made sense to her. But when Janya didn't answer, she added, "You can stay on the steps. I don't expect you to come inside. I'm only going to poke my head in."

"I can do that."

"You can leave as soon as I know what's up." Tracy stopped in front of Herb's place.

"He has lovely plants, doesn't he?"

Tracy hadn't thought about it. But now she saw that Janya was right. Herb Krause was some gardener. There were at least twenty pots placed strategically around the front yard of the little house. Some were huge. Banana trees, palms, even citrus. She wondered if Herb gardened this way so he could cart his plants from place to place when he moved. If so, maybe he was still in residence. The plants sure were.

Both women exited the roadster and started up the path. Janya paused to feel the soil in one of the larger pots, which was home to a blooming double hibiscus in shades of peach.

"Perhaps he is gone," Janya said. "This is very dry."

"Well, maybe we can tell." Tracy pulled out the ring of keys copied from the master set by the Realtor who had rented the properties for CJ. In those days, renters had been more a way to keep vandals from the property than to provide income.

Tracy knocked and called Herb's name, then pounded with the side of her fist, getting another splinter for her efforts.

"I guess I have no choice." She picked at the side of her hand, then she looked to Janya for confirmation. Janya shrugged.

Tracy held the key ring up to the light and found the one marked Krause. Unfortunately, it didn't fit. As Janya watched, she tried another key on the ring, then another. None of them fit.

"Well, that's a bummer. I guess I'll have to go find the Realtor and get her to dig out the originals."

Janya stepped closer and, without a word, turned the knob. The door swung open. "I didn't think he was a man to lock out others," she said, stepping back so Tracy could get inside.

Tracy felt foolish. "Well, I'm surprised. I bought a dead bolt for *my* door."

"I will wait here."

Tracy felt even more foolish. She was suddenly apprehensive about walking inside Herb's house without permission. Technically, maybe, the house belonged to her, but in her weeks here, she had never taken him up on his offer to see the inside. She had been too busy settling in, and she'd been afraid that Herb would rope her into an interminable conversation, complete with a photo display of places he had traveled, pets long gone, and great-grandchildren. Now, as she stepped over the threshold, she had a flash of regret. This didn't seem like exactly the right moment to accept his warm hospitality.

Cold hospitality. As she had guessed earlier, the temperature inside the little house was freezing, but this was even worse than she'd imagined.

"Lord, it's like ice in here," she told Janya, glancing back at the other woman.

"It is unlikely, then, that he's left for good. Unless you are paying for his electricity?"

Tracy gave a sharp shake of her head. She had noticed something else. A faint smell, and not a pleasant one. Suddenly she was torn between leaving and going forward. But who would she call to investigate? CJ was behind bars; neither of her parents had any interest in her new life, and to date, she hadn't made a single friend in Florida.

She felt completely alone. For good reason. She was.

"I think this isn't going to be good news," she said, stalling.

"I think we had better make certain."

Tracy glanced back at Janya once more and saw written on the young woman's face what she herself now suspected.

Tracy chewed her lip. Then she pressed her lips together, trying not to ask, wanting not to be beholden to a person from a different culture, a woman with whom she had absolutely nothing in common.

"I'll come with you," Janya said. "But we must do it quickly, before I change my mind."

Tracy was relieved, grateful *and* embarrassed. "I'm sorry. I guess I'm a wuss."

"Wuss?"

"Coward."

"We can be cowards together, then." Janya joined her inside the little living room.

"I've never been in here. I guess that's the bedroom." Tracy nodded toward a door to the left. "That's where the air conditioner is."

"He has worked hard on the house. Everything is fresh and new. And clean."

"I'm afraid it doesn't smell clean."

Janya started toward the bedroom. "One peek, then we leave."

"Mr. Krause?" Tracy called, as they strode across the room. She registered plain furniture in good repair, a glass-topped coffee table with newspapers stacked neatly on top. Several wilting houseplants.

They stopped at the door. Tracy knew this was up to her. She took a breath and held it, then she turned the knob and pushed it open.

Herb Krause was not on vacation, nor had he moved away. He was lying fully dressed in cotton trousers and a dress shirt on a bed he had carefully made before his final nap, one arm outstretched and hand turned up. Horrified, Tracy moved a little closer to see what her renter had been holding. A key rested in his palm, fingers loosely trapping it there, but the old man was never going to open a door with this key again.

Herb Krause was blue, stiff, and very, very dead.

chapter three

"If an autopsy was required, the medical examiner could pin-point it, but I'd say he's been dead thirty-six hours, tops. The temperature in here slowed everything and makes it harder to tell."

The shiny-headed deputy from the sheriff's department looked up from his clipboard. Judging by his lack of expression, he had faced a lot of dead bodies. "You can be glad he died across from the air-conditioning vents."

"I'm overwhelmed with gratitude," Tracy said.

He lifted a spindly brow that made it clear the hairless head wasn't a fashion statement. "Then while you're at it, be glad that until you got here, the place was sealed like a tomb. At least the insects didn't find him first."

She repressed a shudder. Under the inevitable odor of death's final moments, Tracy had noted the fragrance of insecticide. Herb Krause had been locked in a war with the insect world. At least he had won the final battle.

Herb's death was just one more piece of business for the pro-fessionals who had been called. The sheriff's department had arrived, surveyed the scene, then called Herb's physician, whose name Tracy had discovered from a prescription bottle beside the bed. After that conversation, the doctor had agreed to sign the death certificate, as law required, then he'd checked Herb's records and told the deputy which funeral home to call. The body was being carted outside by their employees, who had arrived quickly.

The deputy finished his forms, passed the clipboard over to Tracy, then slipped his pen in his shirt pocket after she signed. "If you can stay around a little while, you should air it out some more and get all the bedding to the curb for trash pickup. I'm sure his next of kin will be grateful."

"The trash truck comes tomorrow or Sunday. A private contractor. Next of kin…" Tracy hadn't thought that far. Surely Herb had somebody. But how would she know? She had avoided the old man at every turn.

"The funeral home will need addresses if you've got them," he said. "Mr. Krause prepaid his funeral, but the director tells me there's an annoying lack of information in his file."

"I'll have to look around." Tracy didn't want to admit she was clueless. That sounded coldhearted, as if she had taken absolutely no interest in her renter. Which happened to be true.

"Oh, he had this in his hand." The deputy handed Tracy the key she had noted. "Who knows why. I don't think he was planning to go anywhere. His pockets were empty. Nothing else on him. Just the clothes on his back."

Tracy touched the man's arm as he started to move away. "I was over here knocking on his door yesterday. Do you think he, you know, suffered? That he was just lying here for hours, or maybe days, like…dying?"

"No. I think he probably got up yesterday, got dressed, then felt a little strange. The bed was made, so he'd been up at least that long. He probably lay back down, thinking he'd feel better in a minute, had a massive heart attack and went like that." He snapped his fingers. "We should all go that easy. You saw him. He looked perfectly peaceful. No sign of a struggle."

"I guess."

"Call in that information once you get it, okay?" The deputy gave her a business card and left. Tracy was still staring at it when she heard the minivan from the funeral home head down the road with Herb's body inside. Judging from the diminishing screech of the police radio, the deputy was right behind.

"Well, that's one rent I won't collect this month." She stuffed the card in her pocket.

She didn't feel as cavalier as she sounded. She had never seen a corpse, except on television, and these days you were more likely to see a decomposing body on the little screen than a commercial for something you really needed.

But the real thing? That was different. On a scale ranging from serene to terrified, Herb Krause might well have looked peaceful, but her first thought after the shock was that Herb looked lonely.

Were people supposed to die alone and undiscovered? Was that going to be her fate, too?

Tracy heard footsteps and turned to see Janya Kapur in the doorway.

"I saw them drive away," Janya said.

"The deputy said he died fast and easily."

"He was old. Perhaps he was prepared."

"Is that possible?"

Janya wrinkled her arrow-straight nose. "I brought incense."

"Incense?" Tracy wondered if this was a Hindu or Buddhist thing. Was Janya going to scare away evil spirits or send Herb's soul to his next life on a puff of perfumed smoke?

The other woman seemed to read her mind. "I thought we

should open the windows, then light some to make the house smell better."

Tracy remembered what the paramedic had said. "That's nice of you."

"I'll start with the windows in the living room."

Once Janya was gone, Tracy crossed the bedroom, flipped the air conditioner to the fan setting and cranked open the only window that was still closed. Being in here, where Herb had so recently drawn his final breath, gave her the creeps, but the fresh air helped.

With distaste, she went into the kitchen and found extralarge plastic garbage bags. She stripped off the sheets and mattress cover, and using the bags like gloves, stuffed everything inside another one, triple-bagged it and fastened it tight. The mattress would have to go to the curb, too, but she was lucky this was the worst of it. Television had taught her that much.

Toting a square floor fan, Janya came back in, searched for and found a plug, and turned it on. The fan began to whir demurely.

"I really do appreciate your help," Tracy said.

"I feel sad for him. I want to do something."

Tracy sought out the bathroom, a cramped affair with 1950s tile in shades of pink and gray, and a matching gray sink. Everything was old, and funky enough to be trendy, and she wondered if Herb had found it so or merely outdated, a reminder that the house could not be remodeled to his tastes. She washed her hands, then washed them again for good measure.

The house was warming quickly, but now fresh air and Janya's incense scented the air. Herb's life was over, and by tomorrow, there would be no reminders he had died here.

"I guess I need to get the mattress out to the curb, too," Tracy told Janya, who was waiting in the living room. "But I'm going to wait until tonight."

"I think I'll water his plants. He took such good care of them. I know he would not want them to die."

"Just because he has." Tracy immediately realized how the remark must have sounded. "Right. Thanks." She was glad not to have to worry about them herself. In fact, she probably wouldn't have thought of it.

"Then I'll be going," Janya said. "But first, will you mind if I turn on a lamp in the room where he died? It's a custom in my country." She left, then returned quickly.

Tracy had been scanning the living room, which was almost sadly neat. She didn't know how Herb had passed most of his time, but some portion of it had been spent on the minutiae of daily life.

"Janya, did you know Herb? Better than I did, I mean. I don't see any photos around. The deputy says the funeral director wants the phone numbers for his next of kin. You don't happen to know who they are and where they live, do you?"

"We only spoke a few times. He never told me anything about himself." Janya spoke in a lower tone. "And I never told him anything about my life, either. Although I think he might have liked that."

Tracy didn't want to feel guilty. After all, the only connection she and Herb Krause had shared was the upcoming rent check. Still, she couldn't forget the times she had made sure he wasn't outside so she could sneak by his cottage and avoid a conversation.

"I guess if there's nothing on the rental agreement, I'll have to go through his things to see what I can find. His family will need to be notified. I'm sure they'll want some of his stuff." Although as she said this, Tracy wondered. There was nothing in sight that was anything like an heirloom. The furniture was inexpensive and unremarkable. Knickknacks had obviously never been his passion.

"I hope you find what you're looking for," Janya said politely.

Tracy had given up looking for *anything*. But she knew Janya was only talking about Herb.

Ken was gone, but that was no surprise. Wanda's husband had left the house before she even opened her eyes. She doubted she would see him at all today, even though it was her day off from the restaurant. Most nights he got home after she'd already gone to bed, which was fine with her, since they never did anything interesting on the pillow-top mattress anymore, no way, no how.

She wasn't sure where her husband went and what he did when work was over. She *was* sure she didn't care anymore. Ken could be whooping it up with his fellow officers or with some cute young thing who thought hanging out with a cop was some sort of Dirty Harry marathon. Whatever was going on, she had lost interest. A woman was supposed to fight for her man, but what happened if he wasn't worth so much as a rip in her pantyhose?

Sunlight was pouring through the slits between the bedroom blinds, and she had been sitting on the edge of the bed long enough. She wished, as she always did, that she had not promised her son she would never smoke again. Then she headed for the bathroom.

One squint in the mirror convinced her she had not, as hoped, indulged in genuine beauty sleep last night. She had been plagued with hot flashes. If she'd slept soundly in between, the evidence was nowhere to be seen. She had bags under her eyes, crow's-feet at the sides, furrows shooting up between her eyebrows like twin exclamation points. The signs of aging still surprised her.

No wonder Ken didn't find his way home very often.

After a tepid shower—she really should have put a new hot water heater on the list for that Deloche woman—she changed into shorts and a tank top, and wound her hair on hot rollers. Then she limped into the kitchen to see what she could pull together for a late breakfast.

She was surprised to find Ken was still good for something. He had brewed a pot of coffee, which had cooked down to sludge, but he'd also brought in the newspaper. Armed with her first cup of hazelnut mocha from a fresh pot—sinfully rich with sugar and whipping cream—she turned to her horoscope.

"Aries…" She scanned the column and read out loud. "'You don't lack for romantic interests, but playing the field won't bring you closer to finding your heart's desire. The time has come to narrow your prospects. Friends can help you find your true love. Remember, others can see what you can't.'"

A belly laugh erupted. The laughter felt good, cleansing, as if she were getting rid of something poisonous.

She read the paragraph again. Okay, point one was correct. No question she had to narrow her romantic interests. She had reached a saturation point. In fact, there really *wasn't* enough free time in her evenings for all the men who were begging for her attentions.

Still, Wanda wasn't sure playing the field, so to speak, was a bad idea. So far she'd gotten a lot of fun out of it. And that third part? Well, she didn't have a friend in Palmetto Grove who would care if she found true love or not. The women she worked with at the Dancing Shrimp were all caught up in their own love lives. Most of them were actually young enough to have them. Only Lainie, the waitstaff supervisor, still made Wanda feel like a hot young chick, because Lainie was closing in on seventy. She was the only person, too, who knew that Wanda was one inch from kicking Ken out of the cottage.

More accurately, of course, Wanda was ready to turn over this lease to Ken and buy a place of her own. A condo, something modern and easy to keep clean. Maybe one with a real view of the gulf, and a swimming pool, so the grandkids would fight to visit.

Something lumbered down the road. When she heard the squawk of a two-way radio, she frowned and folded the paper beside her cereal bowl. Nothing ever happened here. Sometimes fishermen drove out to the point near to where the ill-fated marina had been planned, but this time of day anybody who wanted to fish anchored offshore. Spring was the best season for tarpon, but tarpon were fish for a boat, and there was no good place to launch one at this end.

She crossed the cottage, which didn't take all that long, and opened the door, peering into the sunlight for a glimpse of whatever was taking place. Her eyes took a moment to adjust; then she saw a black minivan with no windows disappearing down the road toward town, followed closely by what looked like a sheriff's vehicle.

She pondered the possibilities, none of them pretty. It didn't take a genius to figure out who was likely in trouble. The Indian couple was young, and so was the Deloche woman. They looked healthy, if a little thin for her taste. No, chances were the unfortunate passenger in that van was either Herb Krause or Alice Brooks. Heart attack, most likely. Or maybe pneumonia. Pneumonia could take an old person fast. One minute they had the sniffles, next they were pushing up daisies.

She wondered if she ought to do something. If Alice was in the ambulance, that son-in-law of hers could tell Wanda what was up. But if it was Herb…

She'd seen Herb last week when she made Key lime pie. She'd grown up in the "real" Keys, and she knew what a real pie tasted like. None of those grocery store crusts in tin foil pans. She made her own, like her mama had, crushing the best graham crackers she could buy, mixing the crumbs with melted butter, real butter, not some diet substitute. Then squeezing her own limes—Key limes, of course. What point was there to making a Key lime pie with Persian limes? Who ate Persian lime pie? Nobody who would admit it.

She had her very own secret, also learned from her mama. She grated a fine layer of lime rind on top of the crust before the filling went in; then she garnished the finished product with cream she whipped herself and a few curls of dark chocolate, along with thin slices of lime. When her son got married, he had asked her to make a dozen pies for the wedding reception instead of a cake, and they'd built a special tiered stand to hold them, with a plastic bride and groom at the top in shorts and flowered shirts. Of course the bride wore a veil and the groom a top hat, just so people would understand.

She realized she was standing at the door thinking about pie when she ought to be thinking about Herb or Alice.

Nope, cancel the Alice part. Wanda caught a glimpse of Alice's silver hair just in front of her cottage, then the granddaughter who had taken up residence at her side. As she watched, they both went inside.

"Herb, then."

She was sorry if Herb was heading to the hospital or worse about now. And sorry, too, that on the day she'd made that Key lime pie, she'd eaten almost half of it in one sitting. Then, in a fit of anger, because even though it was *his* day off, Ken hadn't come home to share it, she had wrapped up the rest, plunked it in her best ceramic pie pan—the one with the top that looked like crisscrossed strips of dough with an apple slice for a handle—and marched down to Herb's house. He was puttering with those plants of his, and she'd handed the whole thing right over to him, just because she didn't want Ken to have even a single bite if he ever came home again.

Now her very best pie pan, given to her by her daughter—who was not usually the best shopper—was at Herb's cottage. She sure hoped he hadn't been struck dead from an overdose of Key lime pie.

She had to do something about this mess. That pie pan was hers, and she had to get it back. Wanda went inside to finish her breakfast and figure out just how to do it, and when.

Before she locked the house behind her, Tracy retried the key that Maribel Sessions, the Realtor, had given her for Herb's cottage. She hadn't simply imagined the key didn't fit. It didn't. She hadn't found a similar one lying around the house, either, not on his dresser or bedside stand.

Although the one Herb had been holding when he died didn't look anything like the one she'd been given, she tried it now. As she'd guessed, it had been made for a different kind of lock. Thin and spidery, it looked like something out of a Nancy Drew novel: *The Secret of the Dead Man's Key*. If Tracy had a mysterious garret or a tower to unlock, she might be in business.

Once she got home, she called Maribel, who handled leasing the cottages, and Maribel promised to give her the originals if Tracy hurried over before she left for the day. With the promise of a key that actually fit, Tracy went back and locked Herb's doors, and took off for town. If worse came to worse, she could slit a screen and climb through a window to get back in.

To Tracy, Palmetto Grove always seemed a few shades paler than it ought to. Everything deteriorated quickly on the Gulf Coast. Sun, wind-driven sand, salt in the air, all stole the pigment from the brightest paint and rusted even the most ex-

pensive cars. Patches of sand marred emerald-green St. Augus-
tine grass, despite sprinklers continuously spewing a sulphur-
tinged spray. This time of year, only the hardiest flowers still
nodded their colorful heads.

She pulled up to the curb in front of Sessions Realtors:
Homes of Distinction, and locked her car. In a chilly reception
area, made chillier by white marble tile and Grecian pillars, she
told the receptionist that Maribel was expecting her. The
woman obviously knew her name and jumped up to get
Maribel from somewhere in back.

Tracy hadn't even settled down with a magazine before
Maribel came marching out, a huge smile pasted on a face that
was keeping some lucky plastic surgeon in custom golf clubs and
resort vacations. She had Gwen Stefani hair, which she emphasized with a matching creamy-white business suit. Like the town
she bought and sold, Maribel also looked three shades too pale.

"Mrs. Craimer," she said, extending her hand. "So good to
see you again. Have you decided to look for a house after all?"

"Maribel…" Tracy shook hands, then pulled hers away from
Maribel's slightly damp one. "Tracy *Deloche* now. Remember
all that paperwork?"

Maribel looked charmingly chagrined. "I am so sorry. What
am I thinking? It's just that your husband was such a presence."

"Ex-husband." Right about now, CJ was probably a presence
in the prison laundry, ironing shirts.

"I hope you've decided to have a good look at everything
we have for sale." Maribel lowered her voice, as if the empty
room might be bugged. "The market is just the teeniest bit
slow. You can pick up a bargain if you hurry."

Tracy knew all about slow markets. In addition to the
problems she was having with tree-hugger crazies who wanted
Happiness Key to sit quietly and grow sandspurs for eternity,

most developers were, at best, holding steady. Nobody with the resources to fight intrusive environmentalists wanted to take on Tracy's problems. The economy. The hurricanes. The insurance. Tracy might look as if she were sitting on a gold mine, but like a lot of prospectors before her, if things didn't improve quickly, she was going to be eating beans and sourdough biscuits for breakfast, lunch and dinner.

"I'm not planning to stay in Florida after I sell," Tracy told Maribel, hoping that *this* time the message would sink in. "So I'm just going to stay in the extra cottage for now. But I do need the original keys."

"Yes, I was sorry to hear about the renter. Mr. Cross?"

"Krause. While I'm here, I think I'd better get his file, too. I need information on his next of kin." She paused. "Might there have been a deposit? You know, to give back, after I've assessed damages?"

"Not that I recall. The terms of those leases were so loose. As enticement, really, to get somebody to live out there when they might have to vacate so quickly."

Tracy was disappointed. "Well, that's not very likely now."

"Then you might be around for some time?"

Tracy didn't want to tell Maribel she had no place else to go. That sounded so lame, so fricking pathetic. Almost as pathetic as using poor Herb's mythical deposit to pay her bills. She put a better spin on it.

"I'm a very motivated seller. I want to stay on top of things. I know the market can change in a heartbeat, so I want to be right here for the kill."

"Now that's the can-do spirit." Maribel toddled on impossibly high heels to a wall of wooden filing cabinets behind the reception desk, unlocked one and began to paw through it. "I tell my staff they need to stay on top of things that way, but lately

I've lost some of my best. Of course, I'm planning to sell your land myself, so you have nothing to worry about. You're my top priority."

"I like being somebody's top priority." Tracy tried to remember if she ever had been.

Maribel pulled out a file folder and brought it over. Then she opened the top drawer of the desk, took out a ring of keys and handed her everything.

"I did make copies for all the cottages, so we'd have spares if a buyer wanted to see the inside. Of course, that's unlikely, since whoever buys the property will simply bulldoze them."

Tracy stored everything in the Fendi Doctor B Bag CJ's secretary had picked out for her last birthday, probably the last designer purse she would own for a very long time. She wouldn't be one bit sorry to see the cottage she was living in bulldozed. And now that she'd spent part of an afternoon in the bedroom with the very dead Herb Krause, she wouldn't be sorry to see his cottage disappear, either.

"You must be feeling at loose ends," Maribel said. "How are you keeping busy?"

Tracy had been forced to spend a lot of time cleaning her cottage so she could tolerate sleeping in it, but that was boring and made her sound like a drudge instead of the glamorous ex-wife of one of California's most colorful felons.

"I've spent some of it reading up on Florida and federal wetlands laws," she said.

"Don't you worry. Somebody will come along with the money to make Happiness Key a reality. I promise, we're in this together."

Tracy wasn't sure she wanted to be in anything with Maribel Sessions. Right now Tracy's property was a sizable blip on Maribel's radar. The moment it became clear Happiness Key, as originally envisioned, was completely dead in the water, then

Maribel would throw Tracy overboard and sail off without a backward glance.

The door opened behind her, and Tracy turned to find the most interesting man she'd seen in a long time walking into the office. He was probably just under six foot, lean, and, despite a thick head of silver-gray hair, young. He wasn't sixty, not even fifty. She pegged him in his early forties, a man with enough confidence not to dye his hair. The confidence showed in the way he held himself, the set of his shoulders, the length of his stride. And, when he caught sight of her, his smile.

"Lee," Maribel said. "Come meet Tracy Cr— Deloche. She happens to own your mother-in-law's cottage. Tracy, Lee is one of our agents."

Tracy was trying to digest that when the man stepped forward and held out his hand. "Lee Symington, Miss Deloche. How are you?"

Lee Symington had one of those voices a woman could wallow and drown in. Deep, soothing, yet simultaneously intense. And giddyup! Blue eyes that almost leaped out of his tanned face.

"Tracy," she told him. "Call me Tracy. And your mother-in-law?"

"Alice Brooks."

It came together now. She was just glad Lee wasn't related to *Wanda*. "Sure. Of course. I sort of met your daughter yesterday."

"Olivia. I was just about to hop in the shower when you arrived. I'm sorry I didn't come out and meet you then."

The picture of Lee ready to hop into the shower was more than Tracy could handle, particularly with Maribel watching them.

"Did I understand correctly? Are we neighbors?" she asked.

"That's right. I've moved in temporarily with Alice." He glanced at Maribel to include her. "I haven't had a chance to tell you, Maribel. Alice needs the help, and Olivia's good for her. They're very close. Alice hasn't done well since my wife died. Karen was her mainstay, and I know she would want me to do anything I can."

Tracy wasn't sure what to say. That she was sorry Lee's wife had died? That she thought he was a pretty awesome guy for helping the vague old woman who wasn't really his responsibility? That she hoped he was out of mourning and ready for some company?

"I'm sorry she's had a rough time," Tracy said instead. "I'm sure it's been hard for you, as well."

"It's been a year now. Olivia and I are coping. Alice will, too, now that we can take care of her."

"I'm just here to pick up the key to Herb's house. Mine isn't working, and we haven't found his. You do know he, uh, died?"

"Olivia called my cell. She saw the police. She was worried, and Alice was upset. They weren't sure what was going on."

Tracy added this tidbit to the guilt she was trying not to feel. Why hadn't she thought to tell Alice what had happened, to break the news gently? And for that matter, why hadn't she told Wanda or her husband about Herb? Somebody should pen a how-to book. *The Loveable Landlady*. Only she probably wouldn't bother to read it.

Maribel consulted her watch. "Lee, will you make sure Tracy has everything she needs? I've got a showing in about ten minutes, and I've really got to scoot."

She left in a flurry of goodbyes. Tracy was tempted to follow just to see if the afternoon sunshine turned Maribel a ghostlier white or lobster-red, but she was in no hurry to leave Lee Symington.

"So, *do* you have everything?" he asked. His eyes were warmly appreciative, and Tracy was glad she had taken the time to shower and change into a green sundress with a beaded halter top, as well as spray herself liberally with Island Capri before she came into town. She'd felt the need for some cheer, considering the events of the day.

"Everything," she said. "But you can walk me to my car."

He smiled, something in between the mature Richard Gere and the younger Harrison Ford. She was entranced.

He opened the front door for her, and her skirt brushed his pants—nicely tailored summer-weight wool—as she passed. "I know you're trying to sell Happiness Key. And I know it might take a while, considering…"

"Considering that everybody in every single government and private bureaucracy in Florida and beyond wants to tell me what I should and shouldn't do with it?"

"That covers it nicely."

"You probably know the story," she said.

"Not all of it."

"My ex-husband bought the land to develop it into a luxury condominium complex and marina. All very chichi. Then he had a few legal problems." Which was like saying that Florida had a few alligators.

"And now it belongs to you?"

"It's almost funny. I really didn't know until the smoke cleared. But after he bought the property, CJ put the whole package into a legal liability corporation with me at the head. I signed all the papers, not paying that much attention. He told me it was a tax write-off, and I was busy planning a vacation somewhere and didn't ask any questions. It's a good thing I didn't."

"And now you can't sell it."

"Everybody's standing in line to stop me. But the land's worth a mint. After things pick up, some developer will buy it and pay all the bureaucrats under the table while he's at it. He'll promise to leave something else untouched, or reclaim something he's already hacked to pieces, and they'll look the other way. It's just that I don't have the resources to do that myself."

"So what are you doing while you wait?"

Going silently crazy.

"I may look for a job," she said, as if this were of no consequence, although with Herb Krause's next rent payment a memory and the impending repairs to Wanda's cottage, the consequences of not having one could be serious. For the first time in her life, she might need to get her hands dirty.

"You must be bored. Have you thought about joining the Sun County Yacht Club?"

She tried not to laugh. She wondered exactly who she would give as a reference, and how she would pay for even a few months' membership—not to mention the yacht.

She told a slightly different story. "I'd rather not make a lot of new friends to leave behind. But I thought a summer job might be an interesting way to find out more about the community. You know. Stay busy, learn a little more about how things work around here."

"I wish you had a Florida real-estate license. Maribel could use another good agent."

"Too bad. I shmooze well with the rich and famous. I'd be great for business."

"You know, the yacht club event planner might be able to use a little help. She always gets swamped this time of year. I could introduce you."

Tracy wondered if a more tailor-made job existed. She'd planned or helped plan a host of events as a volunteer, first as second in command to her demanding mother, then as CJ's wife. Charity balls, golf and bridge tournaments, luncheons.

"That's a very kind offer," she said. "I may take you up on it."

"I'll see what I can find out and let you know."

She stopped in front of her car and watched him admire it. The BMW Z3 was a zippy little sports car that, in her extreme youth, had been as good as a sign proclaiming that she was fun-loving, carefree and off-limits to anybody except professionals with excellent prospects. Now she wasn't sure what it said. Maybe something about faded glory.

"You'll probably see me going in and out of Herb's cottage," Tracy said. "Until we find his family."

"I'll ask Alice what she knows."

She smiled her thanks. They assessed each other for a moment. She liked what she saw, but then, she'd been perfectly happy with CJ until the morning he sat her down in their solarium and told her he was going to jail.

"I'll see you around," she said, unlocking her door.

"Sounds like you will. Let me know if you need anything."

She thought about that as she drove away. And she realized that she had no idea what she needed, not really. She'd never had to worry about it. Now nothing was ever going to be that easy again.

chapter four

Janya could count on Rishi to get home by dark, although she knew if she wasn't waiting at home with dinner, he would stay at work eating pizza out of cartons or fried chicken out of buckets. Janya was certain the food must taste like the cardboard that contained it. She could not imagine how anyone who had, at the very least, been *born* in India could tolerate that.

Although Janya's family had always employed a cook, Janya's mother had insisted her daughter learn the rigors of classic Indian cuisine. She had learned to buy and grind only the freshest spices. To toast them until the flavors were perfectly enhanced. To create a plate of vegetables so diverse in flavor and texture that meat eaters wouldn't realize the meal had none. She knew how to mix flour and yogurt for chapati, then to cook it on the *tawa,* a special iron skillet, nudging the edges until the bread puffed like a balloon.

Rishi could not distinguish a chapati from a tortilla. Nor did he care. Janya knew she was supposed to care *for* him, so she tried, because it was expected.

Tonight, when Rishi walked into the cottage, Janya was finishing preparations for their meal. She was married to an American. She had observed his eating habits long enough to know he preferred French fries to rice, corn on the cob to lentils. As a strict vegetarian, she would never cook meat, but Janya attempted to please him by trying American recipes.

Rishi slipped off his sandals, as they always did, at the door. "I'm home, Janya." He said the same thing every evening, as if he were afraid she wouldn't notice he had arrived.

She went to greet him, and he wrapped his arms around her in the American way. She stood close, not relaxing, but not moving away, either.

"Tell me about your day," Rishi said, holding her close.

"After prayers."

Janya's grandparents had been devout and traditional Hindus. From them she had learned the rituals, the devotions and prayers, the festivals and roles of the many deities who were aspects of the one true God. Her parents referred to themselves as cultural Hindus, abiding by many of the traditions, accepting some of the beliefs, but not putting too fine a point on any of them.

Janya was more free-thinking. Educated by Catholic nuns, never discouraged by her parents when she made friends with classmates with Buddhist and Muslim backgrounds, she had learned to look for the similarities in all religions, the distilled essence of what was true, the consequences when people paid scant attention to what they proclaimed to believe. In her home, though, she was determined to hold fast to the most basic traditions of her childhood. She was so far from her beloved India, and she didn't want to move even farther.

A Hindu home, even the poorest, had a special place for prayer, a *puja* room, which was sometimes no more than a corner. The beach cottage was so small that at first Janya had feared she would need to set up her altar in a corner, too. But the moment

Rishi showed her the closet for coats on the east side of the living room, she knew that would be the place for worship. Not elaborate, not built to the specifications of those who gloried in obedience to every man-made rule. But a place, nonetheless, to remember who they were and what they believed.

Now she opened the door to reveal a platform covered with a beautiful blue sari, on which sat the *puja* tray with the items they would need for their worship and a statue of Krishna. She had painted the inside of the closet a dark red, then adorned the borders with silver and gold paint, and designs of flowers she remembered from home.

While Rishi waited, she lit the wick of a small brass oil lamp, then a cone of incense. Finally she made an offering of water from a pitcher she had placed there before she began dinner preparations, and a bowl of freshly cooked rice.

She stepped back, they folded their hands, and Rishi intoned the familiar prayers they had agreed upon, still somewhat awkwardly, since this had been done only occasionally in the home in which he grew up. They completed the familiar rituals, finishing when Janya laid flowers at Krishna's feet. Later she would use a flower to put out the flame, as her mother had always done.

When they finished, Rishi followed Janya to the kitchen. "You know the meaning of the word 'lite'?" Rishi spelled it. "In this country we say something is 'lite' if it's not quite the real thing. We practice Hindu-lite in this house."

"Perhaps you want something more elaborate?"

He laughed. "No, I'm happy, but your mother and father won't be when they come to visit."

This was a game they played. Rishi talked about her parents visiting as if it might actually happen someday. She wasn't certain why. Either he wanted to make her believe it, too, so she would not mourn so acutely for her home and family, or, just as sadly, he wanted to believe he had made a normal marriage, with in-laws who were every bit as happy he was their son-in-law as he was to have them in his life.

Of course neither was true.

She stirred the pot of New England-style beans she had made to go with rice and a plate of raw vegetables. "This is not quite ready. Perhaps you would like a snack?"

Rishi opened the refrigerator and stood staring into it, as if he had never imagined such contents. When her husband had gone to live with his uncle and aunt, he had been granted few liberties, and helping himself to food when he was hungry had not been one of them.

Janya found this sad. Rishi had been a beloved son until his parents were killed in the poison gas disaster at Bhopal. His mother and father, who had worked for the trade union that represented workers at the Union Carbide plant, had worried about increasingly deteriorating safety conditions and sent their young son to stay with an aunt in Delhi, planning to join him there at the end of the year. Before they could leave for good, their fears had come to pass, and Rishi had been orphaned.

Rishi often said he had been blessed to have an uncle who was willing to give him a home in America, but Janya was not always certain it had been a blessing. To her, Rishi was like the beggar children who pleaded for attention and recognition on the streets of Mumbai. Hungry for love, graceless, even frightened. Sometimes she thought he stared into the refrigerator just to be certain that food still occupied the shelves and access was no longer denied.

She did not think her husband was handsome. Rishi was just four inches taller than she, thin, but with a muscular body that seemed at odds with itself, never still, never quite coordinated. His nose was prominent, and a mustache made it seem larger still. He had wiry eyebrows over round eyes. When he smiled, his large, perfect teeth were an eruption against his bronze skin.

Rishi was a kind man, grateful for everything he had. Many times a day she reminded herself that she was lucky to have married someone who did not mistreat her, that indeed, she was lucky not to have a critical mother-in-law, or a father-in-law who insisted his son and daughter-in-law grovel like servants. Rishi's aunt and uncle were not interested in becoming part of their lives. Although they had retired to Orlando, they had visited only once since the marriage eight months ago. They had not been impressed by the apartment where she and Rishi had lived at the time, and they had departed after one night for a long visit with their real son in Ft. Lauderdale.

Now she couldn't stand to watch her husband gazing into the refrigerator. She moved past him and pulled out one of the fruit drinks she had bought at the specialty grocers. As he watched, she poured it over ice and served it to him, then went to finish dinner preparations.

"Have you had a good day?" he asked.

"Not as good as it might have been." She took a spoonful of beans and put it on a plate to taste. The recipe came from an American women's magazine, but as usual, the dish lacked flavor. She began to assemble and add spices as they talked.

"Did you go into town?" he asked.

"The bus came right on time." She listed her activities.

"Then you accomplished everything you set out to do. And that doesn't make you happy?" He sounded genuinely curious. For Rishi, finishing a list of projects was as good as a day at Disney World—to which he compared everything.

Talking about death as she prepared dinner seemed unlucky, although Janya tried not to be superstitious. She told him succinctly what had happened and her part in the events of the day.

She ended her recital. "It was very sad. He died alone. No one to be with him or help him on. No one who even knew he was gone until we arrived. Strangers tending his body. Is that the way of things here?"

"No, the way of things is people dying in hospitals surrounded by machines and *nurses* who don't know them."

She shuddered.

"I'm sorry, I made it sound worse than it is," Rishi said. "People are often surrounded by family, too. And doctors and nurses try to let them pass with dignity."

She didn't feel much better. When she died, she wanted the people who loved her right there. She did not want to die in a hospital bed alone and unloved. And she certainly didn't want to die as Herb Krause had, waiting to be discovered by the very people who had ignored him in life.

"This has upset you," Rishi said.

Like many people in his field, he was not good at understanding feelings, but tonight her husband was stretching to accommodate her. She was grateful, but sad he had to work so hard.

Darshan, the man she had nearly married, would have understood how she felt immediately.

Since it was necessary, she tried to explain. "I wish that I had done more for him while he was alive. He seemed like a kind man...." She bit her lip, but then she decided to go on. "And lonely, Rishi. We could have been more interested in his life."

Rishi looked confused. "Why do you think he would have wanted that?"

"Because he was a human being with no one else nearby who cared."

"What about his family?"

"I don't know if he has one."

"I didn't know."

"But that would be the crux of the matter, wouldn't it? That we didn't know. That we made no attempt to know."

"You're upset because you found him. That would upset anybody. But his happiness was not your job."

"Then whose job was it?" She plunged on. "I have decided to take care of his plants." The moment the words escaped her lips, she wished she hadn't said them. Rishi would not understand. And she didn't want to explain anything else.

"He had plants?"

Exasperated because he saw so little, she sounded harsher than she meant to. "How could you *not* notice? All over his yard. In many, *many* pots."

He didn't speak for a moment. She waited for him to tell her that this was not her job, that caring for the plants couldn't please a dead man, that she had no need to ask this stranger's forgiveness.

He was silent as she took food to the dinner table and he seated himself in the chair in the corner. He didn't speak until his dinner was half-eaten, although his expression changed after a few bites, as if he were thinking very long and hard about something.

Finally he cleared his throat. "I think that's good. That you're going to take care of his plants until they can be taken by his family. You can't help the old man now, but maybe you can help the people who loved him."

She was so surprised, she hardly knew what to say. She had expected an argument, even prepared herself for one. She was chagrined. "Then it's settled."

"Maybe caring for the plants will make you happy. And the dance classes?"

The man across from her wanted her happiness. In this, too, she was lucky. But if good fortune smiled on a woman and she didn't feel that blessing deep inside her, did it matter? Janya managed a smile anyway. Rishi deserved that much.

"Maybe they will," she said.

Tracy's cottage had been stripped to the bare bones, all by her own hard work. Gone was the shabby indoor-outdoor carpet that had covered the floors. Gone, too, were two layers of vinyl. Now she was down to the original linoleum, a dreary brown, speckled with black and gray. Scuffed and torn, it was not a good alternative to the carpeting, so on the way home from the realty, she stopped at a flooring warehouse to price alternatives.

Inside a cavern heaped with carpet remnants and exotic hardwoods, she surveyed her choices. Warehouse or not, nothing was cheap, but a pile of ceramic tile caught her eye. The owner told her the tiles were the tail end of a discontinued line, and she would save a bundle. She had already calculated square footage, and he promised he had more than enough on hand. When she said she wanted them, he threw in all the remaining tiles for good measure, in case some were cracked or broken—and to make room for something more profitable.

At the cash register, the price still made her whistle. Once upon a time she wouldn't have blinked at spending this much on a designer dress. But those days were gone, or at least in limbo. Still, she knew a bargain, and the tile was lovely, a mottled rust that reminded her of the adobe house in Taos she and CJ had used as a getaway until Uncle Sam took possession. She gave the owner her credit card and arranged delivery.

Now at home—or what passed for one—she thought about everything that was still needed to make the cottage liveable. Over the past two weeks she had scrubbed, bleached and patched all the walls, and now she had to seal them before she redid the one-bedroom cottage with a pale wheat paint she had bought in bulk. The kitchen cabinets had been scrubbed both inside and out, and they, too, needed to be sealed, then painted—white, most likely, to match the appliances.

She had arranged to have most of the rotting furniture hauled away with the layers of flooring, and to replace it, she had spent a long weekend visiting flea markets. She had found a wooden table and chairs she could paint or refinish for the alcove beside the kitchen, a nearly new sofa and easy chair covered in Haitian cotton, and a four-poster pine bedframe for the discount warehouse mattress and box spring she had bought new. From the sad array at the cottage she had kept a dresser and a nightstand with so many layers of paint she had no idea if there was actual wood beneath them. But the last layer was white and fairly new. They would do.

Cleaning and clearing hadn't wrought any miracles, but she thought once the tile was down, and the rooms and cabinets were painted, the house might be liveable. She'd bought a jute-and-seagrass rug, and six brass vases of odd sizes, from an import store that was "going out of business"—at least until the next "going out of business" sale. Now after pillaging her savings account, she only had to pay somebody to install the tile, then take care of the painting herself. Maybe afterwards she could walk through the door and not be flooded by memories of a different life.

She'd been surprised to find the physical labor—cutting flooring into manageable sizes, then wrestling it into rolls to haul outside—had been fun. As she scrubbed away mildew, cobwebs and just plain dirt, she'd imagined she was scrubbing away the past two years, getting back to something cleaner and more basic. For the first time since CJ sat her down to tell her that life as she knew it was over, she had looked forward to getting up in the morning to see what she could accomplish.

Now she had a chore she was not looking forward to. One more household item had to be wrestled to the curb for trash pickup. She didn't want to leave Herb's mattress in his cottage. And if she waited, it would have to remain there another week, a reminder she didn't want to face every time she went inside.

She foraged for dinner—not difficult, since she rarely ate much at one sitting. She ate a few strawberries, three whole wheat crackers spread with goat cheese and half a dozen smoked almonds. She was ready to roll.

As she was halfway out the door, the telephone rang. This was so unusual she felt compelled to answer. The voice at the other end was familiar.

"Sherrie." Tracy looked for a place to sit, tossing a couple of home improvement magazines on the floor so she could park herself in the easy chair. "It's nice of you to call." She was surprised at the edge in her own voice.

"I'm sorry, Trace. We've been out in Colorado. Wade had a conference, and I tagged along. I came back to an epidemic of strep throat."

Sherrie Falmouth had been Tracy's roommate at Cal State Long Beach. Her husband was a successful plastic surgeon in Scottsdale, Arizona, and was often on the road presenting papers or donating his skills to selected charities. Although the two women had been almost inseparable at "the Beach," their friendship had waned after graduation. Distance and different lifestyles had been major contributors. Sherrie had married right out of college and started a family almost immediately. She and Wade had two adorable little girls, and when she and Tracy talked on the phone, Sherrie was usually obsessed with preschools, toilet training, or the exhaustion of trying to cope and still have something left over for Wade at day's end. Tracy's suggestion to hire a full-time nanny, so Sherrie could start having fun again, had never taken root.

Still, despite growing apart, Sherrie was the friend who had hung in with her when CJ's exploits became public. It was Sherrie who helped pack what was left after the Feds vanished with their spoils, Sherrie who made arrangements for a van to carry everything to storage. And now, not surprisingly, it was Sherrie at the other end of a line that hadn't exactly twittered with activity since Tracy's arrival in Florida.

"Are the girls all right now?" Tracy asked.

"Just fine. But I'm a wreck. How are you?"

This was a question Tracy had never had trouble answering in the past. Now it presented all kinds of challenges. She knew herself to be a lot of things, some of which might not be that appealing. But she'd never been a whiner.

She concentrated on facts. "I've been working hard getting this place in shape so I can stay here until it sells."

"You're doing it yourself?"

"Yep. Oh, and I've had a couple of setbacks. Actually, *I* just had one, repairs I have to make to one of the cottages or the renters won't pay. But the old guy in the next cottage had a doozy. He died. Just like that, and I found him."

"Wow, bummer!"

"You'd better believe it. That part was really bad for him. The fact he won't be around to pay rent anymore's bad for me, but at least I'm still walking and talking."

Sherrie made a tsk-tsk noise. "Did you know him?"

"Not really." She decided to be honest. "I kind of tried to avoid him. I was busy, and I'm new at this. I'm not sure it's a good idea to get involved with the renters."

"Ah, Trace, who *do* you get involved with?"

"What's that supposed to mean?"

"I mean, as long as I've known you, you've made a point of just dipping your toes into relationships. You never just jump in and risk getting in over your head."

"Well, I was kind of over my head with CJ, wouldn't you say? I mean, I married him, I divorced him, and in between I sort of had fun. Until the big surprise."

"No, if you'd jumped into that relationship and really gotten to know CJ, you wouldn't have been surprised. You were surprised because you didn't bother finding out who he was."

"What kind of psychobabble is that?"

"The voice of somebody who knows you. Like, this is Sherrie, remember? One of the few people you ever let in, and mostly because we were in college and partying too hard to hide anything."

"I wish I was as deep and mysterious as you're making me out to be, but I'm a 'what you see is what you get' kind of gal."

"Right. So you say." Sherrie paused. "Is there anything you need? Anything I can do from here?"

"You could find me another rich husband."

"Do you really want one?"

"Make that a sugar daddy. I'll do an Anna Nicole Smith."

"You don't have the boobs for it."

"Wade could take care of that."

"Over my dead body."

"With CJ's connections to the mob, that part could probably be arranged, too."

"The girls and Wade send their love."

Tracy made smooching noises into the phone.

In the last rays of twilight, the walk over to Herb's seemed twice as long as it should have. As she drew closer, she could hear the sound of waves from the gulf side of the key. Her cottage was closer to the bay, and the view was blighted by mangroves and underbrush. Herb's cottage faced in the same direction, but Alice's peeked out at the gulf. Once the cottages were gone, and the vegetation was plowed under or tamed into submission, the owners of the luxury condos planned for this spot would have million-dollar views, which was a good thing, since they would be paying that much or more.

Tracy wasn't a whiner, and she wasn't a wallower. After life as she'd known it ended, she had taken hold of herself and put one foot in front of the other to get herself to this point. But now, as she approached Herb's door, she wondered exactly what was in store for her future. She couldn't dismiss the possibility that she was going to be living on Happiness Key until, like Herb, she was found dead in her bed.

No, that was silly. That was never going happen, because unless something changed quickly, she wasn't going to have enough cash to hold on to the property. The taxes were enormous. She had enough money for another year, but if the land didn't sell, she was in deep trouble.

But hey, that wasn't the only thing she had to worry about. There was everything else, besides. Tracy supposed she had better take Lee Symington up on that introduction to the yacht club event planner.

Although the temperature was still well into the eighties, once she was standing on Herb's front porch a shiver passed through her. She wished she had let the telephone ring, or skipped dinner. She had hoped to do this as the sun set, so she had enough light to guide her but not enough that her activities would be easily noted by her tenants. She was not insensitive, at least not completely. There was something crass about dragging the old guy's mattress out to the road. It would probably look as if she couldn't wait to clear out his house and rent it again. Find the body, carry the man's stuff to the curb, dust off your capitalist hands and call in a classified.

Now she didn't have to worry. Nobody would see her struggling with the mattress, because not only had the sun gone down, the last light had faded. No moon shone over the key, and an uncharacteristic silence had descended. She wasn't easily spooked, but unlocking the door of a dead man and blithely walking in seemed like the sort of thing the victim in a slasher movie might do. A bad idea. But not as bad as waiting for next week's trash pickup.

Inside, the light Janya had left burning in Herb's bedroom was only a soft glow under the closed door and little help. She felt for and flipped a switch by the door, but nothing happened. Terrific. Herb probably had a lamp connected to it, but he had turned it off at the source. She waited for her eyes to adjust. There were a couple of streetlamps at the front of the property where the rental office for the beach cottages had once stood. But the oyster-shell roads themselves had no illumination except front porch lights. She could make out the shapes of furniture, but not well enough to cross the room.

As she waited, she listened. The silence was like the thick, oozing chill of a San Francisco fog. Now and then it was punctuated by swamp noises, which were no consolation. The moment she judged she could see well enough, she felt her way across the room and found the nearest lamp. She fumbled for the switch—and why didn't manufacturers agree on where to put the darn things?—and had just started to flip it when she heard something clang in the kitchen. She straightened with a jerk, nearly knocking the lampshade to the floor.

Mentally she gauged the distance between the end table and the front door. She told herself that she had imagined the clang. She told herself that the deputy had been sure Herb

Krause wasn't murdered in his bed but had died a quick, natural death.

Of course, mistakes could be made....

Her struggle lasted only seconds. She owned this house, such as it was, and it was her job to take care of the property. If somebody was in the kitchen going through Herb's things, then it was up to her to stop them. She doubted anybody was going to kill her for a spatula and a cutting board. She had noted a vintage kitchen timer shaped like a chicken on the windowsill, but even that, campy as it was, provided no motive for murder.

By now she could almost see. A pocket door separated the kitchen from the living room, and now it was closed. She was almost certain the door hadn't been closed when she was here earlier.

She tiptoed toward the kitchen and heard what sounded like the squeak of hinges, the creak of a door opening. She wasn't imagining this. Somebody was inside going through cabinets. For what? And why? Poor Herb wasn't even cold in his grave. Okay, cold, but not yet in the ground.

She felt along the edge of the door until she found the indented handle; then, with one smooth motion, she slid it open and jumped into the kitchen.

A low-wattage bulb lit the stove top from the hood above. Someone was bending over at the other end of the room, going through the lower cabinets. At the noise of the door, the figure straightened and whirled.

"What are you doing here?" Tracy demanded before she could see the intruder's face. "This is breaking and entering."

"Oh, don't get your panties in a twist." The woman straightened her shoulders and glared at Tracy.

Wanda Gray. Dressed in black spandex leggings and an equally tight black T-shirt, like some sort of white trash ninja.

Tracy felt herself relax, then she tensed again with righteous anger. "You scared me to death! What do you think you're doing here? And how did you get in?"

Wanda reached in her pocket. For a moment Tracy wasn't sure what to do, then Wanda swung a key in her direction on a spiral chain.

"Herb gave me his extra key. On account of him being so old and all. I think he expected me to come over now and then if I didn't see him outside, and check to be sure he wasn't lying on the floor with a broken hip or worse."

"And that's what you're doing?" Tracy tried to sound cooler and calmer than her elevated heart rate dictated. "You're searching the cabinets to see if he's in there with a broken hip?"

"No need to get smart. I know he's gone." Wanda snapped her fingers. "Like that. The Symington fellow told me. Of course, Mr. Symington wasn't the one that found poor Herb. The one that found him didn't bother to tell his neighbors he was dead."

There was too much truth in that, but Tracy didn't blink. "Maybe if you'd used that key the way Herb wanted you to, *you* would have been the one to find him, and you would have gotten all the bad news firsthand."

Wanda didn't say anything.

"What *are* you doing here?" Tracy said.

"I brought him some pie last week, in my special pie dish. My daughter gave it to me, and she's not all that good at gifts. One year she gave me a pair of brown suede earth shoes, like she actually thought I might wear them. That dish is a winner, though. I didn't want somebody coming in and taking it home just because they like it."

"Why didn't you just tell me, so we could look for it together?"

Wanda snorted.

"Not to put too fine a point on it, but I've gone a lot of

years without baking a pie, and I see a lot more in my future." Tracy saw a switch and flipped it so the overhead light came on. "Come on, let's see if we can find it."

"You just want to see if I'm telling the truth."

Tracy supposed that was a little bit true. But mostly she just wanted Wanda to go home. "What does it look like?"

She listened as Wanda described the dish, then she started opening cabinets. Glasses in one, just a few, which gave her a pang. Some plates in another, a few saucers and bowls. More pangs. No need for enough dishes to entertain, she guessed.

"Did Mr. Krause have any friends?" she asked. "You knew him better than I did. I guess, more important, did he have family? Because the funeral home took his money, but not his information."

"Memorial, right? Somebody at work told me Memorial will be after me soon enough, too. They probably got to Herb and didn't take the time to do the thing right. Busy canvassing everybody over fifty who hasn't laid down their money."

"So do you? Know anything about him?" Tracy asked. Her search had turned up nothing, but as she watched, Wanda pulled a ceramic pie plate out of a cupboard, followed closely by a lid that looked like the top crust of a pie.

"Well, here it is." Wanda held it out. "Close enough to my description for you to believe me?"

"I never accused you of trying to steal his pie dish. That chip on your shoulder must tip a lot of scales. You just surprised me by being here in the dark, rummaging through his cupboards."

"I didn't want to have to go into the whole story."

"I guess you don't want to tell me if he has friends or family, either. So I'll have to play detective, maybe? Give me something else to worry about?"

"You having a little pity party over there by the sink? Don't worry none about inviting me."

"Glad you found the pie plate. You can let yourself out." Tracy went back into the living room, snapping on the lamp so the cottage was now aglow.

In the bedroom, she stood in the door with her hands on her hips. The mattress was a double, maybe even a queen size. She was going to have to drag it on its side and hope it didn't flip one way or the other as she maneuvered it through the rooms.

She heard footsteps, and Wanda came to stand in the doorway.

"He never said much about himself," Wanda said. "In answer to your question. Not that I care whether you have to play detective, but Herb deserves a little peace."

"What *did* he say, do you remember?"

"I think he said he was from Florida. Never said exactly where, though, or if that meant he'd been born in the state. I got the impression he'd lived a few places in his time, something of a wanderer."

"He never said anything about family?"

"Uh-uh. And I never saw any, either."

"Friends?"

"He did play chess in Grambling Park with some other old men. I saw him there a couple of times, when I was on the way to the grocery store. Never said nothing about it to me, though."

"Were you interested?" Tracy knew she should be asking herself the same question. "Never mind. *I* wasn't. Why should you have been?"

"I did bring him that pie." Wanda sounded defensive.

"And last week I took him some mail the carrier stuck in my box by mistake. That's about the sum total of my interaction with the guy."

"What'll they do if you don't find somebody to take charge?"

Tracy had no idea. Was it up to her? Was she the next-best thing to next of kin because she owned the guy's house? "I guess if nobody comes forward, I'm going to have to go through his papers. You know. To see what I can find out."

"Guess you didn't know what you were getting into when you took this job."

"I didn't *take* it. It was handed to me. And trust me, it's not a barrel of laughs."

"Is that what you're here for? To look through his things?"

"I'm here to drag the mattress out for the trash pickup tomorrow. He died on the bed. It's got to go."

"You're going to do it by yourself?"

"I was planning to." Tracy waited, hoping, despite herself, that Wanda would volunteer to help. Between them, they could make short work of it.

"That's a big job," Wanda said.

"Has to be done."

"Well…" Wanda hesitated, then she smirked. "I'll leave you to it. Sounds like it's gonna take a little time to get it out there. I won't keep you."

"Lock the kitchen door on your way out, won't you? And leave Herb's key on the dresser."

A minute later Tracy heard the back door close. She wasn't sure whether to be sorry that Wanda hadn't stayed to help or thrilled the woman was gone. In another minute she was too busy wrestling the mattress to worry about it.

chapter five

Wanda was a sucker for sad country songs. Patsy Cline and George Jones made her weep before they paused for their first recorded breaths. But Dolly Parton singing "I Will Always Love You"? That wasn't just a weeper, that was a serious thunderstorm.

Wanda felt around on the kitchen counter for a dish towel, took off her glasses and blotted her eyes before she switched off her favorite radio station. She felt as if she'd been wrung dry. Maybe Whitney Houston *had* made it to the top of the pop charts with Dolly's song, but she shouldn't ought to have. Wanda liked Whitney Houston—although she did wonder some about that ex-husband of hers—but nobody else ought to sing one of Dolly's songs. It was like one of the portrait artists at the downtown beach trying to paint the Mona Lisa.

Wanda wasn't perfect, but drinking was one problem she'd never had. She never drank if she thought she needed to. That was the key, and she'd told a lot of her customers that very thing, too, although most of them ignored her. Now she went to the old Kelvinator that had come with the cottage and rummaged to see if Ken had left her a Corona. She found a couple in the back, opened one and drank it right out of the bottle.

The Deloche woman had trudged by a little while ago, looking tired and bedraggled, or as bedraggled as any woman that looked like *that* possibly could. Wrestling that mattress? Must have been some job. It served the landlady right, sneaking up on Wanda in the kitchen the way she had, nearly scaring her to death. And, after all, what did she owe Tracy Deloche? This month, not even a rent check, unless the repair list got tended to.

Besides, that young woman needed somebody to take her down a peg or two. Whenever she talked to Wanda, she sounded like she was talking to somebody with no sense. Ms. Deloche wasn't even from Florida, while Wanda's ancestors had settled deep in the Keys back when alligators and Seminoles were the only neighbors for miles and miles.

Now she stood at the sink, staring out at the driveway and drinking. Halfway through the Corona, she stopped telling herself she had behaved just fine. That was Dolly's fault. Who could listen to that sweet woman and still tell themselves lies? Maybe Wanda did have good reason not to like Tracy Deloche, but her mother, poor as she was, hadn't raised her to be mean-spirited. Wanda had grown up taking casseroles to neighbors when somebody was sick, watering flowers, and feeding the cat three doors down when the old lady who lived there visited her daughter in Tennessee. Wanda knew you didn't do these things so people would be nice in return. You did them because that was how good people behaved.

She hadn't always been bitter and unkind. When she and Ken had lived in Doral, people had come to her with problems, because they knew she could be counted on for the truth and a helping hand. Wives of other cops had asked for advice and sometimes even taken it.

Now look who she had become.

Tracy Deloche had known Herb Krause for next to no time. Wanda hadn't been the old man's best bud, but still, she had known him longer. They'd swapped a few sentences, waved at each other on a regular basis. She owed him something for all the times she hadn't invited him for supper or at least taken him a plate when she'd made plenty to share. She knew she was the right person to help find Herb's family.

But even Dolly couldn't make her take the first step. Who knew where she might land?

The sound of a car in the driveway interrupted her unwelcome train of thought, although the car was unwelcome, too. She checked the clock over the stove. Maybe Ken had finally gotten up the courage to either move out, ask for a divorce or start acting like a husband again. More likely he just needed a clean shirt before he went wherever it was he went after work nowadays. If he'd done his laundry, he might even find one.

She was wiping the counters when the door opened and he stepped inside the little utility room that led into the kitchen. She ignored him until he was standing right beside her.

"Evening," he said.

"You got the time right, that's for sure."

"Sorry I didn't make it home for supper."

"Nothing to be sorry about. I didn't make you any. A waste of good food."

"I have more paperwork now than I had at Metro. If I didn't stay late, it would never get done."

Ken still referred to the Miami-Dade Police Department as Metro. All the old cops did. She wondered if he did that on purpose, so he could remember it the way it had been in the beginning, before everything had changed for him.

"If you didn't stay late, you might have to remember you're married," she said. "And we can't have that."

"Don't start on me, Wanda."

"Don't worry, the sun sapped all my energy." She rinsed out her dishrag, squeezed it like it was a certain cop's neck, then hung it over the faucet to dry.

"Herb Krause was found dead in his house this afternoon. Landlady found him."

"Yeah. I heard from the sheriff's department."

She studied her husband. He had changed out of his uniform, and wore dark jeans and a subdued Hawaiian-style shirt their daughter had given him. Ken was still a good-looking man. That never seemed fair to her. Men aged differently than women. At fifty-seven, Ken's hair was classic salt-and-pepper, and his tanned skin was lined from sun and wind. But he held himself tall the way he always had, and he hadn't drunk himself a beer belly or eaten his way to an extra chin. Even though his nose had been broken twice in the line of duty, it was still straight. Women continued to look at him with interest, while more and more men looked the other way when she walked by. She had fallen in love with that face, that body, almost on first sight.

Which just went to show that a woman could be swayed by the darnedest things.

"He was a nice old coot," she said.

"They're planning a funeral?"

"Doesn't seem to be a *they*. You don't know anything about a family, do you?"

"I never said more than hello to him."

She didn't repeat the obvious, that these days *hello* was the most anybody could expect from Ken. "There's lunch meat in the fridge if you want a sandwich. I made myself potato salad yesterday, and there's some left." She held up her bottle. "More of these, too."

"I ate lunch late. I need a walk more than I need food."

"Well, have at it. There's a whole beach out there waiting for you."

He didn't leave, the way she expected him to. "Except for the old man dying, you have a good day off?"

She was surprised he remembered she hadn't had to work. "Nothing special." She thought about her encounter with Tracy Deloche. Once upon a time the story would have made him smile, but Ken's gaze was already restless, like he was hoping to find something in the kitchen to think about besides her.

"You get out for a little sun?" he asked.

"I mostly stayed off my feet."

He didn't leave. He looked as if he wanted to say more, but she didn't have a clue what it might be.

"Something happen at work?" she prompted.

"Nothing ever happens."

"I don't know why you sound disappointed. Isn't that why we moved to Palmetto Grove?"

"I was just telling you about my day."

"What else do you want to tell me?"

"Nothing, Wanda. I'm just making conversation. You always say we don't talk anymore."

"Maybe I'm just imagining things changed. Maybe all the years of our marriage were as lonely and miserable as the last two, and I just forgot."

He had looked tired when he came in, and now he looked even more so. "I'm going to take that walk now."

"You do that, Kenny. I won't wait up."

He stood there for a moment, as if he did have more to say. For a moment—fool that she was—she was actually hopeful. Three little words could start their marriage back on the right track.

Come with me.

Despite what she'd said, their marriage *had* been good, the kind of marriage a woman never dares to hope for. That marriage could still be saved—if both of them wanted it to be, if both of them made an effort. But after trying so hard for so long, Wanda was pretty much out of effort herself. Ken had to be the one to make the next move.

He turned, and his hand was on the doorknob before he spoke again. "Maybe I'll see you in the morning."

She could feel her shoulders droop, but she kept her voice even. "Stranger things have happened."

He'd been gone a while before she made her way to the telephone. She wasn't worried he would come back now. Not until she was sound asleep and a new day had begun. She knew the pattern. She had hours on her own until she finally went to bed. But she wasn't going to spend them alone.

She made a pot of coffee, cut slices of the mocha pecan pie she hadn't told Ken about—let him find the pie if he ever looked in the refrigerator. In the bedroom she changed into a peach silk nightgown with silly little satin straps that barely held it in place. She liked the way the silk brushed her thighs and the cut of the gown hid the sag of fifty-seven-year-old boobs. The girls weren't as perky as they once had been, but no matter. They were sure perky enough to make her feel sexy and womanly, and she needed that tonight.

She left her hair up and her makeup on, because she wasn't going to bed. Instead, after she made a tray with a carafe of steaming hot coffee, the pie and real linen napkins, she settled herself on the sofa, lounging like Cleopatra on her barge down the Nile. All she needed to complete the image was the asp. Luckily her personal asp had just left for the night.

She picked up the telephone and dialed a familiar number. "Hey, hon," she said, her voice low and soft. "You're being seduced, 'cause I'm here all by myself." She listened for a moment, nodding as she did. "Now that would be swell. You know that's exactly what I want to do. I'm just lying here waiting."

chapter six

Tracy wasn't sure how she got interested in shells. Apparently moving to Florida did one of two things for people. Either a new resident learned to appreciate Mother Nature's exquisite craftsmanship, her use of color and intricate details and, yes, old nature woman's sense of humor—because what was funnier looking than a sea horse? Or that new resident got so thoroughly sick of shell wreaths, shell-filled lamps, shells with candles inside them, that the beauty became instantly invisible and shells on the beach were just an annoyance to crunch under flip-flops.

She had started in the second camp, victimized by some of the most hideous shell art ever conceived. A previous resident of her cottage had glued shells to everything that didn't move. Furniture and door frames, window ledges and even the toilet-seat cover. Then, as if that weren't bad enough, the "artist" had strung shells into room dividers. Tracy had found a shell-studded nativity scene packed in the closet, with the baby Jesus lying in a conch instead of a manger. She had packed it right back up and sent it to Sherrie, as a thank-you for all she had done to help Tracy during the divorce. It would be just like Sherrie to send her a box of Rocky Mountain oysters in return.

She wasn't sure exactly when she'd begun to appreciate shells. Somewhere along the way, as she removed the offending artwork, she stopped seeing the art and started noticing the motivation for it, the shells themselves. The journey to finding her own shells, unadulterated by craft glue or varnish, had been a short one. And the best time to find them was just before sunrise.

The day after finding Herb's body, Tracy woke in the dark and knew that she wouldn't be going back to sleep. She had dreamed she was home again, dressed in a designer gown she had sold in a consignment shop before leaving California. In the dream, though, the dress still belonged to her, and she looked wonderful in it. Tan, fit, unworried. She sailed through the door of the country club where she and CJ had been members, only to be stopped by two men in dark suits carrying walkie-talkies.

"You don't belong here," she was told. Then, as people gathered to watch, the two men turned into eagles, grasped her in their talons and lifted her high above the building. As she screamed, they flew higher and higher, and finally released her. She was tumbling down to a white sand beach when she awoke with a choked cry.

She didn't need Freud for an interpretation. In fact, once she shook off the worst of it, she was embarrassed. Other people had deep, richly nuanced dreams. Hers were cartoons on steroids.

She got up, and threw on shorts and a T-shirt. The sky was beginning to lighten, and a storm had come through last night, which meant that the beach would be filled with more shells than usual. She had lots to do that day. Find Herb's relatives. Find a job. Find someone to install the tiles that would be arriving that afternoon. But first, she was going to find shells.

She made green tea and poured it in a travel mug. Then she slid into her flip-flops, pocketed her keys and set out to see what treasures the storm had delivered.

She did not expect company.

"Jeez!" Tracy slapped her hand to her chest as an apparition appeared out of the darkness when she reached the shore.

The man took a step backward, as if to show that he had no ill intentions. He held up his hands. "Not to worry. Just out for a walk."

"On my beach!"

"Not exactly." The man gave her a slow grin. It seemed to take seconds. "The wet-sand area of a Florida beach is held in trust for all citizens."

"You're making that up."

"Nope. All tidally influenced waters—and you see this would qualify, right? You've noticed we have tides? Anyway, tidally influenced waters up to the average high-water line, plus bodies of fresh water deep enough to navigate to the same ordinary high-water line that existed in 1845—that's when Florida became a state, by the way—are considered sovereign. In other words, they're held in trust by the state for every cane-chopping Cracker and intruder on our shores."

Tracy stared at him. The man was somewhere on the road to forty, tall, but not tall enough to alleviate some of the extra weight around his middle. He was dressed in ragged cutoffs and a T-shirt that had been new in the 80s, when vendors sold it at Grateful Dead concerts.

"I have a bad, bad feeling I know who you are," she said.

He held out his hand. "Marshall Egan. My friends call me Marsh."

Tracy was very sure she would not be one of them.

As she worked on something to say, she eyed him warily. He

had a nice enough oval face, long hair drawn back in a short sandy ponytail, tan skin. Finally, because it would be too rude not to, she extended her hand for the quickest of shakes.

"Tracy Deloche."

"Yeah, I sort of suspected as much."

"Wild Florida, right?"

"You're up on things."

"Exactly what are you stalking this morning, Mr. Egan? Shells? Waterfowl? New lawsuits to keep me from selling the land you're standing on?"

"You weren't listening. You can never sell what doesn't belong to you."

She waved that away. "Then how about the part *I'm* standing on? Or that part just behind me? Do you have some new regulation to pull out that says the people of Florida own everything I thought I did?"

He smiled again. "We're working hard on it. Right now we're suing the Corps, but you could be next."

"Why? Did I step on something endangered? Some root or weed? Some microscopic beetle?"

"Nah, we're just not going to let you develop this land. We have so many strategies, our strategies have strategies."

"I wonder if I'd find you this annoying if it wasn't *my* land we were talking about?" She considered a moment. "Yeah, you know, I would. I really would. You're enjoying yourself. At my expense."

"'Expense' is a good word. Let's talk about it. Do you know what kind of expenses you're going to incur if you try to knock down so much as a bush?"

"You're right." She scuffed her palm along the side of her head. "I should just sign the deed over to you right now. What was I thinking? Then we can join hands and sing 'This Land is Your Land.' We can write a verse about white sand and mosquitoes."

"You are much too perky for this kind of animosity. It's just not becoming."

She stepped closer. "I used to be married to the greatest real-estate shark of all time. And even though I wasn't paying a lot of attention, I did learn a few things. First, you don't give up. Second, you don't give up. Third, while you're not giving up, you're also not letting people walk all over you. *You* do the walking. I got that much from my marriage, that and this bug-infested slice of Florida real estate. And by the time we're done here, you'll feel my footprints all over you, Marshall Egan."

He examined her as if she were one of those bugs. "Here's the thing," he said, not smiling this time. "It doesn't matter how many times you don't give up. You're not going to win. People are tired of seeing Florida dredged, developed and destroyed. You might say that's our own little 3-D show down here, only nobody needs funny plastic glasses to view the result. So people are throwing money at us right and left to stop it. And we're not stupid. We'd rather spend their contributions on land than lawsuits. Your real-estate agent knows Wild Florida's willing to start serious negotiations."

Tracy had already heard the organization's starting offer, as informal as it was. Maribel had informed Tracy that Wild Florida was talking a fraction of what a developer would pay in a better economy.

"When you get really serious, give me a call," she said. "But let's not play games. Come up a few million so at least we're playing ball on the same continent. This is prime land surrounded by water at a time when everybody wants their own view of blue." She remembered that phrase from one of CJ's brochures. "The economy's in the dumps right now, but soon enough developers will be looking hard for just what I'm offering. I can wait. Can you?"

"You have children?"

She shook her head. "Not that it's any of your business."

"It gives you a different perspective, or at least it should. I've got a boy. He's probably going to have kids of his own someday. I'd kind of like them to grow up knowing Florida has something to offer besides Disney World, golf courses, fancy marinas and retirement villages built on former wetlands."

"Then meet my price." She didn't owe him an explanation, but she gave one anyway. "This land is all I have. I'm not going to give it away. I plan to make enough selling it to live comfortably for the rest of my life."

He gave a low whistle. "That gives 'comfortable' a whole new meaning."

"I think we're done here. The tide's coming in. You stay down there in that…what'd you call it? That wet-sand area? You stay there too long, you'll be up to your knees in water on your way back home, unless you trespass and finish your morning walk on my property. And I'll be watching."

"No, you won't. You're not half as tough as you're making yourself out to be."

"Try me." The sun was peeking over the horizon now, and the sky was as pink as a Canadian sun-worshiper. For a moment she watched it climb; then, forgoing the chance to look for shells, she started back toward her cottage. She had lost all desire to enjoy anything Florida had to offer.

Janya watched the sun rising from her private scrub-shrouded sanctuary. She had found this spot on one of her morning walks. Surely somebody else knew about it, but nobody was ever here when she arrived each morning. She wasn't sure which she liked better, the sun rising in the sky, the very same sun that rose over India, or the way that the tide moved slowly back and forth, erasing all signs of nightly activity. A clean start, isn't that what they called such a thing here? A reminder that the past could be wiped away?

As she walked, she had picked up a long stick, using it to poke at sea creatures who had lost their way, and shells marooned by the tide. She nudged them carefully back to their saltwater home, although Rishi had told her that the shell creatures would die anyway. Perhaps so, but she thought there was still a possibility one might not. That was the one she hoped to save.

The sand where waves had lapped, then receded during the night was glassy smooth, a warm beige like the sleek fur of a lioness. She took a step forward and began to carve the perfect surface with the point of her stick.

Fifteen minutes later, her drawing was complete. She had re-created, as closely as she could, the image of Lakshmi, the goddess daughter of the ocean king. Lakshmi, of whom every other goddess was only a part, who raised up and gave power to the individual. Lakshmi, the goddess of fortune. Janya had drawn her sitting cross-legged in the cupped petals of a lotus, four arms extended, a peaceful expression on her lovely face. Or as lovely as a stick in golden sand could make her.

Exactly what would she ask Lakshmi for if she could?

She stood back and looked at the image, surprised she had created it. Drawing was part of her former life. She'd had no desire to release the images in her head since coming to Florida. Yet doing so now had seemed natural and effortless. Of course, this was only sand, and the tide would soon swallow all signs of it.

If she'd had the time, she would have waited to watch. Instead, she turned back toward her cottage. Rishi was already gone, anxious to start his day. His enthusiasm for software design mystified her, as did his decision to turn down substantial offers from two large corporations to work on their design teams. Instead, he had taken the money he'd earned as a computer consultant during his years of graduate school at Carnegie Mellon, invested it in marketing a suite of programs he'd designed to help small businesses, then used the profit from that to rent a former seafood processing warehouse on Palmetto Beach and set up his own software firm. The warehouse still smelled like fish, the office was furnished with secondhand castoffs from more prosperous businesses, and he worked with a skeleton staff. But Rishi had faith that these lean, hungry years would pay off. He said he was poised to fly.

For a moment Janya wondered where *she* would fly if she could. Back to India, but only if she could also fly back in time. If not? No place came to mind, because anywhere else, she would be a stranger again.

She removed her sandals at the door and brushed the sand off her feet. Then she went inside and set water on the stove for tea. Only when it was brewed, and she had taken time to breathe deeply and visualize herself in a calmer place, did she pick up the telephone. It would be five in the afternoon at home, and her mother would probably have finished her tea, a custom their family always observed with a masala-spiced mixture like Janya was drinking now, and samosas or other savory delicacies. Even if her mother had shopped late, she would still be home, making certain dinner preparations were under way, that the house had been swept and cleaned to her standards, that Janya's brother, Yash, was studying.

Janya's parents had hoped Yash might attend one of the colleges of Oxford, but her brother, though bright, was not a conscientious mathematics student. Instead, now he struggled in a local program to become a chartered accountant like their father. Janya knew that, secretly, Yash wanted to teach, that history was the subject he really wanted to pursue, and that the dream of joining the family business belonged to his parents. But Yash had yet to tell them. She wondered if he was afraid that when he did, his parents would turn their backs on him, as they had turned their backs on her.

Finally, as serene as she would ever be, she dialed the long series of numbers that would bring her voice home to India.

The woman who answered the telephone was not familiar, but Janya remembered that her mother had mentioned in one of their infrequent conversations that she had hired a new maid to help with cooking and cleaning. Janya identified herself to the young woman, but a long hesitation ensued, as if the maid were trying to place her. The muscles in Janya's throat grew tight as the maid finally agreed to bring her mother to the phone.

"Aii," she said in Marathi when her mother greeted her. "It is so good to hear your voice."

"Yes, Janya. How are things in the United States?" No matter the occasion, Inika Desai always sounded exactly the same, as if life was a business to be conducted with economy, each conversation a job to perform with haste. She was efficient and self-contained, and if she felt strong emotions, she had learned to disguise them. Janya couldn't remember her mother ever saying that she loved her, although open affection was less a part of the culture Janya had grown up in than the one that surrounded her now. Instead, Inika had demonstrated her love by giving her daughter a proper start in life.

A start she clearly thought Janya had squandered.

The telephone connection was so good today that Janya felt as if she were sitting in her mother's bedroom, as she had sat as a child, watching her mother fasten gold bracelets around her wrist and brush her jet-black hair.

"We are fine," Janya said. "Rishi works many hours, but he is an attentive husband."

"That is good, then."

"And how is my family?"

"Your family is there, in America, with your husband."

If her mother still felt the urge to instruct her in how to be a proper wife, Janya thought all was not lost. "How is my family in *India?*"

"Well enough. The heat is terrible and causes your father to cough, but soon the rains will come."

"And you?"

"I am always well."

Janya waited, hoping her mother would take the conversational lead, but when she didn't, Janya asked about Yash.

"He is a good boy who tries hard and never shames us."

Janya felt the slap as surely as if her mother's palm had extended across the miles between them. Her throat constricted again. She wasn't sure that words could make their way through the narrowed passage.

"He is not here to speak to you," her mother said, before Janya could force out the next question. "He is with his father during the day, now that school is not in session. Your father wants him to learn what his life will entail once he passes his exams. He has little time for conversation."

Janya asked about other relatives, her uncle and his sons and their families who lived on the top floor of the house the families shared. Her uncle's wife, who had undergone hip surgery, an elderly cousin of her father's who was nearing death.

Her mother gave perfunctory answers and finally reminded Janya that the call was expensive, and she must not waste Rishi's money on news that could be handled as well in a letter. Janya didn't have the opportunity to point out that her mother rarely wrote to convey news, because her mother continued.

"I will be writing you soon anyway. There is something I have to tell you that is best said on paper."

"It will take at least a week to arrive. What could possibly be best said in a letter?"

"The very news I will tell you. I don't want you to over-react. You must take this as if it were meant to be, as you must take every day of your life."

Janya had gotten to her feet to stretch, but now she sat down again. "But now I will worry."

"There is no need. This is something you cannot change with worry. It is simply something that is. No one is newly ill or dying. You are old enough to understand that not everything you want is good for you."

Janya knew there was no persuading her mother. A decision made was a decision chiseled into granite. As a child, Janya had pictured her mother's edicts as Sanskrit text on temple walls.

"I miss you," Janya said, although she knew the words were uttered for herself. She needed, somehow, to say them out loud, but she knew her mother would never acknowledge the emotion behind them. "I miss everything about India, even the things I didn't like."

"It will do you no good, this missing. Surely you are old enough to see that?"

"I don't think so."

"Then you must learn to."

"I hope you and *Baba* will come for a visit. I hope you are saving for it."

"We are saving to help your brother reach his destiny. For our part of his wedding once he marries. For his education and his children. That is our duty."

"I'm important, too," Janya said. Anger was beginning to

simmer beneath a long-nurtured sadness. "I am your daughter, and I'm worth saving for, as well. You will like Florida."

"Look to the future, Janya, not to the past. Your past is best forgotten."

Janya hung up a moment later. Outside, she heard someone passing. Through the window she saw Tracy Deloche, hands on hips, stomping by as if she had somewhere important to go.

Janya was afraid that she would never have a place like that herself, a place she truly needed to go and could. Never again.

Tracy was still furious. Of course she had known Wild Florida was determined to keep Happiness Key safe from development. She had been told Marsh Egan was a pit-bull attorney with hound-dog charm, and that he was capable of doing anything to get his way.

The man was legendary. Once he and other rabid environmentalists had chained themselves in a line one hundred yards long to stop a fleet of bulldozers from gaining entry to acreage they had vowed to protect. By the time sheriff's deputies arrived with bolt cutters sturdy enough for the job, a judge in Tallahassee had ruled that the developer's permits were not, after all, in order, and that the housing corporation he represented was lacking many of the documents needed to begin work. From that point on Wild Florida tied up everything so thoroughly that by the time the dust settled, the corporation was begging to sign over the property, in the end recouping ten cents for every dollar they had paid.

Tracy steamed as she thought about that. She was a woman alone. She had no resources to fight anybody. The best she could do was hang on until somebody else was willing to take on Wild Florida, somebody who could buy this land and make things happen in the courts. But she owned what nobody was making more of—unless she counted all that dredging—and waterfront property was precious for a reason. Marsh Egan might slow things down, but in the long run she would win. She pictured herself, wads of money clutched in her fists, and Marsh Egan sadly shaking his head as Happiness Key was transformed into manicured lawns, vivid hibiscus and soaring condominiums.

She walked back and forth along the road to calm down. She was passing Alice's cottage on the way back to hers when she saw Lee Symington heading toward the dark blue Saab in Alice's driveway. She almost drooled. No golden oldie T-shirts for Mr. Symington. He was dressed the way Tracy liked to see a man. Tailored suit, freshly pressed gray shirt, and a discreetly striped tie that looked as silky soft as a spring breeze.

The little girl she'd never formally met was following with his briefcase.

"You look ready for business," she called.

"I hope. I've got a family ready to make an offer on a house if I can iron out a few details." He put the briefcase in the car, then put his arm around the girl's shoulders and guided her over to Tracy.

"This is my daughter, Olivia. You met through the screened door."

Tracy was no connoisseur of children, but this one seemed pleasant enough. She was pretty, as children right before the onset of adolescence often were. But Olivia would be a pretty adult, too. The heart-shaped face, the smile that didn't look as if it would need an orthodontist's intervention, her father's riveting blue eyes, and silky, straight, brown hair, even with Florida's humidity.

They traded the usual adult-child pleasantries before Olivia skipped back to the house.

"She seems like a sweetie," Tracy said.

"I'm in favor of well-behaved children. I make sure I'm contributing to that vanishing pool."

"Well, good luck with your family. Any sale these days is a big event."

He gave her a smile that clearly said they were in that boat together. She liked the way his eyes lit up. And unlike the sneers that Marsh Egan had aimed at her, this smile was not meant to make her feel foolish.

"Even now, it's not impossible to sell a prime piece of property," Lee said. "It just takes patience and imagination. After we talked, I started making calls about Happiness Key. There's definite interest, but like you said, builders are cautious. So I'm going to get one of our junior salespeople to do a computer search of outside outfits who've done development in this area. And I'm sending a full-color brochure to every developer in the local association. Maribel will agree we need a little push."

"That's really beating the bushes." She thought about Egan's words. "And how are you going to mention Wild Florida's legal maneuvers?"

"Developers are used to that, Tracy." He hesitated. "Okay if I use your first name?"

"I'm a California girl. Casual all the way."

"About as casual as an Hermès scarf."

She *loved* a man who knew quality and designers.

"As for the developers?" he said. "Once they see the potential, they'll find a way to do whatever they want."

"Short of murdering Marshall Egan, I'm not sure what they *could* do."

"Then we'll have to find somebody with very few scruples."

She laughed. "Well, you've cheered me up. And I needed it."

"Let me cheer you up some more. Let me take you out to dinner."

"Isn't that a conflict of interest?"

"Maribel listed the property, and I work for her, remember? But we'll try not to talk about Happiness Key. We'll go to the yacht club, and I'll introduce you to the event planner if you're still interested. There's some kind of private party tonight, but we could do it tomorrow if you're free."

"That will be great."

"Then it's a date. Let's shoot for seven." He smiled, and she felt the warmth tickling her in places that proved she was not invulnerable to a good-looking man.

She put the tickling aside, although she hated to. "Before you go, did you have a chance to ask your mother-in-law about Herb?"

"I completely forgot. I'm sorry."

"No problem. I'll go over later and see what she knows."

"I wouldn't." Lee looked as if he weren't sure how to phrase his objection. "Alice hasn't been herself since my wife died. She had a small stroke, no obvious damage that shouldn't improve with time, but she's still going downhill. The doctors are worried about some kind of permanent dementia."

"Alzheimer's?"

He shrugged. "One of the possibilities. The problem is, trying to remember things upsets her. It would be better if I just approached this casually. I'll tackle it tonight. Will that work?"

"Sure, and thanks."

"I'll let you know if I find out anything. Need a ride to your door?"

He favored her with another warm smile when she said no. She thought those smiles might become an addiction.

Once she was inside her cottage, surrounded by all the considerable evidence of her new start, she smiled, too. She didn't want to be here. Not in this state, not in this place. But it was quite possible being here was going to be more tolerable than she had feared only yesterday.

chapter seven

Wanda wasn't sure when Ken came in from his nightly walk, but the next morning she found the paper on the table again, and the remnants of a pot of coffee on the counter. How the man survived on next to no sleep didn't concern her. Nobody was forcing him to prowl Palmetto Grove Key. Whatever he was doing, he was on his own, and for all she knew he had found a comfortable bed at the end of the prowl that didn't include her.

Since the beginning of April, she had worked the lunch shift at the Dancing Shrimp. She and Lainie, her supervisor, had decided lunch would free up her evenings for more important things, and besides, lunch tips were good in the summer. The Dancing Shrimp sat right on the bay, and Wanda usually took the outside tables. Customers on the deck felt expansive, as if they ought to pay a little more for their superior view of sailboats and pontoons, and besides, Wanda always gave extra special service.

Some servers felt that waiting on people was beneath them. Not Wanda. Life wasn't a beach, just something that sounded like it, and everybody needed TLC now and again just to get through. A person never knew what somebody else was living with. Wanda didn't take sass, but she was good with the grumps, making them smile, even laugh, by the time she handed over their checks. She had that gift, and bringing food, making recommendations, replenishing drinks? It was just a good way to use her God-given talent.

Today, however, by the time her shift ended at two, she was dragging. The outside deck was shaded, and fans kept the air moving, but between the pervading heat, a couple of difficult customers and another server who had a hissy fit because a party of notorious big spenders requested Wanda, she felt as if somebody had turned her inside out. Plus her stomach was bubbling and churning, and she'd eaten a whole roll of Tums by the end of her shift. She figured that making a coconut cream pie in the summer wasn't such a good idea if only one party was around to eat it. And eat it. And eat it.

The doings at work weren't the only problem. She wasn't happy with herself. When things didn't go well at the workplace, but they were fine at home, she could manage. Vice versa, more or less. But when things weren't going well anywhere? Well, life seemed way too complicated. And sad.

Back at the cottage, she changed out of her uniform: blue capris and a red polo shirt with a logo of two jitterbugging shrimp stitched in rainbow-colored thread. She couldn't imagine a frumpier outfit, but at least when something spilled or splattered, it wasn't as if she were emotionally attached. And the shrimp did add a little character, kind of a "dance before they eat you" flavor to the whole ensemble.

In the tiny living room she collapsed on the vintage rattan sofa upholstered with prints so bright Ken used to say—when he was still talking—that a person needed sunglasses just to watch television. She didn't really care. The orchids, palm fronds and what-all in vivid hues of her favorite purples, limes and oranges always made her smile. A plush monkey puppet swung from a shelf that sported a framed photo of Elvis before he went and got fat, and the king was surrounded by smaller photos of her children and grandchildren. Elvis and the monkey made her smile, too, and the grandkids made her feel all lit up inside.

She got up to lower the bamboo shades on the windows and rewound the VCR. In a moment she was immersed in the day's doings on *All My Children*. She had not missed an episode of *AMC* in thirty-one years. The day she did, something terrible was going to happen. She didn't know why or how, she just knew. Still, that was no matter, because that disaster was never going to occur. She had two VCRs that recorded the show, just in case one went down the way VCRs liked to do if they could get away with it. She had asked Ken for one of those fancy TiVo machines for her birthday, but he hadn't even re-membered the day, much less the present. No matter. When she moved out and got her own place, she was going to buy one. In the meantime, that was one less thing they would have to fight over at the divorce.

By the time the episode ended, she felt worse. Julia had gone and got herself shot! Wanda couldn't believe it, but she'd seen it happen with her own eyes. Then she'd refused heroic measures and just up and died. Just like that, written off the show. Wanda felt as if she'd lost a friend. And it looked like old Tad was next.

Something had to change. She flicked off the VCR and rewound the tape to get it ready for tomorrow, and as she did, she tried to think out why she was feeling so bad. As much as she hated to face it, the reason was pretty clear. She had let Miss Priss Deloche get to her, and she hadn't done anything about it. She had hoped that just admitting to herself that she wasn't at her best last night would be enough. But now she knew that just slapping herself on the wrist wasn't going to cut it.

She rolled up the shades and stared out the window. She was a big believer in making amends. Enough alcoholics had explained the concept to her over the years as they ordered club soda and a twist of lime. That was something they learned at meetings, when they tried to sober up. If a person screwed up, they had to make good somehow.

She wasn't all that wrought up over the Deloche woman. Any landlady could stand to be slapped around a little. Sometimes you just had to shake good sense into a body, like salt into chicken and dumplings. You never knew how much it was going to take, either. You just had to add a little, then try some more, until you got it right. In the end, everybody who partook was better off for your doing it.

But none of that excused the way she was letting down old Herb. He'd been a sweet old man, never did anybody a bit of harm. She should have been kinder, and now, with a chance to make amends, she was walking away. She wasn't sure what she could do—that was kind of up in the air—but at least she should try. Guilt was a lot of extra weight for a body to carry. She was carrying enough weight as it was, considering that she was eating all the pie she baked these days, with no help from Ken.

Restless now, she went into the kitchen and got a glass of ice water. From the kitchen window she saw movement over at Herb's cottage. Without wasting more time thinking about it, she went outside and walked up the road to see what was happening. When she got closer she saw that the Indian woman with the funny name was moving slowly among the old man's plants. Wanda was almost at the house before she realized what she was doing.

"Now, that's a good idea," she called, crossing through the open gate that led into the yard. "They would have died in a couple of days, that's for sure."

Janya looked up, hose in hand. The trickle was aimed in one of Herb's pots of hibiscus. "Hello, Mrs. Gray."

"You can call me Wanda. And you're what, Tanya? I'm not good with names."

"Very close. Janya, with a *J*."

"People are always making up new names. I just can't keep up."

"Mine is common enough in my country."

"Here it seems like mamas and daddies just put together any sounds they like, doesn't matter what they are, and that's what they call their poor little kids. Like those Christian names people have been using for centuries aren't good enough for them anymore."

"In many cultures, creating a name makes each child an individual."

"Me, I stuck with the tried and true." Wanda watched the woman carefully rotating the hose so that all the dirt got thoroughly and slowly soaked. "What made you think to water these? That Deloche woman ask you to?"

"No, I just thought it was something I could do for Mr. Krause."

"He's not exactly here to appreciate it anymore."

"He worked hard to make these grow. It seems possible his family will want them. Plants this size are valuable, are they not? I have seen them in nurseries. The prices are extraordinary."

"Yeah, I guess. The kind of plants I grow don't need water. I stick 'em up on a shelf and that's it until they get so dusty I give them the old heave-ho."

"I think I might like to make things grow. At the least I can keep these from dying."

Wanda was almost jealous. Janya with a *J* had figured out something to make herself feel better. She watched the young woman—younger, she thought, than Wanda's own daughter—move the hose to the next plant, some kind of tree with big round leaves.

"You like living here?" Wanda asked, because she was still trying to figure out some piece of this problem she could claim. "Or are you planning to make a bunch of money, then go home and spend it, like so many foreign people do?"

Janya seemed to consider. "I don't think so. I think I will be here forever. But is it a problem when people do that? Spend what they earn in other places, I mean? I think some people can't earn what they need to support their families in their own countries, so they earn it here by working hard."

"All that one-world stuff, right? I don't know, but it just doesn't seem right to me. It can't be good, all that American money leaving the country."

Janya smiled a little. "It is certainly good for the people who work hard and are able to feed their families."

Wanda supposed that was true, although the notion still disturbed her.

"Did Herb ever talk to you about family? Because I know Ms. Deloche wants to find them."

"He talked to me very little. And not about anything personal."

As if she had conjured Tracy Deloche, Wanda saw the woman bearing down on them. She stood her ground, although she wasn't all that comfortable, considering the way she had refused to help last night with the mattress.

Tracy came to a stop in front of Janya. "Thanks so much for doing that," she said. "It really is nice of you to offer a helping hand when it's needed."

Wanda knew a slight when she heard one. Janya nodded

politely. Then Tracy faced Wanda. Her tone was ten degrees cooler. "How are you, Wanda?"

"Not bad. Yourself?"

"I'm still trying to find Herb's family. I'm kind of stymied. From what Lee says, Alice's memory isn't good, so I can't count on her. And I hate going through his stuff if I don't need to. I just wondered if you could describe the guys you saw Herb playing chess with. I drove by the park I think you mean, and there was some kind of chess tournament going on, with about fifty old men in fishing caps sitting under the trees."

"Sounds like you got the right place. And his friends were old men in fishing caps."

"Brutal…" Tracy shook her head. "I guess I'm stuck with asking each and every one of them."

Wanda knew her chance to help had arrived, but she did her best not to listen to the voice determined to have its say. In the end, she just wasn't as deaf as she wanted to be.

"I can't describe them worth a darn, but I can find them," she said after a sigh. "I saw him there more than once."

"I don't suppose you'd come with me to point them out?"

"I guess I could do that."

Tracy didn't hide her astonishment. "Well, that's awfully nice of you."

"Believe it or not, there are people on this planet who think I'm usually awfully nice."

Tracy licked her lips, as if that might help her form a reply.

"Don't waste your time trying to figure out what to say to that," Wanda said. "I've got some time right now. How about you?"

"I've got nothing these days but time."

"Then let's have at it," Wanda said. She glanced at Janya, who had moved to another plant. "Nice talking to you," she told her.

Janya nodded. "Most interesting."

Wanda thought that was a nice reply. Being interesting was a good thing in her book.

Grambling Park, where Herb had played chess, was a green expanse dotted with palms and feathery leafed trees that looked as if they had been planted not too far in the distant past. Flower beds sporting marigolds and zinnias rimmed a spewing fountain. Tracy could almost see the spray evaporating. She parked the Bimmer in one of the few spots in the shade and gratefully fed the meter. She was as glad to be out of the car and the glowering presence of Wanda Gray as she was to be on this quest. If she could find Herb's family, the cottage could be cleared out and a new renter installed. Of course, that depended on finding somebody willing to take a month-to-month rental, just as high summer approached. Happiness Key was surrounded by water, but there were no pretty white sand beaches out at the point for sunning or swimming, not until the developers got through with it.

Wanda took her time getting out, grumbling about having to haul herself out of a car so low to the ground. Tracy bit back a response. She was still in shock the woman had agreed to help, and suspicious, as well. Quite possibly Tracy was missing something, and Wanda was going to zap her yet again.

If so, the time wasn't now. Wanda stood with her hands on her substantial hips, clothed, as Tracy had noted earlier, in bright purple polyester cycling shorts topped with a purple-and-lime-striped shirt that emphasized breasts that must have made her the target of many a preteen boy's uncontrolled lust—or jokes. Wanda was a creature of excesses. Hair too bright, makeup too obvious. And the way she walked? As if she were about to jump into the life of every person who came within ten feet of her. She was a neon sign advertising something, although Tracy had yet to figure out what.

"Do you recognize anybody?" Tracy asked.

Wanda pointed. "See that group on the far edge? The two guys at the table with the one hovering over him?"

"That's them?"

"I'm almost sure."

"Great. Shall we see up close?"

Wanda strutted off, and Tracy caught up with her. "I'd like to get this over with. The funeral home called today. If we don't find Herb's family by the end of next week, they're going to go ahead and cremate him. They said he wanted things to be taken care of quickly, and they have to go ahead."

"More likely they just want the space, people in Florida dying as fast as they do. Comes of an aging population."

"That's pretty cynical."

"Don't get me started." Wanda glanced at her. "Why do you care, anyway?"

"Well, out of respect, for one thing."

Wanda made a noise that said, right, tell me another one.

"And because I need to clean out his house and see about getting another renter."

"Money, money, money." Wanda rubbed her thumb over her fingers.

"You work in a restaurant, right? You wouldn't do it if they didn't pay you. Or is it that much fun to recite the daily specials and refill the ice water?"

"You know all those things that are wrong with my house?"

"Don't worry, I carry your list close to my heart."

"I bet there are just as many wrong at Herb's place."

"So?"

"So you try to rent it the way it is and throw in that crazy lease that says you can kick them out the moment you sell the property, shake that up with predictions of a miserable hot summer courtesy of global warming and the story of an old man who just died in their new bedroom, and just see how many people come running to pay you good money."

"*You* did."

"No, I didn't. *I'm* not stupid. My husband signed our lease. And at the time Palmetto Grove didn't have a whole lot of places to rent. But all those people who want to sell and leave Florida now, only they can't? They're all renting out their houses."

"You're the good-news kid, aren't you?"

"I just tell it like it is. Somebody has to."

"Who appointed *you?*"

"It's a God-given talent."

Tracy knew she had to talk to Maribel, and soon, about the possibilities for Herb's house. But she was feeling glummer by the moment.

"Yep, that's them," Wanda said, nodding toward the old men she had pointed out earlier.

Tracy wasn't sure why this particular arrangement of age spots, crooked spines, badly shaven chins and funny-looking caps could seem so familiar to Wanda, but she went on faith. "Shall I talk to them, or would you like to?"

"Oh, I got you here, now it's up to you."

Tracy approached the old men, who didn't look up. She still sent them her most dazzling smile, hoping it would somehow grab their attention. "Hi, gentlemen. My name is Tracy Deloche. Could you give me a moment of your time?"

She kept the smile firmly in place, because she had expected three sets of eyes to swing in her direction. Instead nobody stirred. The two who were seated on either side of a beat-up card table didn't even look up. The third man, who cast a pencil-thin shadow over the table, gave her the briefest of glances, then went back to silently hovering.

Tracy wondered if they were all hard of hearing. What would it be like to be this old and used up, to have so little going for you that your whole day revolved around a silly game in the park? Out of respect for the obvious depth of their concentration, she waited a few seconds before she tried again.

"Gentlemen, I need just a moment. Then you can go right back to your game."

This time even the hoverer didn't glance her way. She moved a little closer and put on a bigger smile, as if she weren't annoyed.

"You know, a girl just hates to be ignored. And this is about a friend of yours, Herb Krause. I'm his landlord, or I should say I was. He died day before yesterday."

She paused, and for a moment she wondered if she was breaking bad news without preparation and the consequences to their feeble old hearts might be a problem. "Um, you know that, right?" She tried to sound sympathetic.

One of the men at the table finally looked up. He wore thick glasses and what might well be a toupee under his cap. "You have problems with your eyesight? We're busy right now."

She knew when to push an advantage. "I appreciate that, I really do. But I've got a problem, and you might be able to help."

The second man at the table, who sported a mustache that was so thin she guessed it was only two hairs wide, looked up, and the two men stared at each other. Finally the second man turned to look at Tracy. "So you have the problem, but *we're* supposed to drop everything?"

"Just for a second." She put her thumb and forefinger together with just the smallest space between them. "A millisecond. I'm trying to find Herb's family, and I know he used to play chess with you gentlemen. I'm just hoping one of you might remember something about them. See, we can't find anybody he was related to. I have all his stuff, and the funeral home wants to cremate him."

The man turned back to his friend. "You remember anything?"

"Not me."

He looked up at the man above him. "How about you?"

"Nothing."

"Can we go back to our *game* now?" he asked, without turning back around. "Now that we've dropped everything like you wanted?"

Tracy had learned from the master and knew better than to quit. "I don't need a lot to go on. Did he mention children? Cousins? Nieces or nephews? If you'd just think for a minute?"

The hoverer pointed to the man facing Tracy. "You going to take all day to make that move?"

"Now I got to start all over again putting it together play by play. Since I got interrupted."

"Go ahead," the other player said. "We'll wait. All we've got is time, and our little *game*."

"Now, boys," Tracy said in the voice that had usually gotten her anything she wanted from CJ. "If that was you lying over at the Memorial Funeral Home, wouldn't you want *somebody* to help the people who cared enough to find your family? All I need is some little thing to go on. Doesn't it bother you to think of Herb all alone, and the people who loved him finding out when it's too late that they could have been there to see him to a better end?"

"There's some kind of echo at this park," the player facing Tracy told the other men. "Maybe we got a mockingbird up in one of those trees. Or a wild parrot. I hear there's a colony of them down the coast a few miles."

Tracy's smile died. She stepped up to the table, pushing the hoverer with her shoulder until she was right between the seated men. "Now you listen! I think you could help if you wanted, and you're just yanking my chain. That old man died, and it's my job to pack up his stuff and send it on to his family. And I plan to do that. I'm not leaving until I get what I came for. What's wrong with you? He was a friend of yours!"

"Apparently not yours, though." The man with the glasses stood. He was an inch or two taller than she was, but he looked like a good puff of wind would send him sailing out over the gulf. "Herb wouldn't have tolerated *you* for one minute. Go away and leave us alone."

Tracy wasn't sure how she upended the card table. One moment she was stepping closer so she could see eye-to-eye with the old man. The next she was stumbling right into the table. She grabbed the edge to keep herself from falling over it, and as she did, the table flipped in her direction. The chess board, the entire tableau of royalty and pawns, slid off and into the grass at her feet. Behind her, she could hear Wanda screeching "Lordy, Lordy!"

Tracy's arms were like the blades of a windmill as she tried to keep from following the table. She hit the man on her right in the face and socked the one on her left under the chin as she struggled to keep her balance. But she was still standing as the table finished pitching forward and landed on its side.

Tracy jumped backward. "You pushed me!" She grabbed the hoverer by his sleazy rayon sleeve. "*You* did that, not me."

He shook her off with surprising strength. "No such thing, girlie. You nearly pushed me over getting to the table. I was just trying to find my balance."

Tracy felt a hand grip her shoulder and fingernails, long tal-onlike nails, digging into her flesh. "Git now," Wanda said. "Right now. Outta here."

Tracy hated to take advice from Wanda, but this time she

was on the mark. Wanda tugged, and she followed. In a moment the old men were behind her, and in a few more, Wanda had pulled her halfway back to the car at a near run.

"I did not...pull that table...over on purpose!" Tracy said.

"And did you behave like a horse's ass on purpose?" Wanda demanded. "Did you talk to those men like they were little kids instead of men who supported their families, and raised their children, and did jobs that contributed to society before they got so old and retired?"

Tracy noted the way she had said "contributed." Con-tree-beauted. It made her feel better somehow, although the rest of the speech rankled.

"I was nice to them!"

"Like hell you were." Wanda had released Tracy's shoulder now and was sprinting as fast as she could in sandals with four-inch heels, confident, Tracy supposed, that she was going to follow. "There wasn't nothing charming about what you did back there, let me tell you. Just because you're all young and perky doesn't mean you get to treat your elders any way other than with respect. And it served you right they wouldn't talk to you. I wouldn't have, that's for sure. The way you treat people is a downright sin."

"Me? Who was it that broke in to Herb's cottage last night, then wouldn't help with his mattress?"

"Why do you think I came today? I felt bad about that, but now I wish I hadn't."

"I just want to find Herb's family!"

"Well, those men don't have to help you unless they want to. Got it? You're not some fairy princess, and they aren't your serfs. You're in the same boat the rest of us are, milady. *Noblesse* does not *oblige* here. Until you stop acting like royalty, nobody's going to help you do a darned thing."

Tracy wasn't sure which to be most surprised about. That Wanda knew what *noblesse oblige* meant, or that she herself had a most uncomfortable feeling that there might be a smidgen of truth in the things Wanda was saying.

They got into the car without another word, and Tracy backed out of the parking spot. She didn't want to look in the direction of the old men, but she couldn't help herself. One was working to right the table. Two were on all fours, picking up the fallen chessmen. Laboriously, if a quick peek could determine such a thing. Dismay filled her.

Wanda didn't say anything as they drove. The only reminder that she was in the car was the cloying scent of orange blossoms. When they got to Happiness Key, Tracy pulled to a stop in front of Wanda's cottage, and the other woman slammed the door behind her. Tracy watched as she swished her hips on the way up her walk. But she found nothing humorous about it now. Wanda seemed a step classier than she had at the beginning of their drive.

Inside her own cottage, Tracy dropped to the sofa and closed her eyes. Was Wanda right about her? Or had she simply encountered the worst pod of grumpy old men on the planet? She had lost her temper, and in all fairness, maybe she had acted just the teeniest bit overbearing. She could have waited for the next move to finish, could have asked them if they had time to talk to her and made an appointment for another time if not. But they hadn't been mapping a new continent, hadn't been finding a cure for cancer. Chess was a game. Nothing happened if a move got interrupted. No one died. Nobody missed the entrance to the Northwest Passage.

Frustration was an annoying buzz inside her. She sat quietly for a few minutes, going over what she could do next to find Herb's family. Of course this really wasn't her problem, or didn't need to be. She could pack away anything in his house that looked valuable and dump everything else—or at least she assumed she could legally do that. She would have to find out. But she wasn't ready to quit yet. She wasn't sure why, but she wasn't. So what could she do that didn't include the men at the park?

She got up to get herself a glass of papaya juice when she noticed the file folder she had retrieved from Maribel. She had removed it from her purse before heading off with Wanda, but she hadn't looked beyond the first page, which sported a blank beside "next of kin." Now she stopped and paged through it, looking for something, anything, that might help. The last sheet was a list of previous landlords. Two of them.

"Sweet." The references might be outdated and probably wouldn't be much help, but at least she had something to try. She tucked the list under her arm, and went into the kitchen for juice and the telephone. In a few minutes she was settled back in the living room, dialing the first number.

A woman answered, and Tracy started right in once she was sure she had the right person. She explained who she was and why she was calling, then, "I need your help. We're trying to find Mr. Krause's family, and so far we haven't had any luck. So if you wouldn't mind checking your records for me, I can wait. I don't mind hanging on, but this is important."

She thought she'd sounded concerned and businesslike, but the woman on the other end gave a nasty laugh. "Well, you're going to have to hang on for a very long time, honey. I'm up to my elbows in bread dough right now, and I'm not inclined to wash my hands until I'm finished."

Tracy took a deep breath and cranked up the warmth. "I'm probably calling at a bad time, but you see, I really need to find his family as fast as possible—"

The phone went dead.

Tracy sat there and stared at it.

Minutes later she tried the second number. When a man answered, she asked if he had a moment, and when he asked if she was a telemarketer, she assured him she wasn't, explaining quickly why she was calling.

"If this isn't a good time, I can call back," she said humbly. "I don't want to trouble you, but the funeral home wants to cremate the body, and I just hate to let that happen without finding his family first. So, is there a good time to talk?"

The man, who sounded like he might be a few breaths from cremation himself, assured her that now was an excellent time. If she didn't mind hanging on a moment, he would see if he could locate the rental agreement that Herb had signed for him. He didn't remember anything about Herb's family, but maybe he had something in his records.

Tracy sat quietly, despite every instinct to hurry the man along, and simply waited.

chapter eight

The day after she wreaked havoc in the lives of three old men, Tracy spent the morning getting estimates from tile installers. The tile arrived in the afternoon, and because she didn't completely trust her neighbors, she asked the two high school boys who delivered it to pile it out of sight behind her back door. Not that far from spending their summers with a pile of Lego, the boys carefully made six stacks with just enough space between them for the door to open. When she walked between the towers Tracy felt menaced. She really had to get the tile on her floor soon.

The first installer's estimate, produced right on the spot, was so high she tore it up. The salesman at the flooring warehouse had said he was the best, but not cheap. Tracy was planning to be okay with second best, or even third, as soon as the other two drew up formal estimates.

In the midst of the interruptions she still managed to get the first coat of paint on her living-room walls. She wanted to finish before the tile went in, so she didn't have to worry about dribbling paint on her new floor. She was pleased with her choice of color, and the improvement gave her a new shot of energy.

By late afternoon she was tired but proud. She cleaned up her mess, then took a well-deserved shower to get ready for dinner with Lee. While she toweled herself dry in her tiny bedroom, she considered her wardrobe.

Clothes were communication, but she was out of the habit of thinking about the message she was sending. With CJ, there had only been one. He had wanted other men to envy him, and Tracy's role was to be provocative and unattainable, a woman men would fantasize about having, while knowing that the possibility was eternally out of their reach.

As far as Tracy knew, CJ had been pleased with his choice of a third wife—the first two, acquired while he was building his empire, having failed to meet his exacting standards. He had rewarded her with jewelry, with vacation homes and surprise trips to world-class destinations. These had been payment of a sort for fulfilling the unspoken promises she had made to him. She had been a wife he could point to with pride.

Since the divorce and the humiliation and the exile, she had stopped dressing like a kept woman. She'd stored some of her wardrobe, placed some in consignment shops, given some to charities—with the proper deductions. What remained were not things she had bought to satisfy her ex-husband, but things she simply liked to wear. Now, searching through the closet, she wondered what message Lee was looking for?

Did she care?

Lately, those kinds of thoughts plagued her. Her upbringing had seemed normal. At her mother's knee she'd learned that pleasing a man was the road to a secure future, and "secure future" meant a net worth of eight figures, minimum. She'd been perfectly comfortable basing her life on this. Digging deeper hadn't appealed to her. What was the point, when her own plans for the future seemed to be working out just fine?

Now, and not for the first time, she silently cursed CJ Craimer, who had believed that laws were only written to keep the little guy under control. If CJ had been even marginally more upright, Tracy would not have to consider all these difficult questions.

By the time she was ready, she felt wrung out, not from the hard work of the day, but from figuring out who she was and who she wanted to be. And this was only one date. The possibility that the rest of her life might be this complicated terrified her.

When she heard Lee's footsteps coming up the walk, she didn't wait for a knock. She grabbed her purse and a beaded shawl, and opened the door. She saw instant admiration in his eyes, and she forgot she had almost decided admiration didn't matter.

"What a great dress," he said.

She liked the dress, too. Royal blue, with drifts of green, it seemed to float when she moved, light, airy and cool. She'd bought it off a sidewalk rack in some Caribbean island town where an artist had dyed, then painted, the fabric, but she had rarely worn it. At the Riviera Country Club or at Bel Air, where she would have been hobnobbing with Hollywood stars and other notables, the dress would have been out of place. Here, she wasn't sure she cared.

"Thanks." She smiled at him. "I've been looking forward to this."

"And I've been looking forward to having a beautiful woman on my arm again."

"That's very kind."

"No, just very true." He held out his arm. "May I?"

He helped her into his Saab, which was, despite the presence of a child in his life, absolutely spotless. No gum wrappers or forgotten flip-flops. That made Tracy smile again. Clearly Lee had made an effort tonight.

He got in and turned the key. The engine kicked once, then died.

"That's odd." Lee tried again with the same results. The third time it didn't start at all.

"Have you been having problems?" Tracy asked.

"No, but my mechanic was out of town, so I had it tuned up at a new garage this morning. They swore they've worked on plenty of Saabs."

Tracy saw a lovely evening evaporating. "Even if it starts, we don't want to break down. Let's take mine. You can call the garage in the morning."

"I hate to make you drive."

"Not a problem." Tracy opened her door and got out. Luckily he had parked on the road and hadn't blocked the driveway. She unlocked the driver's door of the Z3, watching Lee smooth his hand over the hood as she did. He was looking at the convertible with longing, the way a little boy eyes a neighbor kid's brand-new bike. She reached across the roof and held out her keys.

"You drive."

"I'm perfectly comfortable being your gigolo."

She liked this man. He had shown up at her door looking far better than presentable, his slacks pressed to perfection, his gray sports coat an expensive, tropical-weight linen over a charcoal-colored shirt. She liked the way he could poke fun at himself. She stretched her arm farther so the keys were practically tickling his chest.

"Drive."

"You clearly understand men."

After she showed him how to put the top down and they were cruising along the road, they chatted about nothing, as if they had been friends for years. She felt no pressure to entertain him. He told funny stories about selling real estate; he asked good questions. They arrived before she knew it. She hadn't realized how close the yacht club really was, or possibly it was just as far away as she'd thought, and she'd just been too charmed to notice.

Now she took stock of their destination. The Sun County Yacht Club was Tara in miniature, pretentiously and classically Deep South in flavor, with nothing of Florida in the architecture. A circular driveway bordered by softly glowing lanterns led to the front steps, and as they approached, a young man in a white jacket stepped up to park the car. Lee gave him the keys and sternly admonished him to take care of it. Tracy saw him slip the valet a bill, and she was glad that *she* hadn't been the one behind the wheel.

Lee helped her out, then led her up the steps, which extended between four massive Doric pillars that looked strong enough to hold the entire state of Florida.

Lee put his hand on her back to guide her to the door. "The yacht club's been around for almost a hundred years, but only in this building for ten. As clubs like this one go, it's pretty exclusive."

Tracy saw the humor. "This isn't exactly Palm Beach."

He winked. "Tell them if you want, but I don't plan to mention it. They may not have star power, but they're still sure they're better than everybody else."

"I guess that's a start."

"They turn down five applications for every one they accept. Maribel had to twist a few arms when I came up for review. But it's a wonderful place to make contacts. I've had a few of my best sales strictly because I'm a member."

She liked Lee's casual, self-deprecating style. She suspected it played well here, where the old guard would expect to be catered to by upstarts.

Inside, he was warmly greeted by name by several club personnel. Tracy found herself standing taller. For the first time since leaving everything that was familiar, she felt at home. She *knew* this place. The fresher-than-fresh flowers, air cooled to the perfect temperature, gleaming white Carrara marble floors and crystal chandeliers. Okay, maybe the designers, both inside and out, had lacked imagination, but the effect still cried money and status. She could settle for that.

The dining room looked over a marina with a variety of boats ranging from modest cabin cruisers to the honest-to-goodness yachts that had given the club its name. They were ushered to a seat near the floor-to-ceiling windows, and the view was breathtaking.

"I can imagine working here," she said, as Lee politely pulled out her chair and settled her in the spot with the best view. "I could never get tired of looking at this."

"Happiness Key will have a marina as pretty as this, once the red tape's been cut."

"We'll drink to that when we have something besides water."

Lee asked their server, who had just arrived, to bring the wine steward to their table, and at his urging they chose a California Pinot Grigio that was new to the club's wine list.

Once he'd gone, they ordered mushrooms stuffed with crabmeat to start. By now Tracy felt relaxed enough to feel every sore muscle from her active day.

"You're easy to be with," Lee said. "We seem to have similar tastes."

"Let's not forget being stuck in a couple of neighboring cottages that have seen better days."

"Did they? See better days?"

She giggled. "Probably not. Even brand-new, they must have been awful."

"I'm guessing they were built right after the war. Maybe for returning G.I.s."

"Actually, from everything I've seen, they've always been vacation rentals. In the early fifties a local family owned the land and planned a big resort. They started with ten cottages and a rental office. They were going to add a modest-size motel, miniature golf, even a drive-in theater, the whole nine yards. They were going to call it…" She paused for effect. "Happiness Haven."

Lee shuddered, and she laughed. "My ex discovered that on some document, and that's when he got the bright idea of calling his development Happiness Key."

"What happened to all those plans?"

"The family fell on hard times, but they refused to sell the land until recently, when the last member moved out of the area. Maybe they were still hopeful they could follow through on development, I don't know. When the cottages began to need serious repairs, they bulldozed them one by one. You can still see the foundations of the others if you look."

"So your ex dove in and grabbed the property."

"When it came to finding a deal, CJ was an Olympic champ."

"Maribel says he was something else."

"Right. A felon."

"I don't think that's what she meant. She seems to admire him."

"If she's interested, he's probably ripe for a pen pal."

"I didn't mean to take the conversation in that direction." He put his hand over hers briefly and squeezed. "I'm sorry."

"I'm so over CJ there's nothing to apologize for. He left me a mess, but he also—inadvertently—left me Happiness Key. I figure that makes us even."

"So your marriage was a business arrangement?"

"When a marriage ends, that's when you finally get a clear view of what you had."

She paused and realized what she'd said. "Now I'm the one who's sorry. Lee, I was talking about *my* marriage, not yours. It must be totally different when somebody dies."

"I've never been sure which is worse. When you divorce, there's so much anger, you can't look back on the good times without getting angry all over again."

"You sound like somebody who knows."

"I was divorced before I met Karen. College sweethearts who discovered they had different ambitions. Different everythings."

"That sounds like a recipe for disaster."

He leaned closer. His expression was more than friendly, an inch less than affectionate. "You're easy to talk to."

For a moment she wondered if that was true, and if it was, why? Was this something else she'd learned from her mother? That being a good listener was as important for finding the right man as exposing carefully calculated cleavage and a tightly toned midriff?

"When you married the second time, you knew what to look for?"

"Karen was amazing. We were at a party, and it was like an old movie when everything dims and the spotlight shines on one perfect woman."

"Wicked."

"She'd been married, too, to a guy who drifted from one job to another. He never finished anything, never made up his mind. She wanted a marriage with goals, a family. We were a great fit, and we realized it immediately."

She waited for him to go on, although she was worried that now the whole evening was going to be about his perfect marriage.

"I'm guessing you and CJ weren't the right fit?" Lee asked.

"Not so much. Or maybe we were, and that's the problem."

"What do you mean?"

She shrugged. This was too new a revelation to talk about, and frankly, too embarrassing. If she was right, and she and CJ had more or less deserved each other, that couldn't be a good thing.

"How long were you married?" she asked instead.

"Nine years. Good ones."

"I really am sorry. Was she ill for a long time?"

"Nothing like that. We were fishing in our boat. Fishing was Karen's greatest passion." He smiled a little, as if he were re-membering something good. "After Olivia and me, of course. A storm blew up while we were on our way back. I thought about trying to put in to a closer marina, but Karen was sure we'd be fine. If I'd had any idea how bad it would get, and how quickly, I would have sought the closest shelter. But like Karen, I thought we could make it."

He fell silent.

Tracy wished she hadn't asked. "I'm sorry."

"The waves got huge. Once we turned over, I managed to hold on to the side of the boat. Karen didn't. As the storm was ending, a larger boat found me. Karen's body wasn't found for two days."

"That's awful."

"Afterward I tried to figure out what Karen would want me to do. Before she died, I'd just quit my job to take a position in Atlanta, a big step up. We were all looking forward to it. But when the accident happened, I told the company I couldn't come. I couldn't possibly move Olivia after everything, or abandon Alice, so I looked for something here in the area with a schedule I could work around the needs of my ladies. That's how I ended up selling houses for Maribel."

"She's glad to have you. That's obvious."

"I'm finding I like it, and I'm good at it. I may stay in real estate if the market improves."

She thought Lee had done that neatly. He had dispensed with the sad parts quickly, as if he knew she needed the history. But he hadn't used her as a sounding board or a dump, the way other men might have. The man was pretty amazing. Not only was he a huge treat for the eye, even a simple conversation with him was seductive.

She edged closer. "How are you and Olivia doing?"

"We're getting there. Alice is the one to worry about." He snapped his fingers. "Which reminds me. I did ask her about the Krause fellow. She said he didn't talk about himself."

"I'm not having much luck." Tracy thought of the chess players. "Worse than that, actually. I'm having bad luck. But I do have a possibility in Kentucky. I talked to one of Herb's former landlords, and he gave me the name of a preacher Herb used as a reference. But that was almost fifteen years ago."

"The preacher's still preaching?"

"Retired now, but I was given a new phone number for him by the church and left a message. We'll see if he returns my call."

The wine arrived with a flourish of ceremony, and the mushrooms came a moment later to perfume the table. Tracy realized she was hungry. Really hungry. Not a handful-of-walnuts kind of hungry.

"Maybe it's the ambience, but I feel like I could eat my way through their kitchen."

His gaze moved over her, warm and approving and sexy as hell. "Good, because the chef is first-rate. They stole him from one of the big restaurants in Miami. But I think you'll feel at home here. It's your kind of place."

It was. Certainly not as exclusive or world-class as Tracy was used to, but a place where she might belong. She had missed that, and now she knew how much. She had also missed being with an exciting man.

"There's Carol." Lee got to his feet and beckoned to a middle-aged woman who seemed to be making the rounds. She wore a striped cotton blazer over a red dress, and her blond hair was cut in layers that looked as sensible as the rest of her.

Lee took the woman's hand when she reached them; then he leaned over to kiss her cheek. "Carol, I want you to meet my friend Tracy Deloche," he said. "I told you about her yesterday, remember?"

Tracy held out her hand, and they exchanged greetings.

"Carol is our event coordinator." Lee gestured to an empty chair. "Will you join us a moment?"

Carol sprawled in the chair as if hours had passed since she'd sat down.

"Would you like a glass of wine?" Lee asked.

"No, thank you, Lee, although I'm tempted. We're planning the Tarpon Fest, and I've been making calls, and chasing down craftspeople and vendors since early this morning." She turned to Tracy. "It's a day-long fair, very popular with everybody who hasn't left town for the summer. But it's a bear to organize. I'm working with a committee." She left it at that, as if Tracy would understand.

"Oh, I've been on those committees. I know how much work goes into something like that."

Lee smiled his approval, then turned back to Carol. "I told Tracy you might need help, and I think there's even room in the budget for a little, right?"

Her smile looked tired, and her lipstick was just a bit crooked, as if she had applied the latest coat without a mirror. "The people I've interviewed are clueless. Most of them have never been inside a country club, so they have no idea what to expect. They have visions of hanging out around the pool."

"I have a feeling Tracy's been in more than a few," Lee said.

"Why would you want the job?" Carol sounded genuinely mystified.

"Well, I'm in town for a while. It just seemed like it might be fun to be doing something. To stay busy."

Carol looked skeptical. "This busy?"

Tracy stretched the truth to fit. "Well, it doesn't make sense for me to join the yacht club if I'm not going to be around for years and years. But it would be nice to be involved a bit."

"We have reciprocal memberships. Have you checked with your club at home?"

Tracy belonged—or rather, *had* belonged—to two clubs. She was fairly sure one of the things that had disappeared with her divorce were those memberships. If she remembered correctly, CJ had gone off to Victorville owing both Riviera and the Bel Air Country Club a great deal of money.

She didn't answer directly, something at which she was becoming adept. "I think I'd like the work. I've helped plan so many events. The list goes on and on."

"As a volunteer."

Tracy nodded. "But I do have a bachelor degree in recreation."

"Really?" Lee and Carol asked together.

"Uh-huh, really." It wasn't in her self-interest to add that the moment she had realized she could actually get a degree that focused on leisure time, Tracy knew she had found her major. Of course the classes hadn't turned out to be leisurely at all, but that was beside the point.

"I'd be a natural," she finished.

Carol didn't have time to respond. A woman in her sixties came bearing down on their table. Above a string of real pearls, her second chin wobbled with what looked like barely repressed fury.

"Carol, I must speak to you!"

Carol got wearily to her feet. "Mrs. Swanson. How are you tonight?"

Mrs. Swanson's bloodshot eyes were practically shooting sparks. "Not happy. I can tell you that. Not one bit happy! Have I heard correctly? You've changed the Tarpon Fest entertainment schedule? Without consulting me?" She continued in the same vein for another minute.

Carol turned to Lee and Tracy. "It was nice to meet you, Tracy. Come see me anytime this week, and we can continue our conversation. Lee…" Then she turned back to Mrs. Swanson. "Let's just take this into the hallway, shall we? I'm sure you won't be unhappy once I've had a chance to explain." She led the older woman out of the dining room as Tracy stared after them.

"Well, I'm glad you got to meet her," Lee said.

"Who, Carol or the volcano?"

"I'm afraid you'll have to get used to June Swanson if you work here. The Swansons run this place. But I bet the job is yours. Carol liked you. I could tell. She perked right up."

Tracy thought about Carol's tired eyes and poorly applied lipstick. "That was Carol at her perkiest?"

"Let's order dinner." Lee signaled their waiter. "The prime rib is superb here. And the shrimp scampi is, too."

Tracy leaned forward and put her hand on his arm. "Lee, how many Mrs. Swansons *are* there at the yacht club?"

He didn't pretend to misunderstand. "As many as there were at your club in California."

Tracy thought about that. She ran out of fingers to count on. When the waiter arrived she ordered the scampi and decided to enjoy it. She had a feeling that unless Lee invited her to dine as his guest here again, she would not be enjoying anything about the Sun County Yacht Club in the future.

★ ★ ★

The evenings when Rishi went back to work after dinner seemed to drag on forever for Janya. She wasn't certain which was worse—making conversation with a man with whom she had so little in common, or being in the house alone, where she had so little to do.

In India she had rarely been alone. The pink house, with its balconies and shaded courtyard, was home not only to her parents and her uncle's family, who lived on the top floor, but her grandparents, too, had lived there before their deaths, and other family and friends often came and went. She had never known what it was like to spend a quiet evening with only the sound of her footsteps, the croaking of frogs, the whining of mosquitoes.

This evening she had no desire to watch television, always a reminder that she was a stranger here. Later she might read, but for now she sat on the front steps and thought about how alone she was.

Except that she wasn't. There were scurrying noises on the side of the house, followed by the rustling of shrubs. She wasn't frightened. She had a very good idea what might be causing them.

"There is room for two on the steps," she called. "We could share them."

Silence fell. Just as she thought her invitation would not be heeded, a girl's head peeked around the side of the little house.

"I'm a spy. You weren't supposed to hear me."

"I saw you on your bicycle. And what are you spying on?"

The girl, who looked to be perhaps ten, came out into full view. "Just whatever. My grandmother's watching a movie, but they're shooting Indians, and I don't like that."

Janya patted the step beside her. "You are Alice's granddaughter, aren't you?"

"Olivia," the girl said, moving closer.

"And I am Janya Kapur. You can call me Janya if you like."

"That's like a boy's name, only with an 'ah' at the end."

"Olivia is a lovely name."

"My mom said she never knew anybody named Olivia, so she didn't have to forget what she knew."

"A good idea. Then you could give all the meaning to the name." Janya smiled at the girl. She was pretty, with long brown hair that needed a good brushing, pale blue eyes and a pointed chin. She had the perfect complexion of a child and the accompanying guileless smile.

"What are you doing out here?" Olivia asked.

"I was thinking perhaps I should move some of Mr. Krause's plants to the side of my house where you were spying. I watered them this morning, but it's been a hot day. They dry out so quickly, and that way I can water them more frequently."

"I like plants. I could help."

"That's very kind, but I think it's going to be a big job."

"I'm strong."

"Then let's take a few, shall we? You can help me plan where they should go."

They chatted as they walked down to Herb's cottage. Janya showed Olivia a couple of ferns in small pots that she could carry. Together, with Janya hauling three pots, one tucked under her arm, they started up the road.

"Where are you from?" Olivia asked. "Peru?"

Janya laughed. "Why do you think that?"

"Because there was a girl from Peru in my class last year, and she had long black hair like yours. I wish I had black hair."

"Brown hair is lovely. I'm from India. Mumbai."

Olivia practiced the word out loud. "India is in Asia."

"Yes."

"That's pretty far away, isn't it?"

"Very."

"Do they speak English? Because you do."

"Some people do, but there are many languages in my country."

"Do you know them all?"

"I don't think anybody could. I know some of them. Do you know another language?"

"Sí, señora." Olivia giggled. "We take Spanish in school. My father says it's a waste of time. Do you think it is?"

"I would not want to argue with your father."

"He says that everybody in the world should learn English. Just English."

Janya was afraid she wasn't going to be fond of Alice's son-in-law. "I took English in school before I knew I would move here. Maybe someday you'll move to Mexico or Spain and be glad you learned Spanish, too."

At the side of her house, Janya examined the area, and they found a place for the plants on a rickety bench under a tree beside her small patio.

"Do we need to get more?" Olivia sounded afraid that they might.

"Oh, not tonight."

"Is there something else we could do?"

"I think we need something cold to drink. Would you like some fruit juice?"

"Sure. Thank you."

Janya knew better than to invite her inside. In their brief encounters, Olivia's father had been, at best, civil. She thought he would not approve of his daughter going into a stranger's house, especially one whose first language was not English. "Why don't you water the plants while I get it?"

Olivia turned on the hose, and when Janya returned with

two glasses of orange juice with lots of ice, they sat on her steps again and sipped.

"Is the man who lives here your husband?" Olivia asked.

"Yes, but he works very hard."

"My daddy works a lot, too. He leaves me alone with my grandmother. My mother died."

"I'm sorry. I know how hard it is to lose a mother."

"Did yours die, too?"

Janya was silent for a moment. It was a simple question, one she should not have to think about. "My mother is alive, but very far away."

"Do you have a job here? You know, so you have something to do?"

"No." Janya smiled down at her. "And you, Olivia? Do you have a job?"

Olivia giggled again. "Silly! I'm a little kid."

"Oh, so you are. It escaped my notice."

"I go to school. I'll be in fifth grade."

"What is your favorite subject?"

"I like a lot of things. But I like to make things best. I like to draw people, even if their arms and legs are always too short."

"That is the hard thing about drawing people. I agree."

"Do you like to draw?"

"Yes. Do you have to go home very soon?"

"At dark. I'm supposed to be watching out for Nana, but she said John Wayne could do that. I think he's in the movie."

"There are no children here to play with, are there?"

Olivia shook her head. "And my dad says having my old friends come to play will confuse Nana even more."

"I have paper and colored pencils just inside. Would you like to draw for a little while?"

"Really?"

"I haven't drawn myself for a very long time."

"Then you ought to get busy, don't you think?"

"You sound like my brother, Yash. He would say exactly that. We can sit out here and draw until it's time for you to go home. I'll just be a moment."

Janya got up and went back inside. For the first time that evening, she was in no hurry for the sun to set.

chapter nine

Tracy enjoyed almost everything about her date with Lee. As he'd promised the food *had* been good, if somewhat ordinary. Three musicians—bass, piano and drums—arrived halfway through the meal. Okay, so it was music Alice's generation could have sung along to, but the trio provided a romantic backdrop for conversation. Lee was the perfect date. He seemed to know what she needed and made certain to provide it. She had been dazzled by the sheer joy of having somebody pay attention to her again.

Embarrassed as she was to admit it, she had missed that more than anything. During the past year and a half she had watched friends drop away. Until then, she had never given loyalty much thought. Maybe she, too, had distanced herself when people went through tough times, as if bad luck was catching. But during the divorce she had given loyalty and love a new place in the "what's important" lineup. She certainly wasn't going to mistake one good conversation, one evening with a particularly attentive man for either. But just being with somebody who was interested in her had been special.

After the meal Lee drove them home the long way, along the beachfront road, the warm air blowing through her hair, the moon glinting on the distant water. At home, he handed back her keys and walked her to the door. She thanked him, wondering if he was going to spoil a lovely evening by expecting payment in the form of a romp in her bed. But he simply kissed her cheek, squeezed her hands, then left for Alice's cottage.

For just a moment she'd wished more had been required.

Much later, as she was getting ready to go to sleep, she heard footsteps out front, and when she went to the window she saw Lee slip inside his car and quietly close the door. Miraculously after one hiccup the Saab started, and he drove away. She was glad the problem had been minor enough that he could get the car back to the garage without having it towed.

So, yes, on most levels, the evening had been a success. There was just one problem. She was certain she didn't want to work at the yacht club. She didn't want to watch from the sidelines as others enjoyed the fun she had worked so hard to organize. And while she was being truthful, she also had to admit that the thought of organizing endless parties, fashion shows and charitable events was too much like her former life. That would hurt even more if she was kicked around while she did it by people who didn't look up to her as the ultimate Bel Air success story. If she ever went back to the club, it was going to be as a guest, not a worker bee.

All this went through her mind the next morning as she dressed. She had risen with the sun, found a résumé template online, filled out the form and printed it. There was a job in town with her name written all over it. The position was temporary; she could make a little money; she did not have to hobnob with anybody except snotty-nosed little kids. And the good news? She was bigger than they were, and in a pinch, she could hold them underwater.

By the time she reached the recreation center, Palmetto Grove was fully awake. Sprinklers sprayed rainbow-hued mist over shrubs and lawns; gray-haired women power-walked in groups of three and four; plump men bicycled slowly, showing too many inches of flesh spilling over their seats. The air was tinged with salt and newly mown grass. As she parked, she heard the shrieks of children from a school yard down the street. She imagined that for them, summer was not coming fast enough.

She had a full day of chores ahead of her. On the way home she planned to pick up the remaining tile installers' estimates, then she would slap another coat of paint on the walls and the first coat on the kitchen cupboards. Afterward, if she had time, she would hit the grocery store. She wanted to find something she could keep on hand to offer Lee if he stopped by to see her. If she were lucky, she could quickly dispense with this part of the day.

She bustled to the welcome desk and noted that the same receptionist who was always there appeared to be setting up for the day. The woman had short hair and middle-age spread. She wore a white blouse and no jewelry, and Tracy thought she looked like somebody who ought to work in a school cafeteria. All she needed was a hair net.

"Good morning." Tracy didn't want to waste her time or the woman's. "I came to apply for the swimming instructor's position, and I wonder if you can point me to the director's office so I can give him my résumé?"

"Why don't you let me take a look first? I'll make sure you have everything we need."

Tracy figured she was in luck. Apparently the job hadn't been filled. She dismissed the suggestion with a smile. "I'm not worried. Is there an application I need to fill out, too?"

"No, Mr. Woodley checks résumés first, to save paperwork." The woman paused. "Usually after I've looked them over."

Tracy had told one of the installers she would be at his shop no later than nine-thirty. She didn't want him to leave without giving her the estimate. She checked her watch.

"If you don't mind, I'll just take my chances. I need to get going. If you'll just tell me where his office is?"

"Well, I could do that."

Tracy was getting annoyed, but she tried to sound pleasant. "Good."

The woman still looked unruffled, but she was no longer smiling. "You've had experience?"

"It's all right here." Tracy held up the folder. "Can you tell me which hallway he's on?"

"Do you think you'll be in this much of a hurry with the children? Because they get frightened in the water, and they don't need to be rushed."

Tracy stared at her. "I'm sorry. What?"

"Rushing children. It's even worse than rushing people who are trying to help you. It's not a good thing in a swim instructor."

"Listen, I'm just trying to find out where to drop off my résumé. It's a simple task. I walk down the right hallway and knock on a door. If Mr. Woodley has time, he asks me to fill out an application. If he likes what he sees, he offers me the job." Her volume had strengthened with each word. She wasn't shouting by the end of her speech, but she was surprisingly loud.

"Children also do best with instructors who don't get angry and *don't* raise their voices."

Tracy took a moment to breathe. "Look, I don't want to cause a scene here. But does Mr. Woodley know that you're keeping qualified applicants from submitting their résumés? Is that what he would want?"

"I can ask him tonight over the dinner table."

Tracy had a moment of revelation. She almost put up a hand to stop the woman's next words. She didn't want to hear them. She didn't want to know that, once again, she had screwed up. She was afraid if she closed her eyes she would see visions of three old men trying to find chess pieces in the grass.

But she didn't put up her hand in time, and the woman smiled thinly.

"Yes. I'm Mrs. Woodley. And in order to save my husband a little time, because his is a most demanding job, he asks me to look over résumés before they get to him."

"Oh, Lord."

"You're a religious woman, I take it?"

"I wish. I could use some divine intervention about now."

"Well, yes, that's just about what it's going to take."

Tracy crossed her arms and leaned over the desk. She needed the support. "Why didn't you tell me who you were?"

"Let's review. I did exactly what I needed to. I believe I asked you for the résumé. Then I asked for it again. And possibly I asked for it a third time. Which time was unclear to you?"

"You didn't tell me you were married to the director."

"It shouldn't matter."

Tracy knew Mrs. Woodley was right. It *shouldn't* matter. The fault was her own. Hers. Again.

Her throat constricted. The feeling was so unfamiliar, for a moment she thought she was choking. "You know, you'd think I'd get this. I mean, a year and a half ago, I had everything. You name it, anything, it was mine. Then it all just disappeared. So for eighteen months the universe has been telling me I'm not a spoiled princess after all, that I'm just like everybody else." She had no idea why she was saying any of this out loud. She sniffed. "I never cry."

"Everybody cries."

"Do they?" She sniffed again.

"Of course. And this would be an appropriate moment if ever there was one. Why did everything disappear?"

"Because I was married to a creep, a crook, and do you know what? I knew it!" Now the bewildered Tracy was crying in earnest. Big fat tears spilled down her cheeks, and her nose was running. It was unconscionable.

"Maybe he wasn't as bad as you think, but he changed," Mrs. Woodley said.

"No, he was bad news right from the get-go. There, I've said it. He wasn't just bad, he was worse, and I knew what kind of man he was, but I told myself he was a businessman, that to be as wealthy and successful as CJ was, he had to look at the big picture. So I just looked the other way. And doesn't that make me bad news, too? And isn't that why everything just caved in and keeps caving in? Divine retribution?"

"Possibly it keeps caving in because you still talk to people like you're a spoiled princess."

"I know."

"Then it's time to stop, don't you think?"

"Well, that's the crazy part. I'm trying. I've been hit over the head with this like you wouldn't believe." Tracy took a tissue that the woman offered her and wiped her eyes, but she couldn't wipe fast enough. The tears just kept flowing. "The other day I practically caused three old men to have heart attacks. But I keep falling back on what I used to do best."

"Dear, if that was your best, you need a little work. Maybe that's all the universe is trying to tell you."

Tracy blew her nose. "I thought I was listening. I relapsed."

"We all do that from time to time."

"Why are you being so nice to me?"

"Because you've been kicked enough, and you're starting to come to terms with it. You don't need more." She handed Tracy another tissue.

"I didn't even cry when my divorce was final." Tracy blew her nose again. "I cried when they took away all our bedroom furniture, though. California has a seize and freeze law. Between the Feds and the state, almost everything I owned got carted away."

"How did you end up here?"

"My ex put land in my name out on Palmetto Grove Key. But you want to hear the worst part? I can't sell it. No developer will touch it. Too many restrictions and lawsuits around it."

"Oh, my, I know about that. So that's *you*."

Tracy wasn't thrilled to hear that she had become something of a local celebrity. "'Fraid so."

"Well, you're definitely in a pickle."

Tracy took a moment. After a couple of deep breaths she started to pull herself together. She knew she had to apologize and get out. Her voice was just short of a croak. "I'm so sorry I dumped all this on you. And I'm sorry I came in with so much attitude. I sound like a crazy woman. I'm surprised you haven't called the men with the butterfly nets."

"Can you imagine a world where we really had men like that? We'd all be on the run." Mrs. Woodley smiled, and Tracy managed a watery smile in return.

"Thank you." Her voice sounded a shade more normal, and the tears had finally slowed to a moppable trickle. "And please, please, you won't tell anybody about this, will you? I really *will* sound like a nutcase."

"I won't, but really? You would only sound like a woman under some serious stress. Do you need this job?"

Tracy nodded. "Money's tight. But I guess I can work at the yacht club. The event planner's interested. Only…"

"What?"

"I don't want to."

"And you want to work here?"

"I'm a pretty good swim instructor. And I'd be happier in this environment." Tracy had parted with enough of her life story not to want to go into her reasons.

"Shall I look at the résumé now?"

Tracy couldn't believe Mrs. Woodley still wanted to. She handed it over meekly. "Just wait until I leave before you tear it up, okay?"

"My goodness, you have a degree in recreation and leisure studies?"

"I know it's hard to believe."

"And lots of experience with tournaments, I see. And a variety of social activities."

"Volunteer, mostly, although you'll see I taught swimming in college. And I did a little work for our local park organizing a new swim program before I got engaged. I should have stayed with the program and told CJ to kiss off."

"I will pass this on to Mr. Woodley." Mrs. Woodley smiled. "That makes me sound very Victorian, don't you think? Mr. Woodley? Everybody calls him Woody, including me."

"What do they call you?"

"Gladys."

Tracy liked her. More than that, she admired her for being both forthright and kind. "I'd appreciate your help, Gladys. And thank you. Again."

"If you still need to talk, I'll be here."

Tracy thought about that on her way out to the car. Embarrassment was creeping in. She had behaved like a complete idiot.

Maybe she needed a psychiatrist, only she couldn't afford one. She was one of those millions of Americans without health insurance. When she sold Happiness Key, she ought to check herself in to some clinic and figure out when and why she'd gotten so mental. Other people got divorced. Other people didn't sob all over strangers. They picked up and went on. The way she'd thought she was doing.

She was deep in thought—a more or less unfamiliar destination—when a missile slammed into her.

"Oof!" Instinctively Tracy threw her arms out and grabbed. The missile was medium-size and warm, and it smelled like bubble gum.

Once she realized what she held, she thrust the boy away from her, but she didn't let go. Instead she tightened her grip on his shoulders.

"You almost knocked me over!"

"Y'oughta watch where you're going!"

"I know where I was going. I just didn't expect to get tackled."

"So? You were in my way."

"Yeah? Well, that's going to happen a lot, kid. Because you have to stop for other people if they happen to be there first."

"Let go of me."

She was about to, more than a little anxious to be done with the boy, when she noticed he was looking frantically over his shoulder as he wriggled in her grip.

"Wait just a minute." She held him tighter. "Who are you running away from?"

"Nobody!"

"School's not out yet, is it? What are you doing here? Aren't you supposed to be in class somewhere?"

"You heard of homeschooling?" he yelled.

For a moment Tracy wondered, then she shook her head.

Nobody had the patience to homeschool this kid. Even the most committed parents would need school hours to regain their equilibrium.

"I don't see a mother or father coming up behind you," Tracy told him.

"They let me off. I've got, ummm...tennis lessons."

"Not during school hours you don't," Tracy said, making an educated guess. "They don't teach youth tennis until later in the afternoon."

"Let go of me!" He looked over his shoulder again and struggled harder. Then he turned and kicked Tracy in the shin.

She yelped, dropping her hands to hold the abused leg while hopping up and down on the other one.

Gladys Woodley came charging out of the rec center. "Bay Egan! Don't you move! The school just called. They're looking all over for you."

The kid looked as if he were going to run again; then he sagged. The sagging was followed by a flood of words he shouldn't know, much less repeat.

Tracy stopped hopping and grabbed him again. "Cut that out this minute. Where do you think you are? In an R-rated movie?"

"How'd they know where I was going?" Bay asked the older woman.

"Oh, let me see.... Maybe because you've done it before?" Gladys said.

"I'd have made it, too, if *she* didn't stop me."

Tracy looked at Gladys and shrugged. "I had a feeling something was going on."

"You have a sixth sense for misbehavior." The other woman signaled that she was going back inside, and Tracy knew she was going to call the school. Somebody would be here to pick the boy up soon. Tracy was to detain him.

Tracy turned back to her new charge. "Why did you run away, Bay? That's your real name? Bay?"

"Baylor." He said it as if he were daring her to make fun of him.

"Yeah, Bay is good. It's that last-name-for-a-first-name thing everybody's doing. Tough luck. Anyway, look, school's almost out, right? I mean, just a few more days, if I'm correct."

"So?"

She let go of him, but her weight was poised on her toes, just in case she had to grab him again. "Well, if you run away now, somebody's going to punish you, right? I mean, they always catch up with you."

"How do you know?"

"Trust me on that. And from what I can tell, running away's not your strong suit."

"I don't have a suit on!"

"I mean you're not that good at it. So why don't we get you back to school, and you hang in a couple more days. Then, when summer comes, you'll be free as a bird. Otherwise, the powers that be—"

"Be what?"

"Be your *parents,* that's what. They're not going to trust you to do what you're supposed to do. And they aren't going to let you out of their sight all summer. You'll be inside reading little kids' books and coloring, while your friends are outside playing soccer and swimming here at the center. Got it?"

"You think I don't know all this?"

"I have no idea, but it seems pretty dumb to lose out on a great summer just because you're sick of school."

"I hate school. My teacher hates me."

Tracy could imagine that. She'd only been with the kid for a few minutes, and he was already on her hit list. She studied him for a moment. He had sun-streaked brown hair, eyes a similar golden brown, fat cheeks and a pout. His shirt had a rip at the hem, and one sneaker was untied, the shoelace so shredded it would never form a bow again.

"Do your parents know you're unhappy?"

"My dad says to write down all the bad stuff my teacher says. So I do."

Tracy understood. "Let me guess. Your teacher found it this morning. What was your father going to do with it?"

Bay shrugged.

Tracy suddenly realized something. "Mrs. Woodley called you Bay Egan. Are you related to *Marsh* Egan?"

"He's my dad." His tone said, "What of it?"

Tracy could hardly believe it. Marsh and Bay. How charming. Was there a swamp or a sandbar hiding around the corner? And what had Marsh Egan planned to do with his son's list? Sue his teacher, the way he was suing the Army Corps of Engineers?

Gladys returned. "Come inside, Bay," she said, holding out her hand. "The librarian's on her way to pick you up." She looked at Tracy. "They drew straws. It's her free period."

Now Bay only looked glum. "She hates me, too. Just because I put a stupid book in the water fountain."

"I can take over from here," Gladys told Tracy, motioning for Bay to follow her inside. "Thanks for your help."

Tracy thought it was odd that only minutes ago she'd said the very same thing. She was glad she and Gladys Woodley were more or less even now. She had a bruise on her shin to prove it.

chapter ten

After a successful afternoon of painting, Tracy went outside to stare at a failure. In the scheme of things, useless towers of tile were nothing. Compared to the humiliation of her divorce, the desertion of friends and family, acres of fire ants and mosquitoes nobody wanted to buy—not to mention her crying jag at the rec center that morning—the towers were nothing. Maybe she could glue shells to the tiles and sell them at the beach flea market. She could make endearing little landscapes, coquina seagulls flying toward scallop shell suns. If she started now, she might be finished with the stacks by the time she was ready to draw Social Security. If there was anything in her account.

Tracy stared glumly at the tile. When she'd picked up the two additional installers' estimates, her morning had gone from bad to worse. If she paid either man to tile her floor, one of her tenants would find her lying on it, toes curled, eyes staring into eternity. She would leave a note explaining that she had starved to death, while the installer grew fat off her savings account.

She would *not* explain how to find her family. She and Herb could thumb their noses together from the grave.

A more experienced penny pincher would have known to price installation before buying the tile. She had been so proud of finding a bargain, but she'd still been thinking like a princess. Snap her dainty royal fingers, and the tiles would simply find their way to the floor, snuggle in perfect alignment and affectionately ooze grout in every direction. She hadn't given the realities a thought, but even if she had, she would never have guessed just how much installation would cost.

"How hard can it be?" she asked out loud.

The tile didn't answer, which was one bright spot in a dreary day.

She was contemplating whether to look for additional estimates when she heard a vehicle slow outside her cottage. Hoping it was Lee, she rounded the side and saw a newish pickup. She prayed an apologetic tile installer had mistakenly added a zero to his final total. But the cargo bed wasn't filled with a workman's tools. She saw fishing rods, a plastic cooler, collapsible canvas chairs.

When a little boy tumbled out of the passenger seat, springing off the running board like a gymnast on a trampoline, she exhaled sharply. Catching sight of her, he came to a halt, and his eyes narrowed.

The driver's door slammed, and Tracy was pretty sure who was going to appear. She had less than a moment to inhale and prepare.

"Miss Deloche." Marsh Egan, clad in what looked like the same cutoffs and a T-shirt that read Every Day is Earth Day, went to stand beside his son, slinging his arm around the boy, who was now squirming uncomfortably.

"So, what's it this time?" she asked. "Did I leave bruises when I detained Bay this morning? Are you planning to work that into a court case against me?"

"Bay..." Marsh looked down at his son, who didn't look up to meet his father's eyes. "You know what you have to do."

"I still don't see why."

"Because it's the right thing. And we do the right thing in our family."

"Yeah? Tell Mom that."

Tracy was watching Marsh, and in the fading light she actually thought she saw him flush. Was there really something on God's green earth that could make the man lose his confidence?

"Bay," Marsh said, just a bit more sternly.

"SorryIkickedyou," Bay slurred in a low voice.

Tracy wasn't sure what to say. The boy *wasn't* sorry. He looked sullen, even angry. He scuffed his toe in the dirt like a kid who was afraid if he didn't do something with his foot, he was going to kick somebody.

"Thank you, son," Marsh said.

"Uh, I'm sorry," Tracy said, "but what exactly did you thank him for, Mr. Egan? That wasn't an apology. It was a computer-generated message."

Before Marsh could answer, she moved closer and bent down so she was on Bay's level, resting her hands against the fronts of her thighs. "Listen, I know I short-circuited your plans this morning. But get over it, okay? You're a kid, and I stopped you from doing something that would make your life a lot worse, even if you don't see it right now."

"I would have made it to *freedom* if you hadn't been there."

She pictured his little body hurtling through razor wire. She made certain not to smile, although for a moment, it was hard. "Trust me, while I was limping around all afternoon, I was wishing I'd been somewhere else, too."

"I didn't kick you that hard."

Tracy pulled up the leg of her khaki pants, and pointed to a black-and-blue spot the size of an egg. "Want to see your handiwork? Or should I call this your footwork?"

Bay shrugged out from beneath his father's arm and came closer to peer at her leg. He bit his lip, but he didn't say anything.

"I'm trying to teach him some manners," Marsh said in a tone that made it clear he thought Tracy was interfering.

"Do it somewhere else, okay? I'd love an apology, only not this one."

Marsh started to say something, but Bay interrupted.

"I didn't kick you that hard." He paused. "I didn't *mean* to kick you at all. But you got in my way."

"I know. I kicked somebody myself this morning. Metaphorically, that is."

"What does meta-forkly mean?"

"Metaphorically. It means I didn't use my feet, I used words."

"Did you apologize?"

"Yeah, but I didn't enjoy it. I'm not used to it. Kind of like you."

"I shouldn't have kicked you." He narrowed his eyes again. "And you shouldn't have gotten in my way."

"Thanks for the first part. When you grow up, come back and thank *me* for the second."

Bay rolled his eyes. "Fat chance."

"Well, now that we all know where we stand…" Marsh said.

Tracy straightened. "So, are there more of these little charmers at home? Baby Inlet? Little Estuary? That last has a catchy ring to it. Estuary Egan. I bet you'll have to fight off the boys with a baseball bat."

"Bay, get back in the truck. I'll be there in a minute."

Surprisingly, the boy did as he was told. A few seconds later something distinctly country came roaring from the truck's speakers. Tracy pictured any and all nearby fish heading straight out to sea.

"He looks like you," Tracy told Marsh over the wailing. "Only more presentable."

"You have kids?" Marsh asked.

"I had excellent birth control. Condoms work pretty well, too, I hear. I suggest you give them a try."

"Raising kids isn't as easy as you seem to think."

"I don't think anything about it. Don't want them. Not even sure I like them."

"I can see why. They do compete for attention."

She smiled her sweetest. "It was so nice of you to drop by. Do it again in, say, a century?"

He turned away, as if he were planning to get back in the pickup. "I'm sorry he kicked you," he said. "He was just having a bad day."

She stared at Marsh's back; then she stepped forward and wrapped her fingers around his arm to stop him. "I'm *sorry?* A bad *day?* A bad day is when a kid doesn't make a goal in soccer. It's when his teacher curtails his playtime because he didn't turn in his homework. That's a bad day. This kid of yours has a bad *problem.* He runs away, he can't control his temper, he uses physical violence when he's frustrated. He needs help a lot more than I needed an apology."

He faced her, and she dropped his arm. Gladly.

"You don't know anything about it," he said.

"I know what a well-adjusted kid looks like." She lowered her voice, although there was no chance Bay could hear them over Billy Ray Cyrus's "Achy, Breaky Heart." "I hope you'll think about getting him some help. Bay's really a cute kid, but he won't be in a couple of years. And you'll be so busy bailing him out of jail, you won't have time to chain yourself to anything."

"Not a parent, not a psychiatrist, not an expert," he drawled.

"Your loss, not mine. I'll stay out of his way."

"You do that."

"I don't suppose I could convince you to stay out of *mine?*"

"What are the chances, Miss Deloche?" This time he did round the truck. She stepped back, and in a moment, the pickup was a cloud of dust on its way back to town.

Inside the house, Tracy slapped together her usual dinner, a handful of this, spoonfuls of that. To forget Close Encounters of the Egan Kind, she spent the next hour on the Internet trying to find a cheap handyman who could do everything. A local company called Handy Hubbies fit the bill, but the man who answered told her they usually left tile up to the experts, and he wouldn't be able to get her an estimate until the end of the week.

She wondered exactly what the hubbies were handy with and made an appointment for one to look at the repairs on Wanda's cottage. They settled on Thursday and a time. None of her other phone calls were that successful.

Tracy turned off her computer and stared out the window. At some point between the Egans' happy little visit and her frustrating computer session, the sun had gone down. She poured herself a glass of wine and turned on the news. Two hours later she woke to a reality show. A British nanny was trying to teach a couple to parent a little boy who looked like a younger Bay, and she had slept through everything leading up to it.

She shuddered delicately, rose and went to stand in the doorway. The rest of the night stretched in front of her. Even though the windows were open, the house smelled like paint. She wondered where she could go to get away from it. Shopping had always been her stress reducer, but these days she wasn't even comfortable spending money on a movie.

Beyond the house, a man was walking in the direction of the bridge that led to town. She recognized Ken Gray, and it wasn't the first time she'd seen him on the road at night. She wondered what was up with that, although if she was married to Wanda, she would get out whenever she could, too.

Whatever the tale, she now had a golden opportunity to apologize to Ken's wife. She hadn't told Wanda she was sorry for subjecting her to everything that had happened at the park. Wanda had just tried to help Tracy find Herb's family. And she had been more or less right about Tracy's lack of manners. As much as Tracy hated to face it, she did have a tiny problem with the way she talked to people.

Getting an appointment with Handy Hubbies was a good excuse. She could pop over, tell Wanda they were coming, mention that she couldn't hire the help she needed for her own place, but she was going to make sure Wanda was taken care of. Then apologize quickly and get the heck out of there.

She played that over in her mind, decided it might just work, and went to make herself presentable.

When she left the cottage a few minutes later, a soft breeze cooled the air and night noises had begun in earnest. She hoped the deepest, loudest croaking from the direction of the bay was a frog with bronchitis and not an alligator. She knew alligators lived there, had seen them at a distance before she headed quickly in the other direction. But she could only live with Florida's wildlife if she didn't have to think about it.

When she reached Wanda's door, she rapped sharply, waited, then rapped again. She was about to head home when she thought she heard Wanda call "come in." Opening the door, she followed the sound of Wanda's voice into a room painted a vivid orchid. The cushions on sixties rattan furniture were covered with some of the most eye-torturing prints Tracy had ever seen. Wanda was doubled over on one of them, an arm clutched over her abdomen. When she saw Tracy, she stood up and thrust a telephone at her.

"You talk to him." The bewildered Tracy grabbed the phone just before it hit the floor, and Wanda, white-faced and moaning, took off. In a moment Tracy heard a door slam, then the unmistakable sound of Wanda ralphing up everything she had eaten in the past decade.

Tracy swallowed in distaste and thought she ought to leave, and fast, then remembered the telephone.

She stared at it, perplexed; then she put it to her ear. "Hello, umm... Who is this? May I help you?"

She listened for a moment. She could feel her own eyes getting wider and wider.

"You want me to do what?" she demanded. "Are you kidding me? Do it to yourself, you disgusting pervert!"

Wanda figured if anybody had a right to get back at the Deloche woman, it was her. Of course, being so sick she nearly puked up her toenails hadn't exactly been a prelude to good sense. One minute she'd been talking away, feeling just the teeniest bit wonky, and the next she was turning herself inside out. She wasn't sure what possessed her to hand the telephone to Ms. Deloche. Maybe she'd kept her sense of humor, if nothing else.

Now she wasn't feeling like somebody who had a laugh or anything else left inside her. On the bright side, with nothing there to worry about anymore, she could stay put on the sofa a while, and watch the room twirl around and around. It was kind of entertaining.

"You're running a sex line?" Tracy came in with a bag of frozen corn and more or less dropped it on Wanda's aching forehead. "There, that ought to help."

"Just hit me with a sledgehammer, why don't you?"

"I'm considering it. A very large sledgehammer."

"I'm not running anything."

"Then who was that disgusting creature? And why did he tell me he wasn't paying to be talked to that way?"

"He's a man with a sense of humor. You got one, too?"

"Not tonight."

Wanda supposed that was only fair. She adjusted the corn so it covered as much of her forehead as possible. The cold almost felt pleasant, and the throbbing eased a little. Thinking about it, she realized that her landlady wasn't going to leave until she explained. And Deloche hovering there all night was not a pretty picture.

She sighed. "I'm not running anything. I just do a little work for a friend, that's all."

"Phone sex?"

"More like phone romance."

"I'm sorry? You call that romance? What he asked me to do wasn't one bit romantic."

"Oh, he was just pulling your leg. It's called Get Seduced. *S-E-D-U-C-E-D*. That's the number. And the old farts are chan-neled to me, if you want the truth, 'cause *I* understand them."

Tracy plopped down on the edge of the sofa, and for a moment the room spun faster and Wanda had to close her eyes. "Wanda, what is there to understand? The man wanted me to—"

Wanda waved that away with a limp wrist. "It doesn't matter what he said he wanted. I caught on real early all he and every one of them really wants is to talk to somebody who'll listen. That guy's kinda new, but he'll catch on quick. They tell me all about their youth, when girls couldn't get enough of them, couldn't keep their hands to themselves, you know what I mean. And sometimes they get a little graphic. Like it makes them feel young and virile again just to recount those times, 'cause there's nothing much to recount these days, not even when they sell as much Viagra over at the Rite Aid as they do plain old aspirin. Old men just love to tell stories. What else have they got? And who else is going to listen?"

"As if. You make it sound like a charitable venture."

"Well, not exactly charity. I get paid. Takes a certain kind of woman to make an old man feel young and frisky again. I'm what they call 'in demand.'"

"Is that *all* you're in demand for?"

Wanda opened her eyes and made an attempt at indignation. "Just what are you implying, Ms. Deloche?"

"Oh, puh-leeze, stop with the 'Ms. Deloche,' would you? You know my name, and I know yours. And we've been through enough together to be on a first-name basis."

"I'm trying not to think. It makes my head hurt."

"Is this a hangover?"

"It is not! It's something been working its way out for a couple of days. Could be a virus. There's one making the rounds. Could be pie-related."

"Pie?"

"Coconut custard kept in the refrigerator too long. You got to be careful with custard and eat it quick. I knew better, but there wasn't a soul at home to share it with."

"Next time call me if you need to get rid of it faster, and I don't mean the way you did tonight."

"You never did put a healthy slice of pie in that flat little stomach of yours. And what did you mean about me being in demand for something else?"

"I mean, do you meet these guys for other kinds of favors?"

"You mean, am I hooking?"

"That crossed my mind, yes."

"You just go ahead and take yourself out that door right now." Wanda tried, but indignation really was beyond her. She sounded half-dead.

"It was a question," Tracy said. "You're running a senior citizen sex line here. It seems appropriate to ask."

"I told you, I don't run it! I work with a woman who set me up doing it. All these old guys would come in for the early bird specials at the Dancing Shrimp, and before I started work there, Lainie used to joke with them, make them feel good about themselves, if you know what I mean?"

"I don't."

"Telling a few off-color jokes, poking a little fun, stroking their egos."

"I hope that's all she was stroking."

"You have a dirty mind."

"Talk about the pot calling the kettle black."

"Anyways…" Wanda closed her eyes again. "Lainie started getting calls. She figured out right away this was going to keep going unless she put a stop to it, but she hated to do that. She saw a need, if you can understand that."

"I guess I've never seen that particular need. The men that I know don't have to pay for phone sex."

"I bet they pay for the other kind. And I don't mean by the hour, so don't go getting uppity. I mean fancy presents, dinners out, weekends on some island somewhere."

"It's not the same thing."

"No? Close enough. Anyway, Lainie hated to tell them to stop calling, but she realized there weren't enough hours to have these conversations and get anything else done. So one night she was joking with one of the guys that she was going to have to start charging him 'cause he was taking up so much of her free time, and before she knew what was what, he told her he'd give her a credit card number. That's how it got started. Soon enough she realized she didn't want to listen to callers, she wanted to be the organizer. So she asked me to take calls, along with a few other women she trusted. Lainie talks to the new ones a while, figures out what they need, then figures out which one of us will be good for them. They call her when they want to talk, and if we can take the call right then, we call them back."

"And charge."

"I keep track of how long we talk, yes, and they pay Lainie and she pays me. Do you get paid for the work you do?"

"Not from you, I don't."

"Well, you will, soon as you do some."

"I've got a man coming over next week to give an estimate on your repairs. And by the way, I can't afford him for myself."

"I'm supposed to feel grateful I won't be cleaning up after leaks and breathing gas fumes?"

"I don't smell gas."

"That's because I shut off the valve every time I'm done using the stove. And your man will tell you there's nothing wrong with the line. We had the gas company out here. It's the stove needs replacing. The insides are all corroded."

"Oh."

Wanda wondered what would happen if she sat up. Before she could try, Tracy got to her feet. "Do you want tea or something? Do you have anything you can take for an upset stomach?"

"It's not like you to be all helpful."

"Look, I'm trying, okay? Maybe it doesn't come naturally, but even I can make tea and open a bottle of pills."

"What are you doing here, anyway?" Wanda swung her legs around and pushed herself gently upright. The nausea did not return.

"I figured I owed you an apology. For the way I acted at the park."

Wanda didn't know what to say to that, just like she wouldn't know what to say on Judgment Day.

"Do you want that tea or not?" Tracy asked after a long pause.

"There's some bags in the cabinet beside the microwave. Just put one in a cup of water and stick it in until it boils."

"I can manage."

Wanda remained upright until Tracy came back, but once she had the tea, she reclined against the arm of the sofa, where she could rest her elbows and steady her shaking hands. She took a sip, then another, and decided that was going to be it for a while. Her stomach was still rolling, but with gentler waves. Tracy left again and came back with a wet washcloth.

"You can wipe your face if you need to."

Wanda set her cup on the coffee table and took the cloth, but she was suspicious. "You're being awful nice."

"It's not the first time in my life."

"Well, I guess that's good to hear."

Tracy took a seat across from the sofa. "I know this really isn't any of my business, but I'm curious. Does your husband know what you're doing? Does he *mind?*"

"Kenny?" Wanda managed something like a laugh. "Kenny don't know a darned thing about me anymore."

"I see him walking a lot."

"He comes home, then he lights out of here fast as he can go. But it leaves lots of time to make my calls and make some money to sock away for whenever I divorce him."

"Wouldn't you rather have him? I mean, more than the time and money?"

"That's personal."

"It's kind of a personal night, don't you think?"

Wanda thought it was probably a question worth answering. "I'd rather have the old Kenny," she said at last. "But not this one. This one's not worth the minerals in his body."

"I'm sorry. I was in a bad marriage, too. Only I wasn't smart enough to figure it out."

"This isn't that hard. I'm married to a stranger."

"What happened? To change him, I mean? Another woman? The bottle?"

"He killed a man."

Tracy went silent. Wanda didn't know why she was talking about this, and especially why she was talking about it to this woman. Maybe she was as lonely as the old men who called her. Maybe, when it came right down to it, she was just like them. Tears rose in her eyes, but they didn't dare fall.

"He was a cop with Miami-Dade. We had a good life. Other cop families for friends. Good kids. A house we didn't pay that much for in Doral, then the price just rose and rose until we were sitting on a pot of money. Kenny liked what he did, made it all the way to detective. Him and me, we were happy as could be, even though we're as different as apple pie and lemon meringue."

"So what happened? He killed somebody on the job?"

"A drug dealer, a young one, which made it worse. Down in Cutler Bay, at one of the high-rises. He had a gun in plain sight, and turned it on Kenny and his partner. Kenny shouted his warning in English, and Spanish, too. He took Spanish classes every chance he got, so he'd be able to make himself understood, and not just to the Latin Kings, to any man on the street who wanted to tell him stuff. He was that kind of cop."

"He sounds like a natural."

"He probably couldn't have lived with himself even one bit if he hadn't shouted that warning in Spanish, too. The man heard him, but instead of dropping his gun, he fired. Kenny had to take him down. That's all there was to it. And they investigated, you know, the way they have to. But there were plenty of people, not just his partner, but good people who lived there and saw what had happened and said so, even when they knew it might make trouble for themselves. But they said their piece anyway, because the guy who died was nothing but trouble."

"I can imagine how your husband must have felt."

"Maybe at first I saw how it was for him. Right after. He'd fired before, but nobody ever died. And the kid was from a family that loved him and tried to make things right. That made it worse. Like maybe he still had potential, even though he went off to jail after high school the way some kids go to college."

"So why is it so hard to see the problem now?"

"That was a year and a half ago. And every day since, Kenny's moved away a little more, 'til he's not here at all, even when he's home. We moved to Palmetto Grove so he could work in a quieter place. And he does do mostly desk work now, something he used to hate. Manages stuff, goes to meetings. He rented this place 'cause he said he wanted to be near the water, that maybe he would find peace. Instead he just drifted further and further away."

"Doesn't it take time to get over something like that?"

"He's just getting deeper."

"Man, I would never have believed it, but you and I actually have something in common."

Wanda raised one tired eyebrow. "Well, aren't we special to share bad marriages."

"Of course, my husband went to prison. Yours sticks people there."

"Your apology's accepted."

Tracy smiled. Wanda thought the lovely smile really made the woman. And unlike some of the others, this one looked completely genuine.

"You find out anything more about old Herb?" Wanda asked. "Did you go back and apologize to the chess players, too?"

"I'm afraid they'll beat me over the head with their canes.

No, I tracked down an old landlord, and he gave me a reference Herb had used, a preacher in Kentucky. I heard from him this afternoon while I was painting my living room. He remembered Herb because he used to do chores around the church and never asked for a cent in return. Pastor Fred didn't remember much that was personal, but he did say he was pretty sure Herb had a daughter out of state, that he mentioned her once, then clammed up when he asked more. He said Herb was a man with secrets, and nothing Pastor Fred did or said made him comfortable enough to talk about them."

"Well, that's a kick in the head," Wanda said.

"Until he called, I was feeling good about just telling the funeral home I washed my hands of the whole mess. Now I'm pretty much obligated to go through his stuff and see what I can find. But I'm not looking forward to it."

Tracy sighed and got to her feet again. "I'm going to go now and let you rest. Can I get you anything before I do?"

"You can get me the phone."

"Don't tell me you're going to make more calls tonight. The way you feel? You'll give the old guys heart attacks."

"No, I'm going to call Kenny's cell phone and tell him to get his worthless butt back here in case I need somebody with me tonight."

"You know, I was married to a man I could never have asked for that kind of help. I wouldn't even have considered it in the best of times. Maybe you've still got something left with your husband after all."

Tracy took everything back into the kitchen while Wanda thought about that. She returned with a glass of ice water and a bag of peas, and held them out. "You feel better."

Wanda already thought she might. And that was the strangest part of a strange, strange evening.

chapter eleven

On Monday morning Janya discovered American garage sales and fell in love. She was entranced with the lopsided displays of colorful books, battered baby furniture, and surplus cups and saucers laid out over ordinary lawns. Castoffs transformed an unassuming Palmetto Grove street into a more familiar one of vendors hawking merchandise. Best of all, bartering was encouraged. The sale she visited was a gigantic neighborhood effort, where yards would bloom for a week with old television sets and dresses adorned with funny padded shoulders. An entire block of junk was the best possible initiation.

With Rishi's encouragement, she had taken the bus with a map in hand to find her way to the unfamiliar neighborhood. Rishi had promised if she found something at a good price, she could pay, and he would come at lunchtime to take her treasures home. He had been enthusiastic, and so proud that she was willing to wander streets she didn't know.

Now, on Tuesday, humming the energetic "Dus Bahane"—one of her favorite Bollywood songs—and moving her hands and feet to the music, she rearranged yesterday's purchases. A folding table to hold a simple bronze lamp beside their sofa. A soft green basket to put beside the lamp for mail. A woven rug in shades of rose and beige to place in front of the sofa. A plant stand that was exactly the right size for one of Mr. Krause's ferns.

Of course, when the Krause family was found, she would give back the fern. In the meantime, she had brought several smaller plants into her cottage for safekeeping. One sat on a brass tray filled with different sizes of candles—which she'd also found at the sale. One shared the bedroom she shared with Rishi.

When she gazed at the plants both indoors and out, their greenery reminded her of the courtyard in the house where she had grown up, lush and fragrant with bougainvillea and frangipani, and shaded by a gulmohar tree with flame-colored blossoms that blazed in the months before the monsoon.

Her favorite purchase completed the illusion. She had bought a small fountain to set on a table on their tiny patio, and it reminded her just a little of the one she had often sat beside as a child. She knew this fountain had never been expensive, even when new, and that it was impractical, because she had to run an extension cord from the house when she wanted to hear it. But with more of Mr. Krause's plants on the concrete and under the trees surrounding it, the patio was now a welcoming place. And when the fountain gurgled, and she could bring a chair outside and sit beside it, she knew she would be as happy as she had been for a very long time.

She wondered what all this meant. Was she growing resigned to her new life? Was she, as other people did, relinquishing the dreams she had held for herself and settling for something so much smaller? There seemed to be no point in holding on to old dreams of family, love and happiness. She had called home yesterday, when she hoped her mother would be gone, to speak to her brother. Among other things, she had hoped Yash would tell her the news coming in her mother's letter. But Yash had been gone, as well, and the new maid had told her there was no time when Janya could count on reaching him.

After she had replaced the phone in its cradle, it seemed that losing Yash, to whom she had always been close, was the final sign that life as she had known it was over. Yash had not telephoned since she moved into this cottage. Clearly he, like her parents, wanted to forget she existed.

Thinking about that again made her sad, and the music died. She brewed masala tea, plugged in the fountain, and took a chair outside to sit and think about nothing except the green of the plants and the sound of water cascading over pebbles.

She wasn't sure how long she sat there. The air grew warmer, and she knew the patio would soon be in full sunlight. It was time to go inside, although she didn't know what she would do. She had read both her library books and was waiting until Friday, and the next dance class, to get more. The little cottage sparkled, and the hour was much too early to begin dinner preparations. American food, even the way that she improved on it, was so elementary it was quickly dispensed with.

Last night she had watered the larger plants that still remained at Mr. Krause's house, but now she decided she would check on them again to see if they needed attention before the sun rose too high.

She wasn't far from the house when she saw Tracy striding toward her. Janya admired the way the other woman moved, as if there were a magnet pulling her toward her destination. Every step was infused with purpose. Tracy's arms swung loosely, and although she wasn't really a tall woman, her legs were long, and each step covered a healthy distance. Women here seemed to lack the fluid, languid grace that was so much a part of femininity in India. But Tracy made up for this with sheer energy.

"Good morning," Tracy said, catching up to her. "Heading to Herb's?"

"I thought I would make sure the plants have enough water."

"I wonder if I'm supposed to have his utilities cut off? I hate to. You wouldn't be able to water, and going through his things would be difficult. No light, no air-conditioning. Impossible, actually."

"Then you've decided to look through his papers?"

"I checked the inside of his car. Nothing. I'm stuck with the house now, I guess."

Janya listened as Tracy told her about the conversation with the preacher.

"So he has a daughter," she said once Tracy finished. "And if she lived somewhere else when he lived in Kentucky, perhaps that somewhere was here? Perhaps this is why he moved to Florida."

"I know, but if that's the case, don't you think she would have shown up by now?"

"It seems so. But maybe they were estranged." Janya thought of her own family. "Parents and children often are."

"Tell me about it," Tracy said. "Right now mine are out in California wishing I'd never been born."

Janya felt a stab of recognition, although it seemed implausible that she and this woman had anything in common. "So you are hoping to find her address, perhaps?"

"Hers or somebody who might be able to help me find her. I've been putting it off. I really feel strange going in there." Tracy glanced at her. "Not that I'm superstitious, but it just doesn't seem right somehow. To be in there, rifling through his things. Like I'm disturbing the dead, scaring up ghosts."

"You believe in ghosts?"

"I didn't think I did."

"When my father's mother died, I thought I saw something leave her body. Like a wisp of smoke."

"Oh, thanks. Now I have to worry about Herb hanging around and making woo-woo while I go through his stuff. Do you think he'll haunt me for messing with it?"

"Open the doors and the windows, and let the fresh air inside. You will feel better."

"Maybe I'll find something quickly. Maybe it'll be simple."

"I could help you." Janya hadn't realized she was going to offer. But the long day stretched ahead of her. She had started the week well, with things that were new to her, things that had given her pleasure. Why not continue?

"Let's just be straight with each other," Tracy said. "I'm torn. You're already taking care of the plants. You helped me the day I found him. I would like you in there with me, but I feel kind of…I don't know, guilty."

"There is no need. I have nothing else to do. My days are uncluttered."

"Well, mine are a mess. Like my house. You really wouldn't mind?"

"I really wouldn't." Janya realized she meant it. She was not certain she liked Tracy Deloche, but she wasn't certain she didn't, either.

"Then let's take your advice and get all the windows open first to air it out. I had them open until a couple of days ago, when it rained." Tracy went up the walkway with Janya behind her and unlocked the front door.

The house merely smelled the way tropical houses did when they had been closed up too long—a little moldy, a little damp. Tracy waved her hand. "I switched his air conditioner to the fan setting, so it's going to be hot. It'll be better once the air starts moving a little."

They made short work of the windows and left the front door open with the screen door closed. Janya turned on fans, while Tracy propped open the kitchen door for better circulation.

Back in the living room, Tracy looked around. "I thought I'd start with a tour. It's possible I'm making a mountain out of a molehill. There may not be any papers to go through. I haven't seen any lying around."

"There is mail." Janya sifted through a pile on the coffee table to make her point, letting it drop back on to the glass top.

"There is?"

"You haven't been bringing it in?"

"I guess it never occurred to me that he'd still be getting mail. That was dumb."

"How did it get here?"

"Wanda had a key, but I took it. And I locked up after I closed the windows."

"Was the mail here then?"

"I didn't pay much attention."

Janya lifted the pile and sorted through it. "From the cancellation marks, I would say it came last week."

"Does any of it look personal?"

"Not unless he has a correspondence with the telephone company or the one that provides power." She held the envelopes out to Tracy.

"You know, if I don't pay these, they'll come and turn off his utilities anyway. I've got no frigging clue what I ought to do."

"Perhaps we will find an answer today."

Tracy dropped the envelopes back on the table. Her expression brightened. "Maybe his family's been here. Maybe they found out he died and came to clean up, and brought in all his mail."

"If so, why did they not begin to pack? Or talk to you?"

"You're spoiling my fantasy. I guess at the least we ought to look around to see if anything else has been moved." Tracy started in the direction of the kitchen. Janya went the other way.

The house was not as large as Janya's, which had a second bedroom. Despite that, she found a surprise off the bathroom. She had thought a door beside the shower led to a closet for bed linens; instead, now she found it opened into a room. As small as it was, she wondered if the room had been meant as a nursery, or perhaps, as Herb had clearly used it, an office.

"Tracy, did you know there is another room here?"

Tracy came into the bathroom and stood in the doorway. "I guess I should have figured it out from the footprint of the house, only spatial relations aren't my thing."

There was a small desk in one corner, a wooden filing cabinet in the other, and a narrow bookshelf beside it. The center of the room was taken up by the desk chair, and there wasn't an extra inch of space anywhere.

"You know I'll bet it was a laundry room," Tracy said. "Right off the bathroom, where there's plumbing. Along the way, somebody took out the fixtures and closed it in."

"This is probably the place to start looking for information." Janya took a few steps and opened what actually *was* a closet. Stacked neatly inside were a dozen cartons.

"Oh, I was so much happier a few minutes ago. Look at all that stuff!"

"Did you find any other signs his family might have been here?"

"Nothing. The mail's the only thing out of place."

"Yoo-hoo!"

Janya turned to Tracy. "Is somebody calling you?"

They heard shoes clattering across the floor of the living

room, and in a moment Wanda walked in. "I saw you heading over. Thought I'd see how you're doing."

"You're looking bright-eyed, considering," Tracy said. She gestured to Wanda. "Wanda wasn't feeling very well last night."

"Wanda was feeling like somebody cancelled her birth certificate, that's how Wanda was feeling," Wanda said. "Staying home from work today, just to be sure the green-apple two-step doesn't come back."

"Janya offered to help me look for information on Herb's family. Want to join us?" Tracy asked.

Janya wasn't sure how she felt about that. She might not know exactly how to regard Tracy, but she was fairly certain how she felt about Wanda. The older woman was patronizing, crude, and convinced that Janya and everybody who had not been born right here in Florida was a step below her. Janya had told Rishi Wanda's theory that foreigners should not send money to their families, and Rishi had suggested that Janya stay away from her. There was prejudice in this country, just as there was at home, just harder to gauge. Rishi said it was safest not to try to fight it.

"I guess I could help," Wanda said. "Although I'll plant my behind somewhere comfy while I do it, that's for sure."

"Did you by any chance bring in Herb's mail?" Tracy asked. "There's a pile of it on the coffee table. *Recent* mail."

"How would I have done that? You took the key, remember? Short of breaking a window and tossing the mail on the floor, I didn't have access. Frankly, I never thought about his mail."

Janya looked over the things on the desktop while the other two discussed who could have left the mail on the table. She thumbed through an old edition of Webster's dictionary, then an accounts book with shaky penmanship detailing how much

Herb had paid for lettuce, milk and other groceries each week. There was information on how much he paid for utilities. What was left each month from his meager Social Security check.

"He was not a rich man," Janya said, closing the ledger. "From this, it seems he lived from month to month."

"No addresses, like people he was sending money to?"

"We should look at it more closely, but I think there was no money to send."

"Bummer," Tracy said.

"Where do you want me to start?" Wanda asked.

Janya's search of the desktop had turned up little. She opened the deepest drawer and found a collection of nearly a dozen file folders. "Perhaps with these?" She scooped them out.

"I'll just take them into the living room and see what's what...."

Janya started to reply when Tracy put her hand on her arm to silence her. "What's that?" she mouthed.

Wanda was listening, too, her head turning side to side, as if she were hoping one ear might be better than the other. "Somebody's out there," she whispered.

Janya heard a noise that sounded as if something soft was being dragged across the floor. Tracy's gaze met hers. Together, they shrugged.

Wanda was the first to respond. She turned and marched out of the office, through the bathroom and into the hall leading to the living room. "Okay, I don't know who's here, but you'd better plan to speak well of yourself."

Janya followed, although somewhat reluctantly. No one was in the living room. But now there were sounds coming from the kitchen.

"Great," Tracy said softly.

Janya heard the refrigerator door open and close, then the dragging noise again. By then Wanda was standing in the kitchen doorway, but Janya could see one lavender sleeve and one thin hand.

"Alice! You like to have scared us to death," Wanda said.

Janya and Tracy joined her in the doorway. Alice looked up, as if she weren't surprised to see them. "I brought the mail."

The women looked at each other. Tracy was the first to speak. "You have a key?"

"The door was open."

"I don't mean today. The other times you've been over here. You've been bringing the mail in every day since he died?"

"Herb gave me one." Now Alice looked confused. "Was that…a bad idea?"

"No, no. Of course not," Tracy said. "Only I didn't know, that's all. And I couldn't figure out how the mail ended up on the table."

"He said…" Alice, in a lightweight lavender warmup suit, appeared, as she always did, to be struggling. "Somebody needed one. In case." Her face sagged. "I should have checked.…"

"Oh, please don't worry." Janya understood and hurried to reassure her. "No one could have helped him. He died suddenly. Very quickly."

"I had a key, too," Wanda said. "And I never checked, either, Alice. Maybe he thought if we both had one, he'd be safer."

"I saw you walking over here…today. I thought I would clean out the refrigerator. It's the least I can do. Things will spoil."

Janya was afraid Tracy would dismiss Alice and send her home, perhaps from kindness—which was sometimes the cruelest reason to chase another person away. But Tracy nodded, as if she thought that was an excellent idea.

"That's very nice of you, and something I didn't even think about. We were just going through his things. We're trying to find out if he has family anywhere. We don't know who to notify."

"Oh, he has a daughter."

Tracy looked delighted. "Alice, you remembered! Lee said you didn't know anything."

"Why would Lee say that?"

"He asked...never mind. It's great you did. What else can you tell us?"

Alice looked blank.

"Do you know where the daughter lives? Her name?" Janya asked gently.

"No. I don't think so." Alice stared into space. Janya was afraid she was finished, but she began again in a moment.

"Once I was telling him about Karen. My..." She seemed to lose track for a moment, then she nodded. "My girl. Karen. I said...I think...that it seemed like forever to me since she died. Forever since I had seen her."

"Yes?" Janya said. "That must make you sad."

Alice looked grateful. "He said his daughter..." She bit her lip; then she shrugged.

"That his daughter died, too?" Tracy asked.

"No, I think he said...it had been a long time since he'd seen her, too, but she was still alive." She brightened a little. "Yes, that's what he said."

"He didn't say where she lived, did he?"

"No. At least...I don't think... My head. It's like smoke rising. Sometimes I can see through it. Sometimes? Not."

"That's more than the rest of us knew," Janya said. "It is good you remembered."

"I think there was more."

"More?" Tracy looked perplexed. "What? Daughters?"

"Family. More family. Only I can't think why that seems... right."

"Well, it's pretty clear he had a daughter," Tracy said. "And now we'll see if we can find her name and address somewhere. Maybe we'll come across an address book."

"The refrigerator?" Alice asked.

"It's very kind of you. I really appreciate your help."

Alice smiled, and Janya got a glimpse of the woman she must have been before her daughter died and her health betrayed her. "Good."

The others marched back into the office. Tracy was the first to speak. "Does anybody else on this key want to come to the party?"

"Do you think she knew more and just forgot it?" Wanda asked.

"I'm surprised she remembered that much. Lee said he asked her about Herb and she didn't remember a thing."

"Me, I have days like that. Menopause is turning my brain to scrambled eggs. And hot flashes cook 'em up something awful."

"Menopause can certainly affect good judgment," Tracy said brightly.

"Now listen here, I can walk right out and leave you to dig without my help."

"But what fun would we have without you?"

Janya wasn't sure what was going on, but the two women seemed to have established a truce of sorts. Neither looked angry, but there was tension in the air. To head off problems, she scooped up the file folders again and handed them to Wanda.

"If you go through these, I will finish looking through the desk, then I'll see if there is anything in the big file cabinet. Tracy, you might want to start on the top box in the closet. It was not sealed. Maybe he used it recently."

"Aren't you the organized one?" Wanda said. "Everywhere I turn, somebody from India is telling me how to do things. I called about my cell phone service yesterday, and the next thing I knew I was talking to somebody in Bangalore."

Janya guessed that she was supposed to feel pleased. "India is a large country. I could not fix your cell phone."

"Oh, I'm sure you're much prettier than he was, too." Wanda marched out with her folders.

"I'll just get that box," Tracy said, and did.

Twenty minutes later, Janya joined them in the living room where Wanda was taking up the sofa and Tracy a big chair. She arrived just in time to be served a cola in a glass filled to the top with ice. Alice set one in front of each of them, then gestured to the last chair, as if she wanted Janya to take it.

"How's the refrigerator?" Tracy asked.

"Clear of anything…" She stopped.

"That might spoil?"

Alice nodded. "Now I have to go. Lee will be home."

"How's his car these days?"

Alice looked perplexed. "He drives it."

"Well, I'm glad he got it fixed." Tracy put her box to one side and stood. "Thank you again for coming, Alice."

"Lee was gone." She nodded at the others; then she left, walking slowly out the door.

"She's as sweet as shoofly pie, but that woman's one egg short of a custard," Wanda said.

"She had a stroke about the time her daughter died. Combined with the stress, I'm sure the past year's been difficult. Maybe she's just catching up," Tracy said.

Wanda looked up from her folders. "How do you know so much about her? She tell you that? You're suddenly the sympathetic landlady?"

"Lee did."

"The two of you chat a lot?"

Tracy closed the flap of the box and set it on the floor. "When it comes to *chatting* with men, I'm afraid I'm out of my league. Apparently I have a lot to learn."

"Might be a job in it for you. Pay for some of those repairs on my cottage."

Janya watched them glare at each other. A change of subject seemed in order, although she had no idea why. "Has either of you discovered anything yet?"

"About what?" Tracy demanded. She seemed to realize she'd raised her voice to the wrong person. "Oh, you mean about Herb. Not so far. I think he clipped every article on fishing that the *Sun County Sentinel* ever published. Either of you need information on bait or tides?"

"He used to go out to the point and fish on the beach near every morning," Wanda said. "I never saw him come back with anything."

"I guess we can toss these. They aren't exactly family me- mentoes." Tracy stood and nudged the box to the side. "I'll get the next one."

"Well, here's something," Wanda said, before Tracy could go. "Herb's birth certificate."

"Really? Let me see." Wanda held it out, and Tracy took it. "Herbert Lowe Krause. Montgomery, Alabama. June 22, 1920. That made him—" Tracy wiggled her fingers as if she were counting on them "—almost eighty-eight. That's a good long life."

"Too bad they don't update those things with recent infor- mation. Marriages. Children, that kind of thing. It would have made this easier."

"Which folder was it in?" Janya asked.

Wanda squinted at the folder label. "It's all faded." She leaned closer. "I think it says 'Legal.'"

"Anything else interesting in there?" Tracy leaned over as Wanda skimmed through the remaining contents.

Wanda held up another document. "Look here. Another birth certificate." She leaned over it. "Clyde James Franklin. September 14, 1922. Augusta, Maine."

"Not a brother or a son."

"So why'd Herb have this? Lord, it's so old it looks like the one right from the hospital. A friend who died, maybe? Some kind of memento? You never know what people will keep." Wanda replaced it and kept searching. "Here's something else official." She lifted out another document and scanned it. "Interesting. Discharge papers from the army, looks like."

"I bet Herb served in World War II." Tracy paused. "Is my math right? Two, not One?"

"Math's right, but not the name. Clyde again. Released from duty on November 17, 1945."

"Really? I bet you're right. He must have been somebody Herb was close to, maybe an army buddy."

"And here's a high school diploma. Cony High School in Augusta. For Clyde, not Herb."

"Is there anything about Herb in that folder besides his birth certificate?"

"I'm working on it." Wanda held up another paper and scanned it. "More Clyde. Certificate for some sort of welding course."

"This isn't getting us anywhere," Tracy said. "So some guy named Clyde Franklin could weld."

Wanda put that one back, too. "Okay, here's something with Herb's name on it."

"At last."

"It's some kind of Social Security form. What he can count on getting. When. You get these a lot when you get to be my age."

"Anybody else's name on it?"

"No, just his." She went through the rest of the papers, shaking her head after each one. "More of that kind of stuff. Recent stuff. A car title from the eighties. An old driver's license."

"Nothing with a wife's name? A daughter's?"

"Bills, receipts." Wanda kept skimming. "He had a boat, but he sold it. Bought a fair amount of fishing tackle from some place over in Dunedin. Had some expensive dentures, I'll tell you. More than one receipt from some florist in Georgia."

"That could be significant," Janya said.

Wanda looked up. "And the reason?"

"Are the other receipts from Georgia?"

Wanda paged through. "Not any of these."

"We know he lived in Kentucky for a short time," Tracy said. "The preacher said Herb was there about a year, but he decided to come back to Florida."

"Come back," Janya said. "So perhaps he was living *here* before he went *there*."

"I guess you're right."

"Why was he paying a florist in Georgia?" Janya asked.

"If you ask me, we're barking up the wrong tree," Wanda said, closing the folder. "Nothing about a daughter or any other family member."

"How many receipts were there from the florist?" Janya asked.

"I don't know. Six, seven?"

"Maybe he was sending flowers to this missing daughter."

"You know, that could be true," Tracy said. "I'll call the shop and ask if they have anything in their records."

Wanda smiled. "Maybe I ought to do it. People respond to my prompting a little better."

"Well, you'd be a natural. You do have all that *phone* experience," Tracy said.

"I could call," Janya volunteered quickly.

"No, I'll do it," Tracy said. "It's my job, but thank you."

"I don't know that you'll find out anything," Wanda said, handing her the folder. "The receipts are from a while ago."

"I'll give it a try. Can't hurt."

"You like jigsaw puzzles?" Wanda asked. "This is like putting one together, figuring out who he was."

"It is a shame we didn't take the time to do it while he was alive to appreciate the attention," Janya said.

"I'm feeling a tad weak in the knees." Wanda got slowly to her feet. "I'm going home and rest my bones. But I'll take the rest of these folders, if you want, and see what we've got."

Janya looked at the clock beside the television and realized that the morning had flown by. "I should go, too, but I can take mine, as well."

"I'll take the next box with me," Tracy said, standing, too. "We got a start. Let's stay in touch. Let me know if you find anything, okay?"

They walked together to the door. "If I find anything of interest, I will tell you Friday at the dance class," Janya said.

"Then you're going?"

"I plan to."

"I'll take you over," Tracy said. "It's no trouble. Then you can tell me what you discovered in your folders."

Janya was surprised. She realized she was actually looking forward to it.

chapter twelve

With summer vacation right around the corner, Tracy was positive she was not going to be hired as a swimming instructor. If Gladys Woodley had passed Tracy's application to her husband, she had done so without a recommendation.

On Friday morning Tracy sealed the last of three envelopes, bills she'd put off until she couldn't wait any longer. The balance in her checking account was shrinking as fast as a supermodel on the Hollywood Cookie Diet. Lee's proposed sales pitch to Florida developers was probably in the works, but she knew it wouldn't bear fruit right away. Maribel had brought a couple of men to walk over the property on Wednesday, but afterward the Realtor had admitted that they planned to wait and see what happened with Wild Florida's lawsuit.

As she dressed for the dance aerobics class, Tracy wondered if she should go. She was getting plenty of exercise at home, and she was embarrassed to face Gladys. But she had promised Janya a ride, and she owed the young woman at least that for all the help she had given. A new session would start after next week, and then she could find an excuse not to attend.

Janya, with what looked like books under her arm, was walking toward Tracy's house when Tracy stopped to pick her up. Today the other woman was dressed in a short-sleeved blouse with embroidery around the neck and sleeves, and loose pants. She wore black shoes with rubber soles, although they were nothing like the tightly laced up Reeboks Tracy wore. Her hair was braided and pinned off her neck.

"You look ready to go." Tracy shifted once her passenger was inside and took off again.

"I must stop by the library on the way home, so you won't need to bring me back."

"I was going to stop myself. We can go together, unless you have something else you need to do afterward."

"No, only the library. Although I wonder. Rishi suggested that perhaps city hall might have records for Herb."

Tracy thought that sounded promising. "Maybe we can make a quick stop there, as well."

As Tracy flew along the road to the bridge they fell silent, but when traffic forced her to slow, Janya took a slip of paper out of a small cloth purse. "I made a short list of what I found in Herb's papers. But I don't think any of it will help you. I would have come to your house to tell you if I'd thought it would."

Tracy had a feeling this was going to be that kind of day. "I saw Wanda for a few minutes yesterday. She didn't have anything helpful, either. She gave back her stuff, and I pitched it."

"Before he lived in the cottage, he lived in an apartment in town, but the building was transformed into luxury condominiums—he kept the notice—so it is unlikely any of his neighbors remain."

"It's like there was a campaign to wipe out all traces of the old guy."

"Started by him, it seems. There was so little in his file. Jokes he had torn from magazines. Medical records. Photographs—"

"Really? Names on the back?"

"They were of a dog named Rutabaga."

"He must not have liked the dog very much."

"There were registration papers for his car—no other names listed. An entire file of fishing licenses." She put the paper back in her purse. "Those were the most interesting things I found."

Tracy slapped the steering wheel with her palm. "I might as well just pack up his stuff and put it out by the side of the road."

"Did you say that the funeral home will cremate him soon?"

"It's set for tomorrow."

"Shouldn't we be there?"

Tracy couldn't think of any place she would rather *not* be. Luckily Herb had anticipated that. "I asked. They said his instructions, such as they were, state that no service of any kind is to be held, and no one is to attend."

"This is so very sad."

"Yes, well, maybe if his family protested, the home would ignore his wishes. But we aren't family."

"Then we should gather together tomorrow and remember him."

Tracy wondered what exactly they would remember.

"Did you call the florist in Georgia?" Janya asked.

"Out of business for five years."

"We are becoming, what do you call it, investigators?"

"Private investigators. P.I.'s. Gumshoes. Detectives."

"I hope real detectives have better luck."

"Maybe that's what I ought to do. I'm thinking about finding a job. I could be a detective, only apparently, I stink."

"Could Wanda help find you a job?"

"That's funnier than you know." Tracy smiled at Janya. "But no, probably not."

They parked in the side lot, and Tracy reminded herself not to act embarrassed. She had apologized and more or less vindicated herself by catching Bay. She would simply smile pleasantly, make small talk when she paid her fee, and not ask why she hadn't gotten the job.

Inside, the center was buzzing. One group had just gotten out, and since all the participants were wearing gis, Tracy assumed it was a martial arts class. A flock of toddlers, herded by two young women, wiggled by, and Janya and Tracy waited until they were safely out of the way before they went to the front desk.

Gladys looked as unruffled as usual, but she also looked like somebody who could use help. They waited until several other people finished at the desk before they approached with their money in hand.

"Oh, thank goodness you're here," Gladys said, the moment she saw Tracy. "I called this morning, and when you didn't answer, I was afraid I wasn't going to be able to reach you all day."

Tracy felt hope rise, then told herself that getting a silly little job teaching swimming was nothing.

"Well, I'm here now. What's up?"

"Woody wants to interview you right away. Do you have time?"

"Sure. I'll just skip the class or go in late."

"I don't think you'll be going in at all. He'll want to give you the tour."

Tracy thought that was a bit overdone, considering that she would only be working in the pool area. Still, she knew better than to say anything ever again that could be construed as ungrateful or rude.

She smiled brightly. "Should I go down to his office?"

"Third door on the right along the green hall. His name's on it."

"Should I bring an application to fill out?" She glanced at Janya, who was frowning in confusion. "I sort of applied to teach swimming lessons," she explained. "I think Mr. Woodley wants to interview me."

"He has your résumé," Gladys said. Then she smiled. "But he's not going to interview you for the instructor's job, dear. He wants to interview you for the supervisor's position."

Woody had a round face, a round body, and guileless round eyes that looked as if they belonged on a much younger man. Tracy knew better than to accept any of this at face value. Unless one of the town's politicians owed him a favor, Woody had won the director's position through his own merits.

He seated Tracy in the chair beside his desk; then he joined her in the one beside it and started right in.

"We hired somebody for this position last week. This morning she announced she had a permanent offer at a health club in Tampa. I've been tearing out my hair, then Gladys gave me your application."

Woody had very little hair to tear out. Tracy had very little experience being anybody's savior.

She tried to explain tactfully. "I was actually applying to teach swimming. I taught in college. Nobody drowned."

He had a guileless smile, as well. "I'm glad you have a sense of humor. You'll need it on this job."

"Woody…" She paused. "I'm sorry. May I call you Woody?"

"Of course. Call me anything you want. Just say you'll take the job."

"But you don't know anything about me."

"Of course I do. We called all your references when we were going to offer you the instructor's position. And I've gone over your work experience—"

"There's not much. You saw that, right?"

"Yes, it's mostly volunteer, of course. But it's plenty for what we need, and you have the perfect college degree to augment it. I looked up the course work for your program at Long Beach, and you'll be a wonderful fit."

Tracy tried to figure out a way to explain that she didn't want the supervisor's position. She needed money, yes, and certainly this would pay more than the instructor slot. But this was a real job, the kind careers were made of. The kind that came with huge responsibilities, long working hours, huge responsibilities. Okay, she was obviously stuck on that last part.

"I don't know that I'm up to this," she said, struggling to sound modest, not lazy. "I don't want to sell myself when I have my own doubts."

"Let me be frank with you, Tracy." He leaned forward, or at least as far as he could over a belly that testified that someone in the Woodley household was an excellent cook. "I'm willing to take a chance here. You're short on experience, but you're also the only person with a résumé on file who is even halfway qualified to run this summer program. And it starts immediately. I need somebody now, yesterday, last week."

"What about the woman I'd be replacing? You know, your permanent supervisor? In a pinch, wouldn't she come back and help out until you hire somebody more…worthy?"

"Susan just had twins. She's breast feeding. Can you imagine her running around this center with her blouse open and a baby in each arm?"

Tracy only half listened as Woody listed the duties of the job. She was mulling over this extraordinary turn of events.

"I know this must seem a little overwhelming," Woody said at last. "But I'll tell you what clinched the deal. The tennis tournament you organized to benefit multiple sclerosis. We're going to have our own tournament this summer. We need somebody with experience."

Tracy had really only been a gofer that summer. She had taken the position because she had a crush on the club's tennis pro, and she'd guessed—correctly—that they would be working hand in hand. Jerry, the pro, had done most of the work, of course. Jerry plus his roommate Frank, who had turned out to be a lot more than just Jerry's old buddy from high school.

"How much does this position pay?" she heard herself asking.

He named a figure that would have made her laugh two years ago. Now she whistled. She could take care of all the repairs on the tenant cottages, put more in the bank for next year's tax payment, maybe even hire an attorney to look into the situation with Wild Florida.

"Health insurance, too," he said, like a father promising a child a treat after a tetanus booster. "You'll be covered, since you're a replacement, not a summer employee." He stood, sensing he'd reeled her in. "You'll take it?"

"I…I…guess I will."

"Wonderful." He held out his hand. "We'll be seeing a lot of each other. It's an active job. If you need anything at any time, my door is open. Meantime, I'll give you a quick tour, then I'll turn you loose with Susan's notes. She was very organized, our Susan. By the time you get through them all, you'll have an excellent idea how to move forward. But you'll have to catch up quickly. The program starts in just under two weeks. Susan did a lot of the preliminaries, but there's still a lot left to do."

"I'm overwhelmed."

"Not yet you're not, but just wait. First the tour, then Gladys will handle all the necessary paperwork—and there's a bundle. You can take it home and bring it back Monday, if you prefer. I'd like Monday to be your first day, if possible. Oh, and Gladys will fill you in on the tournament. We're hosting, and it's a big deal for us."

Tracy followed in a daze through a whirlwind tour of the facility. Most of it was more or less familiar, although she hadn't seen the pool up close, or the men's and women's locker rooms. She was impressed anew with the indoor walking/jogging track, the exercise and weight rooms, the multiple classrooms, the game room. The tennis courts looked to be in terrific condition. The shuffleboard and boccie ball courts were amazing, as befit, she supposed, an area with so many retirees. She thought of the chess players and hoped the rec center stayed far away from board games.

Woody hadn't stopped talking. "Your big focus will be the youth program, of course."

"Of course," she echoed.

"They arrive at nine. We don't provide meals, but we have snacks. There's usually juice when they arrive, a midmorning snack of milk or juice and graham crackers, and then, at noon, they have the lunch they brought with them. Afternoons we try to provide fruit, popcorn, pretzels, something that's not too sweet. We have water jugs available at all times, especially when the children are outdoors. You'll need to make sure that whoever is in charge of that follows through."

By now she had figured out that she ought to be taking notes. She was scribbling on deposit slips, since she rarely needed them for their real purpose these days.

He continued in the same vein. By the end of the tour it was clear that for the most part her job was making sure other people did theirs. And if they didn't, she filled in. People got sick? She filled in. People forgot? She filled in. People got lazy? Same thing.

They ended up back in the reception area. Gladys grinned when she saw them approach. She finished printing a receipt and handed it over to a woman in black spandex. Then she folded her hands on the counter.

"So…you took the job?"

"I guess I did."

"I'm going to leave Tracy with you now," the beaming Woody told his wife. Tracy thought his was a smile seen most often on carnival midways. She was as gullible as a farm boy forking over a month's spending money in a quest to win a stuffed gorilla, and Woody was thrilled to take whatever she gave him.

"Well," Gladys said, when they were alone, "I took the liberty of putting everything together for you." She reached under the counter and took out an expanding folder, held together by an elastic band. "You can do most of this at home and ask any questions when you bring it back Monday. I know you're probably not prepared to stay today."

"Wow."

"I put my faith in you when I gave him your résumé."

Tracy heard the message. Gladys believed Tracy could do this, and Tracy was not to fail her.

"I'll bring this back Monday morning." She took the folder and tucked it under her arm. "And Woody said you'd tell me a little about the tennis tournament?" That, at least, was something she could sink her teeth into.

"Tennis tournament?" Gladys looked over Tracy's shoulder and smiled. Tracy had heard footsteps behind her; it seemed to be that kind of morning.

"I've never seen it so busy," she told Gladys.

"Registration for youth camp just opened. People come early to be sure their kids get a spot. It's going to be like this all day."

"Then I won't keep you. You can tell me about the tournament later." She turned and saw that the footsteps belonged to Marsh Egan.

For a moment she didn't know what to say; then she found her voice. "Let me guess. You're here to register Bay for youth camp."

He didn't look pleased to see her. "I'm not sure why you care."

Today Marsh almost looked presentable. Khaki trousers, a pinstriped sport shirt unbuttoned at the neck. A round pin on the pocket that read: It's Not Easy Being Green. Even the end of his ponytail was tucked under.

"Registering him for the *whole* summer?" she asked.

"You got it."

"We may have to require a ball and chain with your deposit."

"We?"

She smiled sweetly. "I'm the new recreation supervisor. I'll be in charge of every breath he takes."

She heard Gladys clear her throat and remembered that the other woman was counting on her. "Of course he'll be so happy to spend his summer here, doing things he loves, learning to get along with people. You came to the right place."

"I thought so—until a few minutes ago."

She had done her part. She turned to say goodbye to Gladys, who was standing, leaning forward. Before Tracy could stop her, Gladys reached over the counter and clapped an oversize cap on Tracy's hair.

Tracy reached up with alarm and felt it sitting there like a bad bouffant hairdo. She snatched it off, but Marsh was already laughing.

The hat was bright red with white lettering. She turned the brim and read the slogan. Palmetto Grove Shuffleboard. Get

A Cue. Under the letters was a logo of two long poles crossed like swords. She could still hear Marsh laughing as she squashed the hat in her hands. "I'm not sure I get this."

"It's not a tennis tournament, it's a *shuffleboard* tournament. Tell me you know the game."

She had probably studied shuffleboard in some class or other, but Tracy didn't remember. Time had passed, and some of the games had been remarkably dumb. "I probably played it on a cruise ship."

"Well, you'd better bone up. You're in charge of the Coastal Florida Adult and Youth Singles and Doubles Tournament. Labor Day weekend right here in Palmetto Grove. I'll tell you, our shuffleboard players take this very seriously. There'll be no greater test of your skills than keeping them happy."

"You so clearly hired the right woman," Marsh said, taking the hat from Tracy's hands and plopping it back on her head. "She's just going to be a natural, isn't she?"

Janya watched Tracy fidget as she drove. She knew little except that Tracy had just been given a job at the recreation center. How she felt about it was a mystery, although the fidgeting was a clue.

"I can't believe I said yes," Tracy exploded as they pulled into the municipal parking lot in front of city hall. "Really! What was I thinking?"

"Perhaps that the salary would pay your bills?"

"It's a huge job. Why on earth do they think I can do it?"

"*Can* you do it?" Janya asked.

"Well, how would I know?"

"Perhaps this is a good way to find out."

"We have to be quick about this. I've really got to go to the library now and learn everything I can before Monday."

The sidewalk was hot enough to melt the soles of Janya's shoes, and the sun beating down on her head felt familiar, if not pleasant. City hall was three stories and modern, with siding so blindingly white it hurt her eyes. Inside, they were hit by a wall of air-conditioning. Janya wondered why the city paid so much to air-condition a hallway.

In a room on the second floor Tracy explained their situation to a man with a crewcut and wrinkly ears; then she asked for help. He seemed more interested in Tracy than the question, but perhaps that was the reason he so quickly agreed to see what he could find.

They waited, leaning against the counter.

"He's going to run a records check," Tracy explained. "If this doesn't turn up anything, maybe we can nose around some of the other offices another day."

"You asked about Clyde Franklin, too."

"Well, you know, if they were friends and Clyde has family around here, or he's still alive, maybe he can tell us whatever he knows. I did search the Internet without any luck. But I thought it was worth a try. And this guy is eager to assist."

"Do men often look at you that way?"

"What way?"

"As if they want to devour you."

"Don't they look at you that way? I bet you have to fight them off."

"In India I was usually with someone, my brother, a cousin, a servant. They would do the fighting if it was necessary."

"Always? You were chaperoned everywhere?"

"For safety, yes."

"Well, I guess I can understand that. There were plenty of places in L.A. where I only went if I was with somebody else."

They chatted about the dance aerobic class until the man

with the crewcut returned. "I did a quick check for you," he said. "On the computer. The only records I found for Herbert Krause were fishing licenses."

"Oh, we actually found a bunch of those. Nothing else, huh? Nothing that would help us locate his next of kin?"

"Not that I could find."

"Well, we appreciate your help."

"I did find something for a Clyde Franklin."

Janya had already started to turn away. "You did?" she asked before Tracy could.

"A Clyde Franklin married a Louise Green right here in Palmetto Grove back in 1942. Would that be the one you're looking for?"

"I guess it could be," Tracy said. "Did you find anything else about him?"

"No, that's all I saw." He leaned over the counter. "I could maybe do a more thorough search if both of you come back tomorrow."

Janya saw Tracy wink at him. "We might just do that."

Back in Tracy's car, Janya pondered what little they had discovered. "Mr. Clyde Franklin lived in Palmetto Grove. Perhaps this is where he and Herb met. Neither of them was born here. They met, and perhaps they became friends and went into the military together. Could Clyde have died in the war?"

"No, remember? We found *his* discharge papers, not Herb's."

"Oh, that's correct." Janya reconsidered. "So he survived the war, and of course we know that Herb did, too. But Herb had Clyde's papers. So they must have been friends, and when Clyde died, he took them as mementoes."

"Why didn't this Louise take them? Clyde married a Louise Green, and it only makes sense she would have had Clyde's papers after he died."

"Perhaps they were divorced? Or perhaps she gave them to Herb afterward."

"No, that doesn't feel right. You don't give away things like discharge papers, birth certificates, diplomas, not as mementoes. You give a favorite pen, or books he loved, a ring or tie clip, remembrances, not documents."

"Why would a person have another person's papers?"

"I have no idea. It makes no sense."

"Maybe Clyde and Louise were no longer together, and when Clyde died, Herb took care of matters and kept them."

"I guess it's possible."

Tracy pulled into the library parking lot, and the two women got out. "I'm going to be a little while, do you mind? I'm going to see what they have about shuffleboard."

"It's played on a table?"

"Not this kind. It's played on a court. It's the stupidest game known to man, and suddenly I have to be an expert. I also have to see if I can find a book on installing tile."

Janya listened as Tracy explained about the stacks of tile.

The explanation took them inside. "I will wait for you in the computer room," Janya said. "I would like to check my e-mail."

"Doesn't your husband work with computers?"

"Yes, but we have a problem with our Internet connection at home."

"I hope that's your problem, not mine."

"It is related to our telephone, but I'm afraid our leaking air conditioner *is* your problem."

"Great. I've got a guy coming to look at Wanda's cottage. I'll send him down to yours, too, and now I really am going to have to install my own tile. I'll see you in a little while."

Janya returned her books to the front desk; then she browsed the aisles, settling on a thick novel about eighteenth-century Russia, and a cookbook with traditional American recipes. In her opinion, Rishi had a poor appetite, and she didn't want him to waste away, not even if it meant she could go back to India.

After she checked out her new finds, she wandered back to the computer room. The librarian explained what she had to do to get online, then checked her card. Finally Janya followed the simple steps and logged on.

In a moment, thanks to the miracle of microchips, she was gazing at her mailbox, plump with messages. Delighted, she saw that she had an e-mail from Yash. She opened it and quickly scanned his words, written not in their native language but in English.

I can understand that you are busy adjusting to your new life. But please let me know when it would be convenient to talk to you. I miss you, and I'm surprised you haven't phoned me.

For a moment she was so angry she wanted to strike the screen. Her parents were intentionally trying to keep her from contacting her brother. None of her calls had borne fruit because they hadn't told Yash she was trying to get in touch. Apparently they had told him that she wanted to be left alone to adjust to her new life.

She fired back an e-mail, using English, too.

Yash, I have called many times. It is clear that our mother does not want me to speak to you. Please telephone when our parents are not at home. Please do not let them separate us.

★ ★ ★

She typed in her telephone number, then paused before she pressed Send.

Did she want to create problems for Yash? If he confronted their parents, trouble would certainly ensue. She could almost hear the argument that would follow. Her entire history would be recounted. How she had shamed the family. How Yash's own future depended on distancing himself from Janya. How Janya was so selfish that she did not see the harm she was doing by trying to remain a viable part of her brother's life.

Was this the news her mother had wanted to impart in her letter? That she was barring Yash from any communication with Janya? The letter had not yet arrived. Mail delivery between India and the United States could be excellent or poor, with no apparent explanation. Had Inika Desai written to demand that Janya separate herself from the family for everyone's good? Was she demanding that Janya forget she had a brother?

Janya reread her e-mail. Yash would expect an answer. His e-mail was dated four days ago. He would wonder if she was ignoring him completely, and more than anything, she didn't want to hurt him.

She struggled with herself. She had done nothing wrong, yet she must pay and pay again for someone else's sins. Yash was her brother, and they deserved to continue what had always been a close, happy relationship.

In the end, though, she could not be the rebellious daughter her parents claimed she already was. She deleted her e-mail and wrote another, without recriminations.

Yash, I would very much like to talk to you. Here is my number. Please telephone when you are able. I miss you.

★ ★ ★

She signed her name. The e-mail was a compromise, but she refused to give up her brother when she had already given up so much.

Her delight in her in-box had evaporated. She looked up and saw Tracy coming toward her. Once the Internet connection was repaired, Janya could access the rest at home. By then, perhaps, she would be calmer, more able to appreciate what her friends had to tell her.

She went to close the program, and as she did, her gaze drifted through the list of messages waiting to be read. She froze. There at the bottom was an address she had never expected to appear again.

Dtambe@tambeindia.com

"Darshan…" She whispered the name, and her heart began to beat faster. Darshan, the man she had loved, the man who had asked her to marry him.

The man who had set her aside because of the scandal that had swirled around her.

Her hand hovered over the computer keys. Then, with sadness weighting her fingers, she deleted the message without opening it and exited the program.

"Ready to go home?" Tracy asked.

"Yes." But the word was a lie. Janya had finally realized that she would never be able to go home again.

chapter thirteen

In the days when she was married to CJ, Tracy almost never rose before eleven o'clock. Their social life had extended into the wee hours of morning, and CJ had a fondness for closing trendy bars and nightclubs with politicians and entertainers he wanted to impress.

Since arriving in Florida, Tracy's entire schedule had changed. Now she rarely slept past seven. Most of the time, by seven-thirty she had already walked along the beach. After she stowed what treasures she found, she jogged, sometimes as far as the little general store a mile short of the bridge, where she bought plain black coffee—no lattes in the place, but plenty of bait—and sipped it on her walk back home.

This morning, as she passed Alice's cottage, she spotted Lee going to his car. Summer might officially begin next month, but Florida was already well in the throes, and her jogging mornings were doomed. She was sweaty and disheveled, and she had sucked in enough humidity to seed her own thunderstorm.

Her hair was twisted on top of her head, she was sans

makeup, and her T-shirt was soaked. She hoped Lee appreciated athletic women.

"Well, look at you," he said, when she waved. The sun glinted off his silver hair. His blue eyes were as clear as a tide pool, and he wore a crisply pressed shirt that matched them exactly. She wondered if Lee ever worked up a sweat.

"I've got a busy day. I thought I ought to tackle it at a run," she said, with her prettiest smile. "Are you a runner?"

"I'm more apt to work out at the gym. Not that I have lately. I like being here when I'm not at the office."

She heard what he didn't say, that he felt responsible for Alice and Olivia, and didn't want them to spend more time alone than they had to.

"I'm glad I caught you," she said. "And this won't take you far from home. I thought you might like to come to my place tonight for a drink. It's not fancy, but maybe we can sit outside if there's a breeze."

"I haven't had an offer that good in a long time. But I've got showings tonight and tomorrow. Weekends are my busiest times."

"Then how about Monday?"

"Great. You're far enough along on your renovations?"

"As long as my guest doesn't expect a palace. But if we don't do it then, I might be too busy later." She told him about her new job.

"Did you ever call Carol about the job at the yacht club?"

She didn't want to go into her reasons for not following through. She just turned up her hands in defeat. "Before I could, this fell in my lap. So I thought I would give it a try."

"I'm considering sending Olivia. Do you think she'll like it?"

Tracy would know more by day's end. The folder Gladys had given her contained more than paperwork to fill out. It bulged with information on the program, including copious notes the former supervisor had kept for each week of the previous summer.

"I'll make sure she likes it," she said. "I can watch out for her."

"You must appreciate children."

Tracy wondered. At least she had never actively disliked them. Sherrie's little girls even made her question her decision not to have her own.

"I like Olivia." She was pretty sure that was true, although she'd seen little of her. "Now Marshall Egan's son? Not so much."

"If he's as pushy as the father, I can understand."

She found herself lowering her eyelashes and tossing her head. Hot as she was, and drenched with sweat, Lee was still looking at her like something good to eat. Desire trickled through her, along with hunger to have a man in her life again. And this time, one for whom she was more than a mannequin to dress up and show off. There had been a lot of bling in her marriage to CJ, but after the first few months, very little zing. She would not make the same mistake twice.

He moved closer; then he reached across the space dividing them and stroked his thumb just under her eye. Whisper soft. "It looks like you picked up some pollen out here."

She smiled slowly and was sorry when he dropped his hand. "What time would you like to come on Monday?"

He didn't move away. "About seven? That'll give me time to get home and get things organized here."

He was always thinking about the women in his life. That was an excellent recommendation.

The front door of the cottage opened, and Alice stepped out, reaching for the ever-present broom before she saw Lee and Tracy. Dragging her feet a bit, she moved toward them.

"Lee, I forgot to ask…for a little cash."

As his mother-in-law approached he stepped back from Tracy. "We talked about this," he said gently.

"When?"

"Earlier." He put his hand on her shoulder. "You don't remember?"

"I guess not." Alice looked confused.

"Don't worry. Olivia was talking a mile a minute. She probably distracted you."

"There's a sale...in the paper. I want to buy a few clothes."

Lee looked distressed. He glanced at Tracy. "Alice, I think you need to conserve."

For a moment she looked taken aback. Then she straightened her shoulders and said with surprising dignity, "Fred took care of me."

Lee looked defeated. "Yes, he did. But we've talked about this, remember? The stock market's taken a beating, and there were some...irregularities? I guess that's the best way to say it, some strange withdrawals before I took over your account that I'm checking into. So you're going to have to take it easy on spending for a while. Do you really need whatever it is?"

"Better to buy on sale."

He reached in his pocket and pulled out a wallet. Then he counted out several twenties. "I don't want to take anything more out of your nest egg this month. Will this help?"

She looked bewildered. "Fred made good money. Good investments."

"A lot of people all over this country are in the same boat," he said sympathetically. "But look, together we can turn this around, Alice. I don't want you to worry. We'll get you back on your feet. Meantime, take the money, okay?"

When she didn't reach for it, he took her hand and put the

bills in her palm, folding her fingers over them. "Buy something pretty. You deserve it."

Alice wandered off, looking dazed and unhappy. Lee looked troubled. "This is my fault. Karen helped her with finances, and in the months after she died, I should have jumped in. But I was so numb, I just didn't realize Alice wasn't coping. By the time I did…" He stared up at the house. "I don't know where the money went. After her stroke she sold some of her best investments, put the money in places she shouldn't have. Some of it just disappeared."

Tracy felt sorry for both of them. "She's lucky she has you. What would she do if she was here on her own?"

"We've got each other. She's a great old gal. We'll get through this."

They agreed to Monday at seven; then, with a wave, Tracy started back toward her own house. When she arrived, she found Janya sitting on her front steps.

Surprised, she wondered if the young woman had come to complain about the air conditioner again. But Janya got right to the point.

"In my country, there is a mourning period after cremation. Ten, sometimes many more, days of fasting, and on the last, we have a feast and offer the food to the gods in the name of the departed. The next day the priests absolve the family, and we resume our regular lives."

"Don't tell me you expect us to do that for Herb? We aren't even related to the man."

"Not that, exactly."

"And besides, don't they burn the widow with her husband's body in your country? I mean, are these funeral customs we want to follow?"

"Suttee was a cultural, not a religious, custom, and it has

been outlawed for nearly two hundred years. Besides, some say it was brought to India by Europeans."

"Not the best of imports."

Janya got to her feet, brushing off the back of jeans worn with a long embroidered tunic. "The exact ritual is less important than that there *is* a ritual. Mr. Krause lived a long, useful life—"

"We don't know that, do we?"

"We can guess. And he was kind to us. He always had a smile for me."

"You're reaching."

"Would you feel better if we just forgot him? Or if we marked this day together at his house?"

Tracy thought of all the reading she needed to do. Then she thought about the guilt she would feel if she said no. "When?"

"Three. I have already talked to Alice. Wanda I will leave to you."

"You know, I don't think she's as obnoxious as she comes across."

"There are many people in the world like that."

Tracy just hoped Janya wasn't including her in their number.

Saturdays were never good at the Dancing Shrimp. Businessmen and ladies who lunch were replaced by tables of screaming toddlers and young families straight from the beach without money for a decent tip. Wanda understood that—remembered, in fact, when her own children had shared the more economical super-size platters of shrimp and fries, and when every leftover at the table went home in a doggie bag.

Today, though, she had little patience for cleaning up spills, moving booster chairs or finding quieter tables for old ladies who didn't want to listen to babies screech. Worst of all, she was afraid she might be turning into one of the latter herself.

The moment she could, she left for home, promising herself a hot shower and a cold beer. Instead she found a note from Tracy about the gathering at Herb's.

"Five minutes?" She kicked a pointy-toed pump against her own door. She could skip it, sure, but what would they say about her if she wasn't there?

She had just enough time to throw on a clean dress and slide her steaming, aching feet into sandals. Smelling like fried fish, and sticky with perspiration and the remnants of a preschooler's soft drink, she headed straight to Herb's.

The others were already assembled. By the time she joined them in the living room she was hotter still, out of sorts, and sorry she had come.

"I thought the man didn't want a funeral," she said, fanning herself with her hand.

"It's a memorial service." Tracy nodded at Janya. "Janya thought we needed one."

Janya was wearing one of those long scarves that wrapped around and around and fell into some kind of a skirt. Wanda couldn't remember what it was called, but this one was light blue, almost silver. Her hair was parted and knotted at her nape, and her forehead sported a red dot. Wanda thought she looked like some princess out of an exotic fairy tale.

"I only thought he deserved to have someone thinking of him today," Janya said.

"Well, it ought to be his family," Wanda said. "Not a bunch of strange women."

"Stranger than most," Tracy agreed.

Tracy was wearing a flowered dress with a high neck and long skirt. The back was low, and her shoulders were bared by the cut of the bodice. Wanda thought *she* looked like a Holly-wood starlet out on a photo shoot.

Now Wanda felt even older and greasier. Even Alice looked as if she'd freshly showered and put on a little makeup. She was wearing a dress that didn't even snap up the front. It had a waist and everything.

"Is somebody going to read a prayer or something inspirational?" Wanda asked.

"I'm turning this over to Janya," Tracy said.

"I'm a Christian." Wanda nodded to emphasize her words. "I can't be part of any heathen death rituals."

Janya gazed up at her. "I thought we could each tell a memory we have of Herb. Will that offend you?"

"Not if that's all we do, it won't."

"Then I thought someone might say a prayer. But if that is a problem…?"

Wanda knew she was being chided. As badly as she wanted to, though, she couldn't find a way to strike back. Nothing Janya said was unreasonable.

"As long as there are no graven images. You folks seem to have a lot."

"I have left all my graven images at home where they belong."

"Wanda, please sit," Tracy said. "We've got this under control. Let's all take a deep breath and a moment to think of something we can say."

Wanda sat, smoothing her skirt under her like the lady she should have been. She wasn't sure where all that about heathens and graven images had come from. She couldn't even remember the last time she'd gone to church. Not since she'd moved to Sun County, that was for sure. She was too mad at Ken to risk sitting there and getting struck by lightning.

Alice was the first to rise. Personally, Wanda was pretty sure *she* never wanted to stand up again, at least not for the next ten years. She slid her tingling, sweaty feet out of her sandals and leaned back in her chair.

"When Karen died, Herb came to my house. He…" Alice paused, as if she were trying to find the words or the right way to finish. "He wasn't rich. He was a working man, a welder—"

"That's where he met Clyde," Wanda said, sitting forward suddenly as the information clicked. "There's our connection!"

"Shhh…" Tracy said, waving her to silence.

"Welders are not rich," Alice said. "It's a hot job. Hard work. Especially in Florida."

"So Herb came to see you," Janya said, as if to steer her back.

"He brought me dinner. I think they had coupons at the Golden Grill across the bridge…."

"Yes?" Tracy said, when she didn't go on right away.

"And sometimes you could buy two entrées…you know, for the cost of one? He shared. When he could have saved it all for himself. He wanted me to feel better." She nodded and sat down.

They shared a moment of respectful silence. Then another. Then, when Wanda thought for certain nobody was going to have anything else to say, Janya got to her feet, feet that were adorned with a slender bracelet around one ankle and several toe rings.

"Every day trees fall and houses are built. The world's rain forests are diminishing."

"Herb was a lumberjack *and* a welder?" Wanda asked.

Without even looking, Tracy waved her to silence again.

"Some people use up the world's resources, and some people take care of them," Janya said.

Tracy interrupted this time. "I hope this isn't a commercial against selling Happiness Key to developers."

Janya lifted one elegant brow and waited until the room was

silent once more. "Mr. Krause was one of those who nurtured plants and trees. Even though he owned no home of his own and could not plant his own little forest, he kept many plants in flowerpots so they could move with him. Plants in flowerpots are not easy to care for. They must be talked to, fussed over."

"You won't catch me talking to a plant," Wanda muttered.

Janya waited, as if she wanted to be certain Wanda had finished. "They must be watered regularly, with no lapses. They must be fertilized, pruned, and when they outgrow their flowerpots, they must be repotted. These things take a great deal of time, of love, of good instincts. So though I know little of Mr. Krause, I know he was a man who could lavish love when it was needed, who was willing to work hard and take time from easier things to do what was required, a man whose good instincts produced a forest in flowerpots that the rest of us can admire and enjoy today, even though he is gone."

She nodded and sat down.

Tracy looked uncomfortable, but when it was clear Wanda wasn't going to speak next, she sighed and stood. "When I moved here a few weeks ago, I really wasn't happy to be in Florida."

"You're saying that's changed?" Wanda asked.

Tracy ignored her. "My life was topsy-turvy. Suddenly I was living here, and I've got to tell you, I'd only been to Florida once, and we stayed at the Ritz Carlton in South Beach. I know all of you will agree with me. Nothing out here on Happiness Key is much like the Ritz."

"Amen," Wanda said with feeling.

"Mr. Krause came over when he saw me moving in. And I guess he thought I might need some help. Of course, he was too old to carry things, but he brought me a folder with all kinds of brochures, and lists of his favorite places to shop, to take dry cleaning, to eat. It had flamingos on the front."

She stopped and cleared her throat. "I guess I didn't appreciate it. I'm not even sure where that folder went. Anyway, the point is that he didn't have a lot to share, but he made certain to share what he had. And he always had a smile and something nice to say when I saw him." She glanced at Wanda, or Wanda thought she did, although it was quick. "And he never expected anything out of me, either. He just took care of his place by himself."

She sat down.

Wanda got to her feet, because now she knew exactly what she was going to say. "That brings back a nice memory. One day I was having an awful time with my screen door. It was such an old one, you know, all bent out of shape, and the screen was peeling back from the edges so bad every time I went to open it, I got scratched. And I wasn't born yesterday, so I know all about lockjaw. Those little wires were all rusted, and I was just waiting for the morning when I woke up unable to open my mouth—"

"That would be the day," Tracy said softly, but not softly enough.

"I am speaking here," Wanda said. Tracy didn't look one bit guilty.

"Anyway, I did try to get that woman at the realty to have it seen to, but of course, she wouldn't do a thing, said we could just move out if we needed to. Mighty big of her. So I decided I'd take it off myself and just put it outside for the garbagemen. Better not to have one than to have one that could kill me."

Tracy sighed audibly.

"Well, there I was, struggling with that stump-ugly door, and by then it was just hanging from one hinge, rusted there like the Tin Woodman right when Dorothy finds him. And here comes Herb, with a can of WD-40, like he'd just been hoping to find somebody who needed it. Between us, we got that door off in a jiffy. And it wasn't the only time he helped me like that. These days my Kenny's as worthless as a doodlebug, and Herb always helped out when he could. Like once when the rain was just coming down, down, down in my bathroom, he came over and helped me soak it up. Too bad he's gone now, 'cause next big rain, the same thing's gonna happen."

She smoothed her skirt and sat again.

Everyone was silent. After she had waited a while, Janya stood. "Here in his home, I know we hope that wherever he has gone, he will find peace and unity with God. Would one of you like to pray?" She waited, looking for all the world like somebody Aladdin would scoop up on his magic carpet.

Alice hefted herself out of her chair. Then, while Wanda listened in amazement, she recited the twenty-third psalm. Perfectly, with only a hesitation or two. Then, she sat down again.

"That was beautiful," Janya said. She waited, and when no one else spoke she said, "This is from my own religious tradition." She paused for a moment. "I am death, that snatches all, and the source of all that shall be born. I am glory, prosperity, beautiful speech, memory, intelligence, steadfastness, and forgiveness. I am the divine seed of all lives."

"Ashes to ashes, dust to dust," Alice said.

"Amen," Tracy said. Everybody else, except Janya, followed suit.

Wanda wasn't sure exactly what had just happened, but she did know she felt better. There hadn't been hellfire and brimstone, nobody pointing a finger at the living to remind them that they might be the next one lying in a casket. She just hoped that if Herb was someplace where he could hear this, he could forgive them all for having so little to say, when there should have been a lot more.

"The best thing we can do for the man now is find his family," she said, getting up. "Where are we on that?"

The tension in the room eased; everybody's shoulders drooped a little, as if they were glad to have that done.

Tracy stood and stretched. "Janya and I went to city hall yesterday. We didn't find out anything about Herb, but we did find that Clyde Franklin, probably the same one considering the dates, was married back in 1942 to a woman named Louise Green. Here in Sun County."

"And you think he's the same one?"

"No guarantee. I guess we might be able to get a copy of their marriage license. Wouldn't it have their birth dates on it?"

"Put that down, somebody. Something we can do," Wanda said.

"If we just assume it's the same one, the most important thing is whether either he or Louise is still alive," Tracy said. "And if we can find them and ask about Herb's daughter."

Something was nibbling at Wanda's brain. "You say the name was Louise?"

"Louise Green, until she married Clyde. Then she would have been Louise Franklin."

"Louise Franklin..." Wanda chewed her lip, which didn't matter, since she hadn't had time to put even a dab of lipstick on it.

The ground rumbled and the cottage shook. It was trash pickup day. The private contractor who threw their garbage in the back of a dump truck could only be counted on to arrive sometime over the weekend, and she often forgot to put out her own stuff, because the times were so irregular. Luckily Ken—apparently he was good for something besides making coffee, after all—had remembered to put the can by the road that morning before he took off for wherever.

"Is there an agency that keeps records of people who have died?" Janya asked. "We could check that first. Clyde and Louise would both be old by now, and may be gone like Herb."

"Social Security," Tracy said. "But I'm not sure they would just give us that information. I could call—"

"Louise Franklin!" Wanda clapped her hands. "In the folders I checked. Herb had a bunch of newspaper clippings. I scanned them. None of them seemed important. More fishing holes, that kind of thing. But when I was flipping one of the clippings over, just to be sure, there was a news article about a woman named Louise Franklin. I knew I remembered that name. And I wondered if that was why he'd cut it out, because it was cut to the size of that article, and on the other side, whatever it said, it was chopped off at the end, like it hadn't been that important, although it *was* about tides or something."

"You have a good memory," Janya said. "Do you remember anything about the article?"

"No. But let's get it and see. Where is all the stuff I gave you?" she asked Tracy.

"You said it was worthless, so I threw it away."

The road outside was quiet now. The women looked at each other with alarm. "Did they just pick up the trash?" Tracy asked.

"Sounded like it." Wanda was sprinting toward the window in her bare feet. "Yep, I can still see the dust they kicked up. They'll head out to the point to turn around. They'll be back in just a minute."

"We've got to head them off," Tracy said.

"Last week I tried to get them to wait while I ran back in for a second bag, and they just laughed at me. The first bag barely made it in before they took off down the road. And they wouldn't stop on the way back, even though I was standing there holding it up for 'em. Those guys don't stop for anything."

"Oh, no?" Tracy threw the door open. "They had better stop for me."

Wanda wanted to see this. She liked Tracy marginally better than she had, but the woman still needed some comeuppance. She hobbled out to Herb's front steps to watch.

Tracy was heading for the road, and Wanda felt someone brush by her. Janya in her sari—that's what it was called!—had taken off after her. Before Wanda knew it, Alice was following.

"You watch they don't run you three down," Wanda called. "I wouldn't put it past 'em."

The point wasn't far, which was what made this land so valuable and environmentally fragile. By the time the women were lined up along the road, Wanda could hear the truck returning. The engine coughed and sputtered, but she was pretty sure the truck was speeding up. The women were already jumping up and down, waving their arms, but she knew nothing they did was going to be any good.

Before she knew it she was back inside, slipping her throbbing feet into her sandals and grabbing for her purse. She left by the kitchen door, sprinting toward her own cottage through Alice's yard, fishing for her car keys as she ran. Her feet felt like they were on fire, but she was moving so fast she didn't have time to feel the worst of it.

Behind her, she could hear an irritated honking, then the driver of the garbage truck put his hand down on the horn and held it there without release.

She had parked on the road when she returned from work because Ken had put the trash cans so close to the edge of their driveway, she had been afraid she might hit them. She jumped into her car and backed around. She could hear the truck bearing down on her. The other women had done little more than slow their speed. She imagined the workers laughing at the sight of three women—one gray-haired, one exotically dressed, one Hollywood starlet—so convinced they could make the truck stop, trying so hard to wave them down as they sped by.

Wanda pulled on to the road so her car spanned the width of it, jumped out and leaped to the side as the garbage truck roared into view.

Just in case.

Brakes squealed, and it took precious seconds for the tires to grip the oyster-shell road and slow to a crawl, then finally to a stop, just inches from the side of her old Ford Escort. Wanda didn't even wince. She'd told Ken she needed something sassier than the old sedan. They didn't even make Escorts anymore, for pity's sake. She had her sights set on a Miata, the first thing she would buy after the divorce.

The men in the truck were cursing. Wanda went to the driver's open window. "You got something belongs to my friends back there, mister. And it will be right on top, so it won't be one bit of trouble to find it. Now you get out and throw down that last bag you put in there, and I'll let you go past. I won't even call your boss and complain about the way you treated us."

"We got a job to do, lady!"

"You just bet you do. So you'd better go about doing it." Wanda saw the others coming toward her. "Quick-like. They're going to be hopping mad."

Cursing, the man leaped down from the truck and went around to the back, climbing in and holding up a bag. "This one?"

Tracy had arrived by then. "That's it. Just toss it down. We'll take care of it from here."

He did, and the bag split five ways 'til Sunday. But Wanda didn't care. She nodded as he scooted by her, then she went to move her car.

The truck was halfway up the road again by the time she'd parked and joined the others, who had already cleaned up the worst of the mess.

"That was brilliant," Tracy said.

Wanda didn't care what Tracy thought, not really. But she had to admit, the words sounded nice coming out of the younger woman's lips.

"Now, can you find the right article?" Tracy held up a file folder with articles hanging out the side. Wanda thought it was a lucky thing that whatever Alice had cleaned out of old Herb's refrigerator must have gone into a different bag. The folder was bedraggled, but not coated with broken egg yolks or soaked in milk.

Wanda took it and thumbed through it. "This is the one." She held it up.

"What's it say?"

Wanda handed the rest of the folder back to Tracy and scanned the article.

"It says a woman was walking across a street downtown and got hit by a car. The hospital reported she was in critical condition when she was brought in, and they were unable to save her. The driver was somebody in town on vacation with a carload of kids, and apparently she didn't see him coming." She looked up. "And I was right. The woman was named Louise Franklin."

"Is there a date?"

"No, darn, it's cut from the middle of a page. But guess what else it says?"

"What?" Janya asked.

"I guess I didn't read far enough the first time, else maybe I'd have realized this was important. Louise Franklin was a resident of Palmetto Grove, a widow. Her husband died in 1951. She had one daughter."

"No names?"

"Not in the article, but I bet they're named in her obituary."

"So Clyde and Louise are both dead," Tracy said. "No help there. But maybe this daughter knows something about Herb or Herb's daughter."

"I'd still like to know how Clyde and Herb knew each other, and why Herb had Clyde's birth certificate and discharge papers. Clyde had a wife. He had a daughter, just like Herb does. Why doesn't the daughter have his papers?" Something seemed off to Wanda.

"Now we know when Clyde died," Tracy said. "Maybe we can write off for his death certificate, and see if it tells where he died and of what. See if we can find a connection. Meantime, we can look for this daughter and see if she stayed in town. The newspaper might have a real obituary for Louise with the daughter's name."

"Clyde's death certificate seems unlikely to help," Janya said.

"No, it's a good idea," Tracy said. "These two men are connected some way we haven't figured out yet. Every little bit of information's important. I'll research this and send off for it if I can."

Alice had been silent, tying up what was left of the trash. Now she spoke up. "Do you think the men will come back for this bag now that we've finished with it?"

The other women turned to her, and Alice grinned. "I'm joking."

Wanda put her arm around Alice and gave her a hug.

chapter fourteen

Tracy didn't have an office so much as a rec room. The recreation supervisor was housed off the indoor swimming pool in a large rectangular expanse dotted with sofas, tables for strategizing with staff, and shelves filled with games and supplies. The saving grace was a wall of glass doors that looked over the shuffleboard courts. Good, too, was the picnic table next to the building for lunches or powwows when weather permitted.

Tracy's desk was in the corner closest to the doors, so if she turned her head, she could keep an eye on activities taking place at the courts. She had an antiquated computer and printer, her own telephone line, and a sign on her desk that read Children Should be Seen, Heard and Adored.

She had arrived on Monday morning, and after half an hour with Gladys, making sure she was signed up for every perk, Gladys turned her loose to familiarize herself with the rec room, and to begin planning for a staff meeting on Friday with the ten counselors and six teachers who would be helping her run the youth program.

"Just two little things," Gladys said before she left Tracy to wander the room and take note of all the equipment in the adjacent storage room. "Our arts-and-crafts teacher just quit, so you'll need to find another one. And—"

Tracy held up a hand. "Umm, Gladys? Recruitment is my job?"

"We assumed you'd want to find somebody you'll enjoy working with. We'll advertise in the usual places, of course, but at this late date, you'll probably need to go out and beat the bushes."

Tracy already knew that even though the counselors were chosen from responsible high school students, the teachers were more mature individuals, at the very least college students home on vacation.

"She?" Tracy asked. "The arts-and-crafts teacher?"

"She," Gladys confirmed.

"She must have had an excellent reason to quit so close to start-up." Something about the way Gladys was glossing over this made her suspicious.

"She just decided she would prefer a job…" The other woman turned up her hands. "Okay, when she found out Bay Egan was enrolled again, she quit on the spot."

"And the reason?" Tracy kept a calm tone and a friendly smile.

"Last summer he glued her flip-flops to the floor." Gladys inclined her head toward a far corner. "You can still see the residue if you look, even though we sanded and painted over it. Then there was an incident with scissors and bathing suit straps."

"And we're letting this kid come back?"

"Woody and I know Bay and his father rather well. The boy's been through a rough time. When Marsh and Sylvia, Bay's mother, divorced, Marsh pressed for joint custody. He hoped Sylvia would take more of an interest in Bay that way. She's an attorney in New York, and very intent on climbing the corporate ladder. But even though she has every right to see Bay whenever she chooses, she's more or less abandoned him."

"I'm sure that's tough. But he lives with his father, right? Is their relationship a problem?"

"Marsh may be a bit permissive."

Tracy was forming a picture here. "Permissive because he's too lazy to be a good parent? Or permissive because he wants to make up to Bay for everything that's happened?"

"Oh, the second, no doubt about it. You do have some insight into families," Gladys said, sounding genuinely pleased.

"Maybe I need a five-hundred-pound gorilla teaching arts and crafts."

"Until you find one, you'll have to teach the craft segment yourself, so I'd get right on this. Oh, and the second thing I wanted to tell you. The shuffle board—isn't that cute? That's what they call themselves. Shuffle board. Anyway, the board wants to meet with you at four. There are three of them, dear men every one. They'll meet you on the court."

Tracy made certain not to roll her eyes. She had spent yesterday reading up on the game, and she was even more certain shuffleboard was just for old people who weren't strong enough to sock a volleyball over a net.

Gladys turned at the doorway. "Oh, one more thing. The outdoor pool is officially open now, but the swimming program hasn't moved outside yet, so you'll hear lots of activity next door. Make sure you introduce yourself to the instructors and anybody else who comes through. They'll have lots of good ideas for you."

They did, too. As the day progressed, Tracy was greeted by an assortment of men and women from the janitorial staff, and the executive, sports and teaching staffs, all with strong opinions. The rec center employees ranged from barely courteous to friendly. One of the friendliest explained that some of the barely courteous had applied for Tracy's job, but they would come around when they saw how well-suited she was.

The more she delved into the varied facets of what had to be an overly optimistic job description, the less sure Tracy was that anybody would praise her. Very clearly her predecessor had not been obsessive so much as certain that the only key to success was a schedule organized down to the minute, accompanied by copious notes. Tracy told herself this wasn't going to be any harder than keeping track of CJ's personal schedule and social obligations. But by four, she knew she was lying. Friday's staff meeting was fast becoming a war council. She had a list half a mile long of items for the agenda. She hoped the counselors and teachers had been well-chosen.

Her head ached, and her vision was blurry. She was afraid she was going to have to dig up the cute little Jimmy Choo reading glasses her ophthalmologist had prescribed back in the days when she still had money for doctor's visits. She was even more afraid that before the summer and all the paperwork were over, she might need something stronger. At least now she had insurance.

She stood and stretched, almost glad she had to meet with the shuffle board. The court was in shade now, and apparently a swimming class was in session next door. The chlorine fumes and the shrill blowing of a whistle were making her headache worse. She was ready for fresh air and relative quiet.

Just outside the rec room door, she stood on tiptoe and stretched. The outdoor pool glistened beyond the shuffleboard courts, which were state-of-the-art. Hedges separated the two, but they hadn't yet grown high enough to be a real demarcation. Turning back toward the table, she noted that the wall along the side of the building was a dirty beige and looked in need of repainting before the tournament. But there was potential here, after a little sprucing up. Room for more picnic tables, and places for people to rest in the shade of the building while they watched or waited to play.

She was examining the shuffleboard courts when she heard footsteps behind her. She turned to greet the board and froze. Despite temperatures in the low nineties, she was a block of ice. Then the blood rushing into every extremity set her free, and she was ready to run. But it was too late.

"What are *you* doing here?" A familiar-looking man with a narrow mustache bore down on her. There was no chessboard in front of him today, and she was surprised by how quickly he could move. He was flanked by two others who, unfortunately, looked every bit as familiar.

"Who told you we were coming here?" he demanded.

Tracy ran through half a dozen responses. She hadn't realized her mind could work that fast.

"Let me guess," she said, since none of the other choices were better. "You're the shuffle board."

"Are you stalking us?"

The thought was so preposterous that she couldn't help herself. She giggled, but she sobered immediately when she saw she was the only one who found the question funny.

"First, I want to apologize," she said, trying for sincerity and humility, although without much practice neither came naturally. "I didn't realize how rude and demanding I must have sounded the other day, but I was so focused on finding poor Herb's family I wasn't thinking of anybody else. And upsetting your table was absolutely accidental. I figured at that point, the best thing I could do was to leave. But I really am sorry."

They circled her, and she felt like a gazelle in the middle of a pride of lions. Ancient lions, but still…

"Who are you?" the man with the glasses demanded, lifting a fist in the air. "And why are you still after us?"

She edged away from the court. "I'm not after you."

"Then what are you doing here? Who told you we'd be—" The truth must have occurred to him, because he stopped and stared in disbelief. "Tell me it's not true."

"Here's the truth, and really, it's not so bad. I *am* the new recreational supervisor, but I had no idea you were the shuffle board. I mean, let's face it. Palmetto Grove's not a raging metropolis, but there are more than a few people walking the streets, so I didn't expect the three of you."

"Who the hell hired you?"

"The usual suspects." She smiled brightly, although she remembered as she did how poorly that had gone over before. "So who won the chess game?"

They stared at her.

"I guess it doesn't matter," she said, backtracking quickly. "I hope you found all your pieces."

The skinny man she'd nicknamed the hoverer squinted at her. "I know the Woodleys. I'm going to tell them what you did."

"Well, you can, but honestly? I think they're between a rock and a hard place, and they need me to organize your tournament. So they aren't going to be all that thrilled to fire me on my first day at work. Wouldn't it be more productive if we just tried to get along?"

"Do you know one end of a cue from the other, girlie, or how long a regulation cue even has to be? Do you know how much a disc has to weigh? What the penalty is if a disc is touching a line? The differences between a hook shot and a hesitation shot?"

She was starting to get annoyed, but she tried to remain pleasant. "I know the basics, but if we work together, I can learn the rest."

"I bet you think shuffleboard is about as stupid as chess," Mr. Mustache said, moving closer and pointing his finger at her chest.

She hesitated one heartbeat too long. He nodded with more vigor than she expected. "You *do* think it's stupid. The Woodleys went and hired a supervisor who thinks the game is stupid!"

"I never said that!" Tracy stepped backward and found herself on the grass between courts. "I admit, the other day, I was overbearing, because I wanted to help one of your friends. Now, get over it, okay? I apologized. I'll do everything possible to make your tournament a good one."

She never got to hear a reply, because suddenly a child came hurtling through the open door of the rec room. His head was turned, as if he were trying to outwit pursuers, and before Tracy could yell a warning, the boy was on the court heading straight toward her. She leaped forward, and, fanning out her arms, she swept the old men to either side, then lunged for the all too familiar boy. Bay saw her just in time, spun around, dodged the stumbling old men and Tracy, and kept running.

Right across the courts, over the hedge and into the outdoor pool.

"Unbelievable!"

Water sprayed everywhere, and the splash befit a whale. Tracy took off after him, sending her sandals flying as she ran. At poolside, she spotted Bay floundering in the deep end. She wasn't exactly certain whether he was trying to put an end to his miserable little life or simply recovering from the sudden shock of finding himself in the water. Whichever it was, tempting as it was to let him sink to the bottom, it was not a good idea—especially on her first day at work.

Cursing under her breath, she dove in fully clothed, aiming for a spot a few feet away from the place where he struggled.

She surfaced, spotted the boy and with, one splashing sweep, hauled him against her and tried to pull him to his back.

"Let go of me!" He kicked out at her, and when that didn't work, he tried to punch her. Expecting this, she was ready. She'd taken lifesaving at summer camp in the Sierras, a skill that had been required later as part of a class in college. And she knew exactly what she had to do.

Outmaneuvering all his attempts to drown her, she towed Bay to the ladder and shoved him against it.

"Climb!" she sputtered.

He pushed away, twisting and squirming, but she grabbed him again, this time by the nape, and shoved him at the ladder.

Arms reached down and hauled Bay out of the water. Tracy climbed out and shook back her hair. She recognized the woman in a black Speedo. They'd been introduced earlier, but she couldn't recall her name.

"Appears you lost something," Tracy told her.

"Bay Egan!" The woman, in her forties and comfortably maternal in appearance, gripped Bay's shoulders. Clearly she was so upset she could hardly speak. "Did you tie all my lockers shut?"

Bay struggled, but the woman gripped him harder. "Well, did you?"

"It was a 'speriment!"

Tracy shook herself like a Labrador retriever, and water flew everywhere. "What did he do?"

"He brought a bag of zip ties in his swim bag this afternoon, then he said he had to go to the bathroom. When he didn't come back fast enough, I left the other kids with the parents and my assistant, and went looking. When I caught him, he was threading ties through the holes where the padlocks are supposed to go, pulling them as tight as he could. He'd gotten more than half!"

"What kind of experiment was that?" Tracy asked Bay.

"None of your business!"

"You know what? I think you were experimenting with making everybody furious," she guessed.

By now the shuffle board had arrived.

Mr. Mustache was shaking with anger, wheezing as if he were trying to find words vile enough. Her forbearance was used up. She stuck her finger in his chest. "Don't you dare say a word. I was trying to keep him from running you over. He would have knocked the three of you off that court like so many shuffleboard discs. So zip it!"

"What is this commotion?" Gladys came forward. Tracy hadn't realized she was there.

"Bay took it on himself to make sure half the lockers won't open again without some major intervention from our janitors," the swim instructor said. "When I caught him, he came barreling out here and ended up in the pool."

"I dove in after him," Tracy said, hoping that might win points. She was almost sure she needed them. Gladys had probably been standing there long enough to hear her lecturing the old man.

"That's a little like diving in to save a dolphin," Gladys said. "Bay's the star of our swim team."

"Swim team." Now Tracy remembered the introduction to the woman in the Speedo. Joan Somebody or other. Swim team coach. The noise next door had been practice, not classes.

"Well, okay, I didn't know," Tracy said. "But better safe than sorry. I really didn't have time for a swimming test."

"You hired a real corker here," Mr. Mustache told Gladys, finally sucking in enough air to speak. "Nearly knocked us over, every one. And it's not the first time she's been trouble for us!"

Tracy wondered if employees got severance pay after eight hours on the job.

"Nonsense," Joan said, in a voice three degrees chillier than Tracy's. "She saved the three of you from going down like bowling pins."

Joan still hadn't released Bay, and now she turned back to him. "And that was it. We're finished. This young man is off my team. For good. And I would suggest he be banned from the summer program, too."

Tracy had been with her right up to that point. But she was watching Bay's expression. She expected tears, pleas, but Bay looked triumphant. For some reason, that moved her more.

She reached over and gently loosened Joan's grip on the boy's shoulders. Then she bent over so she and Bay were eye-to-eye. "That's what you're after, isn't it, kiddo?" she asked quietly.

He squinted at her, his gaze rebellious now. "I hate this place. I hate everything here. I don't want to be here."

"That's not true," said a masculine voice, and not one that belonged to any of the old men.

Tracy recognized the drawl. She straightened and turned to Marsh, who was standing, with his arms folded, next to Gladys. He had probably dropped in to see his son swim, then taken the necessary detour. "What's the alternative if he doesn't come here?" she asked.

Marsh was in his official lawyer garb again, and he was glowering. "A babysitter."

"No!" Bay wailed. "No! I'm going to New York."

"So that's the deal," Tracy said. "He's trying to get kicked out so he can spend the summer with his mother."

"It appears so."

"Mr. Egan, is there a place for Bay in New York?" Tracy asked. "Will his mother take him?"

Marsh's frown deepened. "I don't think this is the right—"

She waved him to silence. "Bay needs to hear the truth loud

and clear, and witnesses won't hurt. If his mother can't take him—" she very carefully did not say "won't" "—then he needs to understand that. Infuriating me or Joan won't buy him a ticket to Manhattan. And running away won't help, because his mother will just send him back. If I understand things, Bay has two choices. Being here, where he can enjoy himself for the summer, or stuck at home with a sitter."

Marsh did not look grateful, but he gave a curt nod. "Bay already knows New York is out of the question. His mom is going to be traveling on business for most of the summer."

"I could go with her!"

"She is not going to leave you in hotels by yourself, Bay. It's just not going to happen. She's told me, and she's told you."

"Now look," Tracy said, leaning down so she and Bay were eye-to-eye again, "I get what you're doing. And really, you get an A for effort. I can see a lot of planning went into this. But can you see this is just not going to work? Causing all this uproar isn't going to get you anything except eight hours of Nickelodeon every single day. This is your last chance to turn things around."

He was blinking back tears. "Why do you care?"

She considered. "I have no idea. Really, my life will be a lot easier if you don't come."

He appeared to consider that. "So…what do I have to do?"

"Grovel."

"What's that mean?"

"Say you're sorry and really, really mean it. Then tell us you'll try to be on your best behavior. Because, you know, if you're not, you're out of here. And make no mistake, kiddo, it will be my call. I don't feel sorry for you, and I can evict you from this program without breaking a sweat."

"I just wanted to go to New York."

She had the oddest desire to put her arms around him, an in-clination so foreign that she almost didn't recognize it. "Yeah, I know. But let's put your talent for planning to better use, okay?"

He was silent for so long that she thought he wasn't going to apologize; then his shoulders drooped. "I guess I'm sorry."

"You guess?"

"Yeah," he said without looking at her. "I'm sorry. And I will, you know, be nicer."

She straightened and looked at Joan, pushing strands of wet hair off her cheeks as she did. "Will you give Bay one more chance?"

Joan sighed. "I was sort of counting on him for the butter-fly at our next meet."

"He's that good, huh?"

"He'll be good if he gets his act together."

"Gladys, what do you think?" Tracy halfway expected Gladys to say she thought Tracy ought to clean off her desk.

"I think Bay can stay." She crooked a finger at Tracy, and while Marsh went to his son and put his arm around Bay's shoulders, Tracy joined Gladys, who was walking back toward the courts. With relief, she saw that the old men had disappeared.

"I think you can stay, too," Gladys said quietly, "but now the shuffleboard is gunning for you. They have clout. Find a way to keep them happy. You understand?"

Tracy wondered how her life had come to this.

chapter fifteen

By the time a bedraggled Tracy drove home, showered and dressed, then drove back into town to buy what she needed to entertain Lee, she wasn't even sure she wanted company. But explaining how she had ended up in the rec center pool fully clothed sounded ridiculous. So she shopped for brie and fresh fruit, chilled white wine and the ingredients for vodka martinis. The supplies put a hole in her budget, but she reminded herself that she had a job now. Until the next catastrophe.

There was just enough time to finish making herself and the house presentable before Lee tapped on her door. She let him in, admiring a patterned blue silk shirt that brought out the mesmerizing blue of his eyes.

"I couldn't resist," he said, holding out a grocery bag. "These just came out of the water, and the sauce is my favorite. It's made locally."

She kissed him on the cheek and took the bag. Inside she saw steamed shrimp and a jar of cocktail sauce. "What a treat. I just realized I'm starving."

"Were you planning to sit outside? I can take everything out." He followed her into what passed for a kitchen.

"Let's put the shrimp on a platter with a bowl of sauce." She gestured to the counter. "I have cheese, fruit, crackers. It's starting to sound like a meal."

While she opened the wine, Lee deftly assembled everything. They discussed the martinis, but agreed to kill the bottle of wine instead.

In a few minutes they were sitting at the funky old metal table that had come with the house. Tracy had covered it with a forest-green cloth, and filled the center with an assortment of flowers and candles from the grocery store. Now she lit citronella candles that were scattered in some of her larger shells around what passed for a patio and settled across from him.

Lee had already poured the wine. "To neighbors." He lifted his glass.

"I never thought I'd be toasting to that." They clinked.

"Well, you were a surprise, too. I never expected a beautiful woman to move into this place."

She smiled the smile she'd learned at her mother's knee. "The beautiful woman didn't expect it, either."

"You've had a lot of changes in the past few years."

"It took upheaval on a grand scale to make me look at my life."

"So are you? Looking at it?"

"Well, occasionally." Since self-examination was still relatively new for her, she hated to discuss it like a hobby she really wasn't very good at yet. "And how about you? You've had a lot to cope with."

"Let's toast to moving on." They clinked again.

They chatted about his day, then the houses he hoped to sell, the dismal state of the Florida economy, the cost of gas. The shrimp was gone, and the wheel of brie she had drizzled with butter and sprinkled with sliced almonds was almost a memory, before they pushed away from the table.

Tracy had indulged in two glasses of wine. Considering she'd eaten very little all day, the wine had gone straight to her head. Lee, too, seemed more relaxed than the wine warranted. The slightest thing sent them howling. She finally told him about diving into the pool to rescue a boy who could probably swim circles around her. When he laughed again, she had to admit that now, hours later, it *was* kind of funny.

By this time the sky was almost dark, with only vague tracings of light where the sunset had been. Tracy had turned on the radio. Now the local oldies station was playing disco hits from the seventies and eighties.

"You weren't even born yet," Lee said, when she started to hum along to "Jive Talkin'" by the Bee Gees.

"When I was little I used to entertain my parents' friends doing songs and dances from *Saturday Night Fever.* I was supposed to be the disco Shirley Temple, only I can't sing."

"Well, I was in high school, and I won the disco contest."

She giggled. "Did you have a white suit, like John Travolta?"

"You're laughing at my white suit?"

"Are you kidding? I bet you were hot. I bet all the girls wanted to dance with you."

He got to his feet. "Come here and find out."

Now she really was laughing. "No, really?"

"You can sing along."

"'Night fever, night fever…'"

"You're right, you can't sing."

"I play a mean game of tennis, though. My mother capital-ized on that with more success."

He held out his arms. "Let's see if you can dance."

She accepted the invitation as if they had always slow danced together under a whirling glitter ball. Now Chris de Burgh was singing "Lady in Red," and Lee pulled her close.

"We can save the spins for later."

She snuggled against his chest. His body was hard and lean. She hadn't forgotten how much she liked the feel of a man holding her tight. CJ hadn't been much of a dancer, and after the divorce, the possibilities for dance partners had dwindled right along with her financial prospects.

"You would look great in red," he said.

"I'll wear it next time."

"You look great in anything." He rested his cheek against her hair, and they moved slowly to the music.

Maybe she should have stopped at one glass of wine. She was feeling woozy, or maybe that was just the effect he was having on her. She liked everything about this. The way he held her. The way he smelled, something faintly spicy and expensive, definitely not overdone. And the faint physical suggestion that he might be as turned on as she was.

The song ended at last, and the deejay, a woman with a sensuous voice, began to chat.

Tracy stepped back, but Lee didn't release her.

"Want to wait for the next one?" he asked.

"What'll we do in the meantime?"

When he kissed her, his lips were warm and practiced. He tasted like brie and shrimp and the sweet tang of a moderately priced sauvignon blanc. She leaned into him and kissed him back, and while the kiss lasted, she forgot everything that had brought her to this place.

She was ready for another, convinced she needed at least one more, but when he started all over again, she found herself moving away. She had taken the step backward before she realized it. He looked puzzled, and not pleased.

"My head's spinning," she said. "Long day, too much to drink."

"That's one explanation." The frown turned into a smile, seductive and very masculine. "There could be a better one."

"Definitely that, too." She struggled to put her feelings into words. She was still surprised at her own reaction. "I like you. I like kissing you. I'm just not ready for more tonight."

"Well, that's a shame."

"It is, isn't it?"

"I understand. It took me time to get over Karen's death."

"I guess divorce—" She cocked her head, realizing what he had said.

He seemed to realize it, too. "Not that I'm over it," he said. "It's just not as immediate. Something like that takes forever, I guess."

"I guess." She thought that was a perfectly adequate explanation. He couldn't have meant to sound blasé about his wife's tragic death only, what, a year ago?

"It's just that at some point, you have to start moving on," Lee said. "Even when you're still hurting. I guess I'm starting to."

She was not mourning her spouse. As she thought about it, she realized that, instead, she was mourning her own culpability, her acceptance of a marriage that had been a balloon filled with hot air. When the balloon exploded, there was nothing left to keep. And she didn't want to make the same mistake. She wanted to believe she had taken something away from her divorce besides Happiness Key.

Lee glanced at his watch. "If I leave now, I can still say good-night to Olivia. She worries when I'm home late."

She didn't apologize. They'd had fun, then she'd slammed on the brakes, but that didn't mean she wouldn't hit the accelerator in the future.

"I'm so glad you came," she said, and meant it.

He smiled, and his gaze lingered on her lips. "So am I."

As they rounded her cottage, they chatted. "I did want to ask you something," she said at the edge of her lawn. "I know you worry about Alice. It's one of the things I like so much about you. But she really seems to come alive when she's with us—us being the neighbors."

"Really? When has she been with you?"

She explained about the impromptu memorial service for Herb. "She brightens up when she contributes," Tracy said. "I know you're afraid she'll get more confused, but I hope you won't mind if we involve her a little in the search for Herb's family. It seems to do her good."

"I think it's wonderful you want to help."

"Good, then you're fine with it."

"I wish. But I've seen this up close too many times. She has good days and bad, but I can tell you that the moment she feels any pressure to perform, she falls apart. She regresses. Sometimes we don't hear a word from her for days."

"That's awful."

"I don't want relapses. You can understand? We take things a step at a time. I stay in close touch with her physician."

"I promise we won't put any pressure on her."

"It's probably best to keep something of a distance. Until she's better and seeks you out on her own."

Tracy didn't explain that Alice had done just that. She heard the distress in his voice, and the concern, and she didn't want to trouble him more. But she thought Lee was wrong. Alice had seemed more confident after spending time with herself and the others. She hoped if that continued, and Alice continued to enjoy being with her neighbors, it would only help. By then, Lee, too, would see the difference.

She rose on tiptoes and kissed him on the lips. "Thanks for the shrimp."

He put his hand behind her head and kissed her again. "Thanks for the wine."

With regret, she watched him walk away. Still, it was regret mixed with something else. She thought that extra ingredient might spell relief.

Wanda liked it when the men who regularly called SEDUCED graduated. That was how she thought of it. Sometimes they found a real flesh-and-blood woman they could spend time with. Sometimes they moved into retirement centers or assisted living, where there were better cures for loneliness than telling stories of sexual prowess to a woman they would never meet.

In the past month, two of her regular customers had moved on. Unfortunately, one had been due to a fatal heart attack, but luckily not while he was on the phone with her. Lainie had broken the news, and they'd held their own private moment of silence before Lainie gave her the numbers of a couple of new men who sounded as if they would be Wanda's type.

She always put her oldest customers at the top of her list, and they knew it. A man grew to trust her. He knew she would be there when he needed the contact. So she was cautious about accepting new callers. Tonight, though, with two recent vacancies, she blocked her own number, as she always did, then tried the first number on her new list. The phone rang five times, and she got a recording. The voice was a woman's, an old one at that. Since Wanda wasn't in the habit of leaving her name and number on answering machines, nor in the habit of talking to married men, if she could spot them, she hung up, scratched him off her list and tried the second.

The telephone rang three times before a man picked up. He sounded far away, and Wanda wondered if he was on a cell phone.

Wanda started every conversation the same way, by making it clear exactly who she was and why she was calling. Her greeting was also a warning that the client was now being charged by the minute.

"You're being seduced," Wanda said.

"I was hoping I would be."

The man had a gravelly voice. She pictured Batman from the most recent movie and hoped this guy was half as good-looking as Christian Bale.

"So what are you doing?" she asked. "Me, I'm lying on the sofa, wearing my favorite nightgown." She never said negligee anymore, because once, when her mind had wandered to the way Ken was neglecting her, she'd mistakenly called it a negligent.

"I'm sitting in my office, staring out the window."

"This a work number?"

"You don't have to worry. I'm all alone here. Nobody will overhear us."

"Well, that will be up to you. I can't control that end of things."

"Tell me about yourself."

Of course she knew better than to tell the truth. "Who do you want me to be? I can be a blonde. A brunette. I can look like Julia Roberts or Christie Brinkley or even Madonna, only not in one of those pointy bra things."

"Who do you *really* look like?"

Carol Burnett popped into her mind—Carol Burnett as the beleaguered Eunice, at that—but that hardly fit the situation. "Blond, sleek and sexy. A woman you *don't* want to take home to your mother."

"Too bad. I've always liked the homemaker type."

"Blond, sleek and sexy in an apron, then. And your mama still wouldn't like me, but only because I cook better than she does."

"So what do you like to cook?"

"Pies," she said, without screening her answer.

"Man, I love a good pie. Tell me about them."

This was certainly unique, but Wanda knew that every man got into the calls at his own speed. And this was refreshing for a change. She was tired of describing more intimate parts of herself that did not exist.

"Key lime's my very best. But I bake a coconut cream that'll make you think you died and went to heaven." She didn't add that the last one had almost sent her there. Vomiting for two days was not in the least romantic.

"Anybody ever done that? Died and gone to heaven while you were talking to them?"

"Not died," she said coyly. "But a man or two's said these phone calls are heaven-sent."

He laughed, a laugh as husky as his voice. "I like a woman with a sense of humor."

She filed that away. Not everybody did. Some men were sure you were laughing at them. This one had a stronger ego.

"Tell me about you," she said. "What are you like? What *do* you like? I'm here, just listening away."

"This doesn't get old?"

"If it did, I wouldn't do it."

"It doesn't bother you that you can't see me? That you can't tell a thing about me?"

"I can tell you're a smoker."

"How?"

"The voice. A smoker's voice. A whiskey drinker's voice, too."

"No, especially not the last. I fight that craving. Hard."

"Good for you. It won't get you anywhere but dead."

"Sometimes that doesn't sound so bad." He paused for just a heartbeat. "But not when I'm talking to a blond, sexy woman in an apron. A pie baker."

She smiled. She didn't always like the men she called, but she thought she was going to like this one.

"What else?" she asked. "I'm listening. I've got all night if you do."

"Do you want to know my name?"

"Just the first one will do."

"You can call me Shadow."

"Like a shadow that hides. A shadow without a face," she guessed.

"That's right. And what should I call you?"

"You can call me Sunshine."

"No secrets? None?"

"Not that you'll ever know."

"I guess I can live with that."

"So, Shadow, tell me more."

"Unfortunately, I have to go now. But you'll call again? Next time I leave my number?"

"You bet I will."

She hung up. She wondered who Shadow really was. She was intrigued by the possibilities. One thing was certain, she would be calling again. It was already something to look forward to.

chapter sixteen

When Wanda woke up on Sunday morning, Ken was sleeping beside her. For a moment she was so disoriented she almost put her arms around him and snuggled. But memory and good sense came to the rescue. Nothing much had changed between them, except now Ken was home a little earlier every night. If, in the immortal words of the Eagles, good old Ken was heading for the cheating side of town, at least this week he was heading back to the married side around midnight.

Still, having him beside her on waking was something entirely new. She supposed exhaustion had just caught up with him. The man had to sleep sometime, and he was, after all, paying most of their rent. Except, of course, they weren't paying a darned thing until the repairs were finished.

"At least Ms. Deloche is doing something about that," she muttered as she swung her legs over the side of the bed. The handy hubby had arrived, and Friday he'd fixed the roof leak over the bathroom, scraped the rust out of the toilet bowl and put in a new stove—okay it wasn't brand-new, but it wasn't an antique, either. Tomorrow he was coming back to work on the water heater and patch up what was left of the holes. Then Wanda was going to pay May's rent. A deal was a deal, and she wasn't one to forget it.

"Make enough coffee for me." Ken pulled her pillow over his head.

"Sure, honey, anything you want."

She pulled on her comfy cotton robe and slipped her feet into ostrich-feather mules her son had given her. Unlike Maggie, Wanda's daughter, Junior's gifts were always right on target. Of course she loved both kids the same. Maggie always reminded her so much of Ken, which at one time had been a gift all its own.

In the kitchen, she brewed just enough coffee for herself and loaded it with the usual suspects. There was one slice of pie left in the refrigerator, something she liked to call lemon delight, and she ate it right down to the last crumb. She was still paging through the latest *People* magazine when Ken, freshly shaved and showered, came to join her.

"Coffee?" he asked.

"Excellent, if I do say so myself."

"I mean, did you leave me any?"

"Sorry. Far as I could tell, you were out for the count."

"You think I don't know what you're doing, Wanda?"

For a moment the pie felt like a lump glued to her esophagus. Then she realized Ken wasn't talking about SEDUCED. He was just talking about coffee.

"Are we going to have a fight?" she asked, interested. "Are there enough hours left in the day to cover everything?"

"It's simple human decency to make enough coffee for me, too."

"And it's simple human decency to come home for dinner once in a while, or just have a pleasant conversation about the kids or the weather."

He didn't answer. She heard him at the counter opening and closing cabinets to get filters, coffee. She heard him rinsing out the pot and filling it with fresh water. She didn't look up from her magazine, even when he surprised her by taking the seat across from her at the table.

"So what do you want to talk about?" he asked.

She looked up. "I don't much care."

"Okay. How are you liking Palmetto Grove these days?"

"Well, I like living in this house a little better, if that's what you mean. Some repairs have been done, in case you haven't noticed."

"Right, I can take a leak now without dodging another one."

"And we have a new used stove."

"You been putting it to any use?"

"Now and again." She closed her magazine. "Me and the other women out here have been trying to find Herb Krause's family."

"What for?"

"Tracy…Ms. Deloche has all his stuff and nobody to give it to."

"She could probably put it out by the road, make a case for not knowing what else to do if his family ever shows up."

"Maybe. But she's not ready. None of us are."

"Why do you care?"

"Because he was a lonely old man, and we didn't do much for him when he was still breathing."

Ken met her gaze. "That soft heart of yours always gets you in trouble."

"Hard as a rock." She leaned forward just a little. "You willing to help if we need you?"

"Me? What could I do?"

"You got access to records. You know you do."

"You want me to see if Herb was a war criminal? A terrorist?"

"More like a drunk driver with a record we can follow to his family, Kenny. For pity's sake, is that beyond you?"

The coffeemaker snorted, as if it were daring them to drink what it had brewed. Ken took the dare, then held out the pot to her. She saw he'd made extra, and some tiny part of her was ashamed—but not very.

She shook her head. "I'm fine. Are you going to help, Kenny, or not?"

"Just let me know what you need. I'll do what I can."

She could think of a hundred more important things she used to need from him, but she was smart enough not to go for broke. There was enough that was broke around here already.

She got to her feet. "I'm going to take my shower. Maybe the water heater'll get fixed and I won't freeze my buns off every morning."

"I'm working all day, and I'll probably be gone by the time you get out."

"Then I'll see you again sometime."

He looked as if he wanted to say more, but she headed for the bathroom. She wasn't stupid. A woman learned to take whatever she could get. That was the only way the female of the species had survived. And she planned to survive a very long time. Even if these days she was eating pie for breakfast.

Friday's staff meeting had gone better than expected. Of course, Tracy's expectations were as low as her opinion of Wild Florida, but even considering that, she couldn't complain. Her predecessor had hired competent, mostly likeable teachers and counselors, many of whom had done this before. The old hands had filled her in on which children needed a little extra attention and which could be counted on for leadership. They had responded well to her agenda, taken her suggestions and even offered their own.

The biggest problem still facing her was an arts-and-crafts teacher. But the counselors had agreed to start lanyards on Monday during the arts-and-crafts period. What was summer camp without lanyards, anyway?

After the meeting, she'd come home armed with the tools she needed to install tile. Everything had been right on the shelf at the building supply store on the outskirts of town, and she'd used a Memorial Day coupon that saved fifteen percent. Even though she'd winced at another expenditure, the money she would save doing it herself carried the day.

Over the past week she had finally removed the last layer of linoleum, and Saturday she patched cracks in the concrete floor, scraped and sanded. She stayed up until midnight readying everything. The floor was turning into therapy. She could visualize the finished product.

She planned to spend all day Sunday snapping chalk lines and laying out tile to be sure she didn't need adjustments. But when she took a break to retrieve and leaf through the previous day's mail, she saw something more interesting than bills.

Wanda was outside hosing down her car, and Tracy beckoned. Wanda wore shorts that left nothing about her rear end and thighs to the imagination, and she had paired them with a tube top of prison-jumpsuit orange. Tracy was reminded of CJ. Orange was not his best color. Nor Wanda's, for that matter.

"You look like you been rode hard and put away wet," Wanda said.

"Thanks. I'm putting down tile in my house."

"You're doing it on your own?"

Tracy glanced gloomily at the ragged stumps that had once been manicured nails. "Too expensive otherwise." She saw Janya down the road watering Herb's trees, and beckoned to her, as well. Janya had a fluid walk, like a river flowing, and as she approached, Tracy simply admired it.

"Tracy here's putting down a tile floor," Wanda told Janya when she was standing beside them.

"The book you borrowed at the library helped?" Janya asked.

"And the Internet." Tracy wasn't usually given to impulse, but she nodded at her house. "Want to see what I'm doing?"

"Got a pie crust in the oven," Wanda said. "I can't be away long."

Tracy led them up her walkway and threw open the door. She hadn't really done much yet, but after removing all the old flooring, things looked pretty fabulous to her. Plus there was a straight line of tile extending across the living room, and with that little visual cue, she could picture how great the floor would look once it was finished.

"Now that's pretty stuff you're putting down," Wanda said.

Tracy was surprised the older woman hadn't taken this chance to razz her. "Glad you approve."

"It will improve things," Janya said. "You will be happy with it. And very tired when it's finished."

"I'm already very tired." Tracy waved a piece of mail at them. "But that's not what I wanted to show you. I got this just now. Clyde's death certificate."

"Sure seems like a dead end to me." Wanda smiled. "Dead end, get it?"

Tracy ignored her. "I tried to get his military records, and Herb's, too. But I'm not next of kin, and on top of that, there was a fire in St. Louis where the records were kept back in the sixties or seventies."

"Seems like a conspiracy to keep Herb's life a secret," Wanda said.

"So you ordered Clyde's death certificate?" Janya asked.

"Fifty years passed, so I could."

"What's it say?" Wanda asked.

Tracy was enjoying herself, and she wasn't even sure why. "Well, it's kind of spectacular, really, although I'm not sure what it means."

"As my mama used to say, you're keeping us in suspenders," Wanda said.

Tracy took the death certificate out of the envelope. "Here's the interesting part. Look where the cause is listed. *Presumptive* death."

Janya looked confused. "What does 'presumptive' mean?"

"It means Clyde Franklin was presumed dead because there was no proof, that somebody asked that he be declared dead after he'd been missing for some period of time. I'm not sure what that period is in Florida, but I can find out on the Internet. Most likely Louise petitioned the court, so she could get survivor's benefits."

"So Clyde just up and vanished, and never came back," Wanda said. "And what does that explain?"

"It explains that we have some more looking to do," Tracy said. "And another mystery on our hands. I'm going over to Herb's after dinner and spend the evening going through the rest of the boxes. Do you want to come? Say about seven?"

"Maybe for an hour or so," Wanda said. "My evenings are pretty busy."

"Indeed they are," Tracy said. "Janya? Is that a bad time for you?"

"Rishi is out of town until tomorrow night. I can be there."

"If either of you sees Alice, you might tell her, too. Just don't do it in front of Lee, okay? He's worried she'll get upset or confused working with us on this. I'd like to show him he's wrong."

"Alice likes company," Wanda said. "What's wrong with *him?*"

"Now I understand," Janya said.

"What?" Wanda asked.

"Why Mr. Symington is not friendly when I stop to visit Alice."

"He's not really unfriendly, is he?" Tracy asked. "Just concerned?"

"Perhaps I misinterpret what I see."

"Seems like that would be easy, you being a foreigner and all," Wanda said.

"Yes, a foreigner. A fact I'm not allowed to forget."

Tracy arrived at Herb's before the others were due, and opened the windows and door. A gentle afternoon shower had cooled the air, which smelled like freshly washed laundry. Since they wouldn't be there long, she decided to leave the windows open and the air conditioner off.

She had hauled the boxes out into the living room and was sorting through the first one when Wanda walked in, a pie plate balanced on one upturned hand and a plastic grocery bag slung over her arm.

"I figure, I don't start sharing these pies with somebody, I'm going to have to roll around in the shower to get wet all over."

Despite herself, Tracy's mouth was watering. "What kind is it?"

"Grapefruit pie. Tail end of the grapefruit season, so they weren't as juicy as I like. But it's still tasty."

"How many pie recipes do you have?"

"Ones I've tried? Maybe a hundred. Half were worth trying again with a variation or two."

Janya tapped on the screen door, then let herself in.

"Wanda brought us pie," Tracy said. "Grapefruit."

Wanda headed for the kitchen. "I'll just put it in the refrigerator until we're ready."

"Did you talk to Alice?" Tracy asked Janya.

"She said she will come and bring Olivia." She glanced at the door, as if to be certain Alice wasn't standing there, and lowered her voice. "She was unhappy. I'm not certain why. But she said Olivia got her hair cut, and that seemed to worry her. I got a glimpse. It is short now, quite short in fact, but she is such a pretty little girl, nothing can spoil that."

"Alice has had so many changes. Any change may just be too much."

"Perhaps."

They heard footsteps, and Alice and Olivia walked in. Olivia had a baseball cap pulled over her head.

"I'm glad you're both here," Tracy said. "Olivia, I hope you won't be bored, but we're going to have pie in a little while."

"I brought a book," Olivia said shyly.

"I hear you got your hair cut," Tracy said. "I bet it's cool for the summer."

Olivia bit her lip.

"Long hair is a lot of work," Alice said. "Hard to keep up with."

"Nobody knows more about hair than me," Wanda said, coming back into the living room. "Let's see the damage, and I'll tell you what I think."

For a moment Olivia looked rebellious; then, as if she were used to doing what she was told, she swept off the hat.

Tracy was surprised Lee had allowed the stylist to make such a drastic change. The little girl's hair had been well past her shoulders. Now it was boyishly short, clipped to the top of her ears in front and trimmed neatly above the nape in back without a wisp to soften it. Tracy was afraid what might come out of that "tell it like it is" mouth of Wanda's.

Wanda surprised her. "Now, that's a sensible hairstyle for Florida. Especially for a little girl who likes to get all sweaty riding her bike up and down this old oyster-shell road. A very good choice."

"You are such a pretty girl, it just makes that clearer," Janya said kindly. "And now your lovely blue eyes are so easy to see."

"I think next you should get your ears pierced," Tracy told her. "Get some cute earrings, maybe sapphires to match your eyes. You have great ears. I had to have mine flattened against my head when I was your age."

"Yuck." Olivia wrinkled her nose.

"Her father does not like a fuss," Alice said.

Tracy winked at Olivia. "Just tell me if you're interested. I'll talk to him and see what he says."

"Will it hurt?"

"Not as much as having them pinned to your head. Just think about it."

Olivia looked a little happier. "May I look around?"

"You bet. Make yourself at home."

The little girl wandered off.

"Well, we all make fashion mistakes," Wanda said.

Tracy motioned the others into the living room, where she had dragged the boxes. "She'll think twice next time she decides on such a big change."

Alice wandered in behind them. "It's always been long. Karen used to brush her hair and braid it. I couldn't keep up... well enough."

"By the time it grows out, you won't have to worry," Tracy said. "She'll be old enough to do whatever the style of the day requires. You'll be so tired of watching her play with her hair, you'll wish it was this short again."

"She was so unhappy when they came home."

Wanda put her arm around Alice's shoulders for a moment. "That's how we learn."

Alice nodded, but she still looked sad. Tracy wondered if Lee was right and being here with them was a bad idea for Alice, after all.

"I've gone through everything else," Tracy told them after everybody found a place to sit. "His dresser, closet, even his medicine cabinet."

"What did you think you'd find *there?*" Wanda sounded interested. "You think Herb was dealing drugs?"

"Not unless there's a black market for Preparation H. No, I thought maybe I'd find some kind of medical ID bracelet, you know, with next of kin."

"You're reaching."

"Am I ever. Anyway, I've skimmed through some of these boxes, but it takes time to look at every little piece of paper and memento."

"Well, dig in." Wanda was already elbow-deep in one. "Maybe we can get through them tonight."

The box Tracy looked through was filled with papers. Receipts, most of them recent, a few from the last place he'd lived, where none of the present residents had ever known him. Tracy had managed to track down the developer who had been in charge of those renovations, and he had confirmed that Herb and all his old neighbors had gone elsewhere.

Herb had conducted a love affair with useless paper, but apparently not with anything important. By the time she reached the bottom of the box, she didn't know one more thing that could help.

"He ate a lot of tuna fish," she said, kicking that box to the side. "Maybe he held stock. Maybe he's related to the Starkists."

"He kept a record of every chess game he played over at Grambling or the rec center," Wanda said. "Every single move he could remember. And he must have gone to a lot of movies when he lived in town, because he kept notes on those, too. What he liked and what he didn't. Maybe he was afraid he'd forget and pay for a movie he'd already seen."

"If he was anything...like me, it wouldn't matter." Alice looked up and smiled a little. "I always forget...."

"She forgets how they end," Olivia said, when Alice didn't continue. "She says it doesn't matter if she's seen them, because the end is always a surprise."

Everybody laughed. "Don't worry, Alice," Wanda said. "That happens to me, too. Ever since the change."

"What did you change into?" Olivia asked.

"A badass, mean-spirited, middle-aged woman."

"Like a witch?"

"You got it."

Olivia giggled.

They worked in silence for a little longer, until Janya held up a small box. "This was at the very bottom. Look inside." She displayed it on her lap. Tracy couldn't see well enough to be sure what was there, so she moved closer.

"Medals? War medals?"

"It seems so, yes."

Tracy took them and held the medals up to the light. The first was heart-shaped, with what looked like the profile of George Washington on it. She flipped it over and read out loud, "For military merit."

Wanda joined her and took the medal from her hands. "I know what this is. This is a Purple Heart. See the purple stripe in the ribbon, even though it's faded? My uncle had one. A soldier gets one if he's killed or wounded."

"Interesting. Would you know what this one is?" Tracy handed her the second, which had a figure like some kind of Greek god with a broken sword.

Wanda turned it over. "1941 through 1945. I guess it's some kind of commemorative medal. If you served in the war, you got one. My uncle had one of these, too. He let us play with all his medals. Said that a man does what he does 'cause he has to, not for some shiny hunks of metal."

Wanda handed them back to Tracy. "This all seems familiar, and not because of Uncle Willie. Maybe Herb told me he got these in the war, only I'm as bad as Alice and can only remember I heard about them somewhere."

Alice smiled, not offended. "That's not likely. He never, well, talked about...the war. Said the whole thing was not something..."

"He wanted to remember," Wanda finished for her, after a long pause. "I can understand that. My uncle wouldn't talk about it much, either." She nodded as if that sealed it. "But there's something nagging at me here."

Medals sounded familiar to Tracy, as well. But she was tired, and her brain was refusing to make connections. She had gotten further on the floor than expected, spreading the adhesive, then combing it with the ridged side of the trowel, placing the tile exactly on the line, placing spacers so the tiles would be straight, setting them in with her new mallet. She had expected to hate the whole process. Instead, she had turned on the radio and sung along, and time had gone quickly, particularly when she began to make real progress. There was still a lot to do, and every muscle in her body ached. But seeing this through to completion might not be as bad as she'd feared.

"We need a break," Wanda said, when no answers were forthcoming. "A pie break. I brought plastic plates and forks. Herb's supplies are pretty lame."

"I think there's coffee and a coffeemaker," Tracy said. "Herb certainly won't mind."

Together they got the coffee brewing, and found powdered creamer and artificial sweetener, which Wanda said was as bad as using canned apples in a homemade pie. There was one small can of ginger ale for Olivia.

"I follow a vegetarian diet," Janya said, as Wanda was cutting the pie. "I will be fine if this is something I can't eat."

"Not a vegetable in sight in this pie, but not one bit of meat, either. We can leave the whipped cream off your piece, if you prefer."

"No, I consume dairy products."

"Never could understand why you people don't eat meat. We'd be overrun by cows, we didn't butcher them."

"If you didn't butcher them, you wouldn't breed them and need to eat them."

"You got cows in India, don't you? Don't you worship them?"

"Hindus respect the lives of animals. The cow's milk nurtures us."

"Well, I respect a good juicy steak most of all."

"Wanda!" Tracy shoved the plates at her. "Will you please—" She tempered what she was going to say. "Dish up?"

"Nothing wrong with a little religious discussion. Broadening to the mind."

Tracy caught Janya's eye and shrugged. Janya continued to look serene. Tracy didn't know how the other woman managed it.

They took their plates into the living room. The pie was scrumptious. Tracy wondered how she had lived her entire life without eating grapefruit pie. Wanda looked pleased by all the compliments.

"This is nothing. You ought to taste my Key lime. No question it's my best."

As they finished, Tracy told them what she'd done on the floor. She'd just completed her description when Wanda slapped her hands together. "I know why those medals sound familiar. Where'd you put Clyde's discharge papers?"

Tracy realized why she was asking. This was the same thing that had eluded her. "I can get them. But are you thinking maybe the medals aren't Herb's? Maybe these are *Clyde's* medals?" She was already halfway into the other room to retrieve the appropriate file folder. "Here we go."

She fished out Clyde's papers and scanned them. "Here it is, and you're right. These medals were listed." She handed the whole folder to Wanda.

"So these are Clyde's. Herb has Clyde's papers, why not his medals?"

"Is that the right question?" Janya asked. "Isn't the right question why Herb had these things at all?"

"Or why Clyde Franklin just disappeared after the war, and Louise had to have him declared dead," Tracy said.

"She did?" Alice asked.

Tracy realized they hadn't filled Alice in on that part yet. She explained about Clyde's death certificate. But as she did, an idea was forming.

"Look, I've got a thought about this, and you may think I'm crazy, but hear me out. Here are some things we know so far. Herb had a daughter. And from the article about Louise, we know Clyde had a daughter. Clyde was declared dead by his wife, but Herb lived on, and he did it right here in Palmetto Grove."

Wanda interrupted. "No, he lived somewhere else for at least a while, remember? Kentucky, for starters. And there was that florist in Georgia he was paying regularly."

"But he came here to finish his life. The preacher I talked to told me that Herb had quit his job in Kentucky and gone *back* to Florida."

"So yes, he lived here before," Janya said.

"And we don't have a single paper for Herb except his birth certificate until *after* Clyde was declared dead. Herb springs to life only after Clyde croaks. Am I the only one who gets this?"

The others stared at her.

"Clyde and Herb are the same man!"

Nobody said anything. Finally Olivia spoke. "I wish I could watch TV."

"Not now, dear." Alice leaned forward. Her eyes were sparkling. "No one can be two people. Either Herb was Herb, or he was Clyde. At least when he was born."

Tracy noticed that Alice had gotten the sentences out without so much as a pause to breathe. "Wanda, you've got the folder. Pull the birth certificates, okay? Both of them. What are the differences you see first thing?"

Wanda got them and held them side by side. "Clyde's looks like the original, folded and refolded and torn around the edges. Herb's is newer, thinner, probably a copy. The kind you write off for."

"When people assume somebody else's identity, they write off for the birth certificate of somebody about their own age who died. I think they can even use that person's Social Security number."

"Not so easy anymore," Wanda said. "Kenny told me about that once. Criminals do it all the time. Used to be easy. Before computers and such, criminal types would go to graveyards and get the names of babies off the tombstones, then get their birth certificates, then get Social Security numbers, and suddenly they could be somebody else. Harder now, though."

"But this happened a long time ago. I think for some reason Clyde Franklin decided he wanted to be somebody else. So he became Herb Krause, wrote off for Herb's birth certificate and got his Social Security number—or applied for one, who knows?"

"But who was Herb Krause to him?" Janya asked.

"Wasn't Herb born in Maine? Or wait, was he?" Wanda looked it up. "No, *Clyde* was from Maine. Herb was from... Montgomery, Alabama. How would Clyde have known somebody named Herb Krause from Alabama was dead? He went cemetery-hopping there?"

Tracy was putting it together, but Janya came up with an answer first. "Herb could have died anywhere, even nearby. But we can't forget the war, because so many men died at that time. Perhaps they served together? We know Clyde was there, perhaps this Herb was there, as well."

Tracy took up where she left off. "Yes, that makes sense. Why not just choose a name he could be sure of? Maybe Herb—the real Herb—died in combat, and Clyde knew enough about him, where he'd lived and everything, to write off for his birth certificate. Maybe they were friends."

"So how do we prove this? Because right now it's just a story we're making up as we go along," Wanda said.

"We find out if a man named Herb Krause with the same birthday died some time ago. Maybe starting with the war, then fanning out."

"How can you find this information?" Janya asked.

"My husband, Fred..." Alice looked up. "Fred was too young to serve, you know. But he told me..." She shrugged. "They brought home his brother's friends, he was older, Fred's brother, and he was at Guadalcanal. And some of the men who served with him were brought home to be buried."

"He could have been buried in a military cemetery," Wanda said. "Like Arlington. Aren't World War II soldiers buried there? Maybe Clyde just went to Arlington and got some name off a grave."

"Or they were buried in the countries where they fell,"

Alice said. "Then brought them home if the families could manage it. They wanted their sons…"

Tracy was making mental notes. "So he could be buried where his family lived. I guess I can make some calls to Montgomery. I'll check online, too, and see if there's a list of soldiers buried in military cemeteries."

"Well, we got us some mystery." After everyone had absorbed that, Wanda made it official. "We got us a man who might not be the man we thought he was. A man hiding himself right here in plain sight until the day he died."

"We need more proof, but I'll bet my life the man we knew as Herb was really Clyde Franklin and declared dead by his wife in the fifties," Tracy said. "And before he disappeared, he grabbed his own documents and medals, which is why Herb had them." Tracy wasn't sure whether to be pleased they had traced things this far or discouraged because nothing they'd found had turned up a family.

"Nana?" Olivia pointed to the clock. "Daddy will be home before long."

Alice got to her feet. "We… Lee's coming back. Thank you for the pie."

"Yes, thank you," Olivia said.

"You think about those earrings," Tracy said, walking them to the door and watching for a moment as the two, old and young, walked hand in hand back to Alice's cottage.

"So what happens next?" Wanda got to her feet. "Besides me putting away what's left of my pie so it don't spoil. The way I make my crusts, that's too likely."

"What do you put in them?" Janya asked. "The crust was delicious."

"My secret ingredient? Lard. Some butter, too, but lard's the real deal. 'Course it's harder to find these days…" She glanced at Janya, and she stopped.

Janya was staring. "What is lard?"

Wanda looked uncomfortable. "Just something I put in my pie crusts."

Janya got to her feet. "What is it made from? Lard is animal fat?"

"I just used a little. I wasn't thinking about that when you asked about meat, you know. I thought you meant the filling. I was thinking about the filling. All that pie had inside it was Jell-O and fruit…"

"Jell-O? Jell-O's made from gelatin, which is an animal product, too." Tracy had been around enough vegans in L.A. to know the rules. "Get real here."

Janya jumped to her feet and headed for the bathroom, kicking the door closed behind her. The house was not big enough to hide the ensuing noises.

"Don't look at me like that," Wanda told Tracy when it was clear the worst was over in the other room, and they could hear water running in the sink. "I wasn't trying to poison the woman. And there's nothing wrong with my crust. It's all in her head."

"It definitely was not in her *head*. That's not where all that noise was coming from. And she asked you outright."

"I just didn't think about the crust! So sue me. Since when is it my job to kowtow to heathen vegetarians, anyway?"

The door opened and Janya stalked out. She went straight to Wanda.

"This *heathen* will no longer force her presence on you. Then you will not have to do this kowtowing, whatever it is. And you certainly will not be required to cook for me, since all foreigners are so foolish we dare to have preferences about what we eat, or who and how we worship."

"Janya—" Tracy started, but Janya shook her head emphatically.

"I will remove myself from this house and Wanda's life. I would go all the way back to India if I could, but since that is impossible, I suggest that you ignore me entirely and pretend my house has no one in residence."

She was gone before Wanda could say another word in her own defense.

"Well, damn," Wanda said, when the door closed behind Janya. "Was it something I said?"

"Oh, go home," Tracy told her. "Titillate old men. At this rate, those are the only friends you'll have left."

Wanda sniffed and followed Janya's path out the door.

chapter seventeen

Janya wasn't certain why she was so unhappy about the way the evening at Herb's cottage had ended. Hadn't she known that Wanda felt superior to her? That every difference between them was magnified in the other woman's mind, and Janya herself shrank in comparison? Wanda was like so many people everywhere. She knew and understood one way of conducting her life. Those who were not like her were simply wrong.

And yet Janya was hurt by the encounter. She didn't think Wanda had set out to trick her. Wanda hadn't set out to denigrate an ancient religion practiced by millions of people. But doing so, without setting out to, was even worse. Because this meant Wanda's feelings were so deeply ingrained that they could never be changed and any appearance of friendship between them was only on the surface. Janya, who had begun to look forward to spending time with her neighbors, now wanted to shun all contact.

On Monday morning she didn't take her usual walk, afraid she might run into one of the others. She wouldn't stay inside forever, of course, but she hoped that in a day or two her feelings wouldn't be so raw. Instead, after the newly returned Rishi went to work, she busied herself mopping and dusting. Although Rishi never seemed to have much appetite for dinner, when she had finished cleaning she searched the cookbook of American favorites she had borrowed from the library and settled on a recipe for spaghetti sauce.

She wasn't certain why spaghetti, which was obviously from Italy, was considered American in this book, but with a few changes to make it more palatable, she was determined to master it. She read the recipe again and made notes. There were far too many herbs and too few spices to suit her, and not enough vegetables. She had bought a perfect cauliflower at the supermarket, and a bag of yellow potatoes. She added these to the recipe, along with a mixture of mustard and cumin seeds, turmeric, cardamon and coriander. When that didn't suit her, she ground cloves and added those, as well.

She decided to serve the sauce on rice. She was not so fond of pasta.

She was chopping the potatoes when somebody tapped on her door. She considered ignoring the summons, but respect won the day. She was relieved to see Olivia. She greeted her with a smile.

"So, to what do I owe this visit?"

"Nana's taking a nap. I thought maybe we could make something."

In the two weeks since Janya had pulled out her art supplies to entertain the girl, Olivia had become a regular visitor. Now that school was officially out for the summer, Janya thought she might be seeing more of her. It seemed a shame that the child had no one to play with here.

"Would you like to sketch?" Janya asked. "You are getting good with charcoal."

"That would be fun."

Janya was glad that this friendship, at least, was uncompli-
cated. She and Olivia were both lonely, and they had found
common ground. Certainly it was a shame the rest of the world
couldn't follow suit.

As Olivia's visits had become more frequent, Janya had put
together a plastic tub of supplies. Now she got it and brought it
to the table. She had an assortment of charcoal and highlight
pencils, different sizes, densities and weights, and she already knew
Olivia liked to experiment. On one of her shopping trips with
Rishi, she had bought cheaper sketch pads for practice. He had
not chastised her for spending their money on a stranger's child.

"It's hot outside. Can we stay here?" Olivia asked.

"Let's work at the kitchen table. You'll not be in trouble for
coming inside?"

"I'll check on Nana in a little while."

Janya wondered who was taking care of whom in Olivia's
household. She knew Olivia's father must be gone, or the little
girl wouldn't be here.

"Would you like to work on your still life?" Last time Olivia
had come, they'd set out a pitcher with dried flowers, a conch
shell, and an open book with a wooden apple sitting on the
pages. Janya had left the items in place.

"Will you show me how to blend the pencils again?"

They settled at the table. In the past, whenever Olivia bent
her head, her hair would fall forward and cover her profile.
With the new short haircut, this no longer happened. Her snub
nose was perfectly evident, as was her cute little pointed chin.

"I think I'll sketch you," Janya said.

"No. Now I look like a boy."

"No, you look like a beautiful little girl. Let me show you."

"I don't even want to look in the mirror. I hate brushing my
teeth."

Janya thought the worst of the adjustment must be over, because this morning Olivia sounded more matter-of-fact than sad. "Change can be hard. But you made a choice, and now you should enjoy what you can."

"It was Daddy's idea. He hates messy hair, and I get hot and sweaty."

"Yes, that is a problem with long hair."

"He made the lady cut it short because I was arguing."

Janya wished they weren't having this conversation. She had spent the morning trying not to be angry, and now she could feel anger simmering again.

"It was my fault," Olivia said matter-of-factly. "Daddy doesn't like arguments."

"Many people do not," Janya said.

"My grandmother argued with him, too. Daddy said I upset her, that I shouldn't do that. I didn't mean to."

"I'm certain that wasn't your intention."

"She was more upset this morning." Olivia looked up. "Do I use my finger to smear it? Or that cotton thing."

"You can use your finger," Janya told her. "Just lightly. Then let's put in some more detail." She waited until Olivia was finished blending some of her lines, then she began her own sketch. "Is Alice all right now?"

"No, her fish died."

"Fish?"

Olivia looked up. "She has an aquarium. A big one with lots of fish. You have to come and see."

Janya thought that was unlikely. "Fish must be difficult to take care of."

"She had a big angelfish. She called him Michael, like some important angel in the Bible."

"I'm sorry he died."

"When she found him floating last night she took him out and flushed him down the toilet, only this morning she didn't remember doing it. And Daddy saw her." She looked up again. "He gets worried when she forgets."

"Your father has a lot to think about."

"I think that's why he got mad about my hair, and you know... He has to take care of me, and of Nana, and my mommy is dead."

Janya thought that was all probably true, but she wondered how often he said this to the child. To be fair, Janya knew she was not an expert in the way Americans reared children, but she did think, from what she had seen here, that girls Olivia's age were usually allowed more freedom.

They sketched in silence. Olivia concentrated on every line, tongue clenched between her lips at the corner of her mouth. She showed natural talent and, more importantly, enjoyment in the process. Janya tried to capture this as she drew the girl's expression.

"Can I see?" Olivia asked, when she realized that Janya really was drawing her.

Janya turned the sketch pad toward her.

"Am I really that pretty?"

"Charcoal can't do justice to your lovely face."

Olivia cocked her head. "Will you finish it for me? May I keep it?"

Janya smiled. "The drawing will be just for you."

Wanda woke up with a headache, and it only got worse as Monday unfolded. By the time she finished her shift—hot day and lousy tips—she felt like a piece of bait cast into the water one too many times.

The heat and tips were just part of it. She was getting tired of feeling ashamed of herself. Shame had its place, but hit a woman with an overload, and she sank lower than an earthworm. Wanda was going to be done with shame and turn herself right back into a shameless hussy. Just as soon as she told Janya Kapur she was sorry about the pie.

Who was she kidding? Truth be told, she was sorry about more than using lard and Jell-O. She'd thought Janya's question was silly and hadn't bothered to think it through. Just maybe she was the teeniest bit sorry for some other things she'd said and done, too.

She'd never thought she was prejudiced. She had preferences about things, but she hadn't considered that maybe those attitudes made the strangers who came to these shores feel even more like strangers, made it even less likely they would care if they melted into the old melting pot.

All morning she'd remembered how she had felt as a teenager when her family moved into a nicer house in a different school district. Her mother had been so proud, but Wanda had spent the first months of the school year without friends. She hadn't known anybody, and nobody made an effort to know her. The other girls made fun of her breasts, and the boys hooted whenever she walked by. She felt alone, and yes, alien. And after she finally began to fit in, she'd always made a point of befriending new girls, so nobody else had to go through exactly what she had.

It was funny, how those lessons just got trampled all over when the new girl had a name that wasn't easy to pronounce, had darker skin, or worshiped differently. Wanda had a bad feeling the God *she* worshiped was not all that pleased with her today. She was back to making amends. If there was a group called Foot in the Mouth Anonymous, she would have to start attending meetings.

At home after a shower and a slice of the infamous grapefruit pie, she was ready to put things behind her. If she felt this bad, Janya must feel a whole lot worse. And Wanda had realized during a long, sleepless night that she liked Janya Kapur and didn't want to lose her friendship. Or Tracy's, for that matter, although she was still waiting to see if that Handy Hubby fellow showed up today for one last session.

She looked around for something to take to Janya's house, some sort of peace offering. The woman liked plants, but none of Wanda's had ever seen dirt, unless she counted dust. She remembered that she'd bought a handful of new magazines the last time she'd gone to the grocery store, and she hadn't even opened them yet.

"Lordy, the things I make myself do." Wanda tucked the magazines under her arm and started down the street. Janya was coming out of her house. The other woman froze, which was a little better than running back inside and slamming the door.

Wanda reached her before Janya recovered and did just that.

"I came to speak my piece," Wanda said, "and apologize for last night."

Janya didn't respond. Wanda could tell she didn't know what to say.

"So here's what I'm sorry for. I'm sorry I didn't think about the lard. But honest, I never thought about what Jell-O was, so I'm kind of blameless there. Who knew it was from cows? Anyway, I didn't pay enough attention. I didn't really think hard enough when you asked me."

Janya nodded. Wanda could almost see the wheels turning in her head.

"And I guess that's not all I'm sorry for," Wanda went on. "I'm sorry for things I've said. I keep pointing out that you're not just like me, only sometimes, you know, that can be a good thing. Because I don't like everything about myself. So maybe you're different from the parts of me I don't like. Does that make sense?"

"No."

"Well, I don't even go to church anymore. So if you're worshiping a bunch of gods, that's a bunch more than I'm worshiping. So that could be good."

"I see."

"And being a vegetarian, that's got to be good for your blood pressure. Mine's creeping up there. It's all that pie, more than likely. Could even be the lard in the crust, so I'm going to find me a different recipe, one you can eat." She turned up her hands. "So see what I'm saying?"

"You are saying that you made a mistake judging me, when maybe there is some value in who I am."

"I'd go so far as to say a whole lot of value. But there's not much value in ragging on people just because they're different. I think maybe Florida's changing too fast for some of us to keep up. Maybe it scares us a little, too. We don't know how to act." She held out the magazines. "Anyway, these are for you. I thought you might like them."

"That is very kind." Janya took them, reading the names out loud. "'*People.*' '*Us.*' '*Soap Opera Digest.*'" She glanced up and smiled just a little. "Now I'll *certainly* know more about your culture. Thank you."

Wanda relaxed. "Well, don't let me keep you from your walk."

"I was walking to the bus stop. I must do shopping before dinner."

"You only have one car, don't you?"

"One is all we need. I never learned to drive."

"Don't women drive in India?"

"In India we say that to drive, all one must have is a good

right foot, a good horn and good luck. I was never certain I had the third."

"Dade County's a mess, but it's not bad here. You could learn."

"Rishi is too busy to teach me."

Wanda saw how she could really make amends. "I taught my son to drive, and I taught my daughter. I can teach you."

Janya started to say something, but she stopped herself. Finally she smiled a little. "This will help you, I think. Teaching me."

"Darn straight. If I was a Catholic, I could pull out my rosary and get this apology thing over with quicker, but I'm a Southern Baptist, so this will have to do. Will your husband let you use your car?"

Janya nodded. "Rishi has suggested a driving school. I didn't want to waste our money, in case I am very bad."

"If you wait just a minute, I'll take you over to the grocery store. I need a few things myself. Then, on the way back, we'll swing by the DMV and see what they require these days to get you started."

"You have the time?"

"I'm not just doing this because I'm sorry. I figure we can be friends, if we work at it."

"This is something you want?"

Wanda met her eyes. "This is something I want."

By the time Wanda dropped Janya off at her house, Janya knew the other woman would be a good driving teacher. She had pointed out road signs, explained rules and driving etiquette. Now Janya had to take an online course and study her driver's handbook, so she could take a test and get her learner's license. As she expected, there would be red tape, too, since she was not yet an American citizen. But everything could be accomplished.

She was humming under her breath when she pulled the mail out of the mailbox and sorted through envelopes as she walked up the path to her house. Rishi paid all their bills, but she organized them to make that easier, throwing out mail that advertised things they didn't need, no matter how friendly or colorful the greetings.

Among the clutter was an airmail envelope from India. Her mother's long-awaited letter had finally arrived. Janya stopped and stared at her own address for a moment. Now that the letter was here, she was reluctant to open it. Had the news been good, her mother would have told her over the telephone. Janya was fairly certain that sending bad news in letter form had been Inika Desai's best hope for avoiding an emotional conversation.

Inside, she brewed a cup of masala tea and went to change her clothes. Then, at last, she sat at the table, the tea steaming beside her, and opened the envelope.

She read the letter, which was perfunctory and factual. The tone was no surprise, considering that the letter had come from her mother. For a moment she couldn't absorb what it said. Then she crumpled the paper in her hand, balling it tighter and tighter, until even if she had wanted to resurrect and read it again, she would not have been able to.

It was past midnight in Mumbai. Her parents would have been asleep for hours, but Yash might not be. It was like him to stay up until two, even three in the morning, reading or doing research on the Internet. She had e-mailed him twice more in the week since she found his e-mail at the library, but she hadn't gotten a response. She wondered if her parents had found a way to keep her e-mails from her brother, as well as her phone calls.

Janya picked up the telephone and dialed the long series of numbers; then she tapped her fingers on the table as she waited.

Quite possibly she would get one of her parents, or one of their maids. They would be angry that she had awakened the household, but she was too upset to care.

Yash answered after the first ring. For a moment she was too choked up to speak. Why hadn't she thought of this before?

"Yash," she said in their native tongue. "Finally. I'm so glad it's you on the other end."

"Janya?" He sounded delighted. "I wasn't sure you remembered how to use a telephone."

She no longer wanted to protect her mother. "I have called many times. They don't want us to speak. I might give you bad ideas. Have they been blocking my e-mails, too?"

There was a pause, and not just the normal pause that was part of any international call, or a sometimes problematic phone system.

"I didn't know about the telephone calls. But the e-mail? That's my fault," Yash said. "I didn't know how to tell you something."

"That Darshan and Padmini are to be married? Our mother sent me a letter. I received it today."

"That sounds like *Aii*. Did she tell you that this was all your fault?"

"She spared me that. For her, my betrothal to Darshan is a thing of the past. And the way Padmini betrayed me is simply my imagination."

"She is looking ahead, in that way she does. Since she can't change what happened, she'll change what happens next. She and *Baba* will go to the wedding and take elaborate gifts to show they have forgotten the unpleasantness between our family and Padmini's. Then all will be as it was."

Tears stung Janya's eyes. "How can she be so blind?"

"It's easier to blame her daughter than her wealthy cousin's daughter. Padmini's family is a connection she's not willing to sever. She has hopes I will marry well and lift the shame that's fallen on us. And she believes the Bhagwats and the Tambes can help make that true."

"I can't believe she and *Baba* will go!"

"Yes, you can believe it."

And in fact, Janya could. Because her mother had always cared most about the way their family looked to others. Janya's feelings in this matter, as they had been so often during her childhood, were irrelevant.

"I got an e-mail from Darshan just over a week ago," Janya said.

"What did he have to say for himself?"

"I don't know. I deleted it. What can Darshan say to me now that I want to hear? The time for saying things is over."

"Perhaps he wanted to tell you why he is marrying the woman who caused all the problems between you?"

"I don't think he believed Padmini was the culprit."

"But you know better."

Janya did. Her cousin Padmini had not stabbed her in the back, she had stabbed Janya directly in the heart. And Janya knew her attacker well. She could not be disguised.

"Padmini and Darshan deserve each other," Yash said. "Don't be a sap and let this get to you. You were fortunate to get out of that marriage before it tumbled all around you."

She felt a rush of warmth for her little brother who wanted so badly to make her feel better. "Thank you for caring."

"So you have been telephoning me?" Yash said.

"*Aii* and *Baba* don't want us to talk."

"*Aii* may stop sleeping forever when she hears we spoke tonight, so while you can, tell me how you are."

"Rishi is a good husband. He's rarely here, but when he is, he treats me well. He wants my happiness more than anything."

"And the place where you're living?"

"Rishi knew how much I loved our seaside cottage at Marve. This was as much the same as he could find. He is very kind in those ways."

"I wish I could see the United States."

"You could come for a visit, Yash. You would be so welcome."

"Can you imagine *Baba's* reaction if I asked him for the time?"

"Are you still determined to be an accountant?"

"No, but they are determined for me."

"I miss you," she said. "My little brother. Soon you will marry and have your own family, and forget your older sister."

"Janya, if I marry, I will first be certain my wife adores you."

She laughed. "You know you can phone me anytime? I'll be waiting to hear from you."

"Check your e-mail. Until our parents figure out a way to get my password, we can always write."

She laughed at the picture of her traditional mother sneaking onto the Internet.

She hung up and stared at the wall. And in her head, she watched a video of her cousin Padmini, who had been as close as a sister, marrying the only man Janya had ever loved.

chapter eighteen

On Friday evening Lee stopped by to see how the week had gone, and Tracy invited him to sit on her patio. He had brought a bottle of wine to celebrate her success in her new job, and she opened smoked oysters and crackers.

"Today the schedule felt right," she concluded, after a brief account of the kids' activities, and the way both staff and campers had adjusted. "They were moving in and out of time slots without a lot of fuss. We've got them sorted into ability groups for sports and swimming. I even found an arts-and-crafts teacher, but she got a better job offer before I could get back to her."

"So what's the craft plan for next week?"

"I guess we're going to do shell art. I bought a bunch of foam balls, and they can glue shells on them. It was the best I could do on the spur of the moment. Crafts aren't my thing. If I can't find anybody to fill the slot, I'm going to see if I can bribe a couple of local artists to share the position. They can make more selling decoupaged beer bottles and knitted tea cozies on Saturdays down at the beach, but I'll try."

She spooned an oyster on a cracker and popped it in her mouth.

"We had a girl drop out. She has some kind of allergy to chlorine and the whole center reeks of it, so she was breaking out."

"That can't be good."

Lee was wearing blue again. Tracy wondered if somebody had told him he ought to.

"That's my lead-in," she said, pulling herself back into the conversation before she started panting. "So now we have an opening for Olivia. Why don't you enroll her, Lee? We have a waiting list for younger children, but no one fits into that slot as well as she would. She's the same age as the girl who left."

"I considered it. But I worry about Alice."

"The regular program's just until three, no different really from school hours. And I saw Olivia on Wednesday, and she says she's already bored. Vacation just started."

"She shouldn't be complaining to you." He sounded annoyed.

Lee was a strict father. Olivia's manners were excellent, and she was a child who knew better than to cause a fuss. Tracy wondered exactly what went on at home, how Lee made certain his daughter toed the line without breaking her spirit.

"She wasn't complaining," she assured him. "I asked her how she was doing. And I know there's very little to do out here except watch seagulls and chase fiddler crabs." She sent him the smile she had practiced in front of a mirror as a teenager. "Lee, I also told her I'd ask you if she can get her ears pierced. That was my idea, not hers, but she would look so cute. Now that her hair's short and her ears are so visible."

"Did she complain about her hair, too?"

She wasn't happy with the way this subject was going. "Olivia isn't a complainer. Like I said, the earrings were my idea."

"She was unhappy about her hair, but I guess she's over it now. Is this what I'll have to deal with when she becomes a teenager?"

"When she gets to be a teenager, she'll just ignore you."

"Oh, I don't think so...."

She laughed. "Mean old Lee. Anyway, I don't think you'll need to worry. She's got a level head. She's a great kid."

"So you really want her in your program?"

"She'll be the best kind of influence on the others. Maybe she'll even teach Bay Egan some manners."

"I'll think about it." He left it at that and went on to tell her about his week. She could see he was discouraged that a sale had fallen through, but he seemed pleased that the brochures he'd printed for Happiness Key were going out in the mail on Monday.

"You're a whiz," she said. "I have a feeling you'll be the one to sell it."

He checked his watch. "The Realtors' association is having a barbecue on Sagmore Beach, and I've got to show up and make nice all night. I would have asked you to come, but I can't imagine doing that to somebody I like so well."

She got up to walk him to his car. "Make some good contacts and get good leads."

"I'll think about the earrings."

"Great. I'll take her to have it done if you like. Just let me know."

The phone rang as Lee drove up the road toward the bridge. "Tracy?"

She recognized Alice's voice. "I'm afraid Lee just left, Alice. Are you trying to reach him?"

"No...I made cake. I thought...you...the others..."

Tracy waited, then filled in the blanks. "Did you want us to come over?"

Alice sounded relieved. "In an hour?"

"Would you like me to call Wanda and Janya? I found out something interesting today."

"Oh, yes."

Tracy hung up and wondered if Alice had waited for the exact moment when Lee would be gone. For some reason, that possibility disturbed her.

Alice's cottage was decorated in soft florals and smelled like lilac air freshener. A flamingo lamp sat on a tinted-glass table beside an overstuffed sofa, but the focal point was a huge aquarium on a knotty pine cabinet. Multihued plants waved from layers of white gravel, a treasure chest opened and closed in one corner, and iridescent fish darted between fronds.

"I tried one of these," Wanda said. She leaned over and squinted through the wide expanse of glass. "I lost more fish than a Yankee on a deep sea charter boat."

Janya joined Wanda, and they leaned over together, staring at the circling fish. "They are so beautiful. This must be work, to keep it so clear and clean."

Tracy had been afraid her two feuding neighbors might refuse to attend the same gathering, but something had transpired between them since the incident at Herb's. Whatever it was, she was glad they had resolved their problems.

"I've had aquariums…" Alice joined them. "Since I was first married. My Fred?" She pointed to the cabinet. "My birthday. He made this for me."

"He was a talented carpenter." Wanda straightened, hands against her lower back. "Kenny now? Give him a hammer and he'll have a black thumb to show for it, and not one thing more."

"How long were you married?" Janya asked Alice.

She didn't hesitate. "Forty-five years."

"Now that's a long time." Wanda leaned farther back. "Kenny and me? We been married almost thirty. I figure that's long enough. I'm still so young I ought to be good for another thirty with somebody else. But no more cops."

"Does your Kenny know he is…what is your idiom? History?" Janya asked.

"It will probably take him a couple of months after I'm gone to notice." Wanda began to wander, lifting a photo in a silver frame and holding it out to Alice.

"You and Fred?"

"Yes. Wasn't he handsome?"

"My, yes, he certainly was. And you look beautiful. All dressed up with someplace to go."

"Ballroom dancing."

Tracy smiled, trying to imagine the Alice she knew whirling around a dance floor. It wasn't as hard as she'd expected. Tonight Alice seemed relaxed and more confident. Even her speech wasn't as halting. And when she held up one hand and did a little dance step in front of the aquarium, Tracy could glimpse the younger woman.

Wanda studied a shelf of multicolored pillars topped with couples in ballroom poses. "Are these your trophies?"

"We were good," Alice said, lowering her eyes modestly. "Fred…tango was his dance."

"I'm certain you were just as good," Janya said.

Olivia came in from the bedroom and greeted everybody. She put her hand on Tracy's arm as the others moved into the next room. "Did you find out if Daddy will let me pierce my ears?" she asked.

"I talked to him, and I told him you'd love the rec center camp, too. Let's keep our fingers crossed on both fronts."

"Awesome!"

The others were still enjoying their peek into Alice's life, and

Olivia brought Tracy up to speed. "Nana's showing them the tablecloth she's making for when I grow up. Come see."

The group was watching Alice carefully remove something from a fabric bag on wooden legs.

"Alice is making a tablecloth," Wanda said. "Crocheting the whole thing."

"You can crochet a tablecloth?"

"Not everything comes from China. Sometimes people *make* things."

"I can glue shells on anything that doesn't move," Tracy said. "Next week I'll make you a Christmas ornament."

Wanda snorted, and Tracy decided she really would.

"My grandmother…" Alice gently lifted the tablecloth from the bag. It was a soft winter-white, crocheted from impossibly thin yarn, or maybe some sort of thread. Tracy knew nothing about yarn crafts, but even she could see how intricate this was, and how beautifully done.

"My grandmother," Alice started again. "She was so accomplished. Sewing. Knitting. Crochet." She unfolded the tablecloth so they could see the lacework better. "She made one…not this…for my hope chest. It was my pride."

"I can just imagine," Janya said. "Do you still have it?"

"No. There was a house fire when Fred and I lived in…St. Petersburg."

"Nana and my grandpa lived there before Nana moved here," Olivia said. "Grandpa Fred owned service stations."

"Started working in a station right after the war," Alice said, as if this were a good memory. "Worked up to owning four."

"And you lost your grandmother's tablecloth in the fire?" Wanda asked.

"I did.… I had wanted it for Karen. I made her things, of course.… But I didn't have…not this pattern."

"Is it the same one?" Tracy asked. "As the one you had?"

"I found an old book. Little antique shop in town. Last year in a pile. Maybe not exactly the same, but very close."

"Nana's making it for *me*," Olivia said. "I told her I might not get married, but I want it anyway."

Tracy laughed and ruffled Olivia's hair. "Anyone would want it. It's gorgeous. It's an heirloom. You have to promise you won't spill spaghetti sauce on it."

Olivia giggled.

"How much more do you need to do?" Tracy asked.

Alice spread her hands about two feet apart. "A month. Maybe more."

"Nana works on it all the time," Olivia said. "When she watches television, when she listens to the radio, when I'm doing homework."

"It's a pineapple," Alice said. "A sign of welcome. And I welcome all of you."

Tracy was touched, and more so when Alice brought out an old-fashioned sponge cake covered with whipped cream and strawberries. Tracy bent to whisper in Janya's ear, "You're safe with that unless you don't eat eggs."

"I will eat them tonight, thank you."

"We'll catch on soon enough," Tracy promised.

They took their dessert plates back into the living room, and Alice carefully brought in a tray with a silver coffee service and set it on the table. She filled delicate china cups, and even Olivia got one, with the addition of lots of milk.

Everyone complimented the hostess and dug into their dessert. When the room grew quiet, Tracy cleared her throat.

"Remember our conversation on Sunday night? Our guess that Herb and Clyde were the same man?"

She got a varied assortment of responses, but everyone remembered.

"Well, this week I discovered I could go online to see if a man named Herbert Lowe Krause was buried in a military cemetery."

Wanda looked up. "And?"

"I drew a blank."

"Oh..." Janya sounded disappointed.

"But I remembered what Alice said, about families wanting their sons nearby, in places they could visit. So I called all the cemeteries in Montgomery I could find numbers for and asked for help. I had a call on my voice mail when I got home this afternoon. One Herbert Lowe Krause, with the same birth date as our Herb, is buried at the Greenwood Cemetery. He died in Sicily in 1943, and his body was returned after the war at the request of his family."

"Well, that clinches it. Clyde was in Sicily, too," Wanda said. "It was right there on his discharge papers."

"So we were right. And more important, now we can be positive the Herb we knew was living under an alias, and his real name was Clyde Franklin."

Janya considered this out loud. "Then, for some reason, Clyde wanted to disappear. He needed a new name, and new identification. So he thought back to the war, and he took Herb's name."

Wanda held up her hand. "Okay, this is important. We have to decide something right this minute. Are we going to call this man Clyde? Or do we go on calling him Herb? I vote for Herb, because the real Herb's not alive to care one way or the other, and Herb's the name we knew our neighbor by."

"I vote for calling him Herb, too, just like we always did," Tracy said. "We know everything we need to about the real one now. That Herb's just a name our Herb appropriated."

"Stole, more like it," Wanda said. "A chicken's still a chicken, even when it's plucked. And now, not to try to outdo you or anything, but as a matter of fact, I found out some things on my own. I figure while Kenny's still hanging around, I should use him. He ought to be good for something."

"Honestly, do you talk about the man that way when you're with him?" Tracy asked.

"Talk?" Wanda laughed. "Did you talk to your ex before you divorced him?"

"CJ was *way* too busy with attorneys. The last real conversation we had was the day he told me life as I knew it had ended. After that, I almost never saw him alone again."

"And when you did, you were too furious to talk to him," Wanda guessed. "Am I right?"

Tracy wasn't sure what to call the feelings that talk had inspired. "There was nothing CJ could do for me. His problems were a lot worse than mine."

"Well, I'm the worst problem Kenny's ever going to have. Anyway, I asked him to check and see if Louise got Clyde Franklin's Social Security for their daughter after she had him declared dead. And she did. Not only that, I found the name of their daughter. Pamela Glade Franklin, born in November of 1943 right here in Palmetto Grove. So little Pammy was just eight when Louise started getting Clyde's Social Security for her, money she really wasn't entitled to, since old Clyde was busy pretending to be our Herb and breathing just fine, thank you very much."

"We've got her name!" Tracy did a fake hand slap in midair. "Congratulations, Wanda."

"Do you think Louise and Herb, our Herb, planned this?" Alice asked. "He was such…a nice man."

Wanda turned up her hands. "I couldn't say. One of two

things happened. The first is that our Herb up and left his family, just disappearing into thin air. Louise looked for him, then she looked some more, and finally she had him declared dead, because she and that little girl needed help. Turns out her timing was fortunate, because in 1950, Congress made a bunch of amendments to the law about who could get Social Security, and Louise was suddenly eligible for some money on her own, since she was a widow caring for a dependent child. She got that, too."

"You *have* done a lot of research," Janya said.

Wanda smiled and looked pleased. "Thank you. I had to ingratiate myself after the unfortunate pie incident. Now, that second possibility? It's darker, you bet. Maybe Louise knew our Herb was just off gallivanting, as men are wont to do. She couldn't get a cent out of him, so she decided she'd just see if she could pretend he was dead and ask the courts to make it happen. Maybe he even told her to go ahead, and he'd just stay out of the way."

"It could be somewhere in between," Tracy said. "Maybe she hoped he was alive. We don't know how long she waited before she had him declared dead, because we don't know when he left her. I checked on the law, and right now Florida says you have to wait five years, but I don't know what the time period was then. No matter what, Louise had to wait a long time, hoping he'd come back or knowing he wouldn't, until she could finally go to court."

"Did we ever find out when Louise was struck by the car and died?" Janya asked.

"I checked on that, too." Wanda pulled out a piece of paper. "Down at the newspaper office. They printed this for me from microfilm. Her obituary from 1963. That's how I got Pamela's name. And you can all read this, but I'll tell you the important thing. There was no other family mentioned. She was survived by her daughter and not one other person."

"That made Pamela twenty when her mother died," Tracy said, counting on her fingers. "I wonder what happened to her, where she went, what she did. Maybe she was in college by then. Now that we have her name, we ought to search the records here in town. Schools, hospitals, down at the courthouse. Maybe Louise even filed a will and we can find that, too. But if we don't find her here, maybe we ought to look for Pamela in Maine, where Herb was really born. His family wouldn't have been in Louise's obituary."

"That's something to do, all right. When he was still Clyde, he graduated from high school up there in Augusta. So we can try that and see. But we're up against a real stickler here. Because Kenny says finding a woman once she's married is real hard. Even if we find mention of her in the sixties, who knows what she calls herself now?"

"I'll run her name on the Internet," Tracy said. "But unless she never changed her name, and unless she has a job or hobby with a public profile, we're back to square one."

Alice had begun cleaning up, so the other women helped her take dishes to the sink. She filled it with soapy water and began to wash. Olivia said good-night and went to call a friend from school, and the women were alone in the kitchen.

"Louise's story is a sad one," Janya said. "Except for her daughter, it seems she was all alone at the end."

Wanda took a dish out of the drainer and began to dry it as naturally as if she did it every day. "You grow up, you think you just make enough friends, marry the right man, you'll end up with people all around you. Then things happen, and suddenly, you're more alone than you imagined you could be."

"Yes, when you think of your future, you do not expect to be living thousands of miles from everyone you loved," Janya said.

Tracy had noticed that Janya was not her serene self. She had attributed it to the fight with Wanda, even though the two women had obviously reconciled. Now she wondered if Janya was homesick. And why wouldn't she be? Maybe Louise had been lonely and maybe she hadn't, but the women in the room understood the word all too well.

"I'm not *that* many miles away," Wanda said. "I can drive back to Miami when I need old friends or my children. But I never expected the man I married to start acting like *he* was thousands of miles away."

"You grow old...." Alice put more dishes in the drainer before she finished. "Those friends? Gone, just like that. They die, or go off to live with children or move...into retirement communities."

Janya was wrapping the cake. Tracy began to wipe the counter with a sponge. She found it odd that they all seemed so at home here, doing jobs women had done for centuries and chatting about themselves as they did.

"I know you don't think I have anything in common with you," she said, "but you'd be wrong there. I lost my husband, my home, my security, my friends and my family right before I moved here. Bummer, huh?"

"What happened to your family?" Wanda asked.

"Well, CJ was a crook, and not above taking money from anybody to shore up bad business decisions. He was also a man who could look you in the eye, tell you he could make the sun come up an hour earlier, and you would believe him. In a place like Bel Air, my father's not what they call rich, but by most standards he made a great living, and he had lots socked away for retirement. He planned to retire by sixty, even though my mother laid claim to her share of his investments during their divorce."

"I might know where this is going," Wanda said. "I can smell it."

"You got it. CJ talked Daddy into investing in his companies. On paper it looked like Daddy would do so well he'd be able to retire on time without worrying about anybody or anyone, old wife, new wife. So he talked my mother into going along with CJ's plan. No problem there. She thought CJ *was* the sun. Only in the end, she got burned like everybody else. Because when CJ went down, he took them right down with him. Now Daddy's going to be straightening teeth until he's eighty, and my mother had to sell the house I grew up in, ten thousand square feet with a prime view of Catalina Island, and move to a bungalow in Del Rey. And this is my fault, you understand. Because it was my idea to marry a crook."

She hadn't realized how worked up she had gotten, but by the time she finished, she'd been clipping her words as closely as a Disneyland topiary.

"And so they more or less kissed you off," Wanda said.

"My father's second wife has given orders that I'm never to cross their threshold. My mother is slightly kinder. She met me for lunch the day before I flew here. Of course, *I* paid and *she* ordered lobster salad."

Wanda sputtered. Tracy glared at her; then she snorted. In a minute they were both laughing.

"How can you laugh at such a thing?" Janya asked.

"Because…" Tracy wiped her eyes. "Because they aren't worth crying over. I was just something to barter with. Right from the beginning. I never realized it until my whole life turned to sh—" She looked at Alice, and changed her mind. "I went along with it all. I guess I deserved what I got."

"This is like an arranged marriage," Janya said. "Your parents steered you to this man? The way mine steered me where they thought I should go?"

"Your marriage was arranged? No way! Really?"

Janya lifted one elegant brow. "And yours? Was it not arranged? Only subtly? You were to marry a rich man who would please your parents. Did they pay for your wedding ceremony and party? Did they give you wonderful gifts to take into your marriage the way Indian parents do? We call it a dowry, but is it so different?"

Tracy was stunned. She had never, *never,* thought of her life that way. Arranged marriages were conducted on the other side of the world.

She was still trying to figure out what to say in return when she heard footsteps in the other room. She realized Lee was staring at them from the doorway. And not happily.

"What on earth is going on here?" he asked.

Alice turned. Tracy caught a glimpse of her face. She looked uncertain, even frightened, although Tracy was sure she had to be imagining that.

"Your generous mother-in-law invited us for cake, Lee," Tracy said. "And we've been having a wonderful time. Alice knows how to entertain a crowd."

"Alice should not be entertaining anybody. Alice needs rest and quiet."

Janya spoke before Tracy could. "Perhaps she has had too much of both and needs friends, Mr. Symington. She has been happy with us, and we've been delighted with her."

"And what would you know?" He sounded as angry as his words. "Somebody like you has no idea what Alice needs. You're not even from here."

Janya did not back down, which surprised Tracy. In fact, she took a step forward. "The country I come from has nothing to do with this. Sometimes strangers can see what's going on better than family can."

"Exactly what do you mean by that? What do you think is going on?"

Tracy stepped between them. "Hey, look, Lee, Janya just means you might be too close to the situation. When we're with Alice, she has a great time. You're naturally worried about her. But maybe she's not as fragile as you think."

He didn't reply. She noted a muscle in his jaw working hard, as if he were suppressing whatever he had intended to say.

"I thought…you would be gone. I didn't want to disturb you." Alice sounded tired, maybe even defeated.

"So you waited until I left."

Silence stretched on, and Tracy thought he wasn't going to continue. Then Lee sighed. "I'm sorry. I apologize to all of you, especially you, Mrs. Kapur." He looked at Tracy, not Janya, when he said it. "I was out of line. It's just that excitement isn't good for Alice. The consequences show up later."

"I'm fine, Lee," Alice said with dignity. "And these are my friends."

He nodded. "Again, I apologize. I had no right to be so upset. There's just a lot to worry about." He smiled at his mother-in-law, a thin smile that looked as if it had been manufactured from next to nothing. "And I worry because I care. You know that."

Tracy was becoming a fan of apologies, but this one did little for her. This was a side of Lee she hadn't seen before, and she didn't like it.

"Shall I go out and come in again?" This time he smiled ruefully, and more genuinely, at all of them. "Could we pretend this never happened?"

"You are very kind to apologize," Janya said stiffly. "And now, I must go home."

"Thank you for understanding." Lee was beginning to sound like the man Tracy had thought she was getting to know. She wondered what, if anything, had happened at the barbecue to upset him.

"I've got to go, too," she said.

"And me," Wanda added. "I've got some work to do tonight." She looked at Tracy and wiggled her eyebrows. "A few phone calls that need to be made."

They all thanked Alice, and Lee saw the women to the door. He pulled Tracy aside before she could follow the others down the path.

"Listen, I thought about this, and you're right about Olivia. I'll register her first thing on Monday morning. And I'm sure you're right about Alice, too. She'll be fine until Olivia gets back in the afternoons. Thanks for nudging me a little. Before and, well, now."

She felt better. Everybody had bad days, and Lee did have a lot on his plate. "You're welcome." She rose up on tiptoe and kissed his cheek to show he was forgiven.

chapter nineteen

Had anyone ever brought up the subject, Tracy would have snickered at the idea of an early-bird special. Had she been asked where she wanted to eat, she would have said any place except a noisy tourist restaurant that flung plastic baskets with greasy clumps of dough on every table right along with the menus. Yet here she was, late on a Thursday afternoon, sitting at the Dancing Shrimp with her neighbors, gazing at the early-bird chalkboard. Worse, as she debated between fried scallops and deviled crab, she was finishing her second hush puppy.

From the head of the table, Wanda was waving a straw like a scepter. "Nobody makes hush puppies as good as we do. Nobody else puts shrimp right inside them."

Tracy was calculating calories in her head, a skill she had learned along with her ABCs. She had eaten a meal's worth already, and she hadn't even ordered. Worse, she could feel her hand struggling to reach for another hush puppy.

"And I told you, Janya, we have a vegetarian selection every single night. See, right there." Wanda pointed to the place on Janya's menu.

"Eggplant parmigiana. I will learn something."

Wanda looked pleased. In fact, Tracy thought Wanda had looked positively radiant since Wednesday afternoon, when all the women had accepted her invitation to dinner. Even Alice and Olivia were with them. In fact, the date had been arranged with Lee's schedule in mind. He was in Tampa at a seminar, and Tracy had promised she would keep an ear out for Alice and Olivia tonight. She just hadn't mentioned she would be doing it at the Dancing Shrimp or, later, the dog track.

She still couldn't believe she was going to the dog track.

A young server arrived to distribute drinks and take their dinner order. Even at this hour—or maybe because of it—the restaurant was bustling. The tables were jammed together, with fish nets, plastic pelicans and loudspeakers playing top-forty music just over the women's heads.

To be heard, Wanda had to raise her voice to something approximating a shout. "So, where are we now with Herb?"

Tracy told herself one more hush puppy couldn't possibly add more than say, an ounce, to her slender frame. What was an ounce?

It was gone in two bites. "Yesterday I stopped by city hall and asked if Pamela's name turned up anywhere. It was a big waste of time. If she's living here, everything's under a married name. I called the local high school and asked if they keep alumni records, but they don't."

"Well, I've got something we can try," Wanda said. "After we're done here, I thought we'd go see if the house Herb lived in before the war is still standing. We've got the address from that welding certificate of his. Hall Street. It's a long shot, but maybe somebody there remembers the family."

"That was almost seventy years ago," Tracy said. "What are the chances?"

"I'll be happy to do something else, but that neighborhood's over by the track, so why not give it a try?"

Tracy was running out of things to try. Maribel had promised to list Herb's house as a rental starting in July, but she wasn't optimistic about Tracy's chances of renting it during the hottest part of summer. For now, Tracy wasn't planning to start clearing out Herb's things, but when the time came to do so, she figured she and the other women would have to move on.

"I don't see what it can hurt, but it's possible we've found out all we're going to." Tracy looked around the table and read the other women's expressions. "Hey, we tried. Don't look so down."

"All his things. His plants, his little mementoes. It seems so sad," Janya said. "And to think that his daughter will never know he's gone."

"Or maybe that he was alive for a whole lot of years when she *thought* he was dead," Tracy pointed out.

Wanda finished the last hush puppy and signaled for a replacement basket. "It's the darnedest thing, but I just feel like we got to keep going."

They changed the subject. Olivia told them about her first week at youth camp, and the women applauded when she announced that her team had won the relay at the weekly swim meet. Alice told them how she was coming on the tablecloth. Wanda gave a rundown of that week's *All My Children*.

They demolished the next basket of hush puppies, too, then their dinners. Tracy had asked if the cook would grill her scallops, but they arrived looking exactly like the hush puppies. Wanda had virtuously asked for extra cole slaw instead of fries, then snitched fries from every plate she could reach. Janya said the eggplant was good, although she thought it needed more spices. Alice beamed through the meal, as if this unexpected treat was the finest thing that had happened to her in months.

Tracy wondered if their quest to find Herb's family was less about Herb and more about them.

When they finished, they piled into Wanda's car, which was just large enough for the five of them, and drove to Hall Street, where Herb had lived when he was still an apprentice welder named Clyde Franklin.

"Well, the chances aren't good anybody will remember the family," Wanda said, driving up and down the street of three- and four-story apartments and condos. They were all a little shopworn and weathered, with narrow windows and flimsy iron balconies. But they weren't old enough to have housed Herb or his wife and baby daughter.

"One step forward, two steps back," Tracy said.

"I guess there's no point in asking around," Wanda said. "Even if his house was still sitting right here, this would have been enough of a long shot."

They drove another five miles or so, and waited in a short line of traffic to pay the parking fee and go through the entrance to the Sun County Greyhound Track. Wanda followed the signals of a man wearing a fluorescent safety vest and parked at the end of a row. The lot was large, but only half-full.

"You are certain Olivia can come inside?" Janya asked.

"As long as she doesn't drink or gamble. You're not planning to do either, are you, kiddo?" Wanda asked.

"Can I drink a Coke?"

"You certainly can."

"That'll be good."

Tracy had been to the Kentucky Derby and Preakness with CJ. She'd been to Monte Carlo in Monaco, and the Bellagio in Las Vegas. She had never been to the Sun County Greyhound Track. And now she knew why.

The complex was smaller than she'd expected. A three-story

building faced what was probably the track itself, and just beyond that stood something that looked like a grandstand. Stepping out of the car into a wave of steaming air, she saw that the asphalt parking lot was buckling, and weeds crowded the cracks. Beyond them, the building was painted a soft Caribbean-blue, but even from here, she could see that the paint was peeling.

"Wanda, you're sure they still have races here?" Tracy asked.

"The last hurricane that came through did a bit of damage, okay? But it's still in business. This is the last week they'll race until November. But they'll have simulcasts from other tracks, and we can still come in and bet."

"You need to explain why this is fun."

"What's not fun?"

"Watching a pack of dogs run around a track when the temperatures are climbing into the nineties every day."

"There's talk they're going to tear the whole complex down and build a fancier place, maybe a casino with slots and poker, if they can get the Sun County voters to agree. That would probably suit you better, but right now this is all we got. You going to make a fuss?"

"Nope, I just needed some education."

"You got that right."

As they crossed the lot, Wanda explained how the races worked, drilled them on the best ways to bet, and defined words like "exacta" and "trifecta." She had a command of the facts that reminded Tracy of a college professor grooming his class for finals. They paid their dollar admissions and found a table on the pockmarked concrete terrace that overlooked the track. Tracy took one look at her program, which was as complicated in its way as half the papers she had signed to end her marriage, and gave up.

Janya did, too, and they smiled at each other as they set their programs on the table. But Alice and Wanda were poring over theirs as if they held all the mysteries of the universe.

They ordered drinks, and popcorn for Olivia, and listened as the loudspeaker squawked a welcome between staticky bursts of vintage rock.

"It's not as busy on a Thursday night as some," Wanda said.

"How often do you come?"

"I was coming a lot...before I started doing other things in the evenings."

"Really? What kind of things?" Tracy asked innocently. "What could keep you away from *this*?"

"I mostly spend a lot of time on the telephone with my friends."

Tracy pretended to look fascinated. "You do have the most active social life."

"I'd be happy to give you a pointer or two. Right now, though, tell me what you want to bet and I'll go do it for you."

"Who do you favor?"

Wanda went into a long explanation, which ended with "...but my favorite dog's named Chase the Suspect."

"Well, that makes sense, considering your husband's profession," Tracy said. "But you're saying, after everything you just told us, odds and all that other garbage, you just go by the dog's name?"

"You got it. Of course, he wins whenever I'm here."

"Your dog's running tonight?"

"First race. That's why we came." She pointed to the program.

"Well, if we're just betting names..." Tracy lifted the program and scanned it. "How about California Girl?"

"Hand over your money. We'll keep it simple. California Girl to win, okay? Give me two dollars."

Tracy remembered being with CJ when he had lost thousands and it hadn't fazed him. She parted with the two dollar bills as reluctantly as if they were glued to her hand.

Alice bet on a dog named Dancing Dervish. Janya abstained when none of the names in the first race impressed her. Wanda left to take their bets to the window. By the time she returned the race had begun. She didn't look happy.

"What's wrong?" Tracy asked.

"Chase the Suspect injured his front leg when they were unloading him from the van. Looks like he won't be running tonight. And I wanted you to see him."

Tracy had her eye on the race, a pack of dogs wearing what looked like colored harnesses and muzzles. She was not impressed. Judging by the loudspeaker, the nearly black dog running toward the end was California Girl.

"So we'll just have to come back in the fall," she said.

"I got the feeling maybe he's run his last race."

Tracy glanced at Wanda and away from the dogs. "What happens to them? They go off to be somebody's pets?"

"The lucky ones, maybe. The guy standing behind me at the window didn't think he'd be one of 'em."

Tracy abandoned the race and her choice, who was now bringing up the rear. "You mean they…" She checked to see if Olivia was listening, but the girl was standing at the railing watching the end of the race.

"He's got so much heart. He doesn't deserve a bad ending," Wanda said. "You should have seen that dog run."

"I can't believe… They just…" Tracy shrugged.

"They got rescue organizations that take them sometimes."

"Then maybe that's what will happen."

"This is kind of a shabby place, case you didn't notice? Kind of second-rate, with second-rate dogs and owners. They have a vet, have to. But the guy behind me was saying this vet would rather put a dog down than try to fix him. Especially if his racing career is about over."

There were a lot of things about the world Tracy had been happier not knowing. And here was another one. Revelations were coming thick and fast, and she wasn't that fond of any of them.

"I'm going to see if I can find him," Wanda said, getting to her feet. "Maybe they'll let me pay his vet bill or something and take better care of him."

"They're not going to let you near the kennels," Tracy said, standing, too. "I'm sure they don't let just anybody back there."

"That dog gave me so much pleasure. I'd come here, and there he'd be, running his little heart out. I used to think he knew I was watching and he was doing it just for me." Wanda reached down and got her purse. "You coming or not?"

Of course she wasn't coming. Tracy couldn't imagine why Wanda thought that was a possibility. Then, in the same way her hands had reached for those hush puppies—six of them!— her legs began to move. She waved to Janya before they could take her too far away.

"We'll be back."

Janya did not look convinced. "Please stay out of trouble. I have not yet had my first driving lesson."

Wanda made a bed for Chase in the corner of her kitchen, using an old blanket and a pillow. She was fairly certain dogs didn't need pillows, having grown up with hunting dogs who slept in wire enclosures with nothing but dirt and straw to keep them comfortable. Still, she figured the pillow wasn't going to hurt anything. And sure enough, the dog curled up on the blanket and rested his head on the pillow, like that was the way he had always slept.

"So, tell me again what your husband is going to say?" Tracy asked.

"You just can't let go of that, can you?"

"I wish I could be a fly on the wall."

"You're sure good at being a fly in the ointment."

"You were going to take this dog and run if you had to, weren't you? If I hadn't been there?"

"To sweet-talk the owner, you mean? I never saw anybody turn on that much sunshine in my entire life. I thought I'd go blind."

"It worked. Along with whatever amount of money you put in his hand."

"It did," Wanda said grudgingly. "But you know he just made you think it was your charming personality and my contribution that done the deed, don't you? We saved him a hassle, that's all. As far as he was concerned, this dog was just a piece of his past. One too many injuries to these legs of his. Chase here would have been lucky to meet his maker at the hand of a vet. I hear sometimes they just take them out back—"

Tracy held up her hand. "No more, okay?"

"He's a mighty good-looking dog, isn't he?" Wanda gazed down fondly at Chase the Suspect, forever more to be known simply as Chase. The owner, a nasty-looking man with an unlit cigar clenched in the corner of his mouth, had told them Chase was a blue brindle. Which meant he was a soft bluish-gray, with streaks of tan and darker gray woven through his coat. The owner had promised to send Wanda the dog's papers, but she was pretty sure she would never see them. And what did it matter? Chase wasn't going anywhere.

"Do you want me to ask around at work tomorrow about a vet?" Tracy asked.

"I'll call that clinic just across the bridge first thing in the morning. Somebody at the Dancing Shrimp mentioned they're good."

The track vet had bandaged Chase's leg and given him a

painkiller. Now the dog seemed comfortable enough. He was already sound asleep. As if he was home. As if he knew, somehow, he was safe. But what did a dog know, anyway?

"Have you ever owned a dog?" Tracy asked.

Wanda pulled her gaze away from the sleeping animal. "Grew up with hounds. Had a poodle when my kids were young. When that dog died, I figured I'd never put myself through that kind of sadness again."

"Tough old Wanda, huh?"

"How about you?"

"Dogs shed and slobber. They yap. No dogs in my family."

"They tear your guts out, dogs in general. See, a dog'll love you pretty much no matter what you do to 'em. I bet Chase will think fondly of his old owner or trainer, whoever that bozo was that had him. He won't know that all that loyalty he gave out, all that heart, well, the best reward he could hope for was being cast aside."

"Are we talking about Chase?"

Wanda looked up. Tracy's tone had been gentle, maybe even concerned. A few weeks ago Wanda wouldn't have believed that the woman had either gentleness or concern inside her.

"I'm talking about the dog," Wanda said. "People? We're raised to know better. We're raised to *suspect*."

"I was raised to get everything I could before the bottom dropped out or the roof fell in."

"Now you're right smack-dab in the middle of the wreckage. Those warnings didn't get you anywhere, did they?"

"Sure. They got me right here." Tracy headed for the door. "I'll be back tomorrow to see what Ken says." At the door she turned. "You know, I think your lease says you can't have a pet."

"You know what you can do with that lease, don't you?"

"I thought you'd probably say that." Tracy winked, then let herself out.

A little later Wanda was nursing a gin and tonic when the telephone rang. She got a couple of numbers from Lainie, who sounded just the same whether she was giving out phone numbers of dirty old men or asking one of the Dancing Shrimp busboys to clear table nine.

She looked them over, then decided not to call the men in order. She selected the second from the end, her newest conquest of sorts, and dialed the number.

The familiar, gravelly voice answered.

"Hello, Shadow," she said. "You're being seduced."

"You been outside? Isn't it a little hot for hanky-panky?"

She laughed. "Honey, I could make it a whole lot hotter if I was in the same room with you."

"Promises, promises. Although you know what I'd really want to do if you were? I'd want to take a walk tonight. Along the beach. Moon's up out there, and you could probably see a mile in every direction."

She remembered nights when she'd walked with Ken that way. Although pretty soon she wouldn't remember, because those hours would be so far past. That made her sad.

"You like strolling in the moonlight, Sunshine?" he asked.

"It's been a long time."

"That's not good."

"When was the last time you did?"

"Too long. At least with a beautiful woman."

"You want to know what I'm wearing tonight?" She looked down at one of Ken's faded T-shirts, something he'd picked up at a Boys Club picnic maybe ten years ago. She had thrown it on after a quick shower.

"No, tell me where you're sitting instead. So I can picture you."

"In my bood-war…"

"All lace and satin?"

"No… Lots of flowers, though. More of a jungle theme here." She eyed her bright upholstery. "Me Jane, you Tarzan. Exotic animals, too."

"Animals?"

"Uh-huh. A monkey…" She gazed at the stuffed monkey. "And a wild beast lurking in the corner."

"Wild beast?"

She laughed. "Just a dog. A sleeping dog, at that."

There was a pause. "Now that's something I never pictured you with."

"Well, you would be wrong."

"What kind of dog?"

She wondered if a man could find a woman by her dog and decided she was safe enough. "A greyhound."

"Who'd have thought?"

"And what about you? Tell me where you are."

"Both feet planted firmly in the Land of Regret."

She thought that was the strangest answer she'd ever gotten, and still, she understood immediately what he meant.

"Whatever got you there? You can leave anytime."

"You got any idea how?"

"First thing would be to say sorry to anybody who needs it. Second would be to realize you got the rest of your life ahead of you, and you don't want to spend it mired up to your knees. So you take steps. A few at a time. Until you're standing in the open again."

"You make it sound easy."

"It's not easy. I seem to be spending time there, too."

"You have things you regret?"

"Honey, I'm just human."

"I don't like you being unhappy."

She realized the man was paying for the call, and he was right. It wasn't her job to bring him further down or complain about anything. She sat up a little straighter, and even though he couldn't see her, she pasted a smile on her lips. "Then I won't be. I'll be as contented as a cat swimming in cream. And I promise, I can make you feel the same way."

"No, Sunshine, I just meant I wish you were happy. Really happy. You deserve to be."

Her shoulders sagged. "We all deserve to be."

"You think we ought to warn babies in the hospital nursery that this life might not turn out the way they hope?"

"What, and scare them back to wherever they came from? It can be a trial, no doubt. But you've had good times, right? Enough to keep you moving."

"A lot of them," he acknowledged. "Talking to you is one of them."

Her heart beat a little faster. She realized how pathetic that was. A stranger who was paying for this conversation said something nice, and she reacted like a high school freshman on her first real date.

"I like talking to you, too," she said. Sadly, she meant it.

"I have to go now. But we'll talk again. Okay?"

"You bet."

"Pet that greyhound for me." He laughed a little.

She hung up and held the phone to her breasts a moment. She wasn't sure whether the man mired in the Land of Regret or the dog she had rescued from certain death had brought the flood of tears to her eyes. She lifted the hem of Ken's shirt and dried them. Then she dried them again. And finally once more.

It really was such a sad, old world.

chapter twenty

Like her predecessor, Tracy planned her workweek down to the minute. By the time the kids arrived, she was already sure all the day's equipment was in place, and all the counselors and teachers were present. If needed, she had made calls to parents and chatted with either Woody or Gladys about lingering concerns. At nine, she positioned herself with the counselors near the front door, trading fist bumps or high fives, and insinuating herself between boys bent on proving their superior testosterone levels. Oddly enough, she didn't hate any of it.

On Friday morning she woke earlier than usual and realized she'd had "the" dream again. This time she was dressed in a silver Hervé Léger bandage dress, tight and short and utterly fabulous on her carefully toned body. She walked through the door of the country club, and before the walkie-talkie men could evict her, George Clooney and Ben Stiller sent admiring glances her way. She waved as the men in dark suits dragged her outside, sprouted eagle's wings and soared into space with Tracy clutched firmly in their talons.

Only this time, she didn't tumble to a white sand beach. This time she was released over the sparkling whitecaps just beyond. And as she fell, she simply positioned her hands in front of her in the classic position and dove into the surf.

She lay in bed and gazed above her, wondering if an early-morning shower had found its way through holes in the roof to write a different ending to her dream. But she was dry, and so was the ceiling. Since going back to sleep was impossible, she dragged on shorts and a tank top for an early run.

When she had the time, she liked running to the point and back. The shelling was best, and few people got up early enough to compete. She usually had the point to herself at dawn, but this morning she had company.

"Hey, Janya!" She waved and jogged faster. "You're up early."

The sun was just rising, and the light was rose-tinted. The gulf lapped lazily at the shore just beyond, but the beauty of the moment seemed lost on the other woman.

"I'm often up early," Janya said. "Rishi is in a hurry to get to work, and I walk so I won't be in his way."

"I never see you."

"One day I'll show you my favorite spot. Perhaps you have yet to discover it." But Janya made no move to do so, as if the words were spoken while she was thinking of something else.

"Are you okay?" Tracy asked. "Your husband didn't mind you being gone last night?"

She shook her head, and her lovely hair was a cloud around her face. "He is a very determined man, my husband. He wants to succeed, so he's often not at home himself. I suppose he *will* succeed. I'm told he's brilliant."

Tracy thought that was a strange way to talk about one's own husband. Then again, what had she really known about CJ? Only what he wanted her to.

She couldn't contain her curiosity. "Was your marriage really arranged? Did you know Rishi at all? Or did you meet him on your wedding day?"

"It is a complicated story, but no, we met before the day of our wedding. And I was free to agree to the marriage or not."

Tracy had a million more questions, but she sensed Janya wasn't in the mood. "You didn't say if you're okay. Something's wrong, isn't it?"

"We know each other that well now?"

Tracy turned her hands to the lightening sky. "Guess so."

"I woke this morning to find all the plants on my patio had been turned upside down. Some pots are in little pieces. Many of the plants were uprooted or broken and won't survive. And my little fountain…" She sighed. "It's good not to get attached to things."

"But that's awful!" Tracy was outraged. "Vandals? They didn't get inside, did they?"

"Rishi is very careful that we should lock our doors at night and while we're away."

"Teenagers, I'll bet. Out to make mischief, maybe find a place to drink beer and hang out. When did it happen, do you know?"

"I found them this morning. I had no reason to check last night after I came home. But I heard nothing during the night."

"I bet somebody was out here while we were at dinner or the track. I wonder if anybody else got hit? I guess I'd better check around my place and talk to the others." Tracy wondered if the tile she hadn't yet installed was now in broken shards.

"What if this was somebody we know?"

"Who do we know? I haven't made any enemies, except maybe Marsh Egan, and even he wouldn't stoop to that kind of thing."

"I think, perhaps, I *have* made an enemy."

"Who?"

"Mr. Symington was angry with me the night we were invited to Alice's."

Tracy almost laughed. "Lee?"

"You think this is silly?"

"I'm sorry. I don't think *you're* silly, but I don't think Lee's that kind of person. Look at him. He's a devoted father, a devoted son-in-law."

"You must have noticed how hard he tries to keep Alice from being with us. And when I…" She looked frustrated. "I can't remember how you say this. Stood on his toes?"

"Stood up to him? Stepped on his toes?"

Janya nodded. "Stood up to him. He was angry. He refused to meet my eyes."

"Janya, he was upset with all of us. There's no question he's overly protective, but he apologized, remember? And he seemed to mean it. Besides, he was gone last night when this probably happened. When we dropped Alice and Olivia at their house, he wasn't home, and I saw him drive by about half an hour later."

Janya was silent.

"Come on," Tracy said. "I'll help you clean up the mess."

"That is unnecessary."

Tracy thought it probably was very necessary. Janya had been taking exquisite care of Herb's plants. Whether it was a good idea to become attached or not, she had. And the sense of invasion didn't help. She needed somebody to lend a hand. Tracy was just surprised it was turning out to be her.

"We'll get the mess cleaned up," she assured Janya. "And we'll see what we can salvage. The sooner the better, if any of the plants are going to survive. I think Herb had some extra pots out by his car, and maybe even some potting soil. After we take stock we'll see what we need. But we'll get this back in shape for you."

"You are very kind."

"I'm so *not* very kind. For some weird reason it's just starting to look that way."

After helping Janya set her patio to rights and salvaging about half the plants, Tracy made it to work just ahead of the campers. A quick glance at her desk calendar wrenched a groan straight from her painted toenails. The shuffle board, who had managed to avoid her since the incident with Bay, had finally agreed to meet and plan their tournament. She had hoped to stop by the grocery store and buy cookies to bribe them. Instead, she hadn't even found time for McDonald's coffee, and without caffeine, she was running on empty.

She left everything on her desk for later and went to greet the kids. Now that the second week of camp was nearly over, they seemed to be finding their niche. Olivia fit in nicely, and this morning when she saw Tracy she was all smiles, walking between two other girls in their identical royal blue T-shirts with the camp logo of a grinning alligator wearing a baseball cap.

A group of boys ran up behind them, pushing and shoving each other until they saw Tracy standing, head cocked, as if to ask what they thought they were doing. They slowed and grinned. She knew from a few conversations she had overheard that these boys, the oldest in the program, thought she was hot. If trying to impress her kept them in line, that was okay with her.

The rest of the kids trickled in, and just as she thought she'd greeted the last of them, she saw Bay Egan bringing up the rear.

Since the start of youth camp, Bay had been surprisingly well-behaved. Before his first day, Tracy had conferred with his counselor, and together they had worked out a plan to deal with problems before they got out of hand. For help Tracy had fallen back on college lectures and experience with spoiled adults. In the end, the differences weren't huge.

But although he had not caused any real trouble, Bay had problems. He was a valued member of the swim team, but when it came to soccer and softball, he was the teammate nobody wanted. He was short for his age, and baby fat hadn't yet hardened into muscle. He wore orthopedic sneakers that didn't completely prevent one foot from turning in when he ran, so he stumbled, sometimes spectacularly, when he was out on the field. He was quick with sarcasm, and much too good at zeroing in on the other kids' shortcomings. On Wednesday his counselor had reported that he'd gotten into a scuffle. So even though he wasn't exactly an outcast, Tracy thought he was probably headed in that direction.

She told herself that changing Bay into a happy, popular camper was not in her job description. Her job was to make sure the camp ran smoothly and safely, to make sure the kids went home at summer's end pleading with their parents to send them again next year. She was not a therapist; she wasn't even a parent. What did she really know about a boy like Bay, who badly missed his mother and blamed the world for his loss?

She did all she could. She greeted him not like a potential serial killer, but like a boy who needed a warm welcome.

By ten o'clock she was ready for her meeting, but Gladys got to her first. She arrived in the rec room looking as crisp and comfortable as an English nanny, Mary Poppins with thirty extra pounds. In the past weeks Tracy had concluded that even if Woody was officially the director of the rec program, Gladys was just as important to its success. She was the day-to-day face, the person who knew all the secrets. She might not rub shoulders with town officials, write grants or search the county budget for funding, but she was the one who kept the building standing.

"About the arts-and-crafts program," Gladys said. "Our parents are wondering if there's more in store for their children than braiding plastic strips and glueing shells on Christmas balls."

Tracy smiled brightly. "Weren't some of those ornaments the best?"

"This is Florida. Every Christmas tree in the state's already in danger of toppling under the weight of them. Please don't tell me that next you'll be glueing seashells to picture frames."

"Well, of course not." Tracy wondered if there was time to cancel the order she'd made yesterday for little pine boxes and another case of craft glue.

"Then you're found a teacher?"

"I've tried, Gladys. Here, look…" Tracy rummaged through the papers on her desk and handed Gladys the record she'd kept of phone calls, some of which had been nothing more than thinly disguised pleas.

"We did leave you in something of a bind, I'm afraid."

Tracy nodded. "I'm afraid you did."

"But you seemed so resourceful. We were counting on that."

"Puh-leese! I even tried the local artists who exhibit in the corridors of the outlet mall, Gladys. I *went* to the outlet mall. I'm at the point where I'm willing to let the same people who paint portraits of collies in fluorescent greens and pinks teach our kids. But even they aren't interested. We don't pay enough, and we don't have a lot of money for supplies."

"No braiding, no shells. Find us a teacher or come up with something to impress the parents, okay? Something that teaches the campers a skill they don't already have. Go to the library and get a book on scrapbooking, or weaving or knitting—"

"Knitting?"

Gladys brightened. "You knit? That would be perfect. They'd be learning something they can use later."

"Of course I don't knit. You think I knit? But my neighbor crochets. Will that do?"

"Even better. One hook per child. Better than two knitting needles. Cheaper. And we have yarn on the supply shelves. I'm sure of it."

"She's older...."

"That's even better. The intergenerational touch is good."

Tracy thought of all the problems involved in getting Alice to say yes, and every one of them began with "Lee." But wouldn't teaching here be great for her? She needed a confidence boost. Her work was gorgeous, and she adored Olivia, so there was an excellent chance she liked children in general. If Alice taught the kids basics for a week, even two, then when most of them went on to something else, the ones who had really caught on to crocheting could continue with Alice.

She thought of another problem. "Boys, too?" she asked. "Are they going to throw a fit at something so girly?"

"Not if we let them make something like a beanbag, or maybe one of those Hacky Sack thingies."

Tracy thought that might just fly. " I'll see if I can talk her into it."

Gladys left, and Tracy went over everything she had gathered for her meeting with the shuffle board. She had information about tournaments in other places, official rules, issues they had to face, like publicity, whether food should be served, and whether to have a referee for every court, how to choose the youth who would compete for Palmetto Grove. The list was long.

She had struggled to be professional. But she wasn't optimistic. The shuffle board were out to get her, and that wasn't paranoia.

The picnic table outside the rec room door was their meeting site. She assembled bottles of cold water from the rec room fridge, and took notepads and copies of the agenda for each man. She was making notes when she heard footsteps. She smiled, but not too brightly, as the three old men, well, *shuffled* in her direction. She tipped her head to acknowledge their presence, but not too far. She waited for them to be seated, but not too long.

"Let's get this explanation over quickly," she said. "I was not trying to knock any of you to the ground when Bay came flying through here the last time we were together. I was trying to move you out of his way. So I hope we can get past that and move on to our agenda. I've given up hope you'll forgive me. I'm way past thinking you'll learn to like me. All I'm shooting for here is a chance to do a good job for you with this tournament."

She held up her copy of the agenda. "So would you like to get started?"

"We want to see you play first," Mr. Mustache said. Tracy knew he had a real name. Roger Goldworthy, retired chemical engineer, but he would always be Mr. Mustache to her.

"Whether I can play or not seems beside the point," Tracy said. "I'm not in the tournament. I'm just the organizer."

Mr. Mustache sat back, arms folded. "It's not beside the point to *us.*"

She didn't want to argue, and she knew better than to question. "How about if I just admit I'm lousy? I'm sure every one of you can beat me."

"Not sure enough," the hoverer said.

Tracy couldn't sing or play an instrument. She'd been a good, but not inspired, student at the small private girls' school her mother had favored because the surnames there showed up so often in *People* magazine. She was pretty, because a pretty enough face was something money could buy. She only had one attribute that set her apart. She had been blessed with superior coordination and stamina, and she used them well. She had been captain of the high school soccer team, the champion goalkeeper in lacrosse, a tennis star in her division at the country club. In college she had set the Long Beach record for the one hundred meter hurdles.

And now she was supposed to take on three old men who made the walk in from the parking lot look like a marathon.

"I'm not sure what point you're trying to prove." She held up her notes. "We have a lot to do today."

"None of which is going to get done until you've played a few frames with us."

She sighed. "Whatever. Pick your best man. I'm not going to play all three of you."

The men conferred. Today they were dressed in their Palmetto Grove Shuffleboard shirts, white polos with the crossed cues logo in red. Mr. Mustache stood. The shirt hung limply from his scrawny shoulders. His shorts were belted so tightly they puckered under the loops. She thought if he lost any more weight, his next tournament would have angels watching from the sidelines.

She got cues and discs from the supply cabinet; then they walked to the nearest court. Children were splashing in the swimming pool beyond, but for now, all the courts were empty.

"We'll lag for color choice," Mr. Mustache said. "Could you possibly know what that means?"

"We're supposed to shoot and see who gets a disc closest to that line…." She used the cue to point. "The person who wins gets to choose their color. Yellow shoots first."

He raised a brow, as if surprised.

"I've been boning up," she said.

"Anybody can read."

"Giving credit where credit's due isn't exactly your thing, is it?"

He stepped aside. "Ladies first. You get one freebie. The next one counts."

She had been reading, not practicing, but she was hopeful. Tracy placed her disc on the ground in what she hoped was the appropriate place and positioned her cue behind it. When he didn't correct her, she concentrated on the line she was supposed to hit and shoved. She pushed too hard, and the yellow disc kept sliding until it was well past the line. She shrugged, placed the second disc on the court and shoved again. This time, the disc stopped just short. It wasn't a perfect shot by any means, but the placement was nothing to be ashamed of.

She wondered how the old man was going to find the strength to shoot all the way to the line. He put his disc down, positioned himself behind it, placed his cue, and then, with what looked like less effort than it would take to swat a mosquito, sent his disc to the center of the line.

"My practice shot," he said.

"Hey, that was slick. I'm impressed."

He turned his head and wordlessly told her that her opinion of his skill mattered less than nothing. He sent the next disc, the one that counted, to exactly the same spot.

"So you choose." She went to the center, and gathered up her discs and put them in place; then she stepped away to let him decide.

"We'll shoot four frames," he said. "If you come out of this with half as many points as I do, we'll work with you. If I blow you off the face of the earth, we'll find somebody else, and you'll pay out of your salary."

"As if."

"And if you don't agree, we'll make your life hell."

She was beginning to get angry. "After what I've been through in the past months, nothing you could do would be a problem."

"I'm on the rec center board. Finance chairman."

"So? I'm a temporary employee. By the time you cut my salary, I'll be out of here."

"Yes, but I'm sure there are other people on staff you care about."

"Me? I just know their names."

"You do know the Woodleys? And how can I vote for extending their rather generous salaries if they've hired a bozo to run our tournament?"

She knew he was posturing. He wouldn't cut the Woodleys down like dead trees in the forest just to get even. But she was so mad that he had even suggested it, she took his dare.

"Okay, we'll do it your way. Just shoot."

He went to the line, flexed the fingers on his right hand, then positioned himself behind a yellow disc and slid it forward in one gracefully fluid motion. The disc seemed to float into place at the tip of the scoring triangle. Ten points.

He made a sweeping gesture with his hand. "Your turn."

Tracy concentrated hard. The position of his disc would make it next to impossible to score. So her job was to knock him out of position. Biting her lip, somehow she managed to do just that. Her own disc stopped on a line after pushing him out of the scoring area, but at least they were even.

Mr. Mustache didn't say anything. They did the same little dance again. Tracy was amazed she was able to knock him off twice in a row. The third time she wasn't so lucky. This time he missed the 10 and slid into position below it, scoring an 8. Tracy tried and failed to knock him off, but she scored 7 in the box just below him.

"So you have been practicing," he said.

"No, if I had, I would have gotten you that time, too."

"You're pretty sure of yourself for a beginner."

Tracy saw no reason to point out that she was good at every

sport she'd ever tried—with the possible exception of skydiving, which had scared her witless. Of course, if she'd known everything she knew today, she would have made good use of the experience anyway. She would have pushed CJ out of the plane before his parachute was in place.

Mr. Mustache put the last disc of the round into the 10 triangle rather than knock her out. She knocked him out again, but as she did, his disc shot forward and knocked hers out of the 7 area. The one she had just shot landed halfway into the 10 off section, but she was safe.

"One frame. I have a score of 8 and you have nothing," he said.

"That was just my warm-up."

He had a truly nasty laugh. The other men were chortling and poking each other on the sidelines as she and Mr. Mustache walked to the opposite end. She wanted to club every one of them with her cue. But now it was her turn to shoot first.

Just as she was about to she heard voices and saw a group of kids standing at the pool's edge watching them. She saw two of the counselors, high school juniors, a boy and girl, standing to one side chatting and batting their lashes at each other, but nothing seemed amiss, except that now Tracy had an audience.

She debated asking the counselors to remove their charges to wherever they were really supposed to be, but she knew better than to draw that much attention to what was going on. She blocked out everything except the next shot. Her disc stopped on the line between the two 8 areas. No points for her.

Mr. Moustache put his neatly into the 10. She managed to knock him out and in doing so, place herself firmly into an 8. She knew better than to rejoice. Mr. Mustache knocked her out but didn't score. She scored another 8 and he knocked her out again, this time scoring 7 in the process. Her fourth disc went into the 10 off section and stayed there. She thought it might be on the line, but she was afraid to look. Mr. Mustache scored an easy 10.

At the other end of the court she saw her problem disc was safely on the line. The score was now 25 to nothing, but at least it wasn't 25 to minus 10.

"Two more frames," Mr. Mustache said.

The kids were getting louder, cheering every time she shot and booing her opponent. She waved them to silence, but not with much enthusiasm. She wished their counselors would stop flirting and pay attention. Silently she prepared a lecture to the staff.

Thankfully the next frame was a draw. Each player scored 15 points. At least Tracy wasn't going to end up without any points at all.

She did the necessary math. Mr. Mustache had 40 points, while she only had 15. She had less than half the points he did, and unless a miracle occurred, she was going down. She had only managed 15 in the last frame because she had been the last to shoot. This time he would have the final opportunity to knock any scoring discs of hers to kingdom come.

The kids were shouting now, but she didn't have time to see what the problem was. She concentrated harder and shot, sliding her disc neatly into an 8 area. Mr. Mustache knocked her off, but didn't score. Of course he had all the points he needed now, as long as she didn't score more. And he was in the perfect position to make sure of that. She concentrated even harder. Two more discs, and two more failures to score. She had one more chance, and she knew that wherever she put this disc, Mr. Mustache would knock it out. She was going down, but not without a fight.

She was halfway through her shot when she heard a scream that sent her arm careening forward and the disc scooting like a rocket across the court. She stumbled, off balance and just managed to catch herself. Then, without so much as a glance to see what was happening, she took off across the other courts and toward the pool. She reached the pile of arms and legs that only a few moments before had been a group of rowdy little boys and began to toss them from one side to the other until she unearthed the two at the bottom.

By then the counselors had halted their flirtation and were gathering their flocks, pulling them to one side or the other. Tracy managed to grab the boy on the top and pull him off the one at the very bottom. Not surprisingly, that one was Bay.

"What exactly is going on here?" she demanded. The second boy, Adam somebody or other—she was in no shape for particulars—came at Bay again. The counselors had their hands full with the other kids, and Tracy caught a small fist and held it while she shielded Bay. Freckle-faced, spiky-haired Adam kicked out, and Tracy turned so Bay was protected, pushing Adam to one side as she did so the kick had no target.

"Cut that out right now!" She felt Bay trying to scramble to his feet, saw the furious Adam coming at him again. And suddenly Adam was up in the air, dangling between two old men in polo shirts.

"You listen to the lady," the hoverer said loudly, holding Adam off the ground with the help of his friend. "Or you'll be in that pool over there."

Bay was hiding behind Tracy now, and Adam stopped struggling. The counselors were still apologizing and pulling all the other kids back to the sidelines. Tracy waited; then, when it was clear Adam had control of himself, she asked the men to deposit him on the ground.

She would never underestimate the strength of the shuffle board again.

"Adam," she said, as calmly as she could, "you will go into the rec room right now and wait for me. Sit on the sofa and don't say a word. Do you understand? Go!" She pointed.

He did. She signaled the male counselor to follow and wait with Adam while the female merged the two groups.

She turned to Bay. "Are you hurt?"

He shook his head, eyes wide. He seemed to have lost his voice.

"I want you to wait with me," she told him. "Then you, Adam and I will sort this out. Understand? Don't move more than five feet from my body."

He nodded.

She caught the eye of the remaining counselor. "We'll talk later."

The girl nodded, too. There was a lot of that going around. Tracy watched as she led the campers away.

Finally she turned to the old men. Mr. Mustache had joined them. "That was much appreciated. Thank you."

They nodded, too, and she wondered if she had suddenly been transported to a world of bobble-head dolls. She didn't know what else to say.

Mr. Mustache broke the silence. "You sent that last disc all the way up to Jacksonville."

She shrugged. "You won. I lost." She wondered where the money would come from for a tournament director.

"I didn't play my last disc," he said.

"It doesn't matter. You still won."

He marched back to the court, and after she made sure that Bay was glued to her side, she followed. She had to cross the court anyway to get back to the rec room. She watched him position himself behind his final disc, and she wondered why he wanted to make her feel worse. Then carefully, slowly, he pushed the disc with a practiced professional thrust. As she watched the disc glided across the court and landed right in the middle of the minus 10.

"So, if my math is right," Mr. Mustache said, "I end up with 30 points, and you have 15. That means we're stuck with you."

She stared at the faraway discs. Then she turned her gaze to him. "Why did you do that?"

"Once upon a time, about a million years ago by your reckoning, I got into a fight pretty much like that one over there and ended up on the bottom of the pile. I still remember how it felt when nobody jumped in to help. Maybe there's more to you than I thought."

"I really can't promise there is."

"Well, I guess we'll see."

She smiled, and miracle of miracles, so did he. Maybe the teeth, or at least some of them, weren't real, but the smile was absolutely genuine.

chapter twenty-one

By the time the afternoon ended and everything was in order for the following Monday, Tracy was completely exhausted. She and Adam's mother had spoken at length about how to handle the boys' fight. Luckily his mother was a sensible woman with two older sons. She said Adam had been growing increasingly upset with Bay, who had been teasing him about his new haircut, and she had planned to call the center that afternoon to discuss it. When Tracy suggested that Adam and Bay be given a choice between picking up litter on the athletic fields Monday morning or missing a week of camp, she agreed. She was certain that Adam, normally an affable boy, would choose the litter.

Tracy wasn't as certain about Bay. First she called Marsh at his office, identifying herself simply as Tracy Deloche, not Tracy Deloche rec-center-supervisor-in-charge-of-his-son's-welfare, and as she'd assumed, she was not put through, the excuse being that he was out. Then she called the Egan home and left a long message, ending by asking Marsh to come in with Bay on Monday morning.

That was so much more fun than actually speaking to the man.

Of course, she knew what Marsh would hear from his son, because she'd heard it herself. Bay wasn't to blame. All he'd done was point out that Adam looked like a woodpecker, so it wasn't his fault that Adam punched him. Tracy had told Bay to get used to being punched, then, because unless he learned to keep those kinds of observations to himself, he would be—and often.

Once she got home, she showered and changed into a white peasant blouse that slid provocatively over one shoulder, and a pair of tight capris in a lizardy print. She sprayed the air with Island Capri and walked slowly through the cloud. She was ready to nail down an arts-and-crafts teacher.

At the door to Alice's cottage, she knocked, then adjusted her blouse, snagging the neck with her index finger and tugging it lower. Lee's Saab was sitting in the driveway, but Alice answered.

"Hi," Tracy said. "I saw these at the grocery store, and I thought you and your family would enjoy them." She held out a plastic tray of dried fruit dipped in dark chocolate.

"My…" Alice took the tray as if it held exotic treasure. "This is a…treat." She smiled happily.

Tracy felt just the tiniest stab of guilt. She was doing this for the rec center, and she really believed teaching a class would be great for Alice, as well. She was just sorry she'd felt compelled to begin with a bribe.

"I have a question. Do you have a moment?"

Alice stepped aside so Tracy could enter. "Please…"

Music, someone like Bing Crosby or Frank Sinatra, drifted from an old stereo. Tracy heard the sound of the television, and Olivia poked her head around the corner and smiled shyly. "You look pretty."

Tracy didn't live for those words anymore, but they were still nice to hear. "It's very kind of you to say so."

"When I grow up, I'm going to dress the way you do."

"When you grow up, we'll go shopping."

Olivia giggled and disappeared again.

Tracy looked around. "Is Lee home?"

"Still at work."

"I saw his car in the driveway."

"He bought a new one. To impress…"

Tracy knew that for a Realtor, a new car was a visible sign of success that reassured new clients. Still, she was surprised that when very little was selling, Lee had been able to afford one. She hoped he hadn't gone too far into debt.

She wondered if she should wait. She'd hoped to ask Alice and Lee about the teaching position at the same time, with the idea that Alice would be so excited, Lee wouldn't have the heart to issue warnings. Afterward she planned to pull him aside and explain that she would keep a careful eye on Alice's classes, and bring her right home if need be. And yes, she had planned to use her feminine wiles. This was all-out war.

Since she was here already, she decided to explain the situation to Alice. Then, if she seemed excited, over the weekend Tracy would talk to Lee.

They sat, and she told Alice the whole story. "So we'd love to have you. We don't pay a lot…." She named a figure broken down by the week.

"You want…*me?*"

"We sure do. We want the kids to learn a new skill they can use in years to come. And this'll be great for their hand-eye coordination. Fine motor skills. Self-esteem. Do you think you could do it, Alice? We need you."

"I taught…before."

"Oh, sweet, you're experienced! What could be better?"

"I liked it." Alice nodded. "Karen's Girl Scout…troop. Scarves."

"Perfect!" Tracy told Alice about Gladys's idea for Hacky Sacks. "I can look online this weekend and see if I can find a pattern. Are you willing?"

Alice looked so pleased; then, little by little, her expression clouded. "Lee will say no."

Tracy wanted to remind her that she was free to do as she pleased. But Alice had to live in the same house with her son-in-law.

"I can talk to Lee," she offered. "I had intended to tonight."

"He won't...budge."

Tracy had been this close to snaring Alice. "Okay, how about we just don't tell him right away? I'll ask Wanda if she'll drive you to the center after he takes Olivia to camp Monday morning. We'll do it that way for a few days. Then, when we tell him how well you're doing, he won't worry anymore."

Alice chewed her lip.

"You'll enjoy seeing Olivia's program," Tracy said. "You haven't seen what we're doing at camp yet."

Alice nodded, as if she had come to a conclusion. "He worries...."

"It's understandable."

"We'll see...." Finally Alice lifted her head. "Yes, I'll be ready."

They talked about what they would need for the first day, and Tracy promised to stop by the craft store and buy a supply of crochet hooks. Alice looked worried but resolute when Tracy waved a final goodbye. Tracy wished there was a way to explain to Lee that being overly concerned about Alice was causing more stress. But people were often blind to the truth, even when it was right under their noses.

Back at home, she realized she was all dressed up with no place to go. That seemed sad. It was Friday night, and she was all alone again. Memories of her former life were almost a physical pain. She was starving for weekend evenings out, for meaningless conversation, for designer labels and celebrity chefs. Even for a husband to take care of her.

Then she remembered the price she had paid.

She supposed the logical solution was to throw on her work clothes and see what she could do on the tile. After a number of failures, she had become adept at cutting tile, and she planned to work on the floor this weekend. She had already made such headway that she hoped to have the tiles in place by Sunday night so she could start on the grout. She already loved the floor.

She was just summoning the energy to change clothes and get started when somebody knocked. She wondered if Lee had gotten home. She hoped Alice hadn't changed her mind and told him about teaching at the center. Without Tracy there to defend her, Alice didn't have a prayer.

She opened the door and found Marsh Egan on her threshold. Before she could decide whether to slam the door, he moved subtly closer, planted one foot in the opening and eliminated the option.

"You've obviously been home," she said, letting her gaze drift down to his sandaled feet. "Unless you went to the office in shorts. So you know we're supposed to talk about Bay on *Monday.* Last time I checked, this was Friday."

"I assume you tried to call me at work?"

"Correct."

"And my secretary told you I was gone."

"You have psychic gifts."

"I *was* gone, as a matter of fact. She wasn't dissing you. I appreciate you leaving a message at the house, too."

"That's why they pay me the big bucks."

"Bay tells me you jumped in to save him today."

"More or less."

"He says Adam would have made toast out of him."

She almost smiled. "He was never in danger. At worst, Adam might have bloodied his nose." She cocked her head. "Bay needs a leash on his tongue."

"He's the progeny of two attorneys. What are the chances?"

"Pretty good, if he keeps getting pounded, because he's also smart."

"Why do you only see him at his worst?"

She shook her head. "If Bay throws a tantrum in the forest and there's nobody there to see it, is it still a tantrum? Your son's problems are completely real, whether I'm there to witness them or not."

"He's a good kid."

She didn't like Marsh Egan, but she did think he was trying to be a good father. "If I thought he *wasn't,* he wouldn't be in our program."

"He likes you."

She realized she was relaxing. Marsh Egan was not going postal, which she'd expected. If he'd been anybody else, she would almost think this was an apology of sorts for his son's behavior.

"Look, I like him, too. Just don't tell him, okay? Somebody's got to make him walk the straight and narrow, and at day camp, that's me."

"So now that we're all touchy-feely, you and me, are you going to sell Wild Florida your land for a hundred dollars an acre?"

"Why no, I was thinking more along the lines of tossing you off of it, now that we're all done with the lovey-dovey stuff."

He smiled. He really did have a nice smile, she had to admit. With twilight approaching, the sun cast interesting shadows on his burnished skin, and for the first time, she couldn't deny he was more or less an attractive man. Not L.A. handsome, and not appealing in the most traditional ways. But she liked the way the skin around his eyes crinkled when he smiled, and the pleasing sweep of his jaw.

"Don't toss me anywhere," he said. "Let me show you something you've never seen."

"A legal document promising I can sell my land without interference?"

"Birds."

"Omigosh, I'm so sorry! I've seen birds already. Was I supposed to wait for you?"

His smile widened. "Were you always like this?"

"It's taken me a lot of years and one hilarious divorce to perfect it."

"I'll tell you what. Come with me, and we can swap divorce stories. Mine for yours. No holds barred."

For a moment she thought he was actually asking her out. She frowned and leaned forward. "Come with you?"

"I promise an evening you'll never forget."

"You're going to take me somewhere and feed me to the alligators, aren't you?"

"No, I'm going to take you somewhere, then I'm going to feed you my cooking."

She realized he wasn't kidding. "Just like that? You want me to drop everything and come with you?"

"Yep. That's what I want."

She considered the alternatives. Tile adhesive or Marsh Egan. In the end, home cooking won, but the margin of victory was narrow. "Should I change?"

"I'd hate to be responsible for that." His gaze flicked down and then back up. "I'd *really* hate to be responsible for that. We'll be careful."

Admiration from Marsh Egan was so odd that she ignored it, in case she had misunderstood. "That doesn't sound promising."

"I promise you'll be in one piece when the trip is over."

"Is Bay coming, too?"

"Bay is staying home for the weekend with no privileges. Plus the indignity of a babysitter."

"Oh…" She was glad to hear Marsh had taken the fight seriously.

"I have everything we'll need," he prompted. "Ready?"

As she would ever be. She grabbed her purse, locked the door and followed Marsh to his pickup.

They drove in silence toward the bridge, passing several small groups of houses and the remnants of an old fish camp, but instead of crossing to town, they followed a sandy path past the burial mound, then through scrubby forest, until it ended at a house that looked as if it had been there since the first European settlers arrived. A steep tin roof hung over a porch that wrapped around the whole structure. Much of the porch was screened, but rough-hewn siding was still visible. The house stood on substantial brick pilings and looked completely at home among trees bearded with Spanish moss.

"These Cracker houses were built with weather in mind," Marsh said as they got out. "Overhanging roofs, air flow underneath, multiple windows with cross ventilation. The south side is completely shaded."

"Do you live here?"

"We do since Bay and I came back from New York. It's been in my family for four generations. I've made some major changes to make it more energy efficient, but it's still the same old house."

"It actually survived all the hurricanes that came through?"

"Not without damage, but yes."

She studied the house. There was an indigenous grace to the design, as if from the beginning the plan had been to ensure that life inside would be comfortable and simple.

She noted most of the windows were open. "Tell me you have air-conditioning."

"When we need it. The breezes are great, and the ceiling fans work wonders, but humidity's always the villain."

"How did those previous generations stand it?"

"My grandmother slept on the porch between May and the end of September. Even when the rain swept sideways."

"So where are these birds?"

"I'll show you."

She hadn't expected a canoe trip.

The canoe was made of wood—hand-crafted, she guessed—and both sleek and light. She saw Marsh watching for a reaction. She wasn't sure what he expected. A protest, perhaps? Or a complaint that her hair might frizz? Instead, as if it were a matter of course, she accepted insect spray, then helped him push the canoe into the water until only the stern remained on the ground. When he gestured, she stepped in and positioned herself at the front. She was ready when he pushed off, paddle in hand. Then she plunged hers into the water and paddled as he guided them into deeper water.

Little Palmetto Bay was, as the name claimed, little enough. The bridge crossing it was only a mile and a quarter long, and relatively low, and until it had been built in the 1970s, Palmetto Grove Key could only be reached by boat. Once a small commercial port, the harbor at Palmetto Grove had silted with time and changes in the landscape, and now was only a pleasure boat destination. Because of this, the bay was in less danger than some in more desirable locales.

"Where are your mangroves?" she asked, surprised that the bay was so easily reached, with nothing but reeds and waving grass to slow them.

"The last hurricane rearranged the coastline and destroyed them. Just a bit farther to your right, they're beginning to come back."

"Mother Nature, the great developer."

"Eventually, I hope, ours will begin to recolonize. In the meantime, I can put my canoe in at my house instead of up the road at the boat launch."

"So explain to me why you can look at this scenery every day, enjoy the water and the sunsets and the alligators, and the people who would buy condos at Happiness Key aren't allowed to."

"You know the difference."

She did, of course. Marsh and his house probably did have an impact on the environment, but not on the scale of a major development. The land he lived on had probably looked much the same centuries ago. When a developer completed Happiness Key, everything in the vicinity would be different.

"What's to say that even if I sold my land to Wild Florida, somebody else wouldn't come in and build another development nearby?"

"Some of the key is protected by the state or county. Some of it's already been left to Wild Florida in trust. You have the only significant acreage in jeopardy. Yours is the only parcel that's both large enough and well-suited for building. Yours is the only one that stretches from one side of the key to the other, and nearly out to the point."

"Which makes it that much more valuable, I'm afraid." They were gliding into the bay. The sun was low in a sky rapidly changing colors. They were bathed in violet and hot pink.

Marsh turned the canoe so they were moving along the shore. From this vantage point, everything looked so different. Not simply patched together by unkempt scrub, but rich in texture and color. Startled birds rose toward the sky, some with snowy wings spread wide and legs dangling low. Tree limbs hung out over the water, and she thought she saw a snake hanging from one. She made certain not to search the bank for alligators.

"Hold up." Marsh stopped the canoe, and she twisted to look at him.

"Let me show you something while we still have good light." He took a quart canning jar and scooped it into the water. Then he passed it to her. She had to lean back to get a good hold on it, but she finally wrapped her fingers around it, brushing his as she did.

"What do you see?" he asked

"Not drinking water, that's for sure." She held the jar up to the light; then, delighted, she smiled. "What are all these creatures?"

"Life begins in places just like this. Brackish estuaries. You're holding the result in your hands."

She saw fish that looked smaller than a grain of rice darting in circles, perplexed, she supposed, that their world had suddenly narrowed. She saw what might be a tiny seahorse and several shrimp, other things too unformed yet to name. But the jar, one random scoop of water, teemed with life.

"When you look at this, it's not so hard to believe we came from the sea, is it?" She gently submerged the jar, then turned it upside down. When she lifted it, the jar was empty again.

"This is a tidally influenced wetland area. We have twelve islands here in the bay. Some are covered with mangroves, some with sea grape and cabbage palms. The number changes from one generation to another. But all of them are habitat for what you saw in the jar, and for birds and animals. I'll take you to one."

Ten minutes later, he made good on his promise. The island Marsh had paddled to wasn't large—under two acres for, certain—but it was thick with vegetation. And as they moved toward it, the little island came alive as birds began to light in preparation for the night.

They stayed back far enough not to threaten them. Tracy was enchanted. Against the rosy sky, the birds were a moving tapestry.

"Herons, egrets and pelicans nest here," Marsh said quietly. "We document them. We've had roseate spoonbills—real movie stars, those guys—though not many, and wood storks, but not this time of year. Someone photographed mangrove cuckoos last summer. But I could list birds and bore you all night. So let's just watch them coming home."

She didn't want to fall under the spell of this place. Her life was too complex, too precarious, to think about the effects of development on the waterfowl and inhabitants of these waters. And she wasn't convinced that developing Happiness Key in accordance with the regulations already in place would disturb any of it.

But she wasn't convinced it wouldn't, either.

Marsh finally turned the canoe back to land. Tracy assisted as he guided, enjoying the feel of the water lapping gently at the sides, the rhythmic pull of the paddle. It was nearly dark by the time they got to his house. She got out and pulled the canoe forward, and he joined her. Together they tugged it up the sand until it was well away from the water.

"You handled that paddle like a pro."

"Well, you know, in between having my legs waxed and my hair straightened, I have learned a few things in life."

"There's that attitude again." He started toward the house, and she caught up.

"What's for dinner?"

"Why, are you hungry?"

She was. Ravenous. "I missed breakfast and had a PowerBar for lunch."

"No wonder you stay so skinny."

"Skinny?"

"Well, something closely approximating it." He glanced at her. "Bay's mother says she lost twenty pounds after I moved back here and stopped cooking for her."

"You're friends?"

"That would be a positive spin, but I don't hold the divorce against her. I just married a woman I had nothing in common with."

"Kind of like if you married me."

This time he grinned. "Nothing that extreme. Sylvia just lives to work, that's all. She's a top-notch criminal attorney. She'll be writing closing arguments on her deathbed. She gave birth to Bay and went back to the office two days later, and didn't see him again for a week. She wasn't even sure it was the same kid when she came home for a meal and a good night's sleep. She thought the nurse had traded him for a better-looking baby."

That description made even Tracy squirm. "My ex was a workaholic, too. If he wasn't in prison, we could introduce them. Of course, since she probably wouldn't have time to spend with him anyway, they still might be a good fit."

"Sylvia might spring him. She's that good. Would you want that?"

"Luckily, I don't have to waste time worrying. CJ really dug his hole deep."

They climbed the steps to the porch and opened the front door. She expected to be greeted by Bay; instead an older woman in a Wild Florida T-shirt and a long salt-and-pepper braid came in from the kitchen, followed by two black labs.

"I let the poor kid watch a video, and he fell sound asleep in front of the television. I think he'll be out for a while."

Marsh introduced Tracy. The woman turned out to be his office manager. She said goodbye, kissed Marsh on the cheek, called the dogs and left.

"I watch her mutts when she goes on vacation. She watches my kid. Actually, she'd do it without the trade. Her kids are all grown."

Tracy's stomach rumbled, and he laughed. "Come on. I'll see what you can gnaw on while I cook."

She liked the inside of his house. She wasn't sure what she had expected. Big Mouth Billy Bass singing from the wall. Lava lamps. Framed photographs of Marsh and friends being hauled off to jail. Instead, the house was open and airy, with lots of exposed wood and rooms that flowed into each other. Sofas upholstered in dark leather, chairs upholstered in red plaid, simple rugs over old pine floors. Embellishments were sparse. Some photos of Marsh and Bay together. Some interesting sculptures, and carvings of woodland creatures and birds. Lots of books on lots of bookshelves.

The kitchen was definitely not the original. In fact, she thought it had probably been recently remodeled. Stainless-steel appliances, concrete counters, Shaker-style cherry cabinets. Pans hung from a heavy steel rack over the stove, well used and well scrubbed.

"Did you do any of this yourself?" She thought about her floor.

"A lot of it. It's a good way to blow off steam."

He opened the refrigerator, and took out a plastic bag of sliced vegetables and a tub of dip. "This will hold you until the real stuff appears." He handed them to her and nodded toward a cabinet. "Plates and bowls that way."

She scooped some of the dip, Southwestern ranch and low-fat, into a small bowl, put it on a plate and surrounded it with the vegetables. Then she went to stand near the stove so he could share.

"Are you one of those women who's going to tell me what to do in my own kitchen?" Marsh was still in the refrigerator removing ingredients.

"Me? I don't cook. What would I know?"

He closed the door. "How do you eat?"

She clicked her teeth together. "Like this."

"Are you one of those raw foodies?"

"No, I love to eat. I'm just too lazy to learn how to make it happen. We had a cook in California, and we ate out when she wasn't there. Mostly now I just eat a handful of this and a couple of spoonfuls of that."

"You had your own cook?"

"How far the mighty have fallen, huh?"

He was rinsing fish fillets in the sink now, and setting them to dry on paper towels. "Tell me if I'm wrong, but when I said I didn't hold my divorce against Sylvia, I didn't hear any shrieks from you. You don't hold your husband responsible for yours?"

"CJ? He was completely responsible, except for that big, big part where I married him in the first place. And it's kind of hard to get around that."

"So why did you marry him?"

"He was bright and charming, handsome, and filthy rich. He needed a trophy wife, and I thought I needed somebody to take care of me."

"Did you?"

"Maybe I did, but I don't now."

"So he's in jail, and you're here starting a new life. And you don't think about springing him?"

"I never said that. I said—"

"That luckily you didn't have to waste time worrying."

"You're making me sound shallow again. You do it so well."

He turned and shook his head. "You're really off the mark

this time. I'm just trying to figure out how somebody gets on with their life after something like that. I've been divorced four years, and I still wake up at night and think Sylvia's—"

"Asleep beside you?"

"No, back at the office. Working on a brief."

"Oh. Got it."

"So?" He took down a cast-iron frying pan and set it on the stove. He poured oil in to heat and began to bread the fish. Turning it, sprinkling seasoning, turning it again.

"CJ set the tone. I—" She looked away, trying to figure out how to say this. Then she shrugged. "From the moment he realized he was going down, he was on a solo ride. I don't think he was capable of worrying about the effect on me or anybody else who was involved. It was all about him. Once the shock wore off and I started to pull myself together, I knew the only way I was going to survive was to do the same thing and just worry about myself. I realized CJ wouldn't even notice if I worried about him, or if I was furious or in total despair. Nobody else was on his radar. Actually, nobody ever had been. But the big bang was what forced me to see the truth."

"That's a big hurt. Knowing you're not even a little bit important to the person who was most important to you."

"Are we talking about me? Or you?"

"It's a scary thing, Trace, to realize you and I have something in common. Even down to denying that the divorce was as bad as having our hearts plucked out of our chests."

"I didn't say that."

"You didn't have to." He glanced over his shoulder. "Was anybody there for you?"

She gave one shake of her head.

"You're a lot stronger than you look. It's going to be harder than I thought to knock you down to size."

"It's going to take an army."

He laughed. "Pour us some wine, will you?"

She moved beside him and peered into the pan, which was sizzling. "Are you really going to fry that fish?"

"You were expecting sushi? In these parts we call that bait." Then, before she could protest, he put a fishy hand under her chin and tilted it, probably leaving crumbs. He bent down and kissed her. Just lightly. The way one friend kisses another. "Be a spoiled brat for the rest of the night, okay? It will make things easier for both of us."

She didn't know what to say. She didn't know what to do. She smiled up at him, her most blindingly expensive smile, then went to search for a bottle of wine.

chapter twenty-two

By the time Wanda dragged herself out of bed on Saturday morning, Ken was gone. No surprise. Old news. Package delivered in last year's mail. Her husband was as useless as a screen door on a submarine, and she'd given up on him. What surprised her was that Chase was gone, as well. The fact that the greyhound hadn't nudged her awake so she could stumble along the road clutching his leash while he peed on everything in sight was even more surprising. *That* was worth pondering.

She pondered on the front stoop, looking this way and that. The fact that the two males who lived in the house were both gone could be significant. Maybe Ken was walking Chase.

"Fat chance...."

The other scenario was more likely. Ken hadn't closed the door securely on his way to wherever, and Chase had let himself out afterward. She wondered if the day and a half that the dog had been with her was long enough that he would find his way home. It hardly seemed likely.

"Well, ain't that a kick in the head?"

She considered what to do, but she realized that whatever

she did, coffee had to come first. She propped open the screen door, in case Chase came back on his own, then went to start a pot. In the kitchen, she found a nearly full one. At least Ken hadn't been gone long, since it hadn't boiled away to nothing. Even if Chase had escaped, he couldn't have gone far. Under normal circumstances he might already be back at the track, looking for the nasty man with the cigar. But Chase's leg was bandaged, so he was running slow these days.

She got the largest mug in the cupboard and filled it. Back in her bedroom, she tried to figure out what to wear. Her brain still wasn't operating properly, not even after two big swigs. She was still staring into the top drawer of her dresser, trying to remember what she was looking for, when she heard the screen door slam and the frantic scurrying of paws.

She turned as Chase came limping into the bedroom. At the sight of her, he sped up the limp and before she could stop him, he jumped up and braced himself against her chest with his one good front leg to lick her face.

Ken appeared next. "You got yourself some kind of dog here, Wanda."

She kissed Chase's nose; then she gently pushed him to the floor. That was easy enough now, considering his injuries, but when he was all recovered, she didn't think anything was going to be easy about having this dog living in her house. Except that he was going to be easy to love.

"Did you take him for a walk?"

"We were both itching to get outside."

"After the money I paid that vet to prevent fleas, he'd better not be itching."

"Hope you weren't worried. I didn't want to wake you and tell you we were going."

"Surprised is all. You've been ignoring that dog like he was a new piece of furniture. 'Course, you've only seen him for a second or two here and there."

"I can tell the difference between a dog and a dining-room table."

She sounded grudging, she knew, but she had to say something. She hadn't drilled gratitude into her kids just to ignore good manners now. "I appreciate the help, Kenny. And the extra sleep."

"Had breakfast yet?"

"A couple swallows of coffee."

"Dog and I are starving. What do you feed him?"

She told him where the food was, and how much the vet had recommended. "His name's Chase. Chase the Suspect, if you want the whole truth."

Ken grinned. Her heart felt as if it were tying itself into a double knot. She hadn't seen him smile like that for what seemed like years. She was instantly wary.

"You picked this dog 'cause you're married to a cop?" he asked.

"I used to watch him run whenever I got the chance. Made a little money on him, too, from time to time."

"Not half as much as you've spent on him now, I bet. Chase and me, we'll put something together for breakfast. Go ahead and take a shower."

"You got some reason to be so nice to me this morning? Last time I looked, this was just a regular day in June. Months after the birthday you probably don't even remember you forgot."

Ken reached down and scratched Chase, who had gone to stand beside him. "I'm just hungry for pancakes."

She didn't know what was up. She was half-convinced Ken was trying to butter her up along with the pancakes, so he could admit to something once she was in a better mood. Like the fact he'd hired a divorce lawyer, or the name of a woman he was having an affair with, or how he'd lost their life savings in a series of all-night poker games because he had been so depressed.

"I bought real maple syrup last week," she said, turning back to the dresser. "Have at it. I'll get there eventually."

"As dogs go, this one's not too bad."

She heard them leave, the man and the dog. Together.

She stared at the neat pile of clothes a little longer. What exactly did a woman wear when she had no idea where her life was going?

Janya was so proud that she had easily passed all the necessary tests to receive her learner's restricted license, but now she was facing her first real lesson. Rishi had taken the bus to his office this morning and left the keys on the table for her. Just looking at them made her stomach churn.

He had offered to take her for her first drive, but she'd told him that she'd promised Wanda that privilege. It wasn't really a deception. Wanda had offered, and Janya had accepted. Of course, the real truth was that having Rishi beside her would be distracting. He would instruct with the same enthusiasm he used when he showed her anything new. He would not understand that she was anxious. He would be so certain she was going to do well that he would chatter about things that didn't matter.

Wanda would chatter, too, but as she did, she would point out the things Janya needed to know. Despite the unpleasantness that had passed between them, Janya thought she could trust Wanda in this. In the matter of teaching someone to drive, strong opinions were not a bad thing.

She was preparing for the lesson when Wanda knocked, then opened the door and stuck her head inside. "I can come back in fifteen minutes if you're not ready now."

Janya was tying her first shoe. "No, please come in. This will give me less time to worry."

"About what? You've been riding in cars all your life...."
She frowned. "Or maybe not."

"The last time I rode an elephant into the jungle, I decided I did not like being so high."

Wanda got the joke and smiled. "Well, I can't help that I've never been to India, Janya. We're not all born in interesting places."

"We do have elephants, and camels. Also trains, buses, cars, rickshaws, tuk tuks and feet."

"Tuk tuks?"

"A motorized cart. Three wheels. Very unsafe."

"Do you miss all that?"

Just weeks ago the question might have brought tears to Janya's eyes. Now she wondered. The country and its people, yes. The customs, culture, sights and smells. Yes. Her parents? That was a different question entirely. These were the people who had chosen not to defend and protect her.

"I think if I spend too much time missing India, I will spend too little time learning to like the United States." Janya got to her feet, but reluctantly.

"Harder for you than me, that's for sure. Sometime we'll drive down to Miami and I'll show you all my favorite places."

Janya realized this wasn't an empty offer. At some time, perhaps when she wasn't paying careful attention, she had moved from the role of colorful neighbor to be watched from afar and distrusted, to colorful neighbor and friend. Wanda was so much like women she had known in Mumbai, friends of her mother's who had protected what belonged to them with a ferocious ardor. The thought made her feel more at home.

"And someday I will show you India," she said. "It would be the trip of a lifetime."

"Can we go to the Taj Mahal?"

"Our very first stop."

"Of course, it might be hard, seeing as it's a romantic destination and all, and I'll probably be divorced."

"I saw your husband walking Chase this morning."

"I'm not sure what got into him. He made me breakfast, too."

"Those are gifts to be enjoyed."

Wanda clicked her tongue, and Janya was not certain what that meant here in Florida. Wisely, she said nothing more.

Wanda made a tour of the room, examining things. "I like what you've done. These colors, are they traditional where you come from?"

Janya had painted the little rooms colors that did remind her of home. Deep gold. Creamy turquoise. Their bedroom was the same dark red as the *puja* room—she had asked Rishi to buy too much paint. Batiks hung on the walls with tribal paintings.

"They make me feel happier," she said.

Wanda stopped beside the table near the sofa; then she lifted the pastel drawing that Janya had done of Olivia and stared at it. "Janya, who drew this?"

Janya was sorry she hadn't put the drawing away. She had worked on it more this morning to calm herself. She had taken the quick charcoal sketch she had done almost two weeks ago and used it as a basis for the pastel portrait. So far she was pleased.

"I did, but I've yet to finish."

Wanda looked up at her. "It's amazing. You've caught every little thing about her."

Janya was warmed by the compliment. She knew Wanda did not come by them easily, making them more precious. "I thank you."

"And what is this?" Wanda lifted another drawing Janya had been working on. "What an elaborate design."

"It's *mehendi*. It came to me last night. Do you know about henna tattoos?"

"Not sure."

"It's an ancient art, a way of adorning the body that is not permanent. We do it for weddings and other special occasions. I have been thinking about trying one. Just for fun."

"It would be beautiful. Anyone would love to have this on some body part or the other." Wanda looked up. "You never told us you were such a talented artist."

Janya's smile slowly faded. "Wanda, perhaps this is not such a good idea."

Wanda understood she wasn't talking about the tattoo. "Are you scared to drive?"

It was nice to admit the truth, something Janya might not have felt comfortable doing with Rishi. "My knees may not hold me."

"We'll just cruise around a little with me at the wheel, so I can get used to your car. That way I can tell you what you need to know about it. Then, when you're ready, we'll just slide you in there and I'll show you everything. Heck, out here at this end of the key, there's hardly one bit of traffic. You can go two miles an hour and nobody will care. But you have to do this, Janya. Driving is what it'll take to have a real life here in Florida. And don't you deserve one?"

Then, as if she understood what was needed, Wanda came close, put her arms around Janya, and pulled her close for a reassuring and very American hug. "Now, off we go, little sister. Just you and me and that car out there. Let's go and raise some hell."

Grouting was not as much fun as Tracy had hoped. She had decided to take a break from cutting and placing the rest of the tile to give grouting a whirl, but there was obviously a learning curve on the use of the rubber "float," which didn't float at all but looked more like the squeegees that her window cleaners had used in Bel Air. She was supposed to squish a nasty-looking toothpastey goo into the spaces, then make smoothing sweeps across the surface. She discovered that an old toothbrush helped pack and smooth the grout to her specifications, but twenty minutes later, when she was supposed to start wiping away the excess with a damp sponge, she hadn't gotten very far.

"Are we having fun yet?" Tracy wiped her forehead with the back of her hand. She envisioned packing the very last seam on the day the wrecking ball came to destroy the cottage. She was beginning to understand why the tile installers had wanted so much for the job.

She got to her feet and stretched. She felt like one of the pineapples in Alice's tablecloth. Knotted and shaped to fit somebody else's creative vision. She stood on tiptoe, just in time to catch a glimpse of Wanda coming up the walk.

She answered the door before Wanda knocked. "Please tell me you want to take me away from this." She gestured behind her.

"It's gorgeous," Wanda said, poking her head in. "When are you going to do my floors?"

"At night. In your dreams."

"Janya and me had us an adventure. Want to hear about it?"

"Will it get me out of here?"

"Far enough. Janya says she's got a special place on the beach. We bought sandwiches at that little store by the bridge. Uncommonly good ones, too. Those little hole-in-the-wall places know how to feed people. Put on your bathing suit. Then we'll come back and get you. It's a celebration."

Tracy tried to follow that. "What are we celebrating?"

"Janya and me are still alive, that's what. We'll meet you back here in about fifteen minutes."

"I have bottled water. And fruit drinks."

"Good. I have pie. Different crust," Wanda said over her shoulder.

Tracy did as she was told. Fifteen minutes later she had donned her bikini and cover-up, slathered her skin with sunblock, knotted her hair on top of her head, found a beach hat, filled a cooler with drinks, and put new batteries in her portable iPod speakers. She was good to go.

Wanda returned with Janya, and she had Olivia and Alice in tow, too. They might as well have waved a sign saying Lee was gone. Tracy wondered about that. He spoke often about Alice and his concerns about her health, but he rarely seemed to be home to monitor things. Either he was struggling hard to provide for them in a difficult economic climate, or he really wasn't as worried as he claimed. She hoped that meant he would be okay with Alice teaching at the center.

"Look what we found," Wanda said. "Are you ready?" She wore a muumuu that looked as if it was straight from a discount beachwear store in Honolulu. Tracy was nearly blinded by orange hibiscus.

Tracy locked the door behind her. Security was a bigger issue now that Janya's patio had been trashed. No one else had been affected, but she felt less safe here than she had a few weeks ago. She had asked Wanda to tell her husband what had transpired, but short of developing an informal neighborhood watch system for the five cottages, there really wasn't much they could do.

Wanda had brought beach blankets. Two of them. And, of course, she'd brought Chase, who was slow on his three good legs, but kept up. Alice had chips and fresh fruit, plus a half-gallon Thermos of lemonade. Olivia wore a frilly bathing suit, over-size sunglasses on top of her head, and flip-flops sporting plastic daisies. She carried a book, too. Tracy glanced at it, impressed.

"*Treasure Island.* Robert Louis Stevenson," Tracy read. "Wow, heady stuff."

"Olivia and I share a love of pirate novels," Wanda said.

"Only she's not quite old enough for the pirates I love best." She wiggled her eyebrows.

Tracy laughed. "The Johnny Depp kind, not the dirty, snaggle-toothed, patch-over-a-blind-eye variety?"

"I don't know about Johnny Depp and all that eyeliner," Wanda said.

"He's even better looking in real life than he is on the screen. Interesting, too."

"Well, that just about says it all. Just think, you went from knowing Johnny Depp to this. No wonder you shake that hoity-toity of yours every chance you get."

Tracy punched her on the arm. "Johnny Depp has better manners than you do."

"Next you'll say he's better-looking, and then we'll know you're lying."

Janya, wearing a long patterned scarf wrapped gracefully over her bathing suit, led them back through some scrub at a point where Tracy hadn't realized there was beach. The area was choked with vegetation, while farther down toward the point the land smoothed out into something approximating a real sand beach, although not much of one. That was the area where Tracy usually looked for shells. But now, she was delighted to see, they were in a protected cove of sorts, and while people from the mainland with prettier beaches wouldn't bother with this one, it was a perfect retreat for the neighbors.

"Can you imagine what a developer would do with this?" she asked, as they set up for the afternoon.

"Somebody'll pay big-time for this view. You got any takers yet?" Wanda asked.

"I don't think my land extends this far, but I'm beginning to think that when I'm ninety, I'll be all alone out here, in the last cottage standing."

"Picking off the folks from Wild Florida, one by one, with a slingshot filled with sandspurs."

That made Tracy think of Marsh, something she had tried not to do all morning. Last night's dinner had been spectacular. The fish had been so fresh, she could have sworn it jumped out of the bay into the pan. He'd done something with sweet potatoes and pineapple that still made her mouth water, and added a salad with tomatoes and herbs he grew himself—the last tomatoes of the season, too, which she hated to hear, although of course she wouldn't be eating with him again. Bay had awakened in time to join them, and he hadn't whined or argued. Not about anything.

Then Marsh brought her home, walked her up to her door and told her he was not fooled by this sweeter, earthier side, and as far as he was concerned, they were still at war.

At which point she'd kissed him. And although the kiss was meant to show she intended to win all battles, by the time it ended, she was pretty sure neither of them remembered which side they were on.

"Are you going to help or not?" Wanda asked.

Tracy came back to earth. "With what?"

"What exactly were you thinking about?"

"You wouldn't believe it." Tracy saw that Wanda was holding two sides of a blanket, so she grabbed the others to help lay it smoothly on the sand. The five of them worked together, and in a few minutes they had set up camp. Tracy set her iPod on the playlist she called Beach Music, put it in the speaker cradle and turned the setting to a comfortable volume.

They settled on the blankets, and Janya took out the sandwiches. They'd purchased Southern-style pimento cheese, crab salad, sharp cheddar and tomato, even hummus with sprouts—something Tracy had never expected to see at a general store and bait shop. They spread all the food in the middle, and everybody dug in, passing around chips and fruit, drinks and ice, until they were all contented. Chase got a rawhide bone to keep him busy.

"So, you promised a story," Tracy said. "About your adventure."

"Wanda will tell you that the fault was mine," Janya said. "But it was really the other car."

"See, I'm teaching Janya to drive," Wanda said. "And today was our first lesson."

Tracy thought how swiftly things had changed on Happiness Key.

"She was doing great," Wanda continued. "Why, I think we'd made it all the way up to maybe ten miles an hour. Then another car came down the road and honked at her. You know where the road jogs, this side of the bridge?"

"I am used to honking," Janya said. "Drivers where I come from steer with one hand on the horn. It is customary—"

"Oh, please, it scared the living whatever out of you! Janya here wrenched the wheel, and went off the road and right on down to the beach. I thought we were going into the water, maybe driving all the way to India."

"Tell me you didn't kill some poor sunbather," Tracy said, not sure whether to laugh or act horrified.

"I did not!" Janya looked offended.

"She came to a stop where the tide always does," Wanda said. Now Alice laughed. "And how…did you get back up?"

"I just sat there and let her figure it out by herself," Wanda said. "The sand was packed pretty hard, so we didn't get stuck."

"I turned, put the car in Reverse, turned some more and went back out to the road," Janya said.

Tracy applauded. "Good for you."

"Is driving hard?" Olivia asked.

"I think I will be good at driving," Janya said. "I have good reactions. But you will be better. It will seem normal to you after all those hours on your bicycle."

Olivia wandered off to look for shells, and Chase limped after her. Tracy noticed the girl didn't get close to the water, which was calm here. "Are you afraid to let her swim?" she asked Alice. Olivia seemed to have no intention of even wading.

"She won't go in...not since Karen... Many things." She paused, then shrugged. "She gets frightened now. Often."

Tracy understood.

Alice changed the subject, although she kept an eye on her granddaughter as she addressed Janya. "So you let Wanda... teach you? Not that handsome husband?"

"You think Rishi is handsome?"

Alice looked puzzled. "There is so much character..." She reached up and touched her own face.

Tracy slid her cover-up over her head so she could enjoy the sun. "You didn't think he was handsome when you agreed to marry him?"

Janya reached for a bunch of grapes and began to slowly pick them apart. "There was another man... One I was in love with." She looked up, as if surprised she had said the words out loud.

Tracy realized Janya felt she'd said too much. "We all have a man like that, Janya. The one who got away. I fell in love with mine in college. He married a sorority sister."

"Mine? High school," Wanda said. "A real low-down skunk, too."

Janya didn't look reassured enough to suit Tracy. "It must have been hard, though, to love someone and not be allowed to marry him," Tracy said.

"We *were* to be married...." Janya picked at her grapes some more.

"Now we're all going to wonder," Wanda said. "So you'd better just spill it. Who would we tell?"

"I think it's a story you will find hard to understand."

"I'd like to hear, if you'd like to try," Tracy said. "And is it worse than my divorce? Did you find out he was a felon who was about to go to jail for the rest of his life? Top that, if you can."

Somehow, that seemed to be just the right thing to say.

"In India, we still have arranged marriages, but not, perhaps, as you think of them. In our villages, they *can* be like that. The bride might even meet her husband for the first time at the wedding. But for most of us, it's not that way. Our families have a great deal to do with who we choose. They introduce us to acceptable men, make suggestions about others. And in the end, of course, they tell us whether they approve."

"Let me guess," Tracy said. "Your family didn't approve your choice?"

"No, quite the opposite. After I finished school, I spent a year in Manchester, England, studying English and living with friends of my father's."

"That explains why your English is so good," Tracy said.

Janya nodded her thanks. "Then, when I came home—changed, of course, from the relative freedom I'd experienced in Manchester—I met Darshan. He was the most attractive man I'd ever seen, handsome, considerate."

"Fairy tale," Alice said.

"I was attending the Sir J.J. School of Art in Mumbai. He was nearing the end of his course work in a connected school of architecture. We met at a party. My cousin, Padmini, introduced us. Padmini and I were like sisters. Her family was wealthier than mine, with more prestige, but we had always spent many hours together. I trusted her with my life and my heart."

"That's never a good idea." Wanda reached for a plum. "I

have a sister, and much as I love her, I wouldn't trust her with a bottle of ketchup, not if I was planning a meat loaf in the next week or so."

Janya talked faster now. "Padmini warned me about Darshan. She said he wasn't free to marry just anyone. His father was high in the government and expected to be the next chief minister of our state. His family was not only powerful, but rich and well-connected. Darshan might not submit to a traditional arranged marriage, but he would follow his parents' lead, and his choice would need to be advantageous to his family and above reproach."

"And you weren't?" Tracy asked.

"Until that moment I had never thought of myself as just anyone. My family was good, my marriage prospects *as* good. I had been told I was beautiful. I might not be technically inclined, but I received a bit of praise for my art, particularly my painting. My reputation had never suffered, and I was convent educated. I thought that the man who wed me would be the lucky one."

Alice had been quiet; now she leaned forward and rested her fingertips on Janya's knee. "He had...no taste, dear."

Janya smiled and covered Alice's hand for a moment. "Thank you, Alice. But as it turned out, he did. I had told my mother of him, of course. And although she was wary, my father and uncle, whose family live with us, put her at ease. Darshan Tambe was so far above what they had expected for me that unless he was unworthy of his family's excellent reputation, we had nothing to fear. Either Darshan would cut off our flourishing friendship and marry another, or he would persuade them to accept me. Whichever it was, unless I put myself in a compromising position, I couldn't be harmed. I would know soon enough which it was."

Tracy poured and passed water around the circle. "Since you didn't marry him, this didn't turn out well."

Janya sounded as if she were reciting a story she had gone over and over. "Darshan told his family he wanted to marry me. I wasn't told what transpired, but they agreed. I accepted, of course, and our families met and made the engagement official. Plans were begun for a wedding. Although Darshan's father asked that no official dowry be given, the wedding itself must be an occasion to be remembered by the many, many people who would be invited."

"A big, fat Indian wedding," Wanda said. "I saw that movie, or something like it."

"Mr. Tambe made it clear that once Darshan and I were wed, he would make certain my father's accounting firm was never overlooked when state contracts were awarded. My father had visions of more work than he could handle, all well-paid. An elaborate wedding was an investment."

"Oh, boy, this is starting to sound familiar," Tracy said. "Dress me up in a sari, and we could be twins. I won't even tell you what my wedding cost."

"So many arrangements had been made, so much money had been paid, so many people had been told. I was so happy. Darshan wanted to stay in Mumbai and practice in the firm where he was getting practical experience. With his family's connections and his father's position, when he graduated it would only be a short time before he began to make a name for himself."

"I can't stand this!" Wanda waved her hand. "What in the heck happened to this paragon of perfection?"

Janya wasn't smiling. "Three months before our wedding, Darshan and his parents arrived at our home carrying Darshan's laptop computer. There were few preliminaries. His father went to the Internet and logged on to a social networking site, one that's very popular in India. There was my photo and information. But not just one photo. Many, many photos, showing me in an equal number of unacceptable situations. Me drinking in a mixed crowd. Me looking as if I'd had too much to drink. Me nearly undressed, making eyes at the camera."

"How?" Tracy demanded.

"Some of the photos were familiar. Padmini and I had joked about what we would put on such a site if we were ever tempted to join one. We had pretended we were not from families that would be scandalized by such a thing. We had pretended, making up names and taking silly pictures of each other with Padmini's digital camera. She asked me to look at the camera the way I would look at Darshan when we were finally alone after the wedding."

"So you told them the truth and they understood?" Wanda said. "I'm betting…no."

"I protested, of course. I got my own laptop to show that I had no links to such a site, that someone had done this to me. I even explained how some of the photos had been manipulated, that the face might be mine but that I did not own clothing like that in the photo. I was an art student, so I knew."

Tracy twisted the top back on the water bottle with more strength than she needed. "And they couldn't see that?"

"Even then, I couldn't bring myself to believe the troublemaker was Padmini. I wanted to believe someone else had come across her computer, found the photos and done this mischief. But the proof was on my laptop. The site had been set up by 'me,' using my equipment. It was all right there. And then I knew Padmini had not been a sister to me at all. When I visited her, I had always taken my laptop with me, so I could e-mail Darshan."

"Well, that little vixen," Wanda said. "Let me guess, she wanted this Darshan person for herself."

"You have more understanding than I did, Wanda. Then I could only think of getting everyone to see the truth. But my protests made no difference. Even if what I said was true, many people had already seen the site. Darshan had been told about it by someone at his firm and asked how he could marry such a woman. Darshan's father had been shown the site by another man in his office. How these men were alerted was another question no one could answer. But again, what did it matter? The Tambes could not be linked to me, even if, by some mere chance, there was merit in what I said."

"And Darshan went along with this?" Tracy asked.

"I had no time alone with him, then or later. He e-mailed me to say how sorry he was that things turned out as they had. But none of my return e-mails were ever answered."

"Not worth a lot, was he?" Wisely, Wanda handed Janya a napkin.

Janya wiped her eyes, which were sparkling with tears. "Padmini was so offended by my accusations she refused to speak to me again. I was alone, under suspicion by my own family, no longer betrothed, and shamed and deserted by the woman who was supposed to love me like a sister."

"Where's a hit man when you need one?" Tracy asked. "I could e-mail CJ in the pen. He has all kinds of new contacts now."

"I'm sorry." Janya wiped her eyes. "What must you think of me?"

"Ummm…that you got screwed? That you're absolutely normal?" Tracy handed her another napkin. "Did I mention you got screwed?"

"So that was it? You never saw this bozo again?" Wanda asked.

Janya shook her head. "Can you imagine my life at home

after that? Much of the money my parents had saved had already been spent on a wedding that would never happen. My reputation was in shreds. My parents refused to let me return to school, because they said my presence on the same campus would humiliate Darshan."

"They worried…about *him?*" Alice appeared transfixed, as if she couldn't imagine any of this being real.

"They do to this day."

"I just don't understand." Alice shook her head.

"Soon afterward, Rishi came to India with his aunt and uncle to find a bride. My parents were contacted by his family in India. We were introduced, and Rishi wanted me, despite the things others said. My parents wanted me gone, so my presence would not taint my brother's opportunities to find a good match. I wanted to leave my humiliation behind. Our wedding was arranged quickly. We came to Florida, and here I am." She balled the napkin in her slender hand. "So do I know if Rishi is handsome or charming or someone I want to be married to? How can I possibly? Rishi was a solution."

"Padmini?" Tracy asked.

"She will marry Darshan in September. My parents will attend and take valuable gifts."

The women sat in silence, as if too stunned to know what to say. Finally Tracy spoke for all of them.

"Surely you see how much better off you are without this Darshan person? I bet he wasn't even the one who let you know about his wedding to your cousin."

"I don't know."

"Either he did or he didn't."

"In the past weeks I have had—" Janya raised her fingers, as if she was counting on them "—four e-mails from Darshan. I didn't open any of them."

Tracy didn't know what to say, but Wanda had no such problem.

"You listen to your big sister Wanda. Don't open those e-mails. You let that man stay a piece of your past, Janya. Whatever he has to say, it can't help. If he tries to tell you he's sorry, that will be all about him having a clear conscience. I know what I'm talking about here. Just don't let him back into your life or your heart, or your head."

Janya sighed. "There's been no one to tell this to. No one except Yash, my brother, who never believed I was at fault."

"Somehow, then…your parents raised good children, even if they are not such…good parents," Alice said.

"It's good to be here. It's good not to be judged. To be believed." Janya managed a smile. "Thank you."

"It would be so appropriate right now to have a big California group hug," Tracy said. "But let's not."

"Right," Wanda said. "Let's eat pie." She pulled a little cooler to her side and opened it. "Peach pie, graham cracker crust, and not one thing in it one of them heathen Hindu types would turn up her nose at. Right, Janya?"

This time Janya's smile almost looked real. She definitely looked grateful.

chapter twenty-three

Tracy spent a large part of the weekend worrying that she had applied too much pressure to convince Alice to teach at the center. By Monday morning she was almost certain Alice wouldn't show up, but Alice arrived with Wanda, just as they'd planned, and although she seemed unsure of herself, she was prepared with simple instructions in neat, legible handwriting.

Tracy made copies and set out supplies she had bought on Sunday. She checked on Alice frequently, but by ten o'clock she was relieved to find it wasn't necessary. The counselors kept the kids under control, and the bright yarn captivated the girls. The boys were less enthused, but when they saw the Hacky Sack instructions and were told there would be a Hacky Sack tournament at the end of camp, they perked up considerably.

"The boys are hooked now," she told Gladys, who pointed out that the pun wasn't worthy of Tracy's talents.

By Tuesday Alice seemed more at ease. Sometimes she had to search for words, but the kids caught on quickly and suggested possibilities, the way Olivia did at home. In one-on-one interactions, she was patient and able to get right to the root of a problem.

On Wednesday, Tracy was at the front desk when Lee came striding into the center. She intercepted him before he got as far as Gladys.

"Is Alice here?" he demanded.

"Let's go for a walk." She put her hand on his arm. "I need to stretch my legs, anyway."

"I don't." He didn't shake off her hand, but he made it clear her touch wasn't welcome.

"I'd like to talk to you about this, and not right here."

"I'm in no mood to talk. I've come to take Alice home."

"She's busy. She's happy. Please, can't we discuss this?"

He was not in a mood for discussion; that was written all over his face. But he gave a curt nod and started back toward the door. She exchanged looks with Gladys, who shrugged. Gladys knew the basics of Alice's situation.

A blast of heat greeted them, and Tracy wilted. Her staff shirt, a polo with the same grinning alligator logo as the children's, plastered itself to her back and breasts. She didn't think the athletic-female gig was going to go over big this morning, so she started her pitch as the door swung closed.

"First, *I* asked Alice to teach the kids to crochet. It was completely my idea. We needed somebody to do crafts, and this is a skill they can carry into adulthood. And your mother-in-law is a champion."

"So you knew I wouldn't approve and went straight to Alice because, what? Because you knew she's not capable of resistance?"

"That's not what happened. I went over to your place on Friday evening to talk to both of you. You weren't home, so I discussed it with Alice. She was so enthused, Lee. She perked right up. And she taught when your wife was in Girl Scouts. I think the idea brought back a good memory."

"You think dredging up her past is helpful? You think re-membering activities they did together will make her feel better her daughter is dead?"

The depth of his anger seemed out of place. She wondered if the possibility Alice might be getting better worried him. Was Lee so entrenched in being her caretaker, in giving comfort and help as a tribute to his late wife, that he wanted to slow down her recovery and keep her dependent?

He was walking so fast she had to put on a burst of speed. "I think Alice needs to find herself again. She's been so lucky to have you taking care of her, but she seems ready for a little independence. She's doing really well with the kids. They already love her, and she's got a bunch of budding crocheters hanging on every word. How can this be a problem?"

"You went behind my back."

"We thought we'd just try this and see how it worked, then we were going to tell you. We knew you might be miffed, but I thought you'd be so pleased Alice was doing well, you'd get past that fast."

"Miffed?" He faced her, stopping just short of the parking lot. "I have to live with this woman, Tracy, and so does my daughter. Do you hear Alice crying at night because she can't remember something? Do you watch her do things, then have no memory of them an hour later? The last two nights have been hell. She paces. Last night she put the kettle on and walked out of the house. When I told her, she said I was mistaken, that it was too hot for tea, even though there was a cup with a tea bag waiting for her to pour the water!"

"And you're saying this is because she's a success at teaching?"

"She can't take the stress!" He pushed his hand through his hair, an uncharacteristic gesture, since it disturbed the perfect symmetry.

"But Lee, she doesn't seem to be under any stress while she's here. Oh, sure, she was a little nervous that first day. I don't think she knew if she could still teach or not. But once it was clear she could, she just, well, bloomed. Maybe you can come in and see for yourself? Watch through the door a little to see what I mean. She loves being here. Don't we both want the best for her?"

"Is that really what you want? Or did you just need somebody to bail you out?"

That was a little too close for comfort, and she didn't answer.

"I don't know what's up with you women on the key. You just can't leave poor Alice alone. And every time she's with you, she comes back upset and more disoriented. She must put on quite a show when you're together, because if she was anything like the Alice living in my cottage—"

"*Your* cottage?" The question slipped out before she could think.

"Oh, for Pete's sake, you know what I mean."

Quite possibly she did. Maybe Tracy knew too well. Because hadn't Lee taken over Alice's house *and* her life?

"The Alice we know has a little trouble forming sentences sometimes, but she always manages to make herself understood. She's funny and wise, and your daughter adores her. That's the only Alice we see."

"You obviously know nothing about dementia. Eventually it reaches a stage when it can't be hidden. But early on, a victim can cover up what she doesn't remember. She can pretend she knows things, or understands them, but can you imagine the stress? That's why she falls apart when she comes home. She's exhausted. This is why you have to leave her alone."

Tracy wondered if all that really could be happening. Was it possible that the Alice she and the other women saw disintegrated when she no longer had to put on a show? Was she caught in some downward spiral that would only become apparent to them in the future? In the meantime, by trying to help, were they making life harder for Lee and Olivia?

She just couldn't buy it. Alice liked being at the center, and Alice liked being with the other women. She had enjoyed Saturday afternoon at the beach as much as anyone. She had enjoyed having them to her house for a complicated dessert.

"Lee, if what you say is true, doesn't Alice deserve a chance to be happy now? To make as many good memories as she can before everything gets swallowed up?"

"You haven't listened to a word I've said."

"Of course I have. That doesn't mean we see things the same way."

"The way I see this is the way that matters."

She tried to sound accommodating, but her voice was noticeably cooler. "No, the way *Alice* sees it is the way that matters."

"Alice no longer sees anything the way it is, and it's my job to protect her. Now, I'm going in there, and I'm going to tell her she needs to come home with me. I hope, when you think about this a little, you'll see I'm right. I'm not trying to upset you or spoil things at the center. I'm not even angry, since I know you were doing what you thought was right. But I have to take care of Alice."

"Then at least let her finish today's classes. Don't drag her out and embarrass her."

"Her—or you?"

"That's not fair." She waited. She didn't know if most of the other things Lee had said were true, but one was not. He *was* angry. He was covering it better now, but she could still see it in his eyes and the set of his lips.

Finally he shrugged. "Fine. But she won't be back tomorrow."

"If you and Alice have a good conversation about this, and she doesn't want to come back, I'll understand."

"Please don't go behind my back again. It's getting so I can't leave her alone."

"But you do," she pointed out, more emphatically than she'd intended. "Frequently. And she seems fine."

"Don't accuse me of neglect. I'm trying to make a living for my family."

She glanced away, trying to get control of *her* temper. She was staring into the parking lot, when she realized she had to be looking at Lee's new car. It was a like a silver swan rising above a pond of squawking ducks. The vanity license plate on the front was the giveaway. *RLEETR*. Realtor, with his name smack in the middle.

"Nice SUV," she said. "I've always liked Infinitis."

"I needed a bigger car to carry clients and open-house signs."

"Well, this will impress them."

"I'm banking on it."

And he'd been to the bank, too, to get a loan or to clean out his savings. She knew something about cars, and she made a guess that this model started at fifty grand or so. She thought about Alice, who had been forced to beg for money so she could buy clothing on sale. For the first time Tracy wondered if Janya's suspicions about Lee had merit.

She tried to push that thought away. If Lee really was going through tough times, it would be unfair to turn against him while he was struggling to help and support his mother-in-law. Still, distrust had completely eclipsed the fleeting attraction she'd once felt for him. Distrust, and quite possibly the thought of another man.

The contrast between Lee and Marsh was enormous, but they did share one thing in common. Her.

Tracy knew if she had half a brain, she would take off running right this very minute and never look back to see if either of them was gaining on her.

After revealing so much about her past to the other women, Janya had expected to feel depressed. She had told bits of the story to school friends in India—the ones who had not been spirited from her presence by families or husbands. But she had never told anyone but her family and Darshan's her conviction that her own cousin had engineered her downfall. The proof was gone. Padmini had probably destroyed everything long before Janya's counterfeit page showed up on the Internet. Had anyone searched, there would have been no doctored photos, no text, no signs of any kind.

Now, having shared the story, Janya felt lighter, as if the weight of it had lifted a little. She could breathe easier. In Tracy's words, Janya had been screwed. And yes, that was exactly what had happened. Certainly she should have been more careful. She should have realized her cousin wanted Darshan for herself and would go to any length to get him. But that was as far as her guilt extended.

There had been signs, of course. Padmini had cautioned her repeatedly about Darshan, how he would certainly marry a woman who was more well-connected than Janya, that his family wouldn't approve such a marriage, so Janya shouldn't risk her heart or reputation. Looking back, she remembered times when messages for Darshan hadn't been delivered. Or others when Padmini insinuated herself between them. Janya had felt sympathy, wondering if Padmini hated to lose her cousin to a man, any man, because once Janya was married, they would never be as close.

When they were heading back to their homes late Saturday

afternoon, Alice had said something important. The two women had been trailing the others, who were throwing a beach ball back and forth with Olivia. Alice put her hand on Janya's arm. At first Janya thought she was having trouble walking in the sand; then the older woman stopped, and when Janya turned to help her, she smiled sadly.

"You made a mistake—" she paused, then she shook her head "—out of love, Janya. They are the hardest to bear, but…" She appeared to search for the right words. Janya didn't try to help.

"But the angels bless us.…" she said at last. "And they understand."

Now Janya thought that, in her own way, Alice had been saying that she should forgive *herself*. She had trusted a cousin she loved. Trust and love, even misplaced, were virtues. She might have been foolish, but she had not been cruel. That had been Padmini's role.

As he often did, Rishi worked all day Sunday, and Janya had spent the day lost in thought. By afternoon she'd decided to paint a portrait of her cousin, but not the affectionate portraits of old. This was a portrait to show the person Padmini had become. Not Padmini as a demon, but as a woman who had planned and executed the undoing of someone she claimed to love, a cunning woman who would not hesitate to harm others to get whatever she wanted.

Janya almost felt sorry for Darshan, who would be chained to Padmini for all the years of their marriage. But that was a waste of sympathy. Darshan had chosen to marry her. Even if his parents had insisted, he was a man. He could say no, just as many months ago he could have insisted that the wedding to Janya would go exactly as planned, and anyone foolish enough to believe she had tried to destroy her own reputation could simply stay at home.

By Wednesday afternoon she was standing at an easel set up in her front yard, putting the final touches on the small portrait. The likeness was good. She had painted her cousin at the corner of her house, peeking around the side as if she were hiding…waiting…but not as a woman waits for a lover. Padmini's expression was shrewd, even deceitful. She was a woman waiting for the right moment to spring. The portrait was subtle. At first an admirer would see a pretty enough woman in the full bloom of youth, waiting expectantly for something. But a closer examination would bring discomfort. This was a woman with secrets. This was a woman who was planning harm.

Janya stepped back and examined what she had done. She thought she was finished. She no longer wanted to view the portrait. It had served its purpose. Painting Padmini had been as good as chasing away her ghost.

When she looked away, Tracy was striding down her walkway. She had been so absorbed that she hadn't heard the other woman approach. She thought Tracy's opinion would be interesting to hear.

Tracy came to stand beside her. She stared at the portrait for a full minute before she spoke.

"Your cousin, right?"

"How can you tell? We look nothing alike."

"Which, I'm sure, makes her very unhappy. She's not half as pretty as you are. And everything you said about her is right there to see. It's amazing. I want to punch her in the nose, and I wouldn't know why if I hadn't heard your story. I'd do it for no good reason."

Janya began to clean up. "Painting this made me feel better. I haven't painted in a very long time. I had no heart for it."

"Janya, have you ever thought of painting on a larger canvas?"

"I'm afraid if I painted a larger likeness of Padmini, she would leap out and strangle us."

"I mean a really, really big canvas. You know, like a wall?"

"A wall? You want a mural in your house to match your new tile?"

"No, I want a mural on the wall beside the shuffleboard courts at the rec center. And I want you to teach the kids to paint it and supervise the process. And—" she hurried through the next part, as if she was afraid Janya was going to refuse "—I'll pay you. You'll be the new arts-and-crafts teacher. And all the children will love you."

"Me? Teach? What would I know about that?"

"You're wonderful with Olivia. She told me today that you've been working on projects with her. And this is a fantastic opportunity. The wall definitely needs help. There's going to be a big tournament, and everybody who comes will see what you've done. Please say yes."

"What kind of mural?"

"Oh, I don't know. Something you and the kids come up with together. But Lee showed up today, and he was furious. It's safe to say Alice won't be back tomorrow to teach, and I'm in a pickle. Gladys can crochet a little, and she's going to help the kids work on the crochet projects they started. But all of them are going to be so disappointed it ended like that. Next week we have to do something big and fun and exciting, or they're going to mutiny."

"Not all children like to paint."

"Are you kidding me? The side of a building? We'll have a table set up with craft supplies for the ones who don't want to. But what kid doesn't want to splash paint around and call it art? Supervised graffiti. It'll be fabulous."

She looked so expectant, so eager. Tracy had a strong will,

but Janya couldn't let her friend determine how she should spend her time.

"You'd be great," Tracy wheedled.

"You are good at asking people to do things."

"I know, and they pay me to do it."

Janya tried, but she couldn't think of one good reason to say no. And the fact that it would help Tracy was the best reason to say yes.

"I will try," she said.

Tracy threw her arms around her and hugged her hard, nearly knocking the breath out of Janya, who was not used to these extravagant displays of emotion.

"You saved my life!"

"The least I could do for a friend."

"You know, you're just bone-deep nice."

"And that's what got me in trouble in India."

Tracy stepped away, but she was smiling. "Yes, but look, it brought you here. And nobody could be more grateful than me."

"Then I can be glad some good has come from it."

Tracy sobered a bit. "I hope in the long run you'll have a lot more to be glad about than helping a new friend. Fingers crossed there will be a whole lot more to your move to Florida than that."

"Will you be able to say the same?"

Tracy appeared to consider. "I have no idea," she said at last. "But at least the trip is turning out to be interesting."

chapter twenty-four

As a teenager, Tracy had appreciated her expensive private school because of the contacts she made. In fact her introduction to CJ had come from a friend in her high school English class. Five years after graduation, Tracy had been a bridesmaid at that friend's Beverly Hills Hotel wedding, and later a guest at her first anniversary party. CJ had come alone to the party and departed with Tracy on his arm.

She really couldn't hold CJ against the school. These days, she even appreciated the excellent education they had tried to give her. For instance, had she not been forced to read Mark Twain, would she have learned about Tom Sawyer?

Now she put a finger to the side of her cheek, as if considering what to do next. "I don't know, Bay. You're kind of short for this job. And it's a cooperation kind of thing." Tracy stared at the wide expanse of wall that needed a base coat of white paint to ready it for the mural.

Bay got between her and the wall, so she would have to look at him. "I'm not *that* short. I can use that stick with the roller, like the other kids."

"You probably could manage the roller. But there's that little cooperation thing. They're all taking turns. How good are you at that?"

"How would I know?"

"Well, I hate to experiment with something so new to you. I mean, what if you get all grabby and whiney on me? Do I have time for that?"

"What do I have to do?"

"You have to promise you'll share."

"I don't like to."

Tracy lifted a brow as if to say, so forget it, kid. Bay looked torn; then he shrugged. "But I will."

"Then you can be in the third group. The one Olivia's in."

He brightened. It wasn't the first time she'd noticed that Bay liked to be around Olivia. But who didn't? She was mature beyond her years, and careful never to give offense or hurt anybody's feelings.

In fact, in Tracy's opinion, Olivia was too careful, as if consequences worried her more than they ought to. Tracy wondered what effect this might have on the girl when she got older. What would she go along with just to smooth the waters? How would she stand up for herself?

The shuffleboard courts were hopping this morning, and Tracy had cautioned the kids that under no circumstances, none, *nada,* were they to go anywhere near the players. Nor, on pain of something or other, were they to splatter paint in that vicinity. The Palmetto Grove Shuffleboard Club was practicing, and would continue to practice on Monday, Wednesday and Friday mornings until the tournament in August. She had carefully negotiated the times, so that once the real painting of the mural began, the club would be finished for the day. But today, as they painted the first of two prep coats, there was overlap.

She was supervising group two, making sure they got paint into every crevice on their section, when Mr. Mustache came to stand beside her.

"I promise, we won't be painting during practice after today," Tracy said, after a glance to see who was there. "We just want to get this coat finished early, so it'll have time to dry before we do the second this afternoon. Then we'll keep the paint far away from your teams and the courts."

"What's going to be up here when they've finished?"

She tried to judge the timbre of his voice. Would it really be worse to work at the yacht club? Would anybody there be more difficult?

She glanced at him again. "I honestly can't say. We're leaving that up to the art teacher and the kids. But the art teacher's wonderful." Tracy realized she was basing an awful lot on one painting of Janya's.

"You ever been to Palatka?"

"Where?"

He snorted. "Northeast of here. Directly south of Jacksonville. They have a bunch of murals all over that town. Local seniors went on a bus tour to see them. You never heard of Palatka for a good reason, but after you saw those murals? You'd never forget it again. Told the whole history of the area."

"That's ambitious." Tracy hoped she could survive just one. "Since you're the resident expert, what should we start with here?"

"Well, considering it's a rec center, maybe something about recreation in Sun County."

"I'll tell Janya. It's a good idea."

He snorted again. She was beginning to worry about his sinuses. "Brighten this corner of the world a little," he said. "It needs it."

Now she wondered about her hearing. "You like the idea?"

"You sure do jump to conclusions about everything, don't you?"

"I'm working on that."

"I can tell." She expected him to leave, but he stayed beside her. "I thought of something Herb told me."

She was surprised by this piece of late-breaking news. "Really? I've learned he had a daughter, but I'm not much closer to finding her."

"Sometimes people don't want to be found."

"I wonder about that. But he died on my watch, in my house, and I can't just ignore that."

"I'd tell you more if I knew more. Herb was the most private old cuss I ever met."

She could have enlightened Mr. M. about a number of things pertaining to Herb, but those were secrets she was going to keep in the old man's honor.

She instructed one of the kids to be careful and signaled a counselor to move in closer. Then she turned back to her new informant.

"Anyway," he went on, "he told us once that when he was a young man, he used to tend bar at a place called Gasparilla's, up north in Cargo Beach. Said in those days it was almost like home."

Tracy had hoped for something like "Herb kept all his important papers in a safety deposit box and left me the key."

"Hmmm…Gasparilla's. I wonder if it's still there?" Although even if it was, who would still be alive to remember Herb? Or maybe…Clyde?

"Couldn't say. I came to Florida to retire. By then my drinking days were long over."

"I appreciate your telling me."

"You make sure these kids paint something bright. Knock a few socks off, while you're at it."

With the sense that she had passed some unwritten test, Tracy watched him head back to the courts. The musical ring of colliding discs and children shouting in the pool was a happy summer soundtrack.

Driving lessons were progressing. Janya was gaining considerable confidence. Today somebody honked—not at her, but at a pesky flock of seagulls—and she didn't even flinch. She was almost driving the speed limit, which meant she was still going at least fifteen miles an hour slower than anyone else, but she no longer stood out. She had crossed bridges, driven on the interstate and pulled into many parking spaces.

She still had more to learn. Parallel parking sounded impossible. But she was determined she would learn, and soon. She wanted her license and the freedom that would come with it. Rishi was already talking about finding her a little car all her own. And she had finally agreed to drive with him, to give Wanda a rest. He had turned out to be attentive, patient and flattering. This attractive husband of hers, with the character in his face.

She wondered what Alice would have thought of Darshan.

On Monday afternoon she was contemplating that as she prepared supper, a dish called red beans and rice from a new library cookbook, when she heard a knock. She had changed the spices to different ones she liked better, and left out the sausage, along with something called ham hocks, which she didn't want to think about. The only thing she had left alone was the rice, because it was the reason she'd chosen the dish. She had made many portions, so if she was late getting home from the rec center, there would be food in the refrigerator. She hoped it was good. It certainly was plentiful.

She still had a wooden spoon in her hand when she found Olivia on her stoop. She smiled at her young friend and gestured her in, quickly closing the door to keep it cool inside. "Does Alice know you're here?"

"My father took her to the doctor. Nana wanted me to go, but I told them I would be okay by myself."

But she hadn't been. Janya could see that. Olivia wasn't a confident child. She was afraid of the water, did not like the wind, and was often worried about Alice's health. If she had friends, they were never invited to the cottage. Janya was surprised her father had allowed Olivia to attend the rec center program, and she suspected Lee had done it purely to distract Tracy the night Alice had invited the neighbors for dessert.

"I'm so glad you're here," Janya told her. "Have you heard that I will be supervising the painting of the mural at the rec center? Perhaps you have a little time to sketch out ideas."

"I don't even really know what a mural is. Just, like, a big painting?"

"That's exactly right, and who better to think of ideas?"

"We painted the wall today. Twice. It's all ready. How will we start?"

"I think tomorrow we will talk about what we would like to see there, then perhaps ask all the children to sketch. We don't have a lot of time to do it, so we will have to move faster than I like. But I think we can make it happen."

"I'm so glad you'll be there every day." Olivia's wide smile said she meant it. "I don't know why Nana couldn't stay and teach crocheting, too. I would like you both to be there. Tracy's already there every day."

Janya knew better than to discuss the reasons why Alice was no longer teaching. To her, this was just more evidence that Olivia's father was a tyrant.

"So now the wall is ready," Janya said. "Did you have fun painting it?"

"I like to paint. Mommy and I were going to paint my new room before she died. She let me choose the color. I chose turquoise."

"Like the color in here?"

"Lighter. And I was going to have pink curtains." Olivia stopped. She no longer looked confident. "Janya, I…"

Janya waited, even though she was afraid the beans might burn. "Something is the matter?"

"The house. Where we were supposed to move. It was a secret. Mommy found the house, and she said when she saw it she knew it would be perfect for us. It was pretty far from here. I would have to change schools, but I didn't care. She only told me because we had to paint before we could move in. She said we would surprise Daddy, and I wasn't supposed to tell him or the surprise would be spoiled. It was our secret."

"I see." But she didn't.

"Then she died. I don't know what happened to the house. I was afraid to ask Daddy. I don't think Mommy had told him yet, and then he would feel worse that we couldn't move in there, the way Mommy wanted."

Janya could not imagine a situation in which a woman would buy or rent a house and *not* tell her husband. Everyone liked surprises. But a house? Far from Palmetto Grove?

"It had four whole bedrooms, one for everybody," Olivia said wistfully. "Mommy was going to use the last one as an office. Someday she was going to start a business all by herself."

"You must miss her very much."

"Sometimes I worry it was my fault she died. When Mommy and Daddy fought, I wished I could make the fights stop. And now they have. Forever."

Janya rested her hand on Olivia's shoulder. "You never wished your mother would die, Olivia. And even if you did, just because you were angry at that moment, it's okay. No one can make things happen just by wishing. If we could, the world would be a terrible place."

"Do you think so?"

"I have often wished my house would clean itself and my dinner would cook itself, and neither one has ever happened." Janya had also wished that Darshan would choose to marry her, despite the scandal, but that hadn't come to pass, either.

"Do you and Mr. Kapur fight?"

She didn't know how to answer that. She and Rishi didn't fight because they rarely saw each other. In their case, this was not a good thing.

She tried to explain. "Many people in love fight. It can be difficult to live together." She hesitated; then she added as casually as she could, "But it is never good to hit another person."

"I'm glad Daddy didn't hit Mommy."

Janya was relieved. "Why don't I get some paper and pens? Then you can sketch while I make dinner. We can think of ideas for tomorrow."

"I like coming here."

Janya leaned over and ruffled her hair. "I'm glad you do."

Rishi came home earlier than usual, and Janya was still trying to make the red beans and rice delicious. As with many of the American recipes she had tried, it would not cooperate.

She reached around to turn off the CD player, which had been loudly trumpeting some of her favorite songs. "I do not understand American cooking," she said. "I can't believe Americans prefer these dishes."

Rishi came to stand beside her and peered into the pot. "And what is that?"

"I got a new cookbook at the library this week. *American Cajun Cuisine*. Very American, so you will probably like it. It's called red beans and rice."

"Someday I'll take you to New Orleans. The food is wonderful. All of it's good."

"Well, there are many recipes here for things I will never cook or eat."

"Red beans and rice is served in Louisiana the way we serve dal and rice in India. Only I've never smelled any quite like this."

"The recipe was not good as it was."

"You tried it as it was?"

Janya put down her spoon and frowned at the pot, hoping to figure out what was lacking. "It would have had no flavor."

"That's not usually a problem with Cajun food."

She glanced at him. "Well, perhaps this cookbook is at fault."

He looked away, as if something outside had captured his attention, and he cleared his throat. "That must certainly be it."

Rishi left to change clothes, and she added what she hoped would be the final touches to the beans. They met to say prayers; then Rishi helped her set the table. Janya went to get the food, but Rishi put his hand on her arm.

"Such a beautiful table needs beautiful flowers, Janya."

There were no flowers in the house, and none growing outdoors. The plants she and Tracy had salvaged were catching their breath on the patio, resting after the assault against them. But none of them were blooming now, as if that was one thing too many to expect.

"I have no flowers to put there." She made a small gesture with her hands, as if to show they were empty.

"Then we must get some outside."

She had no idea what Rishi was talking about. He wasn't a man who cared about the way things looked. Days had gone by after his first business trip before he realized that she had painted their bedroom red.

"There are no flowers outside. Many of the pots were destroyed, remember? I made cuttings from some that would not survive, and I am rooting them. The others are trying to recover their strength."

"I'm sure I saw flowers there."

She no longer sat on the patio to rest and think. The little fountain she had taken such pleasure in had been destroyed, and the sad plants that had survived were not the most charming company. Still, she watered the pots every day, as she always had. She knew what was there and what was not.

"Then go see what you can find," she told Rishi, since he was so insistent.

"Come with me to be sure I don't pick something I shouldn't."

Janya wanted to eat, so she agreed. "Yes, all right." She followed him out the door and around to the patio. Then she stopped.

She couldn't imagine how she hadn't heard the noise. Certainly there had been noise. How else would the table and comfortable chairs have arrived? The large pots from Mr. Krause's cottage been moved into place on the patio? The new pots, four of them, overflowing with flowering hibiscus and gardenias, and jasmine climbing up a small wooden trellis? The fountain, and yes, through teary eyes she saw there was a fountain in the sunniest corner, much larger than the tiny one she had bought at the garage sale, gurgling happily. How had these things appeared without her knowing?

"How did you...?"

"You had music on. You didn't hear me come inside until I

was in the kitchen, remember? The men who brought the furniture helped me get the plants in place, too."

"Could my music have been that loud?"

"Do you like it?"

She wandered across the little space, looking at the ID tags on the beautiful new plants, admiring the way Mr. Krause's had been tucked in here and there to form a screen of sorts for privacy from the road. She ran her fingers over the sleek wood of the table, touched the plastic cushions of the chairs, and imagined evenings here with candles, good food and laughter.

She ended up at the fountain. It was on a stonelike pedestal, with stacked squares ending in a basin, and smaller stacks of squares in the middle, from which water bubbled and flowed.

"There are no wires. How does it work?"

"It's solar powered. I charged the panel at work, which is why it's working now. As long as we keep it right there in direct sunlight, the fountain will bubble away."

She faced him. She saw that how she felt about this was the most important thing in the world to him. When had her happiness become so central? When had an arranged marriage, performed only for convenience, assumed such significance in his life? Because gazing into Rishi's dark eyes, she saw she could destroy him with words now. She could take this beautiful gesture and poison it, simply by not telling him what was in her heart.

But honesty came with risks. She could feel her husband pulling her closer. And was she ready to make that journey?

"This is the most beautiful thing anyone has ever done for me." She stretched out her hand, and he took it. "You know what matters most to me, Rishi. You knew how this would please me."

"I hoped so."

"And spending all this money when we are saving for another car, and someday for a house?"

"So? We will take all this to the house with us. We will put some of it in the new car, if that makes you feel better."

She laughed a little. When he drew her to him, she went. She let him enfold her in his arms, and when he bent to kiss her, her lips were already turned to his.

"There are no flowers to cut," she said, when she finally drew away. "I want them all to remain here, where they belong."

"Then we will eat here, on our new table, surrounded by flowers."

"I married a romantic man."

He pulled her close again. "No, you married a man who only wants to make you happy."

She buried her face in his shoulder and hoped that someday, he would.

chapter twenty-five

Janya expected to adapt easily to a Florida summer. After all, she had lived in Mumbai, waded through monsoons, survived without air-conditioning during her childhood and later during the city's frequent power outages. But the mid-July heat and humidity, even so close to the gulf, was too reminiscent of the worst of home. Now the patio that Rishi had so lovingly decorated weeks ago was never comfortable except just after sunrise and sometimes in the evening after rain had brought a respite. On nights when it was too hot to have a meal there, they sat outside for at least a few minutes before bed, drinking tea and sharing stories of their days.

In the relative peace of the patio, she and Rishi had begun to relax together. To a croaking, chirping soundtrack, she learned more about the man she had married. He was wiser than Janya had thought, and more considerate. Now she was beginning to believe her husband stayed away so much because he wanted her to have time to get used to their marriage. Not only was he working to establish himself, but he also didn't want Janya to feel pressure. She knew Rishi wanted children. He talked about them with longing. But he appeared to want Janya to come to this decision on her own and not feel required to comply.

Janya understood his yearning. For most of his life Rishi had been foisted on others. No one, except his own parents, had ever loved him just for himself. In contrast, a child would look at Rishi as if he held the secrets of the universe in his palm. And didn't he deserve that? Janya hoped someday she could willingly give him this.

This morning she was finishing preparations for something else entirely. She was giving a party for her neighbors. She had risen early to prepare, making some of her favorite Indian food, which the others had asked for. These weren't dishes she prepared for Rishi, but her friends had expressed curiosity. Tracy, of course, had eaten in Indian restaurants in California, although Janya didn't trust that the food had been authentic. But Wanda and Alice admitted they had never tried anything so unusual. So Janya was proudly putting the final touches on a lunch of her favorite dishes, and for once she thought her kitchen smelled exactly the way it should.

Tracy was the first to arrive, banging on the door with her usual lack of patience. Janya answered, and Tracy held out gladiolas. "Congratulations!"

Janya held them to her chest. Yesterday she had passed her driver's test, the cause for this celebration. "They are so beautiful."

"They reminded me of you when I saw them at Publix."

"Come in, please. I will put them in water."

"Janya, you look so gorgeous. What are you wearing?"

Janya held out her skirt. "Do you like it? The blouse is called a *choli,* very sensible in hot weather, don't you think?" The magenta *choli,* with silver embroidery on the sleeves, stopped just below her breasts and was cut low in the back. "And the skirt is called a *lehenga.* Some people call them gypsy skirts." She held out the wide skirt, which fell to her ankles, but left her midriff bare. "There's a scarf, too, a *dupatta,* to match the skirt. This was one of those given to me when I married, by Rishi's aunts."

"It's amazing. All that embroidery."

"As they go, this one is casual. Some are so heavy with beads and sparkling stones you could sink from the weight of them. Brides often wear them."

"Did you?"

"I wore a red sari with gold embroidery." Janya had chosen the sari for a different wedding. Her mother had insisted she wear it when she married Rishi, so as not to cost the family more money. Janya wondered if Inika Desai had also wanted to remind her daughter of the man she had lost.

Wanda came up the walk, and the other women greeted her. "You look like something out of some movie," Wanda told Janya. "One of those Bollywood pictures."

"You've seen Bollywood films?"

"A little dancing here and there, but I don't do subtitles. I don't want to read. Can you dance like that?"

"A little, as a matter of fact." The woman with whom she had practiced the steps and routines as a girl came to mind. Today, even thoughts of Padmini couldn't spoil her good mood.

"You have to show us," Tracy said.

"Perhaps after we eat." Janya hesitated. "Do you think Alice and Olivia will come?"

"I managed to tell her about it without Lee overhearing," Wanda said. "I know they'll come if they can."

The women exchanged glances. Three weeks had passed since Lee stormed into the rec center. He had kept a closer watch on Alice since then, leaving home less often. On the occasions when he was gone, the women got together at the beach, with the unspoken agreement those afternoons wouldn't be mentioned. Olivia always came, too, but as if keeping secrets were part of her childhood, she apparently never mentioned the get-togethers to her father.

"Would you like to see my license?" Janya asked.

"You say yes, she'll point out every single letter on it," Wanda warned.

"I am dying to see this license." Tracy held out her hand.

Janya just happened to have it tucked into a pocket in her skirt. Tracy was properly deferential, and Janya restrained herself from explaining the many things she had done to deserve it.

They were interrupted by footsteps, and Alice and Olivia arrived. Janya was pleased. They exchanged greetings, and Olivia came over for a hug. Janya embraced her and stroked her hair. "You're hot? Your hair is wet."

"It's boiling out there!"

Everybody laughed. Janya wasn't certain how long they would have before Alice and Olivia needed to go back home. She asked everyone to be seated; then she began to bring out the food.

Eyes widened as she came and went two more times. Finally Tracy put a hand on her arm to restrain her. "Umm…who else is coming?"

"This is just for us."

"But it's a feast."

"Just enjoy my party." Janya smiled happily and went back into the kitchen.

She had cooked her favorite *paneer jalfrezi,* cubes of cheese with peppers and onions. To go with it, she had grilled rotis so they were tender and puffy, and made fragrant basmati rice, then, in case that wasn't enough, spicy potatoes with yogurt sauce, and chana masala, with chickpeas, tomatoes and spices. Cooking the foods she loved had made her happy.

At the table, they passed the bowls, and Alice, who asked what was in every dish, said she had never smelled anything better. Wanda was careful not to take much, but as they finally began to eat, she looked up.

"You know, little sis, I've been here when you've been cooking before, and nothing smelled like this tastes. This is good!"

"I think perhaps I have not learned to cook American food well. But this I can cook."

"You don't cook American food, that's the trouble. Nothing I've ever smelled in here tastes like it came out of my kitchen, that's for sure."

"I improve it. Rishi is an American. I have to cook the way an American cooks."

Tracy reached for another helping of chickpeas. "I don't see why. Any American would love this."

"I like it, too, Janya," Olivia said.

Janya basked in their praise.

Wanda had waited long enough to tell a story. "So, we're on our way to the driver's license office yesterday morning, with Janya driving—"

"Thank you for giving me the day off so Wanda could take me," Janya told Tracy. "It took them a very long time to get to me."

"Anything to make it easier for you to get in every morning."

Wanda continued as if she hadn't been interrupted. "We're toodling along, pretty as you please, and just over the bridge, where that new housing development went up, a dog runs out in front of the car. One minute no dog, then cute cocker spaniel, practically right under the tires."

"Yuck," Tracy said. "You had to tell us while we're eating?"

"No, I stopped," Janya said. "Quickly."

"Which was a good thing, too, because a little boy came running after the dog, and she might have hit him, too. Which would not impress the cop giving the test, her arriving with a smashed-in front end and all."

Everybody groaned.

"So Janya is not only a new driver...she's a good one." Alice smiled.

Janya thought Alice looked tired, as if she were struggling to stay awake. But she also looked pleased to be with them again.

"But that wasn't the only thing," Wanda went on. "After she finally got that license, I looked at the time, and I realized I hadn't set my video recorder!"

"You missed *All My Children?*" Tracy asked. "And you lived?"

"Now this might seem inconsequential to certain people, but I figure that the day I miss my show, the world's coming to an end."

"You must have gotten home in time, because I got up this morning, same as always. Sun was shining."

"Janya drove like a bat out of hell, pardon the expression. I got home for the last five minutes. I figure that's good enough, just this once. I can still say I saw it every single weekday. But it was like driving with Dale Earnhardt Jr. She's living proof of my abilities as a driving teacher, that's for sure."

"Wanda worked very hard and was more patient than anyone could imagine." Janya smiled at her friend.

"Well, I can testify that Janya is also a wonderful art teacher," Tracy said. "The mural's coming along, and the kids are having a fabulous time working on it."

"I'm doing tarpon fishing," Olivia said. "Adam and Bay and me. On a ladder."

Tracy patted the girl's arm and turned to the others. "You would know how significant that is if you knew Adam and

Bay. Olivia's teaching them to get along. She's a regular conflict negotiator."

"It's a mural about tarpon?" Wanda asked.

"No, it's about recreation in Sun County, a collage Janya drew for us. Fishing. Golf. Tennis. Shuffleboard. Swimming. Boogie boarders. Bikers. Hikers. Everything fits together beautifully. Everybody loves it, even if it's only half-done."

"The children work very hard," Janya said modestly, but she was pleased at the praise, too.

Tracy dished up yet another helping of the chana masala. "And the mural reminds me. There's something I keep meaning to tell you, then I forget when we're together. But I did get another tidbit about Herb from one of the shuffle board, the man who came up with the theme for the mural."

"You mean those old men you nearly ran down and trampled into the grass?" Wanda asked.

"The very ones." Tracy passed the dish to Wanda, who replenished her plate, too. "A couple of weeks ago, he told me Herb used to tend bar at a place called Gasparilla's up in Cargo Beach. Of course, that was a long, long time ago, and it didn't lead anywhere. I called and checked, and there's no bar named Gasparilla's these days. I'm just hoping he remembers something else, although at this point, I think we've hit our last dead end."

"It wasn't a bar," Alice said, scooping up some of her food with one of Janya's rotis. "Gasparilla's…"

"You know about it?" Tracy stopped eating. "Alice, really?"

"Fred…" She paused, as if putting words together in his head. "We always went to Cargo Beach…for vacation. And Gasparilla's? Everyone knew about it and came. A bar and grill. Right on the water." She looked at Wanda. "Like the Dancing Shrimp."

"I never thought of that," Tracy said. "Mr. Mustache said Herb tended bar."

"He has a real name, right?" Wanda asked. "Mr. Mustache is not this poor fellow's real name?"

"And I use it when I have to," Tracy said, waving her to silence.

"Pirate's Puzzle," Alice said.

They waited for her to explain.

"A stew they made. People…miles around. They came." She nodded. "Then the cook died…took the recipe, too. Place kind of, you know…"

"No, what?" Tracy asked.

Alice was gathering steam. "Fancier places came in. Gasparilla's moved down the road. Some problem with the name, too. Something legal?"

"Did they change it?" Janya asked.

"Sea Breeze." Alice nodded in confirmation. "But it's only a bar now."

"Now?" Tracy asked.

"Yes, it's…still there."

"Cool. Only…that must have been…how long ago? Who's going to remember Herb now?"

"Same family owns it…. Last I heard…"

Tracy looked around the table. "Well, I thought we were done, but I guess we could check that out. Anybody interested?"

"Janya and I can take a spin up there next week, after she's done at the center. She can put in a little more time behind the wheel." Wanda popped the last piece of roti into her mouth. "Dang, this is good. You'll teach me how to make these puppies?" she asked Janya.

"Puppy?" Janya asked. "Like Chase? Like hush puppies?"

"Roti. That's what you called it?"

"You may be speaking my language before you know it," Janya said. "And yes, I will be happy to go to this place."

"See, I figure somebody as gorgeous as Janya could get any

man to talk," Wanda said. "Wear that outfit you've got on today, and they'll be fighting over you."

Tracy pushed away from the table, as if afraid that if the food were in reach, she would be filling her plate again. "Come September, I'll get serious about renting Herb's cottage. I'll have to do a few repairs, but by then the snowbirds will be looking for places, so I'm going to have to move his stuff out."

"You going to do your kick-'em-out-the-door lease with these new folks, too?" Wanda asked.

Alice answered before Tracy could. "Sometimes that's good."

"Who wants to move everything they own, then pick it up and move it again two months later? At least the rest of us have stayed a while, so it hasn't been too crazy," Wanda said.

"Karen said I might not be here long…after I sold, you know, my house. She liked the lease."

"Well, next time I move, it's going to be into some spiffy gulf-side condo, with a pool and one of those cabanas where you can sit and have a tropical drink and meet a good-looking man," Wanda said.

Tracy leaned forward to make it clear she was talking to Wanda. "Don't you meet enough men, you know, at *work?*"

Wanda ran her thumb and forefinger across her lips, as if she were zipping them shut.

Everyone had finished eating. Janya rose to clear the table, and the women all rose to help. This had become a tradition, and one that she was happy to share in, with neighbors who had somehow, while no one was watching, become more than that.

They made short work of what they could, leaving some pans to soak in the sink, because Janya insisted.

"Janya promised to dance for us," Tracy said.

Janya was embarrassed. "No, better yet, I will teach you. It will work off calories."

"I'm for that," Tracy said.

"I don't know." Wanda was hesitant, but Alice was smiling. "I want to learn."

That settled it. Janya chose one of her favorite songs, which was both pretty and peppy. "This is 'Kajra Re' from our movie *Bunty aur Babli*. The man in the song talks about how beautiful a woman's eyes are, her dark, dark eyes."

"What's the movie about?" Wanda asked.

"It's a little like the American movie *Bonnie and Clyde,* only Bunty and Babli are loveable, if quite silly. But this song is sung at a nightclub. It's what you call a showstopper, and exciting to dance to."

"Wait, you have to show us first," Wanda said. "We want to see you dance so we'll know where we're heading. I mean, if this is belly dancing, I've sure got the belly for it, but I don't know if I want to shake it after all that food."

The last time Janya had danced in front of anyone, Padmini had been right there taking photos. They had laughed, because Janya had acted far more seductive for the camera than she would have in front of anyone she didn't trust, and she had paid a price. Now? What did she have to lose? These women were her friends, and they were just interested to see how she interpreted the music. Whatever she did, they would still be her friends.

"Yes," she said firmly. "I can show you."

She put on the CD; then, as they watched, she moved into position. The woman's voice was sweet, and as the song began slowly, Janya moved her hands gracefully and slowly swivelled her hips. Then she kicked off her sandals, and began to move up and down on her toes, rotating her head so her hair fell around her as she moved.

The fun began, and the pace picked up quickly. She moved a hip up and down, closed her eyes and lifted her wrist, letting it fall. Head to shoulders, wrists straight and hands across her closed eyes. Then she turned, thrusting her hips from one side to the other, shifting so they saw her in profile, then turning her back as her hips kept time to the music. Part belly dancing, part classical Indian dance, part folk dance, part salsa. Arms up, one at a time, crossing in front of her, wrists rotating, hands climbing until her arms were over her head. Then she went gracefully to one knee, turning as she performed hand movements that went with the song. On her feet again, her skirts swirling around her as her hips and feet moved fluidly, she lost herself in the song.

She was paying little attention to anything else now, but she knew her friends were with her. The women seemed mesmerized. Hands over her head, she shook her hips one way, then the other, in rhythm to the song. Palms down, hands drawing sharp lines in rhythm, then fluid once more as the music changed.

By the time she and the song had finished, she was elated. She wanted to dance forever. The music stopped, and the applause began.

"Wow, that was the most beautiful thing I've ever seen," Tracy said. "Actually, *you* were. Darn you, anyway. It seems so effortless for you, too. You don't have to do a thing, and you're drop-dead gorgeous."

"You think we can shake our hips like that?" Wanda asked.

"I think you can try." Janya motioned them to their feet.

"Can I do it, too?" Olivia looked at her grandmother. "Am I *old* enough?"

Everybody laughed, but Wanda got up, went over and lifted Janya's skirt past her ankles. "Okay, the dancing is something else, but look at this, everybody."

"What did you do to your ankle?" Olivia said. "Is that a tattoo?"

Janya pulled her skirt higher, so they could see. "It's henna, only temporary. I am trying to learn to do them myself. Just for fun. Do you like it?"

The tattoo was intricate, covering the top of her foot and snaking up her ankle. The pattern looked like strands of lace, with swirls and loops and little bows. She thought she was learning the process quite nicely.

Everybody was fascinated. She stood on one foot and held up the one she had adorned. "You could be models for me. I would like to do a hand, only not my own."

"Count me in," Wanda said.

"Me, too," Tracy agreed. "Except I'll need somewhere special to go and somebody special to go there with."

Janya smiled at Alice and Olivia, to encourage them, as well; then she realized this was not something she would ever be able to do for them. Because a henna tattoo would be so much proof they had been to her house, and she was sure Olivia's father would be furious.

"All right," she said quickly. "Let's dance."

Twenty minutes later, everyone was panting and laughing as Janya turned off the music. Wanda had already collapsed on the sofa. Tracy was still swiveling her hips, trying to move them more fluidly. But Alice was the winner. She didn't move as quickly as the others, but there was an innate grace in every movement she made, an eternal youthfulness. She was by far the best of the lot, a natural dancer.

Wanda fanned herself with her hand. "This has been an afternoon of new experiences."

"I have not…had so much fun…" Alice didn't finish, but she didn't need to.

"I like Bollywood dancing," Olivia said.

"You'll need to use those moves carefully, kiddo," Wanda

said. "Or you'll have more boys flocking around you than you know what to do with."

Tracy flopped into a chair on the other side of the room. She glanced at the table beside her, then lifted something from it. "Janya, what's this?"

Janya fanned herself, too. "A bracelet for my brother."

"Your brother wears a bracelet?" Olivia asked. "Is he sick?"

"I don't think it's a medical bracelet." Tracy held it up so the others could see. Olivia went to look at it.

Janya explained. "It's made with silk thread, and gold and silver beads. I may put a photo in the center. In India, we have a special day called *Raksha Bandhan*. A sister makes a bracelet for her brother and ties it on his wrist, to show how much she loves him. In turn, a brother must then protect his sister. The bracelet is stronger than silk thread, because it binds us together."

"And you're making one for your brother?" Olivia asked.

"Yes. Yash is younger than me, very handsome. I miss him. I will send him this, but for the first time, I won't be there to tie it on him this year. He will have to do that alone. Some brothers wear their *rakhi* until it falls off. But Yash will take it off sooner and keep it safe. He has kept all the ones I made for him." Janya just hoped her mother did not intercept this one first.

"Well, you people do know how to have a good time," Wanda said, checking her watch. "But even though this is more fun than I've had in a coon's age, I've got to run. Janya, I can't thank you enough."

"Oh, my, Olivia and I must leave." Alice got to her feet. "We stayed too long."

Janya understood. "Let me see you to the door." But no farther. She understood that, as well.

Everyone left almost at the same time in a flurry of thank-yous, although when Tracy started to follow the others, Janya held her back.

Janya waited until the others were out of earshot. "I worry about Alice. This is not good, the way we must sneak her here, sneak her there."

"I don't know what else to do, but she had fun today."

"And the whole time she was afraid Mr. Symington might come home to stop it."

"I know.... You won't find me defending him anymore, not after the way he refused to let Alice come back to the rec center."

"Then you're worried, too?"

"A little. I think he's just overprotective, but I'll tell you what, I'll go over there this evening, make nice with Lee, so he still feels like he has connections here. You know what they say, you can catch more flies with honey than with vinegar." Tracy gave a small wave and headed down the path.

Janya thought this was just another strange thing about her new country. Why would Tracy want to catch flies with anything?

Tracy spent the late afternoon grouting tile in the bedroom. Finally the floor was finished, except for the bathroom and for applying a sealant to the grout. Laying the tile had been like putting together a huge jigsaw puzzle, only she'd had to cut some of the pieces to fit. She supposed the best part was the way she felt about herself. The woman who had watched her life fall apart had, at the least, proved she could fix this floor.

The cottage would never be the subject of a photo spread, but now it had a quirky kind of charm, with the jute-and-seagrass rug in front of the sofa, the brass vases scattered throughout the room, filled with driftwood and dried weeds, a few green plants Janya had selected from Herb's collection. Here and there she had a memento of her former life. A seascape of the Pacific crashing against seal-studded rocks. A trio of hand-carved wooden bowls. Twin tapestries she had bought from an artist in San Diego. CJ had liked none of these finds, so they were not things she had displayed in their home—which was the only reason she was comfortable seeing them here.

She showered, and changed into denim shorts and a filmy print blouse with ruffles crisscrossing her breasts; then she pulled her hair off her face with a headband of tiny braided crystals. Today she walked through a cloud of 2007's Stella Sheer. The updated version would have to wait until Happiness Key belonged to somebody else.

She wasn't setting out to seduce Lee, just to remind him that she was still here and interested in what went on in Alice's cottage. The trick was to stay in his good graces, but not too far in. To provide an excuse for her appearance on his doorstep, she printed out an Internet article she had read the night before about the way Florida real-estate prices were now on the upswing.

. As far as she could tell, the article was a load of hooey from an infomercial king who was trying to convince down-on-their-luck investors to buy foreclosures and make a killing. Still, Tracy thought it was probably interesting enough to provide the in she needed with Lee.

Along the path to Alice's, she could hear the crashing of waves. Sunset was still hours away, but the sky was rapidly growing dark, and far off in the distance she could hear the rumbling of thunder.

She wondered what it would be like to watch one of these fabulous Florida storms sweeping in from Marsh's porch. Of course, Marsh's house looked as if it had sprouted from the swamp over the last century or more, like some indigenous mushroom. The architecture had none of the class or style she was used to, and no trilling interior decorator had ever rhapsodized about the magical incandescence of pink with hints of Fudgsicle-brown. The house had a shabby-around-the-edges feel to it. The porch was probably home to ravenous insects and snakes, but she still thought sitting there, watching a storm come in, might be pretty wonderful. It might not even be such a terrible thing to have Marsh there watching it with her.

She had only seen him to talk to twice since the night of their canoe trip. Once when he picked up Bay after youth camp and they chatted about the program. Once when he stopped by the cottage after work to give her a packet of papers. Wild Florida had finally put something on the table, and he brought it directly to her, since he despised Maribel. She had scanned the top two sheets and handed the packet back without a word.

"You're clairvoyant? You can already tell you're not interested?" he'd asked.

"Marsh, what you want to pay isn't anywhere near what I'm asking, what I *need*."

"Just out of curiosity, say some developer is dumb enough to buy this for anywhere near what you want, believing he can bribe his way through all the regulatory agencies without tipping us off. So you pay all the taxes, quit your job at the center—"

"I'm only a sub. I don't have to *quit* anything. The job ends in the fall, when the permanent supervisor comes back."

He shook his head in disgust. "So you pay all the taxes, tell Gladys and Woody you don't want the job, and you hightail it out of here. Where'll you go and what'll you do? Will even *that* amount be enough money to make things right in California? Can you buy back your old friends?"

She didn't know what to say. Choked by anger and a suspicion he might have a point, she was mute.

"Tracy…take this." He shoved the packet back into her

hands. "Get your priorities straight, how 'bout it?" Then he'd turned and sauntered back to his car. And she'd let him.

Now she wondered if there were normal men anywhere on the planet. And even if she happened to find one, would she be attracted to him? Or would he just seem like some kind of freak?

Alice's stoop had not been swept this afternoon. Even the oncoming storm couldn't account for all the sand that had blown across it. But Tracy knew where Alice had been. Most likely she was tired after Janya's celebration.

She knocked and heard footsteps. Olivia let her in, but the girl wasn't smiling.

"S'up, Olivia?" Tracy asked, extending her hand palm out for a hand slap.

Olivia complied, but without force or enthusiasm.

She moved closer and lowered her voice. "Nana's not feeling well."

"Is your dad here?"

Olivia shook her head.

"Maybe I'd better see if she's okay."

Olivia put her hand on Tracy's arm to stop her. "She's not okay. She's—"

But Tracy didn't need additional explanations. On the table, just in front of her, was a tangled pile of crochet thread. And Tracy was afraid she knew exactly what it was, or at least what it had been.

For a moment she simply stood there and stared. She was looking at months of effort and dreams, of memories of another tablecloth and beloved hands extended across generations all the way to Olivia. Alice had already lost so much, and now Tracy was very afraid she might have lost her mind, as well.

She felt sick as she reached over and touched the pile. It seemed to recoil under her hand, and she moved back.

"What happened?" She turned to Olivia and moved her hand to the girl's shoulder. "Is that the pineapple tablecloth?"

Olivia spoke in a low voice. "Daddy found it behind the house sitting on the trash can when he came home this afternoon."

"He *found* it? Just like this?"

"When we got home Nana looked all over for it, and she got more and more upset. I didn't know what to do. She was digging through drawers, taking boxes out of the closet. Daddy brought it in and showed it to her. He said before he left this morning she was upset because she realized she had made a mistake at the beginning. He told her it didn't matter, that nobody would ever notice, but she got more and more upset. He thought she would calm down...."

Tracy gazed around the room, because she was afraid to look at the girl. "Were you here when all this happened, sweetie? I mean, could you tell how upset she was?"

"No, I was riding my bike, and Nana was waiting in the yard after Daddy left, so we could go to Janya's. But she seemed fine. Daddy's so worried about her. He made her take some pills and go to sleep. I'm supposed to stay inside and watch her. He went to get pepperoni pizza for dinner. He said he didn't want Nana to cook tonight."

Tracy didn't know how to phrase the next question. She looked at Olivia and asked it straight out, but softly, as if it didn't matter. "Olivia, did your Daddy know that we had a party at Janya's today?"

"I don't know. He came home after we got back. He didn't say anything."

Tracy wondered if Lee had been right all along. Had thoughts of the upcoming party stressed Alice so much that she had ripped out the tablecloth, maybe hoping to fix it, and destroyed it instead? And had she somehow *forgotten?*

Alice, the same Alice who remembered the name of the new bar in Cargo Beach that had once been Gasparilla's. But didn't dementia work that way? Things from the past were clear, but things that had happened that morning were enveloped in fog?

She pulled herself back to Olivia. The little girl was clearly troubled. Tracy didn't want to make things worse, but she had to ask. "Did your grandmother seem okay to you when you walked over to Janya's?"

"She's tired all the time lately, but she wanted to go."

Tracy wondered if Alice had suffered another stroke. She hated to think that might be the case, but again, maybe Lee had been right all along. Maybe Alice did need quiet and rest. And instead they'd been at Janya's eating unfamiliar food, learning a strenuous Bollywood dance. And at home, the heirloom pineapple tablecloth, Alice's pride and joy, had been just a hideous pile of tangled thread sitting on her trash can.

On her trash can. Tracy wondered. That part didn't make sense. Why wouldn't Alice have lifted the lid and stuffed the tablecloth inside to hide it? Why would she leave the evidence where Lee would find it?

Find it *before* he even learned it was missing.

Had this been anything else, she might not have felt so unsettled. But Alice had been making the tablecloth for the granddaughter she cherished, as a reminder of all the women in their family who had come before her. The Alice Tracy knew was more apt to use a flaw in the tablecloth as a teaching tool. Not everything was perfect in life, but it could still be beautiful. Tracy had never heard her say those words, but she thought Alice believed them.

"Is she awake?" Tracy asked Olivia.

"I don't think so. She was crying. A lot. But it stopped."

Tracy felt sick again. She didn't know what to believe, and she didn't know what to do. She pulled Olivia close for a quick hug.

"I'm going to leave, then," she said. "It's probably not a good idea for your daddy to find me here, but Olivia, you know where I live. You know where Janya and Wanda are. If anything happens, and you think another adult should know about it, just run to any of us and we'll help. I promise."

"Daddy says we can take care of Nana without anybody else."

"Just remember what I said, okay? Because sometimes…" She tried to think of a good way to say this. "Sometimes daddies are wrong about things. Okay? And sometimes another grown-up can help when a daddy gets stuck. You'll remember?"

Olivia nodded. Her eyes were huge.

Tracy let herself out.

Rain was beginning to fall, and now the thunder sounded closer. A lollapalooza storm was on its way. Tracy shuddered and wished she could hide.

chapter twenty-six

Chase adored Ken. In a matter of weeks the dog developed a sixth sense about when Ken would come home. Ten minutes before Ken walked through the door, Chase settled himself in front of it like a living, breathing doorstop, and he wouldn't move a muscle until he heard Ken's footsteps coming up the walk. Since Ken might show up anytime, this was a complete mystery to Wanda. Unfortunately, asking Chase to explain wasn't an option.

Ken adored Chase, as well. Or at least it appeared that way when Wanda factored in the subtle signs. He didn't kick the dog. He didn't complain about dog hair on his pants. He took him on walks, which was probably the source of Chase's adoration. Now that Chase was walking—gingerly—on four legs again, he and Ken disappeared for long periods together. Wanda actually missed him.

Chase, not Ken.

On the Monday after Janya's party, Wanda woke to find Chase in bed beside her and Ken gone. Although he had been coming home earlier in the evenings—making her second job a challenge—last night Ken had come home so late she had awakened only long enough to register his arrival before falling back asleep.

"Who told you this was allowed?" She put her arms around the dog, who snuggled closer and licked her face. Would there be a custody fight when she left? Well, that was too bad; Ken could rescue his own greyhound. Or maybe a pit bull, to keep people even farther at arm's length.

"You two look comfy."

She sat up a little and saw Ken in the doorway, a mug of coffee in his hand. "Thought you'd left already."

"I figured you'd be waking up in a few minutes."

She propped pillows behind her. To her surprise, the coffee was for her. Chase sniffed it, decided it wasn't to his taste and jumped off the bed.

"Well, this is a surprise." She narrowed her eyes. "Buttering me up for bad news? Maybe it won't be as bad as you think. Maybe I'm expecting it."

"What are you talking about?"

"You tell me."

He seemed to consider; then he lowered himself to the bed beside her. "We had an incident last night, that's why I got home so late. I tried to call, but the phone was busy."

She didn't even blink, just inclined her head.

"Man took his wife hostage and held her for six hours at gunpoint."

She hated these stories. In the old days she'd hated them because they brought home how dangerous Ken's profession was. Now she hated them because she knew these situations reminded Ken of that night in Cutler Bay. Usually he retreated further after those reminders. He got harder to reach, and one day she'd just stopped trying.

But she couldn't recall a day in the past year when Ken had told her one of these stories himself.

"Were you involved?" she asked. "Aren't you more or less at a desk?"

"I'm also a negotiator."

Ken had trained extensively in negotiation and worked on Miami-Dade's special response team. But she hadn't known the Palmetto Grove department had tapped him for this skill, as well as his experience and commendations.

"You never told me that," she said.

"Thought I did."

"There's a lot you haven't bothered with, Kenny."

"Maybe I didn't tell you because I wasn't sure I could do it anymore."

By itself, this explanation hardly seemed important. But Wanda realized this was the most Ken had said about his emotional state since that terrible night when a young man died.

"You were afraid it would bring back memories." She kept her voice devoid of emotion, afraid to scare him off.

"I did okay last night. I liked not being the one with the gun."

She didn't know what to say. The world had always been a pretty black-and-white place to her. The drug dealer had tried to kill Ken first. In her mind, that meant Ken's response was justified; it was necessary. But she was learning that simplifying things to black-and-white meant the resulting world was a pretty stark place. If she had stayed with that vision, she would never have let herself become friends with Janya and Tracy, maybe not even Alice.

"I've never walked in those shoes," she said. "But maybe I can understand a little."

"I'm seeing the department shrink."

For a moment she thought she'd heard him wrong. Because the man she married would never have done that. To stay on the force Ken had attended mandatory psychologist appointments after the Cutler Bay incident. Apparently he had convinced that psychologist he was doing okay, because the sessions had ended quickly, even though Wanda had begged him to continue.

"Did you schedule the appointments on your own?" she asked. "Or did somebody notice you're not all bright-eyed and bushy-tailed?"

"I did. Wasn't getting very far very fast alone."

She realized how earthshaking this was. Like any man, Ken hated to admit weakness. And asking for help? She wondered just how bad things had gotten. Now Ken was actually admitting it to her. For what purpose?

"Hang in with me," he said, not looking at her.

She wasn't sure what she was supposed to feel. A rush of sympathy? A wave of love? She only felt numb. Too much sympathy and too much love had hit a brick wall called Ken Gray, bounced back and spilled all over her.

"I'm not going anywhere. Not yet anyway." It was the best she could do.

"I know it's been hard." He got up.

"Kenny, it's been hell."

"I wish it could have been different." He whistled, and Chase stopped sniffing under the closet door and bounded around the bed to join him.

"The woman from last night. She's okay?" Wanda asked.

"We talked him into letting her go. Then he put his gun down and came out, and we took him away. It felt good. Seeing something turn out right."

Man and dog left together. Wanda wondered if something really had changed in their tacky little cottage by the gulf. She was afraid to hope.

According to the tourist literature, Cargo Beach, like Palmetto Grove, had once been a working port, with warehouses and commercial docks, run-down watering holes and cheap vacation rentals. Unfortunately for industry, the beach stretching away from the commercial center was white-sugar sand and the water was shallow enough for easy swimming. Cargo Beach had been a tourist mecca waiting to happen.

Now the town looked like somebody's fantasy of a Caribbean vacation. Pastel shops lined brick streets, with palm trees in planters and sidewalk cafés blasting reggae music. Wanda and Janya wandered a couple of blocks, and as they started back toward Janya's car, Wanda was pretty sure she had seen as many tacky Florida souvenirs here as she had in all of O-Town.

"You kind of feel like doing the limbo on every corner, don't you?"

Janya looked behind her, as if she were worried they were being followed. "I was afraid if I forgot to smile, someone would come out of a shop and insist."

"It's like Disney World, only this is supposed to be real."

"I think it must have been different when Alice came here with her husband."

The mention of Alice made Wanda sad. Wanda and Janya had talked about Tracy's discovery at Alice's cottage. None of the women knew what to do. The story of the beautiful pineapple tablecloth was too sad to contemplate. Wanda couldn't bear to think Alice was descending so quickly into dementia.

She tried to perk up. "Well, it's dinnertime. We can drive

over to the Sea Breeze, eat some food and see if anybody remembers Herb."

"I like Palmetto Grove better," Janya said.

"Do you think you'll stay there?"

"The city is kind to business, and Rishi gets tax breaks. So yes, I think we will be there for some time. Do you think about going back to Miami?"

"My life is a work in progress."

They got into the car and rolled down the windows so the heat could escape. They were three blocks down the road before they could stand to roll them up again and let air-conditioning fill the car.

Janya drove like a pro now, and Wanda found she could stop teaching. She wasn't sure she wanted to maneuver through downtown Miami traffic with her friend, but here on the open road she could pay attention to the scenery.

As they drove, the landscape changed. "Cute" was replaced by "real." Funky one-story motels with rusting jungle gyms and No Vacancy signs missing a letter or two. Convenience stores fronting postwar housing developments. Mom-and-pop dry cleaners next to chain video rentals.

She was watching for addresses now. "You can see why a funky old bar called the Sea Breeze wouldn't fit so well where we were. Not unless they hired a marimba band, and served mojitos and pastel corn chips. But we're in different territory here. And there it is, just up ahead."

The Sea Breeze was almost two miles from the center of town. Wanda had seen a million places exactly like it. Pale green shingles covered cinder block, and neon signs in the window advertised Budweiser and Miller Lite. The roof of a concrete patio along one side was held up by metal pillars with paint probably peeling off in strips. Beach bums and working men sat on plastic chairs at plastic tables and smoked too many cigarettes.

"This is kind of old Florida," Wanda warned. "There may not be a thing on this menu you can eat except French fries and cole slaw."

The inside was shabby, too, except no one could smoke. Booths along one wall, a long bar along the other, the same plastic tables in the middle. A couple was dancing to Alan Jackson's "Chattahoochee" on the jukebox.

"We ought to start out at the bar," Wanda said. "Get our bearings."

Janya seemed fascinated. "I have never been anywhere like this."

"Consider it a learning experience."

"What am I supposed to learn?"

"Not to hang out here."

Wanda walked over to the bar and took a seat on a red plastic stool, and Janya joined her. Wanda had already noted that a couple of men at the end were looking at her friend with appreciation.

The bartender took his time getting to them, cleaning the counter as he went. It was that kind of place. Nobody was in a hurry, because the clientele that came early probably dug in their heels and made merry until they were tossed into the parking lot before the doors were locked and barred.

The bartender was about her age. He had weathered skin and washed-out blue eyes. Judging by his expression, an observer would think the night was nearly over instead of just starting up.

"What'll you two ladies have?" he asked when he finally reached them.

Wanda wondered if he belonged to the original family. While Janya thought simply telling the truth about their visit would work best, Wanda thought that was a tad naive.

"I'll have a Miller Lite. Janya?"

"A Coca-Cola, please."

He came back in a minute with their drinks. "I've never seen you here. You just visiting Cargo Beach?"

Wanda took charge. "My mom and dad used to come, back in the days when the Sea Breeze was called Gasparilla's. They talked about it a lot."

"We haven't been called Gasparilla's for forty years or more."

"Well, that would be about right. 'Course, you must have been a kid when it all changed."

"I was a kid in Michigan."

Wanda was disappointed. "I heard the same family still runs the place."

"They do. That doesn't happen much anymore."

"But they leave you to do the work."

He laughed. "The old man's back in the kitchen. If you know about Gasparilla's, you know the big draw was soup, more or less a gumbo, I guess, called Pirate's Puzzle. Ralph's determined he's going to recreate it. He's been working on it for years. Comes in on Monday nights and makes a big batch, and we freeze it for the rest of the week. That's what he's doing now."

"Has he got it right yet?"

"No, but it's pretty good. Too bad the old cook didn't leave the recipe."

"Why didn't he?" Janya asked.

"He had a big fight with Ralph's father. Ralph says he died just to spite him."

"I'll have a bowl to try it," Wanda said. "And my friend here, well, she's a vegetarian. What've you got she can eat?"

Janya ended up with fried mozzarella sticks and zucchini, and an extra helping of cole slaw.

"You go find yourself a place to sit, and I'll bring it over," the bartender said. "I'll tell Ralph. Maybe he'll come out to meet you."

Wanda and Janya settled themselves in a corner booth, away from the jukebox, which was now wailing "Islands in the Stream" with Kenny and Dolly. Wanda figured that was a good sign.

"Explain again why you told that story," Janya said.

"Sometimes a lie's just a shortcut to the truth. If this guy knew Herb, maybe he'll want to protect him. And if we just go charging in announcing we have to find his daughter, he'll clam up."

"Or maybe he would be so happy we cared enough to find Herb that he would work harder to help."

"That's optimistic. But tell you what, my way doesn't work, you bat those gorgeous eyes of yours and tell him why we're really here."

They chatted until the bartender arrived with their food. Wanda thought the soup was fine, but nothing people would flock here to eat. Pirate's Puzzle might just remain a mystery.

"Eat slow," Wanda said. "Until Ralph shows up."

He made his appearance when Wanda was on her last bite. Ralph looked to be near eighty, or maybe he'd just lived a tough life. His apron was a snapshot of ingredients he had used, but he was wiping his hands on a pristine dish towel. Wanda was hopeful she would survive Pirate's Puzzle unscathed.

"I hear your folks used to come to Gasparilla's," he said, without introduction.

"I heard all about you," Wanda said, and this, at least, wasn't a lie. "And what a treat it was to have a bowl of Pirate's Puzzle."

"Did you like it?"

"Ummm…" Wanda smiled. Something about Ralph was familiar, although she couldn't say what. Maybe she'd just waited on too many old men at the Dancing Shrimp. "I loved having crab legs in it like that."

"How come you're not having any?" he asked Janya.

"I don't eat meat."

His nostrils flared. "You like the zucchini sticks?"

Janya looked at Wanda. Clearly she didn't, since she had eaten very few, but she didn't want to lie after lecturing Wanda. "They are wonderfully filling," she said.

Wanda tried not to smile.

"So who were your parents?" he asked Wanda.

"The Grants. Were you even alive in those days?"

"I was. Too young for the war and too old to escape the stories."

"I had another friend, too, who used to talk about this place. Man name of Herb Krause. Did you know Herb?"

"Can't say I did. Do you want some more of my Puzzle?"

"You absolutely stuffed me to the gills," Wanda said.

"Wanda, didn't you tell me that you knew somebody else who recommended Gasparilla's?" Janya asked.

Wanda was glad Janya had pitched in. "Who's that?"

"Clyde...somebody or other. Or do I have that wrong?"

Wanda snapped her fingers. "That's right. Clyde...what was his name?" She paused dramatically. "Franklin. That's it. A neat old guy."

She was watching Ralph's face, and it changed. She'd been living with Ken long enough to read even the slightest nuances on a man's features. The teeniest lift of an eyebrow, the tightening of lips.

He shrugged. "Not familiar."

Except for his reaction, Wanda might have thought they'd chosen the wrong man to ask. Now she was sure he knew something. "Really? I'm sure he used to hang out there. I guess those were the days."

"Well, I've got to get back to my cooking." Ralph turned, and without a word, he headed back toward the kitchen door.

"What is it you say here? Strike two?"

"Strike three," Wanda said. "You know, we're going to have to bring you up to speed on baseball, you planning to be an American and all." She worried her lip with her tongue. "He knows something. You notice the way his face changed when I said Clyde's name?"

"Why don't you just tell him the truth?"

"Because then he won't tell us for sure."

Janya didn't argue. "He did seem in a hurry to leave."

"What is it about old farts that they protect each other right to the grave?"

"What was it about Clyde that was worth protecting?"

Wanda wondered, but she wondered about something else, too. She had recognized Ralph from somewhere. Did he come into the Dancing Shrimp? Had she run into him in Miami at one of the restaurants where she worked? Or had he shopped at her grocery store? She worried her lip some more.

"What is it?" Janya asked.

"I know him. Ralph, I mean, but he looks pretty much like a hundred other old guys I've—" Wanda slapped the table. "Damn…if that don't beat all."

"What beats what?"

Wanda got to her feet. "You stay here. Eat another mozzarella stick if you can stand it. They weren't cooked in lard, you're safe."

"I think they were cooked in motor oil."

"Get used to it." Wanda stalked toward the kitchen. To get there, she had to go around the bar. The bartender started toward her, but she waved him away. "Ralph's expecting me."

He looked suspicious, but he turned back to the counter.

She pushed through the swinging door. Ralph looked up from what looked like a witch's steaming cauldron. "Hey..."

"Studley," she said. "I thought I recognized you, only it was the voice, not the face. It just took me a minute." She moved a little closer and lowered her voice. "You've been seduced..."

The man was standing over a stove. His face should have been rose-red, but suddenly he was snow-white. "I don't— I have no idea... Are you crazy?"

"About you, sugar. We've had some lovely conversations, haven't we?"

He looked around. There was a young man on the other side of the kitchen chopping vegetables. Ralph left the soup and pulled her into the corner closest to the door. "How did you find me?"

"Well, I wasn't looking for you, if that makes you feel any better."

"You're supposed to be twenty-five and a blonde!"

"Isn't it funny the way that works?"

"So what are you doing here?" He peeked over a collection of pots on the island, then lowered his voice some more. "That was supposed to be private. A–non–y–mous!"

"Well, you know, you've just got the sexiest voice, and how could I help but recognize you when I heard it out there?"

"Look, just leave me alone, okay? I...I don't want anybody to know...."

"Of course not." She sounded properly sympathetic. "And I'm not about to tell a soul. Didn't you stop calling because you had a new woman in your life?"

"What do you want?"

"Everything you remember about Clyde Franklin."

"Why the hell do you care?"

She told him the truth. Quickly, succinctly. "We need to find his daughter. As far as we can tell, she doesn't even know he's dead."

Ralph pulled her even farther into the corner. If this kept up, Wanda figured she would be shaped like a wedge by the time she left.

"I don't know a lot," he said. "But Clyde just disappeared one day a long time ago. We all knew something was up, but out here on the beach, we're the kind of people who don't ask a lot of questions."

"He's dead. What can it hurt? Nobody wants to harm anybody. But if his daughter is still alive, she deserves to know he's gone."

"Who was this Herb somebody or other? Why'd you start with him?"

"Because Clyde changed his name sometime after the war to Herbert Krause. And that's how we knew him. Maybe you don't know another thing that will help." She smiled. "But for old time's sake, can't you try?"

The guy across the room yelled over to say he was nearly done chopping.

"Start on the canned tomatoes," Ralph yelled back.

"Studley..." She smiled coquettishly.

"Clyde used to tend bar here on weekends. I was about sixteen, and I thought he was hot stuff, you know? I used to hang around and talk to him."

"Okay..." She nodded to encourage him.

"He wasn't happy at home. That was obvious. Why else would he spend all his weekends away from his wife and kid?"

"Did you know his wife and kid? Did they ever come in?"

He shook his head. "Not then, anyway." He looked as if he was trying to decide whether to go on.

"I would really hate to have to come back here and bug you again," Wanda said. "I know you're a busy man, Stud—"

"Stop that! Okay… Part of the reason Clyde kept coming back was because of Gloria."

"Gloria who? Gloria what?"

"Gloria Madsen. I remember, because I used to say her name like it was some kind of bippedy-boppedy-boo spell. If I'd been a girl, I would have written it in a little heart in my notebook. She was a cocktail waitress, gorgeous girl. The men came in just so she could get them drinks. And she liked Clyde. She was younger, of course—closer to my age, truth be told. But she wouldn't look at me. She only had eyes for him, even though he was a married man."

"Since when has that ever stopped a woman like that?"

"And you think *you* should talk?"

"I do, regularly, although I'm better at *listening*, aren't I?"

He looked away. "Some of the guys knew Clyde before the war, and they said it changed him. A lot."

"I guess it changed a lot of men."

"Anyway, one day he just didn't show up for work, and neither did Gloria, and that was that. We all knew they'd run off together. Clyde's wife came looking for him, got a friend to bring her up here. She was a plain little thing, almost homely. And she had their little girl with her. Everybody felt bad about that."

"Did she know about Gloria?"

"I couldn't tell you. Nobody here would have told her, that's for sure."

"Did Clyde ever write? Call? Come back to visit?"

"No, and I would have known, too. He was the subject of a lot of speculation. Some guys envied him, and some thought he was nuts. Gloria was the kind of girl had her eye out for the main chance. Clyde was good-looking, and smart, but he was nobody's main anything. Too mixed-up, and he drank too much."

"So drinking was part of it."

"Yeah, he was a boozer. He could hold it, too, so you could hardly tell. But one day it gets to you and you fall apart."

"His wife had him declared dead," Wanda said. "Did you know that?"

"I think I heard there were people snooping around at one point, but that's all. Maybe that was it."

"Anything else?"

"No, and that's the truth. I haven't heard Clyde's name for decades."

"Can you spell Gloria's last name?"

"Like it was tattooed on my arm." He did.

"That little girl of his would be in her…what, sixties by now?" Ralph said.

"Something like that."

"Maybe she ought to go on thinking her father died all those years ago."

"And maybe she'd rather know the truth, so she can really put him to rest."

"Glad it's your problem, not mine."

"Ralph…Studley…" She smiled. "We're done here. I didn't see you, you didn't see me."

"I always knew you were older than twenty-five."

"And I always knew you were one good-looking son of a gun. You can tell a lot about a man from his voice."

Ralph actually smiled.

Janya was tired but elated by the time she parked in front of her house. Driving was beginning to feel natural, and she was increasingly comfortable behind the wheel. Soon she would head back out to pick up Rishi and proudly drive him home. In the meantime, she thought she might spend a few minutes reading the *India Post,* which had come in yesterday's mail. She might get more updated news on the Internet, but nothing was better than holding a real newspaper about her own country in her hands.

She didn't notice the car parked just beyond her cottage until she started inside. Then the driver's door opened and somebody called her name.

"Janya..."

Startled, she turned. The man, outside the car now and cutting through her yard, was familiar.

Oh, so very familiar.

She stopped, and her heart seemed to stop with her. Her limbs felt unnaturally light.

"Darshan?"

"It's you. It's really you." He strode over quickly and stopped in front of her. He didn't touch her, but he stood close, and she could almost feel him pulling her closer.

"What are you doing here?" Her words were choked, uncertain.

"I had to see you."

She didn't know what to say. She was afraid to study his face, and more afraid not to. When her eyes lifted to his, she saw that he looked exactly the same, still tall and broad-shouldered. As an artist, she had analyzed his features many times, trying to understand what made him so handsome, so appealing. Not just to her, but to every woman who saw him.

She still wasn't certain. He had a strong nose, cleft chin, high cheekbones. His eyes were almond-shaped but wide, heavily fringed with long lashes. His hair was thick and lustrous. Taken separately, his features were attractive, but not stunning. Despite that, everything worked together in exquisite harmony. Had he come from a different sort of family, he might have headed right for India's flourishing film industry. All he had to do was flash that enveloping, caressing smile, and every woman in the theater would have fallen in love with him.

"I tried to tell you I was coming," he said. "But you never answered my e-mails."

"I didn't read them."

"You couldn't bear to open them?"

"I couldn't see the point." She was glad she was beginning to sound more like herself. She was not a lovesick girl, devastated by loss. She was a married woman, living in another land, finding her bearings at last.

"The point was that we loved each other," he said, in a voice that was as caressing as the smile. "We were to be married."

"Yes, Darshan. But you let your parents destroy that. And you stood by as I married someone else. And now you're to marry the woman who caused all my pain."

"Padmini swears she had nothing to do with what happened."

"Padmini is a liar."

He didn't protest. "I'm not here to talk about your cousin."

"Oh? You will decide for both of us what we discuss? Suppose you tell me what subjects are safe, then. Not my family, who hate me for what I did to them. Not your family, who believe I was a fool. Not Padmini the liar, not the end of our betrothal. Certainly not my marriage to a man I didn't even know. Shall we discuss the weather? Tell me about the monsoons. I hope everybody who believed the worst of me drowns in them!"

She turned to start up the walkway to her house, but he took her arm.

"Let's talk about what didn't end—what couldn't end—

Janya. I thought I could forget you. I thought your coming here would be best for everyone. I tried to believe it, but I can't."

She didn't turn. "Why are you here? To tell me you're miserable? So I'll feel better knowing you suffer, too?"

"Too, Janya? Then you feel it? You know how wrong this is? You haven't given your heart to this man you married?"

"Given your heart" was such a sentimental, almost feminine, expression, and it surprised her, coming from him. Had Darshan always spoken this way? As if he had practiced phrases to please a woman? She couldn't remember.

She lifted her chin. "I agreed to my marriage. I circled the sacred fire with Rishi."

"It was wrong. It was a mistake."

She faced him again. "Your mistake, not mine. Had you spoken one word of support, I would have fought everyone to stay with you."

"You don't know what went on, Janya. You weren't there."

"And you never told me. Tell me, does Padmini know you're here? Did you mention that you would seek me out on this trip?"

"You're bitter."

"I am realistic. But you haven't yet answered. Why are you here?"

"Because you're the only woman I will ever love."

She stared at him. Darshan's eyes were brimming with emotion. She remembered when he had looked at her this way and she had trembled under his gaze. She was trembling now, and she wasn't certain why. This was too much to bear. All the nights she had prayed Darshan would come back to her. And now, here he was, and their love was impossible.

"Go," she said. "Don't come back."

"You haven't yet listened. You don't know why I'm here."

"Tell me quickly, then, before you say goodbye and mean it."

"I can't do it quickly, Janya. That's not fair to either of us."

"I must pick up Rishi at work. He will wonder what's taking so long."

"Say you'll meet me again. Say you'll come and listen to everything I have to say. Because we can be together. I know a way."

She found this perplexing. Was he suggesting she divorce Rishi? Was he planning to break his vows to Padmini? Did he plan for them to marry and live in a place where no one would know what they had done?

She shook her head. "There is no way."

He stepped forward then, and lifted her chin. "You must hear me out. You still love me, too. I can see it in your eyes."

She was pulled in by his voice, by the deep waves of sound lapping over her. She was entranced by the familiarity of his scent, something masculine, a hint of sandalwood, a touch of cedar. At the same time, the words themselves nagged at her, as if these, too, had been practiced.

He smiled sadly. "I don't know what to say or how to say it. I'm falling back on clichés, Janya, but they express what I feel. I love you. I will not live without you."

"Really? Have I no say in this?"

"Please, hear me out, give me a little time before you decide something that will seal our lives in place."

"You'll make me late. My *husband* will worry."

"I have to leave town. I'm in the United States on business. But I can be back next week. Tell me you'll see me then. Give me this one chance to explain it all."

Explain. That was the word that broke down her defenses. To have this explained. To understand once and for all everything that had happened. And yes, to have it explained by the man she had loved beyond reason.

"When?" she asked.

"Tuesday. I can pick you up here or anywhere you choose. After your husband goes to work in the morning."

"No, I work, too. But I can meet you afterward."

"Where?"

"There's a park not far from where I work. We can sit out-side and talk."

"Do you want to be seen?"

She hadn't thought of that. Was she hiding from Rishi now? Rishi, who had only been kind to her, who was waiting patiently for her to learn to love him. What would he think if someone he knew saw her with Darshan? How would she explain?"

Darshan saw her confusion. "I will rent a room at the Beach Haven Motel. Can you meet me there?"

She knew the place. She and Wanda had passed it on the way to Cargo Beach. It was far enough out of town that very likely no one familiar would see her.

"I'll meet you in the lobby," she said. "At five. To talk, Darshan. Just to talk."

"Of course."

She didn't know what to do now, what to say. She did the only thing she could think of. She turned and went inside the house, and waited for him to leave. And once he had, she wiped her eyes, because of course, in the privacy of her home, she had finally wept.

chapter twenty-seven

On Saturday morning the telephone woke Tracy, who had promised herself a morning of sleeping in. It still rang so seldom that this was an event.

On the other end, Sherrie was bright and chirpy, considering it wasn't even 6:00 a.m. in Arizona.

"Good morning, good morning!"

"Why is it good?" Tracy squinted at the bedside clock again, but the time didn't change. It wasn't quite eight in Palmetto Beach.

"Because a colleague of Wade's is flying into Tampa for a conference, and I gave him your phone number. He's gorgeous and available."

"And rich?" Tracy stretched.

"Not CJ rich, more like your father rich. Before CJ mopped up the floor with him."

"It'll be nice if he calls." Tracy thought it would be okay if he didn't, too. "So how come you're calling now? What are you doing up at this hour?"

"The girls had a sleepover last night. I haven't been to bed yet."

"Ouch." Although, truthfully, Tracy thought that might be fun.

"So what's up with you?"

Tracy told her about the rec center, the mural and upcoming shuffleboard tournament, the joys of taming Bay Egan into something approximating a normal boy; then she ended with her neighbors.

"So the quest to find Herb's daughter's hit a big snag, but it's worse than that." As succinctly as she could, she told Sherrie about Alice and everything that had transpired. "We're all worried about her," she finished.

"Wow. Do you think she really ripped up the whole table-cloth?"

"I don't know what happened, but it seems more and more suspicious. I wish I could be a fly on the wall and just watch what's going on at that house."

"Well, you know, you can. They call it a nanny cam, although in this case it's more like a granny cam."

Tracy knew what a nanny cam was, of course. But she had never considered using one in Alice's cottage—or anywhere, for that matter.

"Isn't that against the law?"

"Well, you'd have to check locally. But I have a friend who was concerned about the way a babysitter was treating her son. He was hyper every time my friend went out and much too quiet after she came home. So she installed one in his bedroom and one on the mantel."

"What did she find out?"

"That the kid was a devil. He tired himself out running around the house and abusing the poor sitter, and that's why he was so exhausted."

"Well, I guess that was worth discovering."

"You *are* the landlady. That probably gives you rights."

"I'll talk to my friends, but it's an idea. I should have thought of it."

"You tend to think the best of people."

"It's easier than wondering."

"You always make yourself out to be lazy and completely self-involved."

"And your point would be?"

"That you just hate to condemn people. So if you see something, you give it the best spin. That's why you stayed with CJ so long."

"You're making me sound virtuous instead of like the spoiled rotten divorcée I am."

"Trace, if you were spoiled rotten, you wouldn't have taken that job. Or tiled your own floor. Or even gone off to Florida to wrestle this property thing into the ground. You're a lot more than you ever thought, and every time I talk to you, you just sound better. You're coming into your own."

Tracy was touched. "Wow, if I look in the mirror, will I see a halo?"

"Don't get carried away."

They talked about Sherrie then, and when they hung up, Tracy was wide-awake and ready to start her day.

She decided against a run. Last night she had sealed the last seam on her new floor, and she wanted to show it off. An hour later she was serving good coffee and coffee cake she'd bought in town as the bakery doors were opening. The coffee cake was a splurge, but this was a celebration.

"So, what do you think?" she asked Wanda and Janya, who had finished wandering through the house, examining her work. "Am I good or what?"

"I've got to hand it to you," Wanda said. "You did a professional job. It's sure a big step up from what you had before. Makes it look like a home."

"And you learned all this from a book?" Janya squatted and ran her fingers over a seam.

"I did. I made mistakes, but next time I'll do even better."

"You planning on going into business?" Wanda asked.

"The clearance center where I bought my tile has a fall sale. We could do your floors, if any of the tile gets cheap enough."

"You're serious? Aren't you trying to sell this property?"

"Do you see anybody busting down my door to buy it?" Tracy thought of Marsh's offer. She thought of Marsh. She'd been doing that a lot lately.

"What's the catch?"

"You have to help, and it takes time. But come September I'll be unemployed, and I could work on it then. It's dirty and messy."

"What if Ken helped instead of me?" Wanda said. "I don't think my knees will take it."

"You think he'll still be around?"

"I'll get back to you on that." Wanda looked down at the floor, then up at Tracy. "But you know, that's a nice offer. I sure never expected it."

"I like tile," Janya said. "Perhaps we could do designs."

"That would be cool. I saw some ideas in one of the books I got from the library." Tracy ushered them into the kitchen and poured coffee into her best cups. "I'm thinking of doing tile on these counters, too. Now that I know how to install it. And up the wall for a backsplash."

Wanda accepted her cup and saucer. "This sounds like more than a slow real-estate market. This sounds like somebody who's moving in to stay. You put all this sweat equity into a place, you still want to see it torn down?"

"I'm a one-day-at-a-time kind of gal. If I'm going to live here, I just want it to be a place I like waking up in."

They took the platter of sliced coffee cake into the living room. The others sank into comfortable chairs, and Tracy made herself at home on the sofa. She wasn't sure how she would spend her weekends now that her big project was completed, but she thought relaxing with friends was a good start.

"I noticed the Lee-wagon was parked in front of Alice's," Wanda said. "That why she's not here?"

"I knew better than to ask."

"Have you spoken to her?" Janya asked. "Since lunch at my house?"

"I've spoken to Lee." He had been polite, but she'd been glad to see that his interest in her had cooled, either because of their difference of opinion about Alice, or because he was no longer optimistic about selling her property. Either way, it didn't say anything positive about him.

Wanda plopped two more sugar cubes in her coffee. "And what's his story?"

"He says when she's feeling better, I can visit. For now she's resting. They think she had another stroke."

"Really?" Janya didn't sound convinced. "She was fine last Saturday when we were together. And if what you say is true, she destroyed the tablecloth before she came. Would we have been so blind as not to see she was distressed?"

"How did he act?" Wanda said. "Like he was really concerned? Or like he was hiding something?"

Obviously Tracy was not a good judge of character. Mr. Living Proof was stamping out license plates in California. "He acted...like he was acting."

"Does this mean you're no longer enamored of the hunky Mr. Symington?" Wanda reached for another slice of cake.

"Me, I think he's as high on the creep factor as a buzzard circling a car wreck."

"Where do you come up with these expressions?"

"I was lucky enough to be born in the swamp, Valley Girl. You have some catching up to do."

"Then you aren't certain he's telling the truth?" Janya asked.

"I don't know what to think. Lee told me he stayed here in Palmetto Grove after his wife died because he wanted to take care of Alice. For his wife's sake. He had to give up a good job in Atlanta. Would he do something like that if he didn't have her best interests in mind?"

"Atlanta?" Janya asked. "He was moving the family that far away?"

"He said after Karen died, he just couldn't do it. I guess he knew taking Olivia so far away would be hard on Alice, even if she didn't need looking after."

"You see, this is peculiar," Janya said. "Because Olivia told me her mother had found a new house for them, but her father didn't know. She told me all about the color they would paint her room, but she said the house was a secret."

"Where?"

"I'm not certain, but not as far away as Atlanta. She said they drove there one day to begin painting. She said she would need to be in a different school, that the new house, the secret house, wasn't right here in town."

"Well, they could have driven to Atlanta, but that's a long trip for a few coats of paint," Wanda said. "And if so, why didn't she say so? Olivia's old enough to remember something like that."

"She said the house had four bedrooms, and her mother would use one as an office." Janya put her finger on the tip of her nose, as if she were thinking. "And she talked about her parents fighting."

They sat in silence a moment. "Four bedrooms?" Tracy asked. "One for Karen and Lee, one for Olivia, one for an office. And who would the other one be for?"

"A guest room?" Wanda guessed. "Pretty common."

Janya shook her head. "No, she said that there would be a room for everyone, and the last room would be her mother's office."

"Alice," Tracy said. "She was planning to bring Alice. That's why Karen didn't care if the lease here at the beach was short-term. In fact, if that's right, short-term was a plus. Maybe they sold Alice's house, then settled her here until Karen could find a place they could all share."

"Of course the interesting question is whether Karen was planning to bring her husband along," Wanda said. "Let's face it, who rents a house without telling his majesty unless she's planning to leave him?"

"Olivia said she had to be careful not to say anything to her father. And after her mother died, Olivia didn't tell him because she thought it would make him sad."

Wanda sniffed. "That child is too good with secrets. That's not natural. None of this makes one whit of sense."

"What exactly did Olivia say about the fighting?" Tracy asked Janya.

"She said when they fought, she wished they would stop. And after her mother died, she thought maybe she was to blame for wishing."

"Poor kid."

"I'm getting a bad feeling here," Wanda said. "Like maybe we're not getting the straight scoop about Lee being a conscientious son-in-law who devotes himself to Alice out of love for his dead wife. He must have found out about the house after she died, at the latest. The new landlord would have tracked him down. If she was leaving him, he knew."

Tracy set her coffee cup on the table. "I can't stand the thought that something might be going on over there that could hurt Alice or Olivia. I check in with Olivia at camp, of course, but her attendance was spotty this week. I think Lee is keeping her home to watch Alice or to keep her away from me."

"She hasn't been to my house," Janya said. "She used to come often, but not since last Saturday."

"I'm trying to stay friendly with Lee. I want him to know we have our eye on things, but that's not enough. We don't have any evidence—not really, anyway—that things are amiss over there. All we have are a few vague suspicions, maybe nothing more than a difference of opinion about what Alice needs. I was telling a college friend about this earlier, and she suggested I install a nanny cam."

Wanda whistled softly. Janya looked perplexed, so Tracy explained. "It's a hidden camera. And it records people without them knowing."

"Is such a thing legal?"

"I can ask Kenny." Wanda dusted the crumbs from her hands and reached for her coffee cup. "He'll know what, if anything, we can do."

"Then I guess we have to decide if we should go ahead with it. It's such a huge invasion of privacy."

"Let's just wait and see what he says. For all we know, it's done all the time."

"That's not a pretty thought."

Wanda turned to Janya. "Now for the fun gossip. Who was that good-looking man waiting at your house after you dropped me off on Monday night? The one you were talking to outside on your lawn."

Tracy thought lawn was a misnomer, but she noted Janya's startled expression.

"You saw?"

"Chase had been cooped up all afternoon while you and I were gone. He needed a walk. I just caught a glimpse. Of course, it's none of my business...." From Wanda's tone, that last was more a formality than anything else.

"A man I knew in India." Janya looked as if she were debating. "Darshan."

"What?" Tracy slapped the sofa. "Are you kidding me? The man you were going to marry? He came here? All the way to Florida? To see you? What for?" She added Wanda's line, with the same lack of sincerity. "Of course it's none of my business...."

"Do you always say that? Here in America, when you want to know everything?"

"Only when we're struggling to be polite."

"I am not sure what he wants. He says he still loves me."

"Get out!"

Janya looked startled for the second time. "Really? This offends you?"

"No, no! That's just an expression. It means, like, you're kidding me, okay? I don't really want you to *go*. I want you to tell us what he said."

"He said my marriage was a mistake."

"A real master of timing, this guy," Wanda said. "Now that you're safely married, he can say anything he wants. What's it going to hurt?"

"But why would he bother?" Tracy could tell Janya was upset, but the question seemed reasonable. "What did he want from you? Forgiveness? A blessing on his new marriage? Or is he married yet?"

"Not until September."

"So what, is this a last-ditch effort? He wants you to divorce your husband and marry him before he ties the knot?"

"Or maybe men in India marry more than one woman," Wanda said, obviously fascinated by the possibility.

"No! Not Hindu men. Please, can you imagine me living side by side with Padmini?" Janya almost smiled, and Tracy was glad to see it.

"He couldn't have come all this way just to tell you he made a mistake." Tracy knew men, and not a one would suck down airline meals on a transoceanic journey just to explain his feelings. Even the best of the bunch.

"He wants me to meet him Tuesday after work. He will tell me then."

"Are you going to?"

"I…" She shrugged. "Should I?"

"Wow." Tracy leaned back against the pillows. "What will you lose if you don't, and what will you gain if you do?"

"I have no answers."

"Well, I have a question," Wanda said. "If you don't go, for the rest of your life, will you wonder what Darshan was going to say?"

"I…I don't think I know."

"I don't know what to tell you," Tracy said. "Except that if you do go, whatever he says, whatever you think you're feeling, you need to go home after you hear him out. You need to think it over before you do anything."

"Most of our lives we are living in the middle of a story. But sometimes we end one or begin another. I feel I'm in that place."

"But which place?" Wanda asked. "The ending, or the start of something new?"

Janya smiled sadly. "I suppose that's what I discover on Tuesday."

★ ★ ★

Wanda couldn't remember the last time she and Ken had sat down to dinner together. She just knew that this morning he had made a point of telling her that he would be home in time to take Chase for his afternoon walk. When he actually showed up on time to do it, she figured it wouldn't hurt to meet him halfway and have something ready for dinner, in case he decided to eat with her when he and the dog got back.

She fried chicken and baked biscuits to go with it. She wasn't ready to bake the man a pie. Some things were sacred, and she didn't bake pies for just anybody. But she did make peach cobbler, which was over and above the call of duty, and an emotional risk, at that.

The chicken was just ready to come out of the oven—where she always finished it—when Ken and Chase returned. The dog bounded in, as he always did, to be sure she was still there. Chase's adjustment to living in a house with a family had been nothing short of amazing.

"I hardly have to do a thing," Ken said. "I walk him off leash now. He comes whenever I call, and in between he chases seagulls."

"I never thought you'd take to him."

"If you'd asked me, I'd have said the same thing. But it's nice to be needed, and he gives back double."

"Kind of like a wife, only his expectations are a whole lot lower."

"My expectations are kind of twitching. Do I smell chicken?"

"You do. If you wash up and act real nice, I'll give you some."

He smiled, the old Ken smile. For a moment she just basked in it. Then he was gone, and she heard water running in the bathroom.

Dinner was on the table when he returned. She'd cooked

green beans and summer squash to go with the chicken, and made cream gravy for the biscuits.

He sat down, looked at the food on the table, then up at her. "I have really missed your cooking."

She bit her tongue. This was not the night to point out that she had been right here cooking all the months he had stayed away. "Well, dig in," she said instead. "Before I change my mind."

She waited until he was halfway through his plate before she asked him the questions she'd been saving for a good moment. She had been married long enough to know a smart woman never tackled a man about anything on an empty stomach.

"I need your advice, Kenny," she said. "Will you take a minute and listen?"

"You've got until I finish what's on my plate and have seconds."

"There's peach cobbler, too, if you leave any room."

"Peach cobbler? With vanilla ice cream?"

"Chocolate ripple, even better."

"Shoot." He frowned. "Maybe not the best choice, that word." Then he shrugged and smiled sheepishly. "So, what's up?"

She figured she had just witnessed a miracle. As always, Ken had been reminded of the man he killed. Probably almost everything reminded him. But he'd pushed it away. Maybe the man's guardian angel had finally woken up from her nap and was seeing to business.

"Okay, there are a couple of things." She split another biscuit and ladled gravy on top. "First, on the Herb front."

"You all still looking?"

"We are. We got the name of the woman Herb left his wife for, back when he was still Clyde Franklin. Gloria Madsen." Ken knew the Clyde/Herb part of the story, so she didn't explain again.

"So you got a name. Anything else?"

"Not really. But I got the feeling she was some piece of work, you know? Kind of a tramp, not above stealing anything she could get her hands on."

"So you're hoping I'll run her name and see what I can find out about her later years."

"It's a real long shot. But it's all we got right now."

"It's no trouble. Just don't go telling everybody and their grandma what I'm doing for you." His green eyes had an affectionate gleam, as if he really wasn't sorry to help.

"I'll write down everything I found out, which was precious little. But with luck, maybe she robbed a bank."

"That would be great, wouldn't it? Maybe she murdered somebody, too, embezzled from a big oil company, even worked on Wall Street."

Wanda put her hand to her chest. "Maybe she was one of the top dogs at Enron. Or…a politician."

"I can hardly wait to get started."

They smiled at each other.

"So what else?" He dished up a second helping that was as large as his first. He had lost weight in the last months. She thought he was on the road to gaining it back tonight.

"Well, the situation at Alice's seems to be deteriorating." She told him everything they knew, not leaving out a bit of it. "So we'd like your advice. There's no good way to watch out for Alice. Lee keeps her shut up in that cottage like it was jail."

"Could he be right? Does she need the rest and quiet?"

"You tell me, Kenny. She's got friends. She knows we care about her, and she, well, *blooms* when she's with us. Take that away, and is she going to be better off? Does that work, staying away from people you love?"

She hadn't meant to talk about *them,* but all roads seemed to lead there.

"Not that well," he said after a moment. "This Lee Symington might just be up to no good."

"Like what?" Wanda said.

"Elder abuse. Not that rare, you know. Old people can be a whole lot of work and trouble. Even the best caretakers have bad days and lose their cool."

"It's not like he's changing bedpans. She cooks their meals and cleans."

"What do you think's happening?"

"He handles her money. He claims she has very little, that her investments went south."

"A lot of people's did."

"What if hers didn't? What if he's robbing her blind?"

"You'd need more to go on for an investigation."

"And if anybody started coming around asking questions, Mr. Lee Symington would know what was up. And that would make all our lives miserable."

"Something tells me you have an idea already, only you were hoping I'd come to it on my own."

"Granny cam. Can we put one in there without them knowing about it? Tracy's the landlady. Would she have cause?"

He didn't laugh her off. He just looked as if he was thinking. "You can't record what they're saying. That's against the law unless both parties agree. But there's no law in Florida that says you can't watch them anywhere there's no expectation of privacy. No cameras in the bedroom or bathroom, in other words."

"You mean, we really can do it?"

"Can, but are you sure you want to? What do you think it'll tell you?"

Wanda thought about that over another chicken leg. "Well, it won't tell us if he's embezzling Alice's money. I guess all it will tell us is whether he's threatening her physically."

"I'll get you some information on hidden cameras. You'll be surprised how sophisticated they are. Her house is so close to old Herb's, we might be able to set up some wireless arrangement so you can view everything there."

"You know the most terrible things, don't you?"

"You'd better believe it."

Over cobbler and coffee they talked about their children. Wanda caught him up on everything she knew. Everything felt normal, simple, like any long-married couple at the end of a day. Wanda wasn't lulled by it, and when Ken announced he was going in to work to finish some paperwork, she didn't protest. She wasn't even sure what they would do if he stayed. She was out of that rhythm.

"I'll be back by ten," he promised. "We can watch the news before we go to bed."

"See you then." She was carrying dishes to the sink, but he stopped her. He kissed her goodbye, the way he always had until his life fell apart. She didn't know what to say, but it didn't matter, because he was gone before she had a chance, anyway.

Dishes done, her third shower of the day out of the way, Wanda propped herself up in bed with the telephone. She was too tired for a whole night of calls. In fact lately, since Ken had begun to come home earlier, she had passed some of her clients back to Lainie and asked her to find them someone new to talk to.

She didn't want to risk an interruption or an explanation if Ken caught her on the phone with another man. More than that, she was just losing heart for the whole thing. She had faced the fact she was doing these calls more to spite her husband than for money. What Ken didn't know certainly wasn't hurting him, and she was losing interest in flaunting SEDUCED after the divorce.

She was losing interest in the divorce, too. But maybe she wasn't losing interest in Ken.

When Lainie answered, Wanda jotted down a list of numbers, but when Lainie finished, she told her she only had time for one call tonight. "I'll call Shadow," she said, "but I don't have time for the others."

"Those calls to him are pretty short," Lainie said. "Maybe you ought to take that second number. He talks forever. Don't forget, you get paid by the minute."

"I know how I get paid."

"Well, next month, don't say I didn't warn you when your paycheck won't cover dinner at McDonald's."

"Okay, I won't say it. Now see if you can find somebody to cover the other fellows tonight. Please?"

"You're letting me down, Wanda."

"I think you'd better get used to it, Lainie." Wanda hung up.

She dialed what was now a familiar number. Shadow picked up on the third ring.

"You've been seduced," she said. "And it's a pretty night for it, isn't it? Stars shining, a crescent moon."

"You been outside to see it?"

"I can see through my window."

"You need more fresh air, woman."

"I need somebody to take a walk with me this time of night. You won't catch me out there by myself."

"Wish I was there."

She wished he was, too, although even wishing felt wrong. But she and Shadow had connected. She'd never really looked forward to calling any of the other men in this same way. She had reveled in their conversations, but she hadn't felt as if she were talking to a friend.

"So what do you need tonight?" she asked. "What's your fantasy?"

"I think I just need a woman's opinion. Your opinion."

"Is that so?" She felt flattered. Being consulted was part of a marriage, an important part that had disappeared in hers.

"I made a mistake. A bad one. And I don't know how to tell somebody I'm sorry."

Little ol' Wanda, phone-sex psychologist. Yet even as she tried to be flip, her heart went out to him. Here was a man who needed help, and he had turned to her. Unfortunately, what did she know of forgiveness? She was so locked into anger at Ken, she could no longer feel his pain. She had lost patience with his suffering, and she had made things harder for both of them.

But Lord, didn't he deserve it?

"Why is saying 'I'm sorry' so hard for a man?" she asked. "Can you just say it and get it over with?"

"Some things are a little larger than a simple apology."

"Yes, but isn't that a starting place?"

"I don't know anymore."

"Do you want to tell me about it?"

"Probably not."

"Well, I've got my own issues with asking for forgiveness," she said. "Sometimes the other person needs to ask for it, too. So who goes first? Do you arrange a time when you both promise to start, say, on the stroke of twelve and spew it out together?"

His gruff laugh was now pleasingly familiar to her. "Maybe that's the way to do it."

"You try it first, then, and tell me if it works."

"Let's say I did that. Then what happens? You know?"

"Then I guess you figure out how to start again. If the relationship has anything left, maybe you figure out how to keep it. If it doesn't, you just part company, but at least you're not so angry anymore, or hurt."

"Maybe that's why a lot of men never say they're sorry. Because they're afraid of that last part."

"Whoever you're apologizing to, Shadow? They'd be crazy to turn around afterward and head for the door."

"You don't know me, Sunshine."

But she felt as if she did. "I'd take a chance on what I do know," she said.

"You're good for my soul. I talk to you, and I feel like I can just keep going."

"You can. Keep going, I mean. I hope you don't think about not going."

"I have. Not anymore."

"That's good. That's important. You just put one foot in front of the other and move on."

"Is that what you do?"

"That's what I do, although sometimes I'm not one bit sure where I'm headed."

He laughed. "You have a good night. I'll call again."

"You be sure you do now."

She hung up. Sometime later she opened her eyes and saw Ken undressing on the other side of the room. She still had the phone cradled against her. She carefully set it where it belonged. Then she sat up.

"Did I miss the news?"

"You didn't miss one good thing. Just war and misery. You were better off sleeping."

She turned over and bunched the pillow under her head. He turned out the light and got in bed with her. She could feel his warmth, the soft caress of his breath against her neck. Then he put his hand on her shoulder, and in a moment, his breathing deepened and slowed.

His hand on her shoulder. Such a simple thing. But didn't it make all the difference?

chapter twenty-eight

On Tuesday afternoon Janya watched the tarpon kids working on their section of the mural. Bay was a perfectionist, and he was intolerant of anybody's mistakes, but primarily his own. Janya and Tracy had discussed this, and Janya had given him the task of painting clouds any way he wanted them. Since he had a good eye and strong creative sense, she knew she was safe. With nobody's expectations to live up to, he seemed to be relaxing.

"He's been talking about this all day. He's proud of those clouds," Tracy said, as she and Janya stood shoulder to shoulder on the shuffleboard court. Bay was on a ladder, but not so high that, if he fell, he would be in trouble.

"He struggles between two selves. One wants to reject everything and everybody. The other wants to do everything exactly so."

"I kind of feel it's my job to help him forget all those voices and just have fun."

"Where do the voices come from, do you think?"

"Maybe he wants to please his mother, even though she's not

on the scene. Maybe he thinks if he does everything just right, she'll come back."

"He's a bright boy."

"Yeah, maybe in the long run that will help him figure things out and move on. But I think his dad's making him behave at home now, and that means Bay doesn't have to make all the decisions anymore."

Janya moved forward to point out something to a child painting a wave, then rejoined Tracy. "He likes you. A lot. He tries to impress you."

"And I let him, but not when he's working at it. When he's just having a good time and being a kid."

"Olivia is a perfectionist, too." Janya had assigned Olivia the largest tarpon, rising from the water like a mythical sea beast. Olivia was painstakingly following the sketch Janya had done to show colors and highlights. The outline was there for the kids to follow, but many had put their own stamp on the design. Olivia had talent, but she was afraid to let herself go.

"Olivia worries she'll make her father angry," Tracy said. "I'm guessing that's what the hair was about. She resisted, and Lee had them cut it short to show he was boss. I think she's always worried something she might do will make him angry at Alice, too. That kid has too many burdens."

"The children seem to like the mural. I'm glad I could come and do it with them."

"Will you be here tomorrow?" Tracy turned just far enough to see Janya's face. "After you see Darshan today."

"Did you think I would just run away?"

"Love can be powerful. Maybe facing life without it could be too unbearable to contemplate."

Janya had been turning this over in her mind. "Is that what Herb thought? That leaving his wife, pretending he was dead and going off with a beautiful woman, was preferable to the life he had chosen?"

"I wonder if we'll ever know."

Janya said no more about her plans. She didn't want to tell Tracy that she had carefully packed a bag and stowed it in her car. That she had lied to Rishi about where she would be after work. She was unclear about many things, but not about keeping those thoughts to herself.

When the campers finished for the day, Janya helped clean brushes, move ladders, take up the drop cloths. By the time everything was put away, it was time to meet Darshan.

She still wasn't used to driving alone, but she avoided what passed for rush hour traffic by leaving well before five. The Beach Haven motel was only twenty minutes away, but she drove slowly, not like a woman going to meet a lost lover. She supposed she was driving like a woman unsure whether what she was doing was right. She had thought of little else since Darshan's surprise appearance, but answers had evaded her. One moment she wished she was already at the motel, and the next she wished he had never come, that he had let her memories fade slowly with time, until he was nothing but a ghost that only haunted her occasionally.

She was early, so she parked in the motel lot and crossed the street, cut through another small parking lot and found a path to the beach. She was gazing away from the sinking sun when she saw a familiar figure walking toward her. Darshan was just close enough to identify. He had rolled up the cuffs of his loose-fitting trousers nearly to his knees, and he carried his shoes in one hand. His cotton shirt was unbuttoned almost to the bottom. He moved with confidence, as if he knew how appealing he was. With loose-limbed grace, he threw a stick for a small spaniel.

After the dog was well beyond him, he turned and continued toward her. She knew the exact moment when he registered her presence on the beach. He stopped for a moment and raised his hand to shade his eyes. Then he started toward her at a faster pace.

Janya didn't walk to meet him. She waited, her hair and skirt blowing in the breeze, but she watched, comparing Darshan to Rishi and hating herself for it. Darshan moved as if he were on display, as if he expected others to watch him, although she thought he probably moved the same way in an empty room. He didn't strut, nothing so obvious, but he seemed to embrace the world, to wrap it all around him so that he was at the very center.

Rishi moved as if he needed to, as if there were so many things he wanted to accomplish and time was his enemy. Rishi would be surprised to find himself on display, and if he did, he would also find it uncomfortable. Darshan had been the petted oldest son, his mother and father's hope. Rishi had been the orphaned nephew and burden.

Yet which of them had reason to be confident? Darshan had done nothing to deserve his handsome face and athletic body. He'd been born to privilege and adoration. And Rishi? Everything that was attractive about her husband was his own doing. His energy, his quick mind. And yes, he had been born with intelligence, but Rishi's constant study, his curiosity, his willingness to delve for answers, those were the things that made him attractive. They gave sparkle to his eyes, a glow to his enthusiastic smile, and yes, as Alice had pointed out, character to his features.

"Janya…" When he reached her, Darshan took her hands and drank in the sight of her. "You have no idea how many times I've wished for this."

"No, I don't."

"There's no number high enough."

Her hands clasped in his felt familiar, and the feeling coursing through her was, as well. Months of longing had made Darshan even more attractive. The sudden severing of their relationship had enhanced what she'd felt when they were betrothed. She was awash in old emotions and unable to separate them from newer ones.

For a moment they just stood that way, the waves sweeping nearly to their feet, gulls flying above them. She knew he wanted to kiss her. She also knew he was waiting for a sign. When she could look at him no longer, she concentrated on a line of pelicans flying low along the water.

"Did you know I was out on the beach?" he asked. "You know me so well, you probably realized I would be."

"No, I was early. Walking was better than waiting."

He let her hands fall to her sides, but his gaze still roamed her face. "I had forgotten how beautiful you really are. I dream about you almost every night. But dreams don't do you justice."

She tried to imagine Rishi saying such a thing, and she couldn't. Even when she and Darshan were betrothed, he had not been so free with compliments. She wondered what had changed him. A sincere realization of what she meant to him, seasoned by months apart? Or something else?

With that last thought, the desire began to ebb. Doubt took its place. Doubt and the reality of this moment. This was not an innocent romantic reunion, as she had so desperately longed for. This was a meeting that could destroy lives. Despite the emotion of the moment, she thought of Herb, who had left his wife and child for another, more desirable woman.

"Let's walk," she said.

"If you're too tired, it's cooler in my room."

"We'll walk." She started around him, and he joined her.

"You said you're working?" he asked. "What are you doing?"

She told him about her job at the recreation center. "And why are you in Florida?"

"My excuse was a paper I'm writing on environmentally sound building practices, based on the work of an architect in Fort Lauderdale."

"I'm surprised Padmini and your parents allowed you to come."

"Padmini knows I still love you. She was distraught."

"She has no reason. She fought for you and won. She should be delighted. Even my parents were taken in by her ploy."

He didn't protest, and he didn't say he was reconsidering his marriage. Instead he changed the subject.

"Do you like living in the United States? Have you found other Indian women to be friends with?"

"No, but I have found friends. And there are many things I do like."

"And your husband?"

"What about Rishi?"

"Is he kind to you?"

"Without question."

"I'm glad."

Anger flashed through her. "Yes, I can see you might be. Were he abusing me, you might feel the occasional stab of guilt."

He stopped. "You say Padmini fought for *me*. Janya, I fought for *you*. I told everyone you would never have been foolish enough to join that Web site and post those photos. I stood up for you many times."

"But not when it really mattered. Not when your parents asked you not to marry me."

"Forgiving you, when all their friends knew and were talking to them about it, that was too much. They are traditional, and they are my parents. It's my duty to take their counsel and care for them as they grow older."

"Then why are you here? Are they not still your parents? And certainly their friends will talk even more if you cancel your wedding to Padmini."

He was silent. She turned to look at him and saw the truth in the way he was looking out at the horizon.

"But you have no intention of canceling your wedding, do you?" She was surprised this didn't upset her any more than talking about the past.

"I don't know what I'll do."

"But I think you do. You didn't come here with the idea of finding me and trying to repair what was broken."

"Would you leave your husband if I asked?"

"Don't turn this on me, Darshan. You're the one who flew halfway around the world to find me."

"I can't forget you. That's why I came. Despite everything. Despite an impending marriage that will bring security to my family."

She thought about his words carefully before she spoke. "I have had many hours to think about all the things that happened. Padmini tried to destroy me, and yet, what she did was merely silly, even if it was hateful. I wasn't found in the arms of another man. I wasn't caught selling my body in Kamathipura. Someone put my photos, some real, some not, on a Web site. Only the most traditional of families would find this a matter for ending a betrothal. And your family is not so traditional."

"Because of his position, my father must always be above reproach."

"Your father could have shrugged this off, railed against silly girls who misuse technology and joked about how I would need to be protected in the future. There were many options, any of which would have ended well for us."

"My father was genuinely appalled and humiliated."

"No, Darshan. Your father was already appalled and humiliated that you wanted to marry *me*."

She had said it, and just uttering the words made her stomach knot. But the suspicion that had been growing right beside her romantic daydreams was fully blossoming now, and Darshan had done nothing to stunt it.

He answered slowly. "Perhaps at first he was against it. He had hoped for a marriage that would bring our family financial security. But when he saw how happy I was—"

"He continued to berate you. That is what happened, is it not? Your father was never in favor of our marriage. Nor your mother. And they worked on you, planted seeds, and when this came about, you knew you had been defeated. This was the excuse they needed to drive home that final thrust."

He was silent.

"I deserve to know," she said.

"My father's businesses began to fail," he said at last. "He was busy with his post in the government and neglected them. He lost a great deal of money, and he must have money if he's to become our next chief minister."

"Well, you were a dutiful son, after one sad flash of rebellion."

He stopped and took her arm. "Janya, what's past is past. Many mistakes were made. But it was my father, not me, who felt you were not suitable. I thought I could change him."

She started back the way they had come, walking faster. Someone had built an elaborate sand castle, but the tide had already begun to eat away the perimeter. Soon it would fall under the assault, and tomorrow it would be gone. She sidestepped it as she had before, in no hurry to hasten the process.

But Darshan wasn't watching or didn't care, and he plowed right through it.

"Why are you here?" she asked. "Do you feel so bad that you finally decided to explain? Because I've understood for a long time how we came to this. You have wasted money on airfare you should have saved for your wedding."

They stopped again. He put his hands on her shoulders. "I want you. It's no good pretending I don't. A life without you? I can't imagine it."

"How can you imagine one *with* me?"

"Janya…"

The weight of his hands was another reminder of better days. They were strong and warm, with elegant, long fingers carefully manicured. His dark eyes were searching hers, and behind them…? She wasn't sure. She had a sudden insight, was reminded of another man, although she couldn't quite make the connection.

"You're married." He rotated his thumbs, going right to the tension in her shoulders. Darshan's hands were magical, as if he understood exactly how to please, exactly how to make sure his hands helped him get whatever he wanted.

"Would you leave your husband for me?" he asked softly.

She knew better than to put herself in his power. She waited.

"I'm about to marry. And after one wedding that didn't transpire, could I back out of another?"

Again she waited for him to answer his own question.

"But I will be in the United States often," he continued. "My new firm wants me to work closely with the architect I mentioned."

She stepped away from him, turned and started up the sand, cutting across it at an angle and back toward her car.

He caught up in a few strides. "We can be *everything* to each other, Janya. Everything that matters. Neither of us married for love. But we can have that, too. We can't be husband and wife, but we can be lovers."

She said nothing. She just found the path, crossed one lot and then the street. She halted before crossing the hotel lot. Darshan put his arms around her and pulled her behind a tree.

"I will never love anyone else. I know you love me. Look at me."

She did. She searched his eyes, and she realized who he had reminded her of, the other man who had come to mind on the beach.

She shuddered. "You said mistakes were made? You're correct. I made two, Darshan. First I fell in love with a man who thought he was better than I was." She pulled away and started toward her car.

He caught up again. "This is foolish. What do we care if the world sanctions our relationship? We would have so many happy nights together."

She couldn't walk fast enough. She unlocked the car with her remote; then she opened the passenger door and took out the bag she had so carefully packed. She opened it and began to draw out objects, dropping them on the ground at his feet.

"The sari you bought for me. The bracelets. The ring. The pashmina shawl. The book of love poetry." She was dropping the items faster and faster, flinging them at his feet now, until the bag was almost empty. "I kept them. I brought them into my marriage, and now I'm so ashamed. If my husband notes their absence, I will tell him they were soiled beyond repair and not nearly as lovely as the things he has given me."

For just a flash he looked at her with the eyes of a cobra. "You fool!"

"I said I made two mistakes. The second? I fell in love with a man who can only love himself. But Darshan, there was a third mistake, too. I didn't see until right this moment that *you* must have helped Padmini plan my humiliation."

His fury was suddenly tinged with surprise, a cobra caught in a net, and she knew for certain that although she had only been guessing, she was right. Now she knew him for the man he was. She also understood exactly what he had been capable of, although knowing gave her no pleasure. She set the facts before him, his very own feast of lies.

"When you finally realized you had been blinded by lust, you knew you had to act quickly. Padmini was willing to do anything to become your bride, even destroy her best friend and cousin, so the two of you found a way to make that happen. *You* were the one who made certain your colleagues and your father's saw that Web site. For all I know, you helped Padmini put it together."

He had recovered his poise. "This isn't true."

She reached into the bag and pulled out the only thing left, the portrait of Padmini. This she handed to him. "Give my cousin this gift, along with all the things I've outgrown, Darshan. And don't contact me again. If you try, I'll telephone Padmini and tell her what you've said. I will call your parents, and the men at this new firm of yours. I will beg them to make you leave me alone."

She rounded the car and got in, glad he didn't try to follow her. She turned the key and drove off without looking back.

Never would she have expected to see Lee Symington simmering deep in the eyes of the man she had loved. She supposed this would be the only time in her life that she would be grateful she had ever met Alice's son-in-law.

She drove calmly, carefully. But she didn't go home. She drove to Rishi's office to insist that he come back with her for dinner on their little patio.

chapter twenty-nine

Wanda wasn't familiar with Tampa, but Ken knew it well. It was a thriving international city, but like any city, it had high-crime neighborhoods. When he told her where she could find Gloria Madsen, Ken warned her that the neighborhood was primarily industrial, but the cops still dealt with illegal alcohol sales and prostitution. A flourishing adult entertainment business was a magnet for people Wanda didn't want to meet on a dark street corner.

"You be careful," he said. "If you want to wait for my next day off, we can go together." But on Friday morning, rather than take a trip to and from Tampa with Ken sitting silently beside her, Wanda left alone. As payment for what was surely going to be nothing more than a wild-goose chase, she planned to treat herself to a real Cuban lunch in Ybor City.

She hadn't been surprised to learn that Gloria Ann Madsen, born in Cargo Beach in 1928, had a long record of arrests, most recently for forgery. She had served part of that sentence, but as the oldest inmate at the correctional institution, she had been moved to a halfway house as soon as it was legally possible. That was where Wanda was heading now.

After the long drive and a staggering portion of paella, Wanda parked in front of a run-down house on a side street she'd spent a frustrating hour trying to find. The house was stucco, with a red tile roof, but anything that had added beauty to the basic Spanish-style architecture had been stripped away. The house number was scrawled on the wall by the front door. Halfway houses were rarely flush; halfway houses for ex-cons were probably the poorest.

She checked the street before she got too far from the car. The sun made her head ache, and if bad guys normally lurked in doorways, today they were lurking inside, where the beer was icy cold.

The walkway to the house had been swept, but patches of sandy soil and weeds bordered it. Apparently, landscape beautification was not on the agenda for residents. Wanda rang the doorbell and waited. A young black woman with short braids and a nose ring answered, and looked her over carefully. Wanda explained who she was and who she wanted to see.

The woman gestured Wanda inside without asking what she wanted. "She doesn't get much company," she said, as she headed toward the back of the house. "Even if you're a bill collector, she'll be glad to see you."

In the living room, Wanda took a seat on a worn sofa. The house smelled like fried onions, BENGAY and urine. Judging from the walker and wheelchair shoved in a corner, this particular halfway house specialized in inmates making their return to a community they had left a long time ago. Of course some, like Gloria, were probably career felons, who hadn't let age stop them from plying their trade.

A dying rubber plant stood against the opposite wall. At some point somebody had draped it with colored Christmas lights. Now the plug was dangling over one leafless branch, along with a sad strand of tinsel. Growing old was bad enough, but doing it here? Worse than depressing.

The woman who finally crept into the living room looked all of her eighty years. She was tiny and frail, with thin hair that had been dyed a pale orangey-red. Several inches at the root were stark white in contrast. She had penciled in eyebrows with a shaky hand and dabbed on coral lipstick. But there was little left of the woman for whom a man named Clyde Franklin had abandoned his family and changed his name.

"Who are you?" Gloria demanded. "You one of those door-to-door evangelists trying to save my soul again?"

"Not hardly." Wanda got up to help her to the sofa, but Gloria jerked her arm away.

"You think I don't know where the sofa is?"

Wanda understood. Most likely this woman was the husk of the person she had been years ago. She was trying, in her own angry way, to maintain dignity. Wanda also understood why Gloria had few visitors.

She waited the interminable length of time it took the woman to seat herself on the sofa. Then Wanda took a seat beside her and handed Gloria a CVS gift bag she had put together the night before. "My name's Wanda. I brought you a few things. I figure it can't be easy living here."

Gloria didn't ask why Wanda cared. She opened the gift bag and sorted through the items. "Postcards? Why the hell do I need postcards?"

"I figured there might be somebody you'd like to write to."

Gloria snorted. She didn't say anything about the other items—a candy bar, some lavender body wash, a new comb and two packages of pantyhose. She closed the bag and set it beside her, a distance from Wanda, as if she were afraid Wanda might snatch it back.

"I ain't got a thing you need, so if you come here to get something from me, you're out of luck."

"That might be true." Wanda looked around the room, and her gaze settled on the television set. "Does that thing work?"

"The picture stinks, but we get most stations."

"You watch *All My Children?*"

"So what if I do?"

"Did you watch today?"

"And if I did?"

"Just trying to find out if Colby mentioned that secret plan of his again."

That sparked something in the old woman. She relaxed a notch. "Better, even. We got to see it. The whole thing."

"You remember what it was?"

Gloria lit into a description. Wanda planned to see the show at home later, since she'd been sure to tape it, but Gloria was on a roll. She gave Wanda a blow-by-blow of the entire hour. Wanda was sorry she'd gotten her started.

"So what, you come to this dump just to get a recap of your favorite soap?" Gloria said once she'd finished.

"No, I came to see what you know about a man named Clyde Franklin. Later on he called himself Herb Krause."

Gloria didn't look surprised, and she didn't look worried. "What for?"

"He died back in May. I'm one of his neighbors. We've been trying to find his family to let them know and see if they want anything of his."

Now Gloria looked interested. "He have anything good? Anything anybody would *want?*"

"Just mementoes, mostly. Nothing valuable."

"No surprise, I guess. Herb never had much get-up-and-go."

Gloria Madsen's own get-up-and-go had gotten her *here,* but education wasn't on Wanda's agenda.

"Did you know him mostly as Herb?" she asked instead.

"That's how I think about him. When we lived together, that's what he called himself. I got in the habit."

"He got the name from a dead war buddy, didn't he?"

"I never paid much attention to what he did or how he did it."

"Do you mind telling me how long you were together?"

"Why?"

Wanda sat back. "I guess I'm interested. He gave up a lot to be with you, so I wondered if he got his money's worth."

Gloria's laugh sounded like an old dog yapping. "I was something else in those days. Men crawled all over me. 'Course, most of them came back from the war right after I grew a big set of knockers." She demonstrated with her hands. If her breasts had really been that big, she would have made Dolly look like Olive Oyl.

"Them guys were looking for a woman, and I was looking for a way out of Cargo Beach," Gloria said. "What a hole!"

"You seen it lately? It looks like they turned Walt Disney loose with a thousand gallons of Easter egg dye."

Gloria yapped again in appreciation. "Herb was my ticket out of there. About a year later I found a ticket somewhere else. Herb never really settled into the life I wanted. He never got over leaving his wife and kid the way he did. Maybe he never got over the war, either, I don't know. So I made it easy for him. I found another guy more to my liking and took off."

"He didn't go back to his family. At least not from what we can tell."

"Maybe his wife didn't want anything to do with him after that."

"Could be."

"He wrote her all the time."

That was a surprise. "No kidding?"

"I'd find letters crumpled in the trash. He never knew what to say. He'd start them, then give up. He addressed envelopes, too. Just in case he ever figured out what he was going to write. But he didn't use a one of them, not that I know of, anyway."

"You wouldn't possibly remember the address, would you?"

Gloria appeared to be considering.

"Maybe it was on Hall Street?" Wanda prompted. "We know he lived there before the war."

"No. It was prettier than that. Allamanda. You know, like that pretty yellow flower you see all over down here. You know why I remember? Because I saw Herb's wife once, Louise. And she weren't no allamanda flower, I can clue you, though she was kind of sallow, I guess. He should have bought her a house on Sandspur or Crabgrass." She winked in appreciation of her own joke. The eyelid took a couple of seconds to rebound, as if it were out of practice.

"That was so long ago. You're sure?" Wanda asked.

"He bought that house right after the war, a little old house in Palmetto Grove, with a screened porch up on concrete blocks. I saw it once. Drove down with another fellow to see how Herb was living. That was before we ran off together. It probably wasn't worth a lot, but Herb figured Louise would sell it for some dough once he was gone. He checked every once in a while, but she hung on to it. She probably got work to make ends meet. He said she'd worked in a laundry during the war. Took their little girl with her. Washed and ironed sheets ten hours a day. He told me that so often I got sick to death of hearing it. Who cared?"

Wanda's patience had extended an unusual length. Had she

been able to reach that far, she would have patted herself on the back for being cordial and understanding. Gloria Madsen was a pitiful wreck of a human being.

Now she sat forward, ready to take off before cordiality made a beeline for the door before she could. "Is there anything you might remember that would help us track down the daughter? Louise died a long time ago. So we're looking for Pamela, or maybe even her children."

"I don't know anything. Like I said, I lit out after only a year with Herb. He was drinking pretty heavy. I'm surprised he made it as long as he did."

"He was well-liked where we live." Wanda tried not to wince as she said this.

"Yeah, that was his problem. He was just too nice. His conscience just kept getting the better of him. We'd have had more fun without it."

Wanda stood, brushing her skirt over her knees. "Well, good luck here. They'll be letting you move out soon?"

"Got no place to go. Myself, I have a daughter somewhere, too. Not Herb's kid, mind you. The next guy's. But she won't want me around. I don't like her that well, anyway."

Wanda couldn't imagine what to say to that. She nodded goodbye and made it to her car in record time. She rolled down the windows, but she sat there and baked for a few minutes, hoping she was wrong. Inside her head the conversation played, then replayed, and every time she reached the same conclusion. Could she possibly have something in common with revolting Gloria Madsen, a woman who had abandoned Herb because he was no fun, because he had a conscience, and just because she could?

She was sweating when she started the engine and started back home.

★ ★ ★

Tracy was finishing her daily report when somebody knocked on the rec room door. She glanced up to see Marsh Egan.

"I haven't changed my mind about Happiness Key," she said. "Just in case that's why I'm so honored by your presence."

"Want to have a barbecue out on the beach?"

Her eyes narrowed, the number one physical response she always had when Marsh was around. Number two was something approximating desire, and she didn't want to think about that. She had to be misinterpreting. She couldn't possibly have the hots for this casual, cynical, too-happy-with-his-own-cooking attorney who was trying to rob her of everything she owned.

She stood and stretched. "Why? So you can harass me about my property?"

"I was thinking more along the lines of us enjoying what passes for a cold spell around here."

"Cold spell? You could fry eggs on the shuffleboard courts."

"Well, you could, but my spareribs are tastier. And it only got up in the eighties this afternoon. It's going to be a gorgeous sunset, and you could watch it with me and Bay."

"Will you promise not to do a hard sell?"

He smiled, a very masculine smile. "Depends. I won't try to sell you Wild Florida's agenda, if that's what you mean."

She was melting, and not from the heat. She tried to remember why going anywhere with Marsh was a bad idea, but nothing came to mind.

He took lack of another protest as yes. "Go home and grab your suit. The beach directly across the key from my house is mostly empty on weeknights, and it's a great place to watch the sun go down. I'll set up my grill." He told her how to get there, and when.

"What can I bring?"

He gave her "that" smile again. "The cutest bikini you own."

"Don't get any ideas."

"I'll have ideas aplenty. I'll also have my son."

"For once Bay will be in the right place at the right time."

"I guess that's all in how you look at it." He gave a mock salute.

She finished the report, then some other business, closed up the rec room and let herself out the side door. So what if she had turned down a blind date with Sherrie's doctor friend for tonight? So what if he had offered to spring for dinner at the ritziest restaurant in Palmetto Grove on this, the only night he had free? She had been sure she wouldn't feel up to going out after a long day at work. A woman could occasionally be wrong.

Once she was home, she showered before she considered her bathing suits. She did not choose the skimpiest. Not even a bikini. She pulled on a black strapless one-piece with a giant poppy a la Georgia O'Keeffe. Then she threw on a gauzy red cover-up and matching flip-flops, left her hair loose, and packed a basket with cheese and crackers, and a bottle of chilled Chardonnay.

She arrived at the beach as Marsh and Bay were setting up a portable grill beside a picnic table on the edge of some small dunes. On the sand below them, she spread a blanket and set up her iPod speakers. Then she sliced cheese and laid out crackers.

Bay flopped down beside her, and she offered him the plate. He helped himself, eating out of the palm of his hand. Marsh arrived with a small cooler filled with drinks and dropped to the blanket beside his son.

"Don't ribs take a long time to cook?" Tracy asked.

"What's a California girl know about ribs?"

"I had a rib of celery yesterday."

"Somebody needs to get some meat on those bones of yours."

"Eating alone's no fun," she said before she could censor herself.

"I precooked the ribs last night, along with everything else."

"You were pretty sure of yourself, if you were planning all this for me."

"You or some other gorgeous female. I had a list."

"You did not," Bay said. "You told me you were going to get Tracy here if you had to kidnap her."

"Children," Marsh said. "There are no secrets."

"I kind of wanted to see him kidnap you," Bay said. "Throw you over his shoulder, like they do in the movies."

"What kind of movies do you watch?"

Bay shrugged.

"The kind with real men," Marsh said.

They discussed movies, Tracy's beach music, Bay's progress on the butterfly stroke, the mural, whether Bay was going to practice hard for the center's youth shuffleboard team, Tracy's new floor, and finally, once Bay went bodysurfing, Alice.

Marsh kept his eyes on his son. Tracy found herself telling him her concerns about Olivia's father and the way Alice was being kept from the other women. She wasn't sure why she told him, except that Marsh, for all his bravado, was a good listener. She even sensed genuine interest, though sensing *anything* genuine was a skill she hadn't honed in the past.

"You're a busy little bee, aren't you?" he asked, once she finished.

"What's that supposed to mean?"

"I mean, you've got some project or other all the time."

"You think Alice's welfare is a project?"

"No, I think it's a sign you aren't the ditzy blonde you pretend to be."

"Have you noticed the color of my hair?"

He reached over and snagged a lock, running his fingers along the length, then tugged gently. "Come closer and let me see for sure."

She didn't budge, so he moved closer to her. "Are you sure you're not a blonde?"

"This is demeaning to women of the blond persuasion and politically incorrect."

"It's not demeaning. I'm comparing them to you, and I happen to like you. So it's a good thing."

"Why?"

"Why what?"

"Why do you like me? I'm standing between you and total conquest of the key."

"I've yet to figure that out."

She smiled, and he glanced her way and smiled back. "And this is where you tell me that you're growing fond of *me,* as well," he prompted.

"No, here's where I tell you that my husband was a sociopath. Plus the neighbor I once thought was charming and kind might be one, too. So you'll have to excuse me if *these* days I'm trying not to grow fond of any human being with a prominent Adam's apple. In fact, I'm thinking of setting up a lie detector in my living room for first dates."

"Well, we already had our first date, but here's what you would find out if you hooked me up now. I'm loyal. I can be trusted with money, secrets and your deepest fears. Even though I'm a lawyer, I make a point of not stepping on people, unless they're stepping on the things I hold dear. I would rather be outdoors than indoors in any kind of weather, which is why I left Manhattan. Florida is my home, and I won't ever be moving again. I love kids and can't believe I married a woman who doesn't. And when you and I finally go to bed together, I promise I'll be as interested in pleasing you as any sane man could be under those circumstances."

"Wow."

His fingers moved from her hair to her cheek, and he stroked it with the back of one. "Now here's the plan for tonight. My son's out in the water by himself, so I'm going to go and join him. But you're just here to have fun. No projects, no plans. You sit, unless you feel so inclined to play with us. When we're done throwing the beach ball or dunking each other, we'll eat. And after that, we're just going to sit here and watch the sun go down. Nothing else. Just sit and let our thoughts have their way. Afterward you'll go home, and I'll go home and put my son to bed. But when I do, I'll be wishing for a different ending to the night."

She was absolutely entranced. She didn't know what to say, so she said nothing.

"Good," he said. He kissed her nose; then he got up and took off for the water.

Tracy wondered exactly what she was getting herself into. Then she asked herself if she really wanted to know.

Wanda did some shopping before she left Tampa, which meant she hit rush hour. Summer traffic clogged the roads going south, and an hour from Palmetto Grove, she was so hungry she had to stop for dinner.

Then she had a flat.

By the time the road service came and changed the tire— no way was she going to ruin her nails—the sun had gone down. She tried Ken, but cell service was spotty, and she was disconnected twice, just as she reached their voice mail. By the time she was able to try again, her phone battery was dead.

She cruised into her driveway about ten. Ken's car was there, which surprised her. Assuming he would go back to work after he let the dog out and made himself something to eat, she hadn't been concerned enough to find one of the last of that vanishing breed—telephone booths—to leave a message. She figured she would be home for the night before he came home for good.

All the lights were on when she walked in, and Ken was standing just a few feet from the door. Chase was on the sofa, head on his paws as if he were waiting for disaster to strike.

"Where have you been?"

She blinked at the lights. "You know where I went."

"I know where you went this *morning*." He slashed a hand through the air as he spoke, an uncharacteristic gesture.

"Well, Kenny, that's where I've been." She started into her litany of woes, but he cut her off with another slash.

"You couldn't call me? You thought that wasn't important?"

"If you would let me finish? I tried. Twice. No cell service, then my battery was dead. And where do you get off yelling at me? You're the one walks out of here any time of the day or night and doesn't look back. How many nights do you think I've had to wonder where *you* were?"

He turned and stomped into the kitchen, but Wanda followed.

"An answer, please," she said. "Exactly why is this so different? I wasn't trying to worry you, things just happened."

"You know I can take care of myself!" He spun and faced her.

"I can take care of myself, too. In case you haven't noticed, I've been the only one taking care of me for a very long time."

When he didn't answer, she gave up and stormed into the bedroom, where she stripped off her clothes, pulled on a robe and went into the bathroom to shower and brush her teeth. She was hot, tired and pissed. She had begun to hope maybe things between them were improving, but now it looked like they were moving from silent mad to yelling mad. Considering that she was bone-deep tired of mad in general, she wasn't going to take well to this new stage. She figured their relationship might be at the very end, stage four malignant marriage. A breath short of terminal.

When she went back into their bedroom to get her night-gown, he was sitting on the side of the bed. She was so tired she could hardly put one foot in front of the other, and she wished he had taken off for wherever, like so many other nights. The one night she didn't want him here, there he sat.

She dropped her bathrobe and shrugged into a thin little nightie that made the hot nights and hot flashes bearable.

"If you'll excuse me, I'm going to sleep," she said. "I've had a long, hard day, and I want it over with fast."

He got up, and she got in bed, expecting him to turn off the light and leave. Instead, he turned off the light, slid out of his clothes, letting them drop audibly to the floor beside the bed, and got in beside her.

She turned over so her back was to him. She expected him to do the same. They'd been sleeping that way for what seemed like a hundred years now. But Ken didn't turn over. She felt him lying rigidly on his back, probably staring up at the ceiling.

"Wanda?"

"Just say it. Whatever it is, so I can get some sleep."

"I thought I'd lost you."

For what seemed like a long time she lay there, wondering if he had. She didn't dare tell him. She wasn't even sure she should speak.

"Come here," he said, at last. Then he reached out and pulled her against him. He put one arm under her and turned a little so he could stroke her hair.

"I hope to God you never, ever, go to the place I've been," he said softly.

"Kenny, if you had let me, I would have followed you there."

"How could I ask you to?" He pulled her a little closer; then he kissed her. Lightly at first. Then harder.

She resisted for only a moment. Then she put her arms around him and held him tight as the kisses deepened. When his hands began to wander, she welcomed him. Tonight she didn't know if their marriage was ending or beginning anew. She just wanted to be sure she gave it every chance.

She wanted to have nothing in common with Gloria Madsen. She was holding out for hope.

chapter thirty

"Maybe she's chained to the bed. Or maybe she's come down with some kind of tropical fever, and that son-in-law of hers is nursing her back to health day and night, mopping her forehead and forcing cool liquids down her throat. Could be one or the other, but how are we going to find out?"

"Do you get a charge out of exaggerating everything?" Tracy put her pie plate into Wanda's new dishwasher. The dishwasher was one of Janya's garage sale finds, and Tracy had paid Handy Hubbies to install it last week. Wanda had invited them both for lunch and a slice of her famous Key lime pie to thank them.

"How do you know I'm exaggerating?" Wanda asked. "We haven't seen hide nor hair of the woman in so long, I'm not sure I'd recognize her anymore."

In the weeks since Sherrie had suggested a granny cam, things had deteriorated at Alice's. Now the women almost never caught a glimpse of her. And Olivia, whose attendance at the center had become more inconsistent, seemed increasingly unsure of herself. When Tracy tried to talk to her, she had little to say, as if she were afraid she might make a bad situation worse.

"If Alice's health really is declining, that could account for everything," Janya said, although she sounded as if she didn't believe her own words.

Tracy knew illness was a possibility, but the whole situation seemed suspicious to her. "When he sees me now, Lee barely nods in my direction. A couple of times I've tried to signal I want to talk to him, but he avoids me."

"It was bad enough we let poor old Herb die alone...." Wanda shook her head. "We didn't learn what we needed to from that?"

"Trust you to put this right on the table. Okay, next time I'll plant myself in front of his car and wave until he stops."

"*If* he stops," Janya said. "If I was waving, he would charge, like a bull at a red cape."

Since closing the door on Darshan once and for all—a scene she had related to her friends—Janya had seemed more confident and assertive. Nowadays she was outspoken about her dislike of Lee. Tracy thought Lee charging anyone was an exaggeration, yet she couldn't ignore the other women's fears. Something just wasn't right at Alice's cottage.

"I've talked to Ken about Alice." Wanda poured detergent into the dispenser, closed the door and turned the dishwasher on. "There, doesn't she purr pretty?"

"It came from a very nice house," Janya said. "Many bedrooms."

"Only the best secondhand furniture need apply. But Ken says since Alice already suffered one stroke, this *could* be the aftermath of another."

Even if that were true, the setup still didn't seem right to Tracy. If Alice was ill, then Lee had to know the neighbors would be happy to help. Instead, he was shunning them all, even her.

"I really wonder if we ought to make a complaint," she said.

"Staff at Adult Services are underpaid and overworked, the

way they are all over the country. Ken says there's no way to guarantee a thorough or quick investigation."

Tracy still wasn't ready for the granny cam.

"You could always just go on in and look around," Wanda said. "You have a working key."

"Unless he's changed the locks."

"He's a Realtor. He knows that would raise a red flag. The place is for sale. He knows somebody might need a quick look."

"If he *has* changed them and I complain, he'll know I was trying to get in."

"I guess you need a good excuse."

"Smoke detectors," Janya said. "Is that something a landlord might provide for tenants?"

Tracy winced. "Great. I never thought about smoke detectors. Another strike on the landlady front."

Wanda snapped the dish towel at Tracy; then she dried her hands. "Janya's got an idea there. You're worried about fires all of a sudden. Let's say somebody told you if there's ever a fire at one of our houses, you could lose everything."

"Lost everything already, remember? Been there, done that."

"You still have this property. Makes you that much more worried, since it's all you got."

"I guess my insurance agent could have mentioned smoke alarms."

"There you go."

Tracy continued to think out loud. "I could run out and buy a couple, then wait until Lee leaves the house...."

"I'll save you a trip to the dreaded Wal-Mart. I've got a couple extras out in the utility room. Ken's been to one too many fires. He stocks up."

"This doesn't sound bogus? It's believable?"

"It's all we got right now."

Janya glanced at the clock over the door, a bright pink plastic tulip surrounding a black-and-white dial. "I must go, but Tracy, I advise you to be careful. You may think I'm wrong about the plants, but if I'm not, Lee's a violent man."

"I agree. Let us know if you're going in," Wanda said. "I'll come, or I'll watch your back."

Tracy smiled. "Is that how cops' wives talk?"

"It's right there in the manual. I'll get you those detectors. The sooner you find out nothing's going on in there, the happier we'll all be."

Tracy left with the detectors and a full stomach. At home, she set the smoke detectors beside the sink and worried about what she should do next.

She didn't have more than a few minutes to consider. The mail truck passed. On the way outside to see what was in her box, she saw Lee's car pull out of Alice's driveway. Normally she wouldn't have been able to get to his car before he was gone, but he stopped, then got out to retrieve a package on the ground beside the mailbox. She had just enough time to get out to the road and no time at all to think about what she was doing. When he saw her bearing down on him, she thought he was actually going to leap in and leave without acknowledging her.

He didn't. He opened his car door and stood behind it, like a knight behind his shield. Unfortunately, she was more and more afraid Lee was nobody's knight.

"Hey, long time no chat," she said. "How are you?"

His smile was anorexic. "On my way out for a while."

She glanced in the car and saw Olivia, but not Alice. She smiled at the girl, who smiled back, then looked straight ahead.

"I'll just keep you a minute," she promised, casting about for a way to penetrate his defenses. "I talked to Maribel last week.

Her optimism about the market is always higher than mine. How's yours?"

"Attitude is everything."

"Have you had any responses from the flyers you sent about Happiness Key?"

"They only generated a couple of calls, and none of those went beyond the first inquiry."

"Bummer, huh?"

"I'll continue to talk it up."

His initial flush of interest in the sale and in Tracy had faded. This was as obvious as his desire to get in the car and speed away. Since she had complete faith in her own attractions, she was even more suspicious.

"Has Olivia told you what an asset she is painting our mural at the center? We miss her when she's not there."

He looked as if he were casting around for something to say that wouldn't put her in her place. Under the veneer of good manners, he was fuming.

"Summer is a good time for a child to be a child," he said stiffly. "Sometimes she likes to hang out at home and unwind."

Tracy was not that clueless. "I imagine she's needed at home." She pulled as much warmth as she could from a rapidly diminishing supply. "We haven't seen Alice for some time. We're all worried. Isn't there some way we can help you?"

"I wish, but she's very fragile and confused. She's under doctor's orders to rest and stay calm, which means visitors are out of the question. She needs quiet, familiar surroundings, no challenges."

"Lee, is it just the teeniest bit possible you've misunderstood what the doctor wants? I'm sure he doesn't expect you to wear yourself to a frazzle. And why would he isolate her? We could come and sit with her when you need us. We're not strangers. I think Alice would find us comforting."

A muscle throbbed in his jaw, but that made sense, since his teeth were clenched so tightly. "I know what the doctor wants," he said, once he'd unclenched them enough to release the words. "The moment she's ready for company, I'll let you know."

She smiled, glad for the first time in months that she'd been trained to smile anytime it might benefit her. "Be sure you do. In the meantime, we'll stay out of your way." That last part was true enough. If the neighbors were going to find out what was going on, they would have to do it without him around.

He relaxed a little. "It's a difficult time. I'm sorry if I sound rude. But sometimes the best thing anybody can do is nothing."

"I am so sure you're right." She nodded in emphasis. "And hey, I'm the queen of doing nothing. But I'll be right here when you need me." She stepped back from the car. "I know you're taking good care of Alice. You take care of yourself and Olivia, too, please. We're all rooting for you."

The moment the crunch of oyster shells under his tires was no longer audible, Tracy took off for home. She grabbed the bag of smoke detectors, but she knew better than to think that ploy would work if Lee came back while she was inside. He'd just warned her off. She could pretend she had simply forgotten to mention the detectors, but he would see right through that.

Still, what choice did she have? Wait another week and try it? Who knew what the situation would be at that point? She was more convinced than ever that something had to be done quickly.

She took a moment to dial Wanda before she left for Alice's, but she got a busy signal. It was too early in the day for seduction, but Wanda often called her children and grandchildren. Hopefully Tracy would be in and out before Wanda hung up. She tried Janya, but there was no answer, and Tracy gave up. She didn't have time to rally the troops. She had to go, and go right now.

Alice's keys in her pocket, she took off the way she'd just

come. The street was deserted. Lee hadn't dropped a hint about where he was going, but she hoped his destination was somewhere across the bridge. Maybe Olivia needed school clothes, or they needed a good grocery shopping, since they hardly left the house anymore. She told herself that if Lee just needed bread or milk, he wouldn't have taken Olivia with him for the trip.

On the other hand, maybe he wouldn't have taken Olivia if he wasn't planning to be back home in a matter of minutes....

She sped up so much that she almost slammed into Alice's door. Stopping just in time, she flipped open the screen door and jammed the key into the doorknob, praying as she did that Lee hadn't changed the locks.

He hadn't, most likely for all the reasons Wanda had suggested. Or possibly because he believed Tracy was just a ditz with a key ring.

Inside, the house was not as clean as she remembered, although nothing seemed out of place. A healthy Alice would never have allowed dust in corners, or streaks on the glass doors of the cabinet that held her dance trophies. The lilac smell was fainter now, as if the plug-ins were overdue to be changed. The aquarium looked murky enough that Tracy hoped the fish had written their last will and testament.

"Alice? It's Tracy. I'm here to install a new smoke alarm."

The air conditioner came on with a whine, and she jumped at the noise, her heart pounding harder.

"Jeez, Wanda," she muttered, "if you hear me screaming over here, come quick."

Pretty sure she knew which room Olivia and Alice shared, she started down the hall and knocked on the closed door at the end.

"Alice?" She listened. "Alice, it's Tracy. Are you all right?"

No one answered.

She stopped, heart nearly in her throat now. The last time

she'd checked a renter's bedroom, she'd discovered a corpse. She closed her eyes. All she had to do was put her hand on the doorknob and turn it. Then all she had to do was open her eyes and take one good look. Still she couldn't make herself move. She hadn't forgotten how it felt to find Herb.

"Okay, here I go. It's like sex. It's got to be easier the second time. Everything's easier the second time." The pep talk didn't work. "I'm doing this for Alice. No matter what I find, it's got to be better than not knowing."

She still wasn't moving.

"Lee could be on his way back home by now."

That did the trick. She forced herself to turn the knob. Then she pushed the door open and stuck her head inside. She screwed up her face in anticipation of the worst. She took one step in, then another.

Alice was lying in bed, as Herb had been, but Tracy could see she was breathing. Slowly. Maybe too slowly. But regularly.

Her whole body sagged; then she remembered she didn't have time for relief.

"Alice?" Tracy crept over to the bedside. The room was small, the spreads on the twin beds frilly and girlish, as if chosen to please Olivia. Alice was curled up on her side, her hands under her face in an attitude of prayer.

She moaned and made an attempt to sit up.

"No, it's just me, Tracy. Don't get up, it's okay. I just wanted you to know I came in to put up smoke detectors. My insurance company insisted."

Alice's eyes were wide open now. "Lee?"

"He and Olivia just left. I don't want to bother you. I'll be out in a jiffy. You don't even have to tell Lee I was here. In fact, please don't."

Alice stared at her. Her eyes were unfocused and seemed to

grow more so as Tracy watched. Her eyelids drifted down again, but before they closed, she exhaled two words. Tracy couldn't hear clearly, but she was very afraid Alice had just said, "Help me."

Tracy put her hand on Alice's shoulder. "Alice? What did you say? Help you? Help you do what?"

Alice moaned.

"Alice, do you need something? What can I do? I'll do anything. Are you afraid? Are you being mistreated?" Tracy realized she was babbling, but now she really was frightened.

Alice didn't respond. Her breathing slowed again. Tracy tried shaking her a little, but Alice was deeply asleep once more.

Tracy straightened. What did she know that she hadn't before? That Alice wasn't well? Lee had told her as much. That things had reached such a serious state the woman needed help? But Lee claimed help was exactly what he was giving her. He said he was following the advice of Alice's doctor, and how could Tracy refute this? What had she seen that proved things were anything but what Lee said they were?

Help me? Even if she had heard Alice correctly, what was Tracy supposed to help her with? Maybe Alice needed a glass of water or a trip to the bathroom, and she'd hoped Tracy could assist.

Or maybe she needed someone to protect her from Lee.

She might only have minutes before Lee and Olivia came back. Unfortunately, she was getting used to snooping through her renters' lives, but this time she knew better than to touch Alice's belongings. Lee would know if anything was moved. Even the hairs on the man's head seemed to have been assigned specific coordinates. Trudging through a hurricane, he would still look exactly the same.

She walked through the house, checking to see if anything was in sight that might provide information. She noted two smoke detectors, which meant she had even less reason to be there, but everything she might find interesting had been put away. Short of rifling through drawers, she had no alternatives.

She had reached an impasse. She had to have more information, and she knew there was only one way to get it. Olivia was too young to turn on her father. Alice was too sick. Only Lee himself could tell the story. Tracy had grown up with the children of actors, lived on the same streets, shopped at the same grocery stores. Film stars had been her neighbors, but she had never expected to make a neighbor a film star. Not until now.

"Granny cam, here we come."

She locked the front door and let herself out the back, making sure the door locked behind her. Then she zigzagged behind the house until she was far enough away that she could safely walk along the road again. Halfway to Wanda's house, Lee's new Infiniti passed, and she gave a friendly wave, although she couldn't see anyone through the tinted windows.

She could act, too. She just hoped her performance was going to be good enough.

chapter thirty-one

Janya decided to cook, really cook. Not a library-inspired recipe, with ingredients, smells and tastes she wasn't familiar with. She was hungry for food she understood, food that satisfied her hunger for all things Indian. If the women of Happiness Key enjoyed the dishes she prepared, wasn't it time to take a chance on Rishi, who, at the very least, had been familiar with Indian cooking during his childhood?

More important, she had finally faced something she had hidden, even from herself. Although she'd couched her attempt to learn American cooking as a gesture to please her husband, not cooking the foods she loved best had been a rebellion. She'd moved to the United States to leave an unhappy life behind, but she'd brought unhappiness with her. She kept this part of herself, along with others, close to her heart. On the outside, she tried to conform to Rishi's desires, but on the inside, she carefully hoarded secrets. What kind of marriage could be built on such a foundation?

She hoped that when Rishi came home tonight, he would see and appreciate more than the food she was preparing. She hoped he would also see her effort to express who she was through cooking it for him.

In the midst of considering this, she heard a key turning in the front door, and, surprised, she went into the living room to investigate. Rishi walked in.

"Rishi." She heard the welcome in her own voice. "So you decided you don't need to work all day?"

He smiled, and she smiled back. "The house smells wonderful. Like my childhood in Bhopal."

Surprised, she confessed, "I've tried and failed to be a good American cook. I'll take lessons at the rec center in the fall, but tonight we eat food I understand how to prepare."

"Janya, I want you to be *you*. If the smells are any indication, I want you to cook what you want to cook. Please. Forever."

"You really think you might like it?"

"I don't know when you got the idea I didn't want you to cook what you're familiar with. Yes, I'm used to American food. Too much of the time as a boy I was given money to walk into town and buy my own meals, because no one was going to be home to make dinner, and I wasn't allowed in the kitchen. So yes, that's what I'm used to. But I never wanted it to be that way."

She was touched, and she didn't know what to say. How many other things had she misunderstood? How many false assumptions had she made?

How many terrible meals had she served while she was keeping herself from the man who wanted only whatever she could give him?

Since Darshan's visit, she had opened to Rishi more and more, feeling what he felt and hoping for better than mere tolerance. Now she went to him. There was still one thing that stood between them, and she hoped if they could find their way around it, perhaps someday, sooner than she had thought possible, they might have a real chance at happiness.

But he didn't kiss her, which surprised her, since the moment was so right for it, and he was just American and romantic enough to find it so. Instead he stepped back.

"I have a surprise, too."

She encouraged him with a smile. "Can it be as delicious as mine?"

"I think you'll find it delicious. In a different way."

"Tell me."

"I haven't been at work this morning. That was just a story I concocted. I went to the airport."

For a moment Janya didn't understand. Then Rishi stepped aside and she saw Yash—handsome, smiling Yash—walking through the open doorway.

She stood perfectly still for a moment, wondering if she were imagining her brother coming toward her. Then she clapped her hands. "Yash!" She ran forward and grabbed him, dancing up and down. "Yash, what are you doing here?" she asked in their native tongue.

He wrapped his arms around her for a brief embrace. "Have you forgotten what day it is, big sister?"

"No. Yes! Yes! It's Saturday."

"Today is Raksha Bandhan. And since you weren't in India to tie the bracelet you sent, I had to come to America so you could do it here."

That evening when her mother phoned, Janya was not surprised. Soon after his arrival Yash had left a message telling their parents where he was, but, exhausted from his travels, he was asleep by the time Inika Desai finally returned his call.

Janya listened as her mother accused her of kidnapping her

brother, of scheming to separate Yash from his family, of refusing to be a repentant, respectful daughter and distance herself from those for whom she had caused so much trouble.

When the harangue ended, Janya took a deep breath. "I was as surprised as you that Yash came to visit, but I shouldn't have been. You see, nothing you can do will make him less of a brother to me."

When the next flood of accusations ended, Janya replied simply. "I hope someday you'll want to be part of my life again, *Aii*. But it will be up to you to let me know. I'll stop calling. When your grandchildren are born, I won't bother you with the news. But know if you change your mind, our door will be open." Then she replaced the receiver.

She had not felt half as calm as she sounded. Now tears washed away what was left of the pretense. She had no control over the things her mother did, but she *could* control what she herself did about them. Perhaps in the future her mother would understand how much she had lost and try to find her daughter again. But for now, Janya told herself, she still had a family. She had Yash.

She had Rishi.

She felt a hand grip her shoulder, and she turned and rested her head against her husband's chest. He put his arms around her and held her until the tears finally ceased.

She stepped back and wiped her tears with the tail of her shirt. "Rishi, this isn't the only sorrow in my life. I need to tell you something."

He covered her hand and held it to his cheek; then he kissed her palm before he released it. "Not here, with your brother sleeping in the other room."

She thought of her favorite spot on the beach, where she had never taken him. "I know where we can go."

The evening was warm, but it felt familiar and comforting,

except that the salt tang of the air was bracing in the way city air never had been.

They walked side by side, not holding hands, but their bodies brushing as they moved. Rishi was silent, as if he knew she was deep in thought and would not want to be disturbed. This was just another example of the ways he had changed, and how hard he struggled to be sensitive to her needs.

She wound through the brush, even when he protested that it was growing dark and they ought to be careful. "It's not as wild as it seems," she said. "This is my favorite place on the key. I should have showed it to you a long time ago."

They emerged in the little cove where she and the other women had so often come to sunbathe and gossip. She thought of all the centuries when women in her own country had found places to be together and talk about things that mattered to them. Those places in villages and small cities were often associated with household chores like washing clothes or hauling water. But no matter where they were in the world, no matter who they were or whatever their differences, women always found other women to share their lives.

She stood looking out at the water, arms folded over her chest. Evening melodies were beginning, and Janya could see the lights of a ship moving slowly against the horizon.

"Yash told me that you helped him pay for his trip," she said.

He sounded embarrassed. "He shouldn't have told you. It's no matter."

"Of course it is. You are so good to me. You knew what having him here would do for my spirits. I'm so grateful."

"He's our family. I hope he'll come often."

"Rishi, that's not what I need to tell you." She faced him. "I don't know how to begin."

"Say it quickly. It will be easier."

"Nothing can make it easier. I am ashamed."

"Let me decide if you need to be."

She wanted to turn away, but she knew she had to face him, to see his expression. "Darshan Tambe came to see me. He was on a business trip. I didn't invite him, and I refused to open the e-mails he sent before he came, so I was not expecting to see him again. That much I did right. But he found where I lived and came here, to our house, and waited until I was alone. He asked me to meet him somewhere while you were away at work. He said he had to explain everything that had happened."

Even though she was still facing him, she couldn't read his expression. He was trying hard to keep his feelings to himself, but he nodded. "Go on."

"We had been betrothed. I had been sure I loved him. I... That experience haunted me. It was so painful. Can you understand?"

He nodded again, but said nothing.

"I went. I had to know. This was a door that had been left open."

"And you had to know where it led?"

"No, no! I had to close it. Once and for all. So I did. I'll never see Darshan again. I made certain of that. I brought some of his gifts into our marriage. It was foolish, I know, but I... When you and I married, I just wasn't ready to let him go, Rishi, I'm sorry. Now he has them back, every one. And I told him if he ever contacts me again, I will tell Padmini and his parents everything."

"He still wanted you?"

She looked down at her feet, deeply ashamed of her own actions and Darshan's assumptions. This was the hardest part, but she owed Rishi a full explanation.

"Not as his wife. Never as his wife. As we talked, I realized he and Padmini had made certain of that together. Marrying me was not advantageous enough, so he made sure our betrothal would end. But he still wanted the things that come with marriage. He's a very bad person. I'm so lucky he's gone from my life."

"Truly gone now?"

She looked up. "Forever. If I were a better person, I would even feel sorry for my cousin, who probably doesn't know what she has ahead of her." She paused. "But I'm not that good."

He touched her cheek. "Why have you told me, Janya? I never would have learned this."

"Because we've made a fresh start, but *you* didn't know we had, and you needed to."

He smiled. Gravely. "And what kind of start will it be?"

"The kind we should have made at the beginning. The kind where our pasts are forgotten and our future can be created together."

"Americans believe in love at first sight."

"Americans are not always right."

"Until I met you, I thought it was silly, too. You were just one of the women my aunt and uncle thought I should consider, but I knew the moment you walked into the living room of your parents' home that I had found the one I wanted to marry. I know it was different for you, that you were still caught up in a part of your life that had ended. I was warned to choose someone else because you would always yearn for the man you had lost, but I hoped someday you would put the past behind you and feel what I felt that afternoon."

She was touched, as she had been earlier, but with much more than sympathy now. She really was happy to be standing here, enveloped in the deepening August twilight with Rishi, to know that he accepted her as she was, that he cared about her in a way no man had ever cared before. And he would care for her always, without reservation.

For the first time since their introduction, she thought their marriage might bring them both happiness.

"I've had love at first sight," she said. "This time, I'll try love that grows steadily, the kind that comes from building a life and a family together. The kind that's taking root here now, Rishi."

His eyes said it all.

She was the one who moved first, who slipped her arms over his shoulders and brought him closer. Behind them, the waves lapped at the shore, as if searching for purchase. Seabirds squawked and called to each other as they scanned the beach for perches for the night. Janya wished them well. For the first time she understood what it was to feel truly at home in her new country and life. She had found safe harbor.

chapter thirty-two

"Air freshener?" Tracy said as Wanda held up the package she'd just delivered to Tracy's house. "Nanny cam air freshener? I'm never going to feel safe again. Never going to scratch or pull up my pantyhose or pick my nose anywhere in the whole world."

"You never once picked that debutante nose of yours."

"Well, I'm definitely not going to start now."

"This is the most expensive air freshener in the world, and it doesn't freshen a darn thing." Wanda removed a slotted plastic box about the size of a deck of cards, which looked a lot like the ones plugged in at Alice's house wafting lilac fumes through the air. "What do you think?"

"I think we've got a good shot." Tracy took the device out of Wanda's hand and turned it over. It looked completely innocuous. "And all I have to do is plug it into a socket?"

"It's the easiest way to go. It's got a built-in motion detector, so it only records when something's moving. Works like that for maybe three to four days, even has time-stamp technology, then you remove it and play back whatever you filmed on your computer or a television set."

The removal part sounded like bad news to Tracy. "So I have to go back to Alice's in a few days and retrieve it?"

"Yeah, you have to remove the whole thing, and I know that's bad. But Kenny says the other alternatives are worse. Most cameras either have battery packs that don't last more than a few hours, or they have to be wired in place. Then they have to send their signal to a receiver, and that would have to be positioned somewhere else, and reception—"

"I get it. The sooner I install this, the better. You didn't say how he got hold of it."

"The department impounded a roomful of spy toys from a business under indictment for doing a little too much spying on their own. We lucked out, but it's not something we're going to tell just everybody, okay?"

Tracy thought ahead. "Now I've got to wait for Lee to leave."

"That's another good thing. You can plug this in and get out in a matter of seconds. He doesn't have to be gone more than a minute or two. Just take one of the old fresheners out and put this in its place."

"I'm sure it doesn't look exactly the same as the ones she has now."

"He's a man. More or less. Do you know a man anywhere who pays attention to what air freshener looks like?"

Two days had passed since her last trip to Alice's, and Tracy wasn't willing to let more time go by. She wasn't sure what they might record, but she hoped it would be enough to get a full investigation.

"I don't know for sure that she said 'help me.' If she did, I don't know what she wanted me to do." Tracy had said this before, but none of the women were convinced. Both Wanda and Janya were as worried as she was.

"This time, if my phone's busy, you just wait before you go

inside, you hear? Don't take it on yourself like you did last time. Lee came back right after you left the house. That's cutting things way too close."

"Even if he changes his mind a block away and starts back home, I'll be finished."

"You do like I say, Miss Priss. Don't go in without telling us. Here's my cell phone number." Wanda jotted the number on a piece of paper and handed it to Tracy. "Now, I've got to scoot, but we'll have this taken care of shortly. Don't hide the camera so it can't take pictures, but don't put it in a real obvious place. Replace one of the old ones, whatever you do, and bring it home. Then you can put it back when you go over to retrieve this one."

"You and Janya are going to try to keep an eye on the house and let me know if he leaves?"

"She's busy with that good-looking brother of hers, but she says she'll be watching whenever she's home. Me, I got to go buy dog food and who knows what all, but I'll be back in an hour or two."

Tracy saw Wanda to the door. A thunderstorm was brewing, the spin-off of a tropical storm that was moving slowly up the coast, and even though it was only late afternoon, the sky was as dark as if the sun had just set for the night. Wind kicked sand along the road, and palm trees and live oaks bowed and bobbed in an eerie dance. Earlier that afternoon Marsh had suggested she come to his house and watch the storm blow in. As much as she'd wanted to, she had declined.

In the weeks since their barbecue, she and Marsh had fallen into a pattern. A couple of times a week they got together, sometimes for nothing more than a walk on the beach. Bay was always with them. The boy's presence was a safety valve. Although she and Marsh never discussed a relationship, she knew Happiness Key was the log in the water their little love boat just couldn't get around. Until that was resolved and they could view whatever damage they had sustained, going forward was just too hazardous.

So for now they didn't owe each other explanations. Which was good, since Marsh was a lawyer, and she was pretty sure he would have something to say about what she was planning. Something she didn't want to hear.

She closed the door and turned the camera in her hand. The ominously dark skies reminded her of the afternoon when she had gone to Alice's and seen the unraveled tablecloth. She had never been creeped out by thunder and lightning, but storms on the gulf were so impossible to ignore that she had developed an acute appreciation for their power. Now she wasn't sure if it was weather or the permanent cloud that seemed to hover over Alice's cottage that made her the most uneasy. She wished the evening were over.

Hoping to snap out of her funk, she stripped off her camp clothes and showered, slipping into comfortable shorts and a tank top. She dried her hair, then pinned it up off her neck. She was looking at the television listings, trying to figure out how to spend the evening, when the telephone rang.

"Miss Deloche?"

Tracy recognized Maribel's voice. She almost complimented the Realtor on finally getting her last name right. Maybe Tracy had exorcized CJ's ghost at last.

"Sold Happiness Key yet?" she asked instead.

"Well, not that cut-and-dried, but I do have a couple of developers who are very interested. We've been down twice to look at it."

Tracy plopped down on the sofa. "You're kidding."

"I know it's been touch and go, but didn't I tell you somebody would be willing to take on Wild Florida and the economy? It was just a matter of wait and see. They're talking less money than you want, of course, but we're in the early stages of negotiation. Leave it to me. I'll get them higher."

"I talked to Lee a couple of days ago, and he didn't mention anything. In fact, he was pretty pessimistic."

"Lee?"

Sometimes Tracy worried about Maribel. "Lee Symington."

"I'm not sure why he was talking to you at all."

Tracy was confused. "Umm…he's my neighbor. And he works for you."

"Not anymore."

If she hadn't already been sitting down, that would have put Tracy in a chair. "I'm sorry? What?"

"Lee and I parted company a week ago. Maybe somebody else hired him and he's still hoping to sell your property." There was a pause. "Although nobody's asked for a recommendation. I would have remembered that."

Tracy wasn't one to read between the lines, or at least she hadn't bothered to very often. But she was quickly piecing together all the things Maribel hadn't said.

She went straight to the heart of it. "I need you to be honest. Will you tell me why you parted company?"

"That's not exactly legal."

"Maribel, I'm not going to tell anybody, but it would help. He's, you know, sniffing around this listing with a lot of energy. Can he be trusted?"

Another long pause ensued. "Sometimes it pays to be careful," Maribel said at last.

"Can't you be more specific?"

"Let's just say I wouldn't trust the man or anything he says."

"Wow."

"I particularly wouldn't let him near my bank accounts."

"Double wow."

"You didn't hear this from me, understand? I don't want him suing me, and he's the kind who will, if he thinks he can make a buck."

Tracy didn't triple wow, but her mind was racing. "Okay, you didn't tell me a thing, and I didn't listen. But while I'm not listening, let me get an opinion. Everyone here's worried about Alice, his mother-in-law. Lee seems to be keeping her out of sight. Do we have cause for concern? Is he capable of violence?"

"I'll deny I said this. You're not recording me?"

Tracy knew more about spying in Florida than she'd ever expected to. "Can't. It's not legal."

"A few months ago Lee was on the verge of making a sale to a family moving into Palmetto Grove. At the last minute the buyers changed their mind and backed out. The father's new job started looking shaky, and he decided they'd better rent a little longer, just in case."

Tracy remembered Lee being down about a sale that had fallen through. "And?"

"The morning after they told Lee they had changed their mind, the father went outside, and all his tires had been slashed. To shreds. On top of that, the car had been keyed. You know what that means?"

"Somebody took a key and scraped the paint."

"Exactly. Only this was more than a few scrapes, this was extensive damage. Gouges, the kind somebody with a serious grudge inflicts. The father came to me, and of course I told him it couldn't have been Lee, but now I'm not sure. I know he's dishonest. I know he has a temper. Unfortunately, I've seen both up close. Let's just say ever since I fired him, I'm parking my own car in my garage, and I've got neighbors watching the house."

"Fired?"

"I can't say more."

She had already said enough. Tracy's stomach felt like a pretzel. So all along Janya had been right about the destruction on her patio. And what about Alice's tablecloth? The one she didn't remember unraveling?

Because she hadn't. Lee had. Maybe he had come home and discovered that Alice and Olivia were at Janya's with the other women. How easy it would have been to just destroy the tablecloth, then pretend Alice had done it herself.

She thanked Maribel and hung up; then she went to the window and looked out over the street. Now she was even more anxious to get the camera in place. If Lee was trying to make sure nosy neighbors didn't visit, might he wait to leave until the weather was unpleasant enough to scare them off?

She couldn't see Alice's driveway from her window, but she wondered if Lee would use the approaching storm as cover and slip out for a little while.

Slip out in his brand-new car. And what about that? Where had the money for the Infiniti come from? She was afraid she knew.

Her phone rang again, more calls than she normally got in days. Janya's musical voice greeted her.

"He just left."

Tracy felt every muscle in her body tense. "Let Wanda know, okay? I'm heading over. Did he have Olivia with him?"

"It's so dark, I wasn't able to see."

"Just keep your eyes open. And wish me luck."

Tracy hung up. Fifteen seconds. Unlock the door, switch the real air freshener for the fake. Lock the front door and leave again by the back. The last visit had been a practice session, and this would be easier, because she wasn't going to check on Alice. She would just pop in and out.

Right.

Of course she would check on Alice.

She slipped on a waterproof parka and slid the camera into her shorts pocket. She made sure her tennis shoes were tied, made sure she had the key ring with Alice's key; then she left her own front door unlocked and took off down the road.

The street was empty, but the storm was closer now. The weather forecasters had feared it might turn into a hurricane, but it had weakened en route. Now the dark skies were her ally, as was the lack of streetlamps, although she was uncharacteristically spooked by both. She wondered if Wanda would call Ken. She hoped so. At least he would know something was in play.

Halfway to Alice's, she remembered that Wanda was at the grocery store. Tracy had Wanda's cell phone number at home on her kitchen counter, but that wasn't going to do any good. And she'd been in such a rush to leave that she hadn't brought her own cell, so now she couldn't call Janya to alert her to the slipup.

There were no lights on at Alice's, which seemed odd, because all the other cottages were softly lit. Even Herb's had a lamp on a timer to discourage vandals. She gazed up the road, but she didn't see headlights. She cut across Alice's grass and up to the porch. Then, heart pounding from more than exertion, she unlocked the door.

The house was so dark that she had to pause near the doorway while her eyes adjusted. Why hadn't Lee left a lamp on for Alice? Perhaps he'd planned to return so quickly he figured it didn't matter.

Or maybe Alice was no longer in need of one.

She didn't dare turn on a lamp herself. She waited until her eyes adjusted, then she let the slashes of lightning give her an extra boost. With the next burst she spotted an outlet near the door, on the opposite side of a small end table. She bent over, checking the line of sight. As far as she could tell, nothing would block a view of the room, but the outlet wasn't obvious because of the table beside it. Best of all, Alice had one of her own plug-ins installed there, which explained the faint puff of lilac whenever somebody walked through the door.

Tracy pulled out the real air freshener, which was smaller and shaped a little differently from the one housing the camera, but the two were enough alike that she thought Lee would only notice if he were suspicious enough to investigate. They were probably safe. She doubted he would give any of the women enough credit to consider this possibility.

She was furious with herself for falling prey to a sociopath after she had just divorced one. When this was over, she was going into therapy.

It only took seconds to install the camera air freshener and pocket the other. Then she crossed the room and started down the hall. Olivia wasn't here. Either she'd been with her father in the Lee-mobile, or she had gone home with a friend after camp. Tracy had been relieved to see Olivia at the rec center that morning. The girl was more subdued than ever, and less inclined to chat, but at least Tracy knew she was still okay.

Except who was watching over Alice?

At Alice's door, Tracy paused and listened before she knocked. As expected, there was no answer, even when she called and knocked louder. She turned the doorknob and pushed. It opened an inch or two, but she couldn't push it farther.

"Alice?" Tracy put her shoulder against the door and shoved. "Alice, are you in there?"

"Tracy…"

Tracy had envisioned a body on the floor against the door,

Alice's cold dead body. She was filled with such relief that tears sprang to her eyes. "Alice, are you all right?"

"Lee…"

"It's okay. He's not here. He left, but I don't know when he's coming back."

"Trying…"

Alice fell silent.

"Alice, can you open the door? Can you let me in? Look, we'll get you out of here, okay? Whatever's going on, we'll fix it. But we have to get you to my house first."

"Dress…"

Tracy tried to translate. "We'll get you dressed, don't worry. Just open up."

"Dresser. In front…"

Now Tracy understood. Somehow Alice had managed to shove her dresser in front of the door. There was only one reason Tracy could think of for that. Alice was frightened that when Lee came back, something horrible was going to happen.

The old woman was not in the early stages of dementia or delusional. Maribel's phone call had laid that possibility to rest. Alice was justifiably terrified.

Tracy tried to think what to do. If Alice could move the dresser away from the door, she would. But moving it in the first place had probably taken all her strength. Tracy tried to picture Alice's windows. Were they the kind that opened out? Or were they the old-fashioned jalousie windows that she herself had in several rooms?

"Alice, can you open your windows? Are they large enough for me to crawl through?"

No answer.

"Alice, are you awake in there? Can I get through your window? Then I can move the dresser and we can get out of here."

No answer.

"Alice, open the windows if you can. Please. I'm coming around."

She took off for the front door, planning to leave it unlocked so she could get back in if necessary. As she passed the kitchen phone she lifted the receiver to call Janya, but the line was dead. She hung up, then tried again, but either the storm had interrupted service or Lee had disabled it.

She picked up speed, darted through the front door and around to the back, giving one brief glance up the road. No headlights in sight, a good sign. With relief she saw that the room at the end had windows that cranked out, but they were closed, and most likely locked against intruders.

Or old women fleeing for their lives.

She picked her way through overgrown shrubs and banged her palm against the window. "Alice, open the window." When there was no response, she flattened her face against the glass and peered inside. With horror, she thought she saw Alice sprawled on the floor between the beds.

She grabbed a chunk of concrete from the ground nearby and smashed it hard against the glass. The window shattered, and she grabbed the jagged pieces that remained, tossing them to the bushes beside her and away from the frame. When the frame was clear, she rattled the screen. It came loose in her hands and followed the glass shards to the ground.

She lifted herself up by her palms, one stinging badly from a cut as she forced it to bear her weight. But she managed to swing herself inside the room, saying a brief prayer of gratitude that she had spent the summer at the rec center chasing children and hauling equipment.

Alice was lying face down on the floor. Tracy grasped her shoulder and shook it. "Alice, wake up. You've got to wake up."

She was rewarded by a moan. Tracy threaded her arms under Alice's torso and tried to lift her to a sitting position, but it was like lifting a rag doll, a one-hundred-pound-plus rag doll. She tried again, and this time, using every bit of strength, she was able to pull Alice into something approximating a sitting position, so she was lying against Tracy's chest.

Tracy shook her, and not gently. "Alice, we've got to get you out of here."

Alice's eyes opened, but she didn't speak.

Tracy debated what to do, and as she did, she heard the sound of a car pulling to a stop out front.

"You get here now," Wanda said into her cell phone. "And turn on that siren of yours, Kenny. I mean it."

She hung up and motioned to Janya. "It's going to be a while before he arrives. Grab those flowers." She pointed to a motley silk bouquet in a basket on her coffee table. The bouquet had been ready for the trash can for months. The only thing that had stopped her from tossing it out was inertia. "We're going to call on our neighbors and see if they're home."

Janya grabbed the basket. "Tracy has been at Alice's house for more than ten minutes."

"I told her not to go unless I was here!"

"She told me to call you. She didn't want to wait."

"Yeah, well, good thing *you* had my cell number." Of course it was too bad Janya's call hadn't come five minutes later, after Wanda had already checked out and put her groceries in the car. Now she was going to have to go back and shop all over again. She just hoped she got a different cashier.

Outside, Janya peered up at the sky. "It's starting to rain."

Wanda had noticed that, too, although the lightning worried

her more than the splatter of raindrops. "And that husband and brother of yours are coming home when?"

"Rishi is showing Yash his office."

"Well, we're on our own here, then. Let's get going."

As they sprinted toward Alice's house, Wanda saw Lee Symington's SUV driving up the road toward it.

"Lord have mercy." This time she wished she were a Catholic, so she could cross herself. Not only did they have confession, Catholics had an edge over Baptists in emergencies.

Janya was making plans out loud. "We will tell Mr. Symington we bought these flowers for Alice. Then we'll keep him talking."

"I'm not sure that's going to do it. We don't know where Tracy is. And if he hears her opening the back door to get out…"

"By then your husband will be here."

Wanda thought of all the times Ken had failed her. "Don't count on it." She glanced at Janya. "You happen to know karate or kung fu? Something like that?"

"You only have the continent right."

"This isn't my lucky day."

Wanda took a deep breath and turned up the walk to Alice's house. Lee was just getting out of his car. She'd been a fan of *All My Children* for so many years, she figured she would just pretend she was on camera, walking through her part. She would be Erica, who always got what she wanted.

"It's going to be a gully washer," she called cheerfully. "Good thing you got home when you did, Lee. Someday that road's just going to wash away. Shame the city doesn't take better care of it."

Lee slammed his door, but he stayed in place.

Wanda marched right up to him, as if he had welcomed her with a smile and extended his hand. "Janya and I have a little gift for your mother-in-law. I hear she's having a hard time of things. We want to cheer her up."

She saw Lee glance down at the arrangement in Janya's arms. "You *must* be worried about Alice to come out in a storm."

"Well, we are, you know. We never see her anymore. And we miss her."

"The doctor says no visitors."

"Does he? You just never know what a doctor's going to say these days, do you? One minute they're preaching this, then the next they're preaching that. Now, Janya here's a vegetarian, and some doctors think that's the way to go, but then you read about iron and protein and all that other slobber. And you have to ask yourself if anybody knows anything, whether they have letters tagging along behind their names or not."

"I'd love to debate this with you," he said in a tone that made it clear he would rather tie his incisors to a doorknob, "but I need to check on Alice."

"Mr. Symington," Janya said with a pleasant smile, "I have wanted to share with you some thoughts about Olivia's artistic talents."

"Yes, I understand she's been bothering you at home. She won't anymore."

"She's a lovely little girl and never a bother. I wonder if you have time to come and see some of her artwork?"

Now he looked annoyed. "I just said I have to check on Alice."

Wanda broke in. "You certainly did, but I could check on her for you. Why don't I, while Janya shows you Olivia's drawings? I can take her the flowers, too, let her know we're thinking about her. I won't tire her out."

"Ladies, it's starting to rain. I'll let you know when it's appropriate to see Alice." He moved around them and toward the house.

Wanda kept up with him. "You know, I hate to say it, but you're right about the rain. I don't think we *can* make it back now without getting soaked, not until it slows a little. What were we thinking?"

"Oh, I think you'll be okay if you head right home. You can probably beat the worst of it."

On the steps, he opened the screen door and reached in his pocket for his key. There was a slight overhang, and Wanda got right up next to him so that opening the door would be a challenge.

"I wish it weren't so," she said, "but I always catch a cold if I get caught in a downpour like this. Something about the change in temperature, maybe. Would you mind too much if we just wait inside a little while?"

Now his anger was unmistakable. "What is it with you women?" Then he frowned. "What's going on here?"

"Just the rain, far as I can tell. They say it's linked to that tropical storm coming up the—"

He ignored her, and, without inserting the key, he twisted the knob. The door opened with a flourish, nearly knocking Wanda in the face. He cursed; then in a moment he was inside and Wanda heard the lock click into place.

"Around back," she told Janya. "Ditch the flowers."

Until she heard the car pulling up, Tracy had hoped she could move the dresser and get Alice to the back door. Now she knew that was impossible. Her best chance was to get Alice out through the window, the same way she herself had come in. In the time since she'd heard the car, she had managed to drag Alice upright and almost far enough. Alice had awakened twice and attempted to help, but Tracy was sure she was heavily drugged. Alice's mental state was no longer in question. She had managed, even under the influence of something mind altering, to try to protect herself.

No, *Alice* was not the problem.

Tracy could hear voices out front. The low rumble of a man's, the higher pitch of a woman's, maybe even two. She knew her friends had come to help, that they were trying to keep Lee from entering the house, but she also knew it was only a matter of time until he did. She wasn't sure what he could do. Or what he *would* do when he found her here. She was close to panic. Then the voices stopped, and she heard the front door open.

Alice slumped against her. Tracy summoned what strength she could and dragged her a little farther.

She heard the bedroom doorknob turn, heard Lee cursing when he realized he couldn't get in. The storm had arrived with full fury. Rain was pouring through the broken window and flooding the floor, but she continued to haul Alice upright and position her at the window. Figures materialized on the other side, and through the sheets of rain she saw Wanda and Janya.

Wanda immediately realized what to do. She reached inside, beckoning. "Quick, a little closer."

Alice rallied. Maybe it was the water streaming over her, but she revived a little and tried desperately to reach for Wanda.

Tracy heard Lee kicking the door, and she knew they had only moments before the dresser was shoved aside.

"Killed Karen…" Alice shook her head, as if she were shaking away fog. "Trying to kill…me."

Tracy got behind Alice and wrapped her arms around her, pushing her toward Wanda and Janya, who was now perched on the sill grasping Alice's nightgown.

The door flew open with a bang, and Wanda screamed. "Watch out!"

Tracy turned just enough to see Lee charging into the room.

She pushed Alice toward the other women and faced him. Then she threw her hands in front of her and shoved him with all the strength she had left. He stumbled backward, then caught his balance and leaped toward her, grabbing her around the throat.

"That's enough!"

A man's voice cracked like a pistol. Over the storm. Through the panic. Lee pushed her away. Tracy saw him turn, then, with one jerk of his elbow, shove his way past Ken Gray, who was standing in the doorway.

Ken took off after him. Tracy didn't know what to do. Wanda had crawled through the window, and now she was holding Alice with Janya's help. Tracy ran after the men, afraid Lee was going to escape. She ran through the house and out on the steps just in time to see Lee on the ground and Ken standing over him, gun drawn.

Lee was lying in the rain with a pistol trained on him. He had lost. The man *had* to know he had lost, yet he scrambled up, and Tracy was sure he was going to run again.

"You wouldn't shoot me," he shouted. It sounded like a taunt. It sounded like he believed it.

Between flashes of lightning, Tracy saw Ken extend his arm and point directly at Lee's chest with the steadiest hand she had ever seen.

"No?" Ken almost sounded as if the two neighbors were having a normal conversation. "I've killed better men than you, Symington. So just give me an excuse. I only need one."

Tracy forgot to breathe.

Finally, almost in slow motion, Lee raised his hands over his head. Tracy went back inside as Ken began cuffing him.

chapter thirty-three

Tracy positioned herself so she had a clear view of Olivia and Bay. The two children were ten feet from the water, creating a sand castle with carefully molded parapets and sawtooth battlements. Bay had explained the blueprint in mind-numbing detail. They would be busy for a while.

Marsh lowered himself to the blanket, and gave her a cold bottle of spring water and a quick neck rub. He had strong, sensitive hands, and it was wonderful to be pampered a little.

"You think Olivia's doing okay?" he asked.

"She refuses to talk about what happened, and she hasn't cried. She was up two or three times last night, when she should have been asleep, but I think she'll feel better once Alice is out of the hospital."

"Are you going to tell me everything?"

Tracy thought this was one of the endearing things about Marsh. He was interested in her life, but he was also patient. In the three days since Lee's arrest, there had been no opportunity to discuss details. Marsh had dropped off dinner every night, and when Tracy agreed it was time, he'd organized this

Friday-night barbecue to help Olivia take her mind off every-thing. Afterward they would go back to his house until it was time for Olivia to visit Alice.

"Well, you know the basics," she said. "Lee's in jail, hopefully for a long time. Alice is in the hospital recovering, and Olivia's staying with me until Alice comes home, probably Sunday. So far, Alice's doctor is hopeful there won't be any long-term effects."

"Has anybody pieced the whole story together?"

"Some of it will be tricky to prove, maybe impossible, but here's what we think so far. You know about Olivia's mom?"

She waited until he nodded. "After Karen died, Lee claimed he and Olivia had to move in with Alice to help out. Nobody knew Karen had been making plans to leave him. With a friend's help, she'd rented a house in Lakeland, and gotten a job. As part of her plan, she moved Alice out to Happiness Key, where she only had a month-to-month rental agreement. When every-thing was set, Karen was planning to move her to the new house. Unfortunately, she never explained this to Alice, because she didn't want to worry her. I think she figured the less said the better, because she was afraid Lee would turn violent."

"I'm guessing she was right."

"Somehow Lee found out, and her worst fears were realized."

"Or so you think."

"So we think. Lee and Karen went out on their boat, and Karen didn't come back."

"So why the sudden suspicion on Alice's part?"

"Because a couple of weeks ago, the friend who'd helped Karen tracked Alice down and told her Karen had been afraid of Lee, and planning to leave him. The friend asked Alice if she wanted her to go to the police and ask for a more detailed investigation into Karen's death."

"But she didn't?"

"By then, what would they have found? Karen drowned, and her body wasn't discovered for days."

"Too bad reality's not one long episode of *CSI*."

She linked her hand with his, the good one, not the one that had required twelve stitches after her adventure with Alice's window. "The police will have to find out a lot more before they can charge Lee for Karen's murder. But it's going to be easier to prove he tried to murder Alice."

"It doesn't hurt that he went charging into her bedroom and choked you." Tracy still had bruises on her neck to prove what had happened that night. In their own way, they were as valuable as the diamond necklace CJ had given her on their first anniversary.

"That's a good start," she agreed.

"So after the friend's visit, Alice came to believe Lee had killed Karen?"

"It never made sense to her that Karen would be out on the water during a storm, particularly not without a life jacket, because she was a fanatic about water safety. On top of that, Alice had turned all her finances over to Lee, and suddenly her retirement money was disappearing. So her suspicions were growing anyway. Of course, she was afraid to go to the authorities. If she was wrong, and it was just a bad economy as Lee claimed, he would be so angry, she would never see her granddaughter again."

"He really had her trapped, huh?"

"She tried to think the best of him, but she was getting more and more concerned. Then Karen's friend mailed Alice copies of e-mails Karen had sent her, all of which said pretty much what the friend had reported. But having the printed e-mails in her hands changed everything, only Alice still didn't know what to do or where to go."

"So when did Symington decide to go after her?"

"As near as anybody can figure, either Lee found the packet of e-mails, or Alice said or did something that made him suspicious. He wasn't ready to leave town, because he wasn't finished draining her investments. I guess you don't just go in, close accounts and take the next flight to Buenos Aires."

"Our vulnerable senior citizens. It happens more often than anybody realizes."

The kids were bringing buckets of wet sand up to the castle again, but Tracy thought Olivia looked tired. She sped up her explanation.

"At that point, we think Lee decided that if Alice died, whatever money was left would just pass to Olivia, and he would have unfettered access. Plus, he was probably sacrificing a lot by cashing out Alice's accounts when stocks were so low. He could make more if he let the funds sit where they were for a while. So getting rid of her was the best option. Only there was just one problem. Us."

"The neighbors."

"Exactly. When he moved out to the cottage, Lee must have figured he could keep Alice isolated, that nobody would pay attention to anything that was happening. To make it easier, he planted the idea Alice was in the early stages of dementia, so people would discount whatever she said. Only that didn't work, because we all got to be friends, and we started noticing things weren't right. If a so-called accident had occurred, we would have been all over it—and him."

"So it wasn't as easy as dumping an old lady out of a boat."

Olivia looked up toward the blanket and waved, and Tracy smiled and waved back. After a few seconds Olivia started in on the castle again.

"I get all that," Marsh said. "What I don't get is how he planned to end this story without putting himself under suspicion."

"Well, he set himself up to look like an attentive son-in-law. As Alice got more and more upset, her blood pressure naturally went up, too. He was still taking her to the doctor for checkups, probably because if he didn't, it might come back to haunt him during an inquest. Only at the last checkup, the doctor played right into his hands. Since the hypertension meds Alice had been on weren't working, the doctor prescribed a different class, one they rarely use unless the others aren't doing their job, something called MAO inhibitors. Heard of them?"

Marsh shook his head. Tracy was beginning to like the way his ponytail flip-flopped when he did that. She figured she was losing her mind.

She looked away. "The big problem is that a number of foods interact badly with the drugs, even fatally. Common things like cheese and bologna, a surplus of caffeine, too much chocolate, lots more. Swallow the wrong stuff and the drugs can actually cause strokes, instead of preventing them."

Marsh guessed the rest. "And if they did, nobody would be the wiser. Lee could just say that despite all his warnings, Alice had, in her befuddled state, fixed herself a cheese sandwich and a cup of cocoa."

"Exactly. Lee started feeding Alice foods that would cause another stroke and kill her. One night Olivia even told me he was bringing home pepperoni pizza, so Alice wouldn't have to cook. Of course, that didn't set off any alarms, because I didn't know about the meds."

"Why didn't it work?"

"Because he hadn't factored in how stubborn Alice can be. She realized what was happening, so she refused to eat or drink anything he gave her except water. By then Lee was drugging her big-time, giving her extras of everything the doctor had prescribed, but she managed, somehow, to continue refusing to eat. He disabled the phone and told her the telephone company was slow getting out there to service it. And, of course, he had already staged incidents to make it look like she was losing her mind. I'm sure part of that was to confuse Olivia. That way the poor kid would be afraid to do anything Alice asked her to. It was all pretty diabolical."

"So she stayed alive by refusing to eat or drink?"

"That's pretty much it. She was so drugged that he couldn't really force food down her throat or she might choke, and that would trigger an autopsy. So when she was awake, he just presented her with the forbidden foods and told her they were safe. I guess he figured eventually she would forget, or maybe get so hungry, she would start to believe him."

"Poor Olivia."

"I don't think the kid fully knows what's up yet. Ken Gray sat her down and told her the basics. She knows Lee was trying to hurt Alice. I don't think she understands a lot more than that, certainly nothing about her mother. She knew something was terribly wrong, but Lee told her he was trying to keep Alice from going into a nursing home. He probably warned her that the authorities would take Alice away if Olivia told anybody Alice wasn't eating."

"She was at a friend's house when all this went down, wasn't she?"

"Lee was probably afraid we were about to report him. He'd lost his job at the realty, and he must have known I would find out from Maribel at some point. So he got Olivia out of the house. By that point Alice was so weak, he probably figured it was worth the risk of her choking to try to get enough of the wrong things down her. Then the whole thing would be over with and he could get out of town."

"He was that sure she'd die?"

"In her weakened state? He was probably right. Plus he was giving her twice the medication she was supposed to have, hoping a bad reaction would be twice as strong. I guess he figured that would take care of it."

"So how are you with all this?"

Tracy hadn't had time to think about herself. On Tuesday night, after Lee's arrest, she had given her statement to the police; then she'd made half a dozen phone calls until she discovered who Olivia had gone home with after camp. Finally she had undergone an extensive interview with a woman from the local child protection agency to make sure Olivia would be safe with her until Alice was released. From that point on, Olivia had been with her constantly, unless the little girl was visiting Janya.

"I just wonder if we could have done anything differently. Of course now that we know what was happening, it seems like we should have figured it out faster. But Lee set this up carefully, and there wasn't anything we could point to and say 'Look, here's proof something bad is happening over there.' So I guess we did what we could. We paid attention, we cared, we tried to intervene, and in the end, we put ourselves in the middle."

He reached over and tickled her under the chin, as if he understood she needed to lighten up. "You know what I think?"

His opinion mattered, which was scary. "I'm sitting down."

"I think if that old guy Herb hadn't died on your watch, you might have looked the other way. But you learned something."

"Right, it's all about taking care of each other. Duh. Can the lessons stop now?"

"For a smart-ass California girl who says 'duh' way too much, it took a lot of courage to go in there the way you did and try to get Alice out. Even when you knew Lee was coming in after you. Why didn't you tell me what you were planning that night?"

"So you could tell me not to go?"

He looked genuinely surprised. "No, so I could lend a hand. Didn't you know I'd be there if you needed me?"

A shadow fell over the blanket, and Tracy looked up. Olivia was waiting to get her attention. "I'm tired."

"How about a walk along the beach?" Tracy rose and brushed off the seat of her bathing suit.

"You two go ahead," Marsh said. "Bay and I will light the charcoal so we can cook the burgers."

Olivia didn't agree or disagree; she just followed Tracy down to firmer sand, but she let Tracy walk on the side closest to the water.

"That's a pretty extravagant castle you and Bay are building."

Olivia didn't answer, so Tracy fell silent. At the beginning of the summer she would have considered herself the worst possible choice to help Olivia. Since then, she'd learned she had a sixth sense when talking to the youth campers. She understood when to hang back and when to step up. She had no idea how or where she had gotten that or some of the other qualities that seemed to make her good with kids, but she was going to have to make use of them now. Olivia deserved time and space to figure things out.

They walked until the beach nearly ended in an inlet surrounded by a flurry of scrub. Tracy was about to suggest they turn around when Olivia stopped.

"Tracy, my father's a bad person, isn't he?"

Tracy could hardly refute that. She scrambled to put a better spin on it, but in the end, she had to be honest.

"He's done some very bad things. I wish it weren't true."

"Why are some people like that?"

"I don't think anybody knows. Maybe something happened when your father was a kid, maybe he just started making bad choices, and one led to another. But it's not something people inherit from their parents, Olivia. It's not like blue eyes or brown hair. You're nothing like him."

"He says I'm too much like my mom."

Tracy waited until she could speak calmly. "Sweetie, from what I understand, being like your mom is a good thing. Everybody loved her."

Now Olivia was looking out at the water, as if she wished her mother would materialize and walk through the waves toward her. Tracy was afraid she knew what Olivia was putting together in her mind. She wished somebody else was there to help the girl, but there was nobody else. Just her.

There seemed to be a lot of that going around.

Olivia's voice was tentative. "Daddy was angry at Mommy the day she died. She didn't want to go out in his boat, but he talked her in to it."

She looked at Tracy. "He told me I should never tell anybody about the fight they had that morning. He said if I did, they might take me away from him and Nana. And he told me not to tell anybody about Nana being sick and not eating. What if I had, Tracy?"

Tracy rested her hand on Olivia's shoulder. "There are a lot of things we don't know about what just happened, but in no way is this your fault, Olivia. You did what you were taught, which was to listen to your father, and I'm afraid he made sure you couldn't do anything else. So the grown-ups had to make things right, not you. Even if you had known, you're a little girl, and people don't always listen to everything children say."

"You do."

Tracy smiled. "I'll always listen to *you.*"

"My nana's old, and she's been awfully sick."

This, at least, was something Tracy could reassure her about.

"But her doctor's sure she's going to pull through just fine. You've seen how much better she is when you visit."

"What if she dies?"

"I don't think that's going to happen."

"Tracy, it will happen someday. People do."

Uttered in Olivia's most grown-up voice, this unfortunate truth broke Tracy's heart. "Okay, you're right. So what's the question?"

Olivia lowered her voice. "I think I'd be an orphan. I don't have cousins or aunts and uncles. What will happen to me if everybody's gone?"

Tracy tugged Olivia close and put her arms around her. For a moment she couldn't speak.

She finally summoned her voice, although she had to clear her throat first. "Olivia, sweetie, if your grandmother dies before you're all grown-up, or she gets sick and can't take care of you anymore, you can come live with me. We'll even fix it so it's all legal, okay? And Janya and Wanda will always be here for you. You're one of our gang. We love you."

Olivia relaxed against her. Then she finally began to cry.

Tracy stroked Olivia's hair and realized that she had just promised she would stay in Florida until the girl became a woman. Because how would she be able to keep an eye on Alice and Olivia unless she was living right here, watching over them?

She waited for the jolt of an anchor hitting bottom, the familiar sensation that she was a sleek yacht moored in a fleet of dinghies. Instead, she looked up the beach and saw Marsh and Bay ambling toward them. She felt her anchor dropping gently into a bountiful estuary, the place where life begins.

Wanda felt like an actress on opening night after an exhaustive dress rehearsal. Even the care she took dressing and doing her hair and makeup was the same care a Broadway star took before walking out on stage.

She chose a scoop-necked peach T-shirt and under it the new flesh-colored bra she'd bought at Victoria's Secret. She passed over her comfortable capris for white linen slacks that hid her varicose veins. And she painted her toenails a brilliant scarlet. She was ready to meet Shadow at last.

That afternoon she'd gone back over her records, to see how many times she and Shadow had talked. She'd counted eleven, none of them for long. She hadn't made enough money off the guy to buy a good pirate romance and a bottle of wine. Of course, with Shadow, the relationship had never been about money. They had connected. From the beginning, she had understood him and looked forward to his calls. He was the only caller she took these days, and Lainie had finally given up and found someone else to permanently take her place. Wanda wasn't sorry.

Last night, when Shadow asked her to meet him, she hadn't hesitated. For some time, probably almost from the first, she had known this was inevitable. They were soul mates. The phone conversations had only been a prelude to something more intimate and important. She was ready for both.

They had decided to meet on the beach near the Indian mound. She'd told him what she would be wearing, and he'd told her to look for a man in a light blue sport shirt and jeans. She supposed it was possible he would take off once he saw the real her. But she didn't think so. Shadow just wasn't that kind of man.

After a short walk, she put Chase in the house and got in her car. She hadn't been more nervous than this when she'd seen Lee Symington charging up behind Tracy and Alice in Alice's dark bedroom. On that occasion she'd also been furious, and if she had been able to leap in and throttle the man, she would have done it. She had never been happier to see her husband, and never prouder of the man Ken was and what he did. She thought the encounter with Lee had proved he could still do his job, that he wasn't trigger-happy or gun-shy, but simply a good cop with a conscience. She supposed she had Lee to thank for that, if for nothing else he had ever done except sire Olivia.

The drive to the stretch of beach Shadow had suggested took only five minutes. She arrived right on time, parked, took a deep breath, then another for good measure, and stepped into the parking lot. She crossed it, the heels of her sandals ringing against the pavement. There were other cars parked here, but none she recognized. In her opinion, Palmetto Grove was just the right size. A woman could make friends, find her own little community, but she could also be one of a larger crowd. And that was what she was hoping for this evening.

The sun had another hour to go before it melted into the horizon, but the sky was streaked with rose and flame. Most of her life she had taken Florida sunsets for granted, but she knew she could never live in a place where this sight wasn't a short drive away. She understood why Ken had hoped to find his way back to life by walking for endless hours on this beach.

Not too far beyond where she'd parked, a man in a blue sport shirt was looking out over the water. He was broad shouldered, and he stood tall, as if he were stretching toward the sky. He had a narrow waistline for a man pushing sixty, and his jeans were tight enough to outline a nicely shaped behind. His hair was cut short, and it made the integrity written on his features that much easier to see.

She stopped beside him, and he turned.

"Hey, Kenny."

He nodded. "Wanda."

They stood shoulder-to-shoulder, staring out at the water.

"So when did you know it was me?" he asked at last.

"The voice had me fooled for a little while. You use one of those voice changing thingies from that closet of spy toys the department's got?"

"Yeah."

"And some kind of cell phone? Maybe one of the throw-aways?"

"You've been married to a cop for a lot of years."

"I guess it was easier to talk to me if you could pretend you were somebody else. Easier to tell me what you were thinking about."

"It was never easy."

They were quiet a little longer. Then she turned, forcing him to turn, too. "And when did you know it was me? Right from the first?"

He nodded.

"How?"

"I tried to call you a couple of times in the evenings, and our line was always busy. One night I came home early and heard you talking to some man. After that, tracking what you were doing and who you were doing it for was easy enough."

"I guess I always figured you'd find out one way or the other."

"So why did you do it?"

"To get even. To feel sexy and special for somebody, since I wasn't either of those things for you anymore. To have somebody to talk to at night while you were gone."

"That's it?"

"No. I guess I wanted to have a secret, too, because it seemed like you had so many."

"Sounds like you've been thinking about it."

"You could say that."

"I can't tell you I'm sorry for feeling the way I did. You see that sun going down over there? It was like that for me. Everything good, everything special, just disappeared over the horizon. But believe it or not, you were the moon that kept my sky from going all black, Wanda. Maybe I didn't know how to tell you, or even how to reach out my hand, but you were the only thing helping me see at all in that darkness."

He was not a man who spouted poetry, but she thought being compared to the moon was a fine thing. Tears filled her eyes.

"Kenny, I wanted to hurt you, and that's a fact. I just felt so lost. You expect to lose a lot in this life, and I knew someday I might lose you to some crazy person with a gun. But I never thought I'd lose you when you were still coming home most evenings. I just didn't know what to do about it."

"That crazy man with the gun? I shot and killed him down in Cutler Bay, and when he died, I guess he just took me along. So I can't say I'm sorry for feeling like I was down in that grave with him, but I am sorry I pushed you aside when I was trying to claw my way back up and you were standing there with your hand out. A real man doesn't ask for help, and he doesn't take it when it's offered. And for me, trying to be that real man, a real cop, was all that was left of the man I used to be."

She put her arm around his waist and rested her head on his shoulder. "I'm sorry, too. Sorry I was talking to strange men when I should have been trying harder to talk to you. But just for the record, except for Shadow, they were just lonely old farts who needed to talk about the times when they weren't lonely and they weren't old. That's all the job ever was."

His arm crept around her waist, and his hand splayed over her hip. "We're some pair, aren't we?"

"Are we? Still a pair?"

"You're going to hang up that phone of yours?"

"Well, if Shadow ever needs to talk to me again, I might take his calls."

"I think maybe now he can say what he needs to right to your face."

"It will be better that way, Kenny."

She hugged him hard. She had come to this beach thinking it might be the end of her marriage, and now what had passed for one since that awful night in Cutler Bay was gone. But this new marriage, with both of them talking and trying together? She thought maybe these would be the best years of all.

chapter thirty-four

Frail and a little unsteady, Alice still looked so much better than she had a week ago that the women broke into applause when she walked proudly to Wanda's car. Since her release from the hospital four days ago, she had been using a cane Janya bought at a garage sale and painted in pastel swirls. All the women had signed it with get-well messages in silver and gold, and Alice claimed that even when she didn't need the cane anymore, she planned to use it occasionally, just because it made her feel so good.

"Nana, you sit up front," Olivia said, holding out her hand to help her grandmother into the car.

"Like…a queen."

"Queen Alice," Wanda said. "Queen of Happiness Key."

Olivia made sure her grandmother was comfortably tucked in; then she got in the back with Tracy and Janya. Tracy swung her legs to the side so Olivia could crawl over her and sit between them. She knew Olivia felt most secure being sandwiched between her friends.

"The new earrings really are so beautiful," Janya told the girl. "They suit you perfectly."

Olivia smiled shyly. Last week, with Alice's permission, Tracy and Olivia had made a trip to a local jeweler, where Olivia had picked out sapphire chip studs to match her pretty blue eyes. She held Tracy's hand when the man pierced her ears, but Tracy figured that after everything else, Olivia had found the pain a minor inconvenience. They would be almost healed by the time school started next week.

"Now you're sure you feel up to this?" Wanda asked Alice before she started the car.

"Ready and willing."

Properly medicated, well-fed and hydrated, Alice had regained much of the strength and mental clarity she had lost in the weeks before Lee's arrest. She had also regained some of her funds. A forensic accountant who worked with the police department had discovered an extensive paper trail leading to accounts Lee had set up for himself, guaranteeing prosecution on those charges. Although some of Alice's money would never be recovered, it looked as if her final years might be comfortable enough.

Wanda pulled away from the cottage. While Alice had been in the hospital, the neighbors had scrubbed every inch of her house, repainted, and rescreened all the windows and doors, hoping to remove some of the unhappy memories of the past weeks. The aquarium was pristine once again, and they had added several fish, including the prettiest angelfish Olivia could find. The bedroom Lee had used now belonged to his daughter, who had helped Yash paint it turquoise. Tracy had found curtains of just the right pink, and a fluffy pink rug, and two days ago they had added a pine bookcase, and a matching canopy bed and dresser, more garage sale finds of Janya's. There were no traces of Lee in the house now, except in Olivia and Alice's worst memories.

"Well, our reservation's not until seven," Wanda said. "No early bird for us tonight. We're celebrating Alice's return, and I recommend the grouper to all you meat eaters. Nobody cooks grouper better. Our cook said he'll do a special vegetarian lasagna for Janya."

"Why so late?" Tracy asked. "That's an hour away."

"We're going to scout out Allamanda Street. According to Gloria Madsen, that's where Clyde was living right before he turned himself into Herb."

Tracy leaned forward, intrigued. "Wait a minute. I thought you couldn't find a street with that name. Didn't you look it up after you talked to her?"

"I did. But I said something to Kenny about it last night, and he said Gloria's memory might be fine. Seems the city regularly changes the names of streets, and I should look it up in an old directory instead of a new one."

"This being married to a cop's a good thing."

"In more ways than you know. Anyway, I called city hall. Turns out back in the sixties, somebody got it into his head to change all the streets over by the bird sanctuary to bird names. Big stink when they did it, too. Allamanda Street is now Pelican Way."

Tracy knew the area. She'd actually been to the sanctuary with Marsh and Bay to see a bald eagle's nest. Even harder to admit, she'd enjoyed herself.

"They built a lot of condo complexes in that area," she warned. "Wild Florida forced the developers to donate an extra hundred yards of property rimming the sanctuary before they got the permits. And they had to use native foliage and build special storm drainage ponds."

"That boyfriend of yours will make an environmentalist out of you, you don't watch yourself."

Tracy didn't correct the title. She wasn't sure what Marsh

was, but "boyfriend" was as accurate as anything else, even if it sounded like a word from another era.

"Anyway, if Alice is up to it," Wanda said, "we'll just wander a little, see if anybody there remembers the Franklins. We can take a little walk in the sanctuary, nothing else turns up."

Since Alice's return, they had mastered the art of mundane conversation, taking care not to bring up the subject of Lee. Now they chatted about the search for Herb's family. Tracy had given up looking and was planning to pack up his stuff as soon as her job ended and she had time. Wanda had arranged this side trip as an excuse to stretch their legs and give Alice some exercise, but even she didn't expect to turn up anything.

"I'm sorry we didn't find that daughter of his," Tracy said, "but nobody can say we didn't give the whole thing a good try. I guess in the end we did everything we could for the old guy."

They talked about the upcoming shuffleboard tournament and mural unveiling on Saturday, the need to buy Olivia's school supplies with the school year starting in less than a week, the election. By the time Wanda consulted her directions a third time and found the right turn, they were ready to get out.

Pelican Way was one long block, a dead end made up of a mixture of small houses and two-story apartment buildings that looked like snowbird rentals. The street was at least a quarter of a mile from the water, and the houses that remained were run-down and might be rentals, too.

Everyone got out, with Janya helping Alice. Children were laughing and calling to each other behind one of the houses, and a motorcycle roared past before it cut into an apartment lot. Sidewalks were pot luck, so they walked on the side of the road instead. The street ended at a swampy creek with a couple of picnic tables and a disintegrating volleyball net. A short footbridge crossed the water to where a new street began.

"I'm trying to imagine this place right after the war," Wanda said. "Baby boomers running helter-skelter, parents sitting on their screened porches, maybe having the neighbors over for highballs. Men talking about where they'd been, women talking about what they'd done while the men were gone."

"A good place," Alice said.

"Was it like that where you lived?" Tracy asked.

"Neighbors paid attention." Alice had been walking carefully, feeling her way slowly with the cane to be sure she didn't take a tumble. Now she looked up and smiled sadly. "Like mine."

Olivia slipped her hand into her grandmother's.

"I hate to say it, but I doubt anybody living here will remember Herb," Wanda said. "Clyde, I mean. That was a long time ago. But I'm game to knock on a door or two."

"We could try the houses." Tracy silently counted seven, including one that looked as if it had been built as a duplex.

They started back up the other side of the road, walking slowly and chatting about which house to try first. Somebody's television broadcast the evening news into the humid evening air.

Wanda stopped and pointed at a house sporting a poodle tied to a railing. "Gloria said Herb's house was little, and the screened porch was up on concrete blocks, like that one right there."

"And the one over there," Tracy said, pointing across the street. "Not to mention that in the decades since she saw it, it might have gone through a renovation or two."

"Okay, Miss Smarty Pants, you think we ought to start with the ones that don't look anything like her description?"

"Whatever, but you're going to be so embarrassed if that poodle takes a chunk out of you."

"Me, I understand poodles." Wanda sniffed and marched up

the walkway, admonishing the little white dog as she got closer, until it slunk off into the bushes.

"I'm glad Wanda wasn't *my* mother," Tracy said.

Wanda tapped on the porch door and yoo-hooed, but nobody answered. She finally gave up and joined them at the curb. "What's next?"

"I think the woman crossing the street might be," Janya said.

Tracy turned and saw a woman Alice's age or older bearing down on them from another house across the way. She looked like a leaf blowing in the wind, impossibly light and fragile, with skin desiccated into alligator hide.

"I'm not signing petitions, and I have my own political party and church, so I don't need to hear about yours." The woman recited the lines in a weary voice, as if she had said them too many times.

"I guess that's the advantage of living on the key," Wanda said, holding out her hand. "Too far for hustlers. My name's Wanda Gray." She introduced the others. "We're not looking for signatures, votes or converts. Just trying to solve a mystery."

Tracy watched the woman's eyes light up. Silently she congratulated Wanda on an inspired approach.

The woman didn't introduce herself, as if she was still wary, but she gave a little nod. "I like a good mystery."

"Well, here's the story. A neighbor of ours died. We think he was related to some folks who used to live on this street. It's a long shot, but we thought we'd see if we can find them. As far as we can tell, none of his relatives know he passed on."

"What's the world coming to?" the old woman asked.

Again Tracy thought Wanda's approach was inspired. No need to go into the Herb-Clyde-altered identity story. As far as Wanda had taken it, her version was true.

"Have you lived on Pelican Way very long?" Janya asked.

"Since back when it was Allamanda. Nobody's lived here longer."

"Then you're the one we want," Wanda said. "The way people up and move these days, we didn't think we'd find anybody of consequence."

"This is Florida. Where else would I retire?"

Olivia was sifting through pebbles in a nearby driveway, and Alice was leaning heavily on her cane. Tracy figured they ought to get right to the point.

"So did you happen to know the Franklins?" Tracy smiled. "Clyde and Louise Franklin?"

Tracy waited for the head shake that had been the answer of choice almost every time they asked a question. Instead, the woman shrugged.

"I didn't know Clyde. I moved here after he died. But I sure knew Louise. We used to play gin rummy every Wednesday night. Is that who your neighbor was related to?"

"To Clyde." Wanda's eyes were sparkling, but she made her answer sound as if this were just a regular conversation. "We know Louise was killed in a car crash some years back."

"Awful thing. Poor woman deserved better. Everybody on the street liked Louise, even if they felt a little sorry for her. That Clyde of hers?" She lowered her voice. "She had him declared dead, you know. Never found out what happened to the man."

"It's a crying shame," Wanda said. "Living with something like that, then dying without knowing."

"I felt bad for Pam. She was a good girl, serious like her mother, and kind. A hard worker, too. She finished putting herself through college, but she never came back here to live. She moved up north. Most of the houses left on the street are rentals now, you know, with people coming and going so fast

I just stopped trying to keep up. I have a group of friends from church and my bridge club, and I spend summers with my daughter's family in New England, so I'm not home a lot."

Tracy felt her hopes deflate again. "Which house was Louise's? Is it still there?"

"Oh, yeah, down at the end." She pointed away from the footbridge. "Between the apartments."

Tracy couldn't see the house well, but they had parked right in front of it. From her vantage point it looked a little larger, a little more modern than the one they were standing in front of.

"It's a rental, too?" Wanda asked.

"Right. Has been since Pam left. See, vacation apartments started going up, and people sold off their houses one by one to builders. A few of us held out, but after a while everybody who'd kept their houses moved away, and now they just rent them out. Except me, of course. We'd probably all sell if we could, but these days nobody wants to build apartments, not with all the condos on prettier streets around here. I guess when it's time to move out for good, I'll be renting mine, too, the way Pam does. Or sell it for peanuts."

Tracy nearly missed the part about Pam, but Wanda didn't. "So Pam still owns the house and rents it out?"

"Oh, right from the beginning. I've never seen a For Sale sign over there, although I'm not sure why. And some parade of tenants she's had. From what I can tell, they change about every year or so."

"Have you seen her, then?"

"She's got somebody managing the rentals, somebody else taking care of the property. She doesn't have to show up too often, but she drops by once in a while to check on things. Four or five years ago she came by around Christmas time and left me a note, but I was visiting my son in Orlando."

"Would you happen to have her address?"

"No, it's been a lot of years since we had a chat."

"The renter…" Alice leaned forward, propping herself on the cane. "They would know?"

"Seems like it. I don't know her name. I think she might have moved in back in early spring when I was off on a cruise, and then I came back and left again for the summer. Just got back last week. A sweet girl, though. She has a little boy, just a toddler, and she always waves. I guess now that I'm home again, I'll get around to meeting them."

"I think we'll just check with her," Tracy said. "Maybe she can put us in touch with Pamela."

"Good luck to you. You must really have liked your neighbor to go to all this trouble." She headed toward her house, and her poodle slunk out of the bushes to go with her.

"It can't be this easy," Tracy said, as they started back toward their car and the house that was almost directly across from it. It was frame construction, like the one they'd just visited, but the stoop was enclosed in red brick, and the windows were all new. The house had recently been painted a mustardy-yellow, and if there had once been a screened porch, it was gone now. A riding toy shaped like a banana stood between them and the door, and a beach ball adorned the stoop.

"Easy?" Wanda snorted. "You got a slow leak in your head somewhere? We've chased garbage trucks, hobnobbed with felons, hung out in bars, batted our eyelids at clerks down at city hall, read newspaper articles so old they turned to dust before we could finish them. Don't you remember? This hasn't been one bit easy."

"Maybe not. Maybe it's going to seem weird to have it over with."

"Maybe it's going to be great."

"Tracy is afraid we will have no need to spend so much time together," Janya said.

Tracy realized that, as usual, Janya was right. "Okay, I'll get over it if you all promise to hang around."

"Is anybody planning on going somewhere else?" Wanda asked.

Tracy didn't dare tell them about the developers, who every day, according to Maribel, seemed closer to making an acceptable offer for Happiness Key.

Nobody spoke until they were skirting the banana and walking up to the house that had once belonged to Clyde Franklin, alias Herbert Krause.

"Okay, who's going to do the talking?" Wanda asked.

"I guess I will." Tracy licked her lips. "I just don't know what I'm going to say."

"Oh, grits and gravy, woman. You should have been practicing all these months. How much more time do you need?"

Tracy knocked, but Wanda gently pushed her aside. "You never seen one of these?" She turned a metal loop that protruded from the door frame, and a doorbell clattered inside. The doorbell looked like original equipment.

"Sweet," Tracy said. "So what, you shocked some poor little elf in the woodwork, and he ran up and hit the doorbell with a hammer?"

"Back before cell phones and the Internet, people still managed to get the job done." Wanda twisted the loop again.

But the job didn't get done, because nobody answered.

"I guess I'll have to come back," Tracy said.

There was a collective sigh. They'd been so close. Tracy took Alice's arm to help her down the steps just as a car pulled into the driveway.

Tracy held up her hand to keep everyone where they were. A young woman, in age somewhere between Janya and Tracy, got out of the car. She had curly blond hair that just brushed her collar, and a slender figure. Before she started up the walkway, she went around and retrieved a small child from a car seat, then a bag of groceries from the passenger side The child was sound asleep, his blond hair a halo of ringlets. The woman must have seen them as she parked, because she didn't look surprised to find them waiting for her.

"Carolers?" she joked once she got to the stoop. "It's a little early, but I'm game." She was pretty, a wholesome corn-fed beauty as pale as if she hailed from Wisconsin or Iowa.

Tracy stepped forward. "A lady down the road pointed us in this direction. She said you might be able to help us."

"Well, you don't look like muggers." The woman handed her grocery bag to Tracy and gripped her son harder so he wouldn't fall forward. "Hold this a sec, will you? I'll get the door." She fished around inside her purse and pulled out a key.

She held it up for them to admire. "That's the good thing about one of these old relics. It's always the first thing I feel. It's impossible to lose it."

Tracy looked down at the key, then over to Janya. Janya was looking at the key, as well. Both women had seen one exactly like it. In fact, the key Herb had clutched in his hand as he died was now at home at the bottom of Tracy's purse.

"Do you want me to unlock it for you? That's really an antique, isn't it?" Tracy wasn't as good at disguising her feelings as Wanda. She knew she sounded elated, but the woman didn't seem to notice.

"As old as the house. My mother gave it to me when I moved here." She nodded at a new dead bolt inches above the knob. "There's a modern lock, too, but I like to use this key. I guess it's sentimental, but it's the same one my grandmother used when she lived here."

"You're Louise Franklin's granddaughter?"

The young woman turned, surprised. "How did you know her name? Voter rolls or something? I'd better warn you, I'm a Democrat. If you're here to get me to register as anything else, you'll do better somewhere else."

"No." Tracy drew a deep breath. "We, well, we didn't know who you were. In fact, we just found out this was Louise's house, and that her daughter, Pamela, still owns it."

"Pamela's my mother. Pamela Bishop. I'm Katie Bishop Ayres, only daughter and heir. Not, I hope, that there will be all that much to inherit. Mom and Dad deserve to enjoy retirement." She leaned over carefully and inserted the key, playing with the lock until there was an audible click.

She faced them. "So what is this about? You're not political, and if you sang 'Silent Night,' you did it silently."

"We're actually here because of a man named Herb Krause."

Katie sobered. "Poor Herb. I heard he died. I guess there was no funeral?"

Tracy didn't know what to say. "Well, no…"

"Were you friends of his?"

"Neighbors."

"Please come in. You can explain inside where it's cooler." Katie opened the door and went in, leaving them to follow.

Tracy looked at the other women. Everybody appeared as perplexed as she felt. She shrugged and followed Katie into the kitchen. From the shape of the living room, she guessed the very front part was the missing porch, now enclosed. Katie tucked the little boy into a corner of an L-shaped sofa and put a cylindrical pillow in front of him. He slept on.

The kitchen was tiny, but the appliances looked newish, and the cabinets were a pretty white beadboard with mottled blue counters accenting them. Katie took the groceries from Tracy and set them on the counter.

"So you were Herb's neighbors," Katie said. "He stopped by a couple of times, just to make sure Frankie and I were doing okay. He was such a sweet old guy."

Tracy was stumped. She didn't know what to ask, but Wanda had no such problem.

"So you didn't know him well?" She started unpacking the bag and handing the items to Katie to put away. A half gallon of milk. A loaf of French bread. Fresh mushrooms.

"Oh, no, not at all," Katie said from inside the refrigerator. "But after the help he gave Mom all those years, I was glad to make his acquaintance. She always said she couldn't imagine what she would have done if Herb hadn't been in charge here."

Tracy repeated that. "In charge?"

"May I have a glass of water?" Olivia asked.

"You bet." Katie closed the refrigerator and got a glass from the cupboard beside the sink. "Anybody else?"

The water break did nothing to help Tracy put the story together. "I'm sorry, Katie, but we're, like, megaconfused here. Your mom knew Herb, too?"

"Well, not the way you know a good friend. But Herb took care of this property for years. And she met with him every time she had to come and check on it. She liked him a lot. She said he took care of the house and the yard like they were his. You can't buy service like that."

Tracy's feelings must have been obvious, because Katie stopped talking. There was a long silence, and at last she said, "Maybe you just need to tell me what this is about."

"I'm trying to think of a way," Tracy said honestly. "It's pretty big, Katie."

"Herb left Mom a million dollars in his will?" She was joking, but she wasn't smiling.

"No, but, well, he did leave her something. His name. Herb Krause wasn't really Herb Krause at all. His real name was Clyde Franklin. He was your grandfather."

chapter thirty-five

Every surface of the Palmetto Grove Recreation Center had been cleaned and polished, and the hallways repainted and decorated with photo montages of the summer activities. The photos were Tracy's idea, and some of the older campers had shown real ability in snapping, printing and presenting them. The floors in the classrooms gleamed, and the children she had tapped and trained to be guides were politely showing visitors through the complex.

"Everything came together so well. This is a big day, Tracy, and you've done most of it." Gladys was all dressed up in a red skirt and blouse to support the shuffleboard team. Her hair had been styled, and she wore makeup. Woody, who was racing from one end of the building to the other to make sure he didn't miss anybody, was wearing a suit.

Tracy was equally happy at the way the day was progressing. The Coastal Florida Shuffleboard Tournament was underway, and so far, everything was running smoothly. The opening ceremonies had been upbeat, and the caterers, who had laid out a continental breakfast for the players, reported success. Now they were getting ready to serve lunch.

With rounds one and two completed, the home team was doing well. The adults were wiping up. They had already beaten their opponents from the yacht club, and Tracy felt sorry for Carol, the events coordinator. The youth camp kids had taken a beating, but their best players were competing in the afternoon rounds.

Downstairs the shuffle board was decked out in all their team finery, along with the special gold cue pins Tracy had bought for their shirts. A member of the women's team had sewed a gold star on Mr. M.'s pocket, since he was the captain. Tracy hoped there might be more than a little Betsy Ross support going on there. She was rooting for them.

Now she gave Gladys a farewell wave. "I'd better go make sure lunch is ready. You're coming down?"

"Can you hold up a minute, dear?"

Tracy skidded to a halt. "Do we have a problem I don't know about?"

"Woody asked me to talk to you. He'll track you down later to make this official, but it's so crazy today…"

"Right." Tracy smiled brightly. She wasn't worried. The Woodleys seemed thrilled by the way everything was unfolding, and besides, her job ended this weekend. Monday she would come back to clean out her desk, but maternity leave was now up for Susan, the woman she had replaced. Whatever Tracy had done, for good or bad, she was finished.

"Woody's going to ask you to stay on, Tracy. Everybody's so pleased with your work here. You're by far the best supervisor we've ever had."

Tracy wasn't sure she understood. "But Susan's coming back next week."

"She really doesn't want to leave the babies, and, well…let's just say Woody encouraged her to stay home with them. It's a win-win for everybody."

Tracy's head was spinning. This was completely unexpected. "But she was so organized. I couldn't have done it without all her notes. She even counted rolls of toilet paper and figured out how many trips to the bathroom we could count on from each one. I mean, get real, she factored in things none of the rest of us will ever want to think about. You can't beat that."

"Between us, she's great with toilet paper and lists, but not half as good with kids as you are. You worked a few miracles here. Woody thinks you're the right person to keep our program moving in the right direction and give us a fresh look. I know it's a big job, but you won't have to work quite so hard during the school year. You can take a nice long break over Christmas. I think you'll like it. Say you'll stay. There may even be a raise…."

"I… Well, I don't know…."

"Think about it. You don't have anything else lined up yet, do you?"

"No. No, it's not that. It's just that everything is changing. I can't seem to keep up. The minute I figure out something, that changes, too."

"Welcome to adulthood."

Tracy wondered if she would ever feel at home in that particular locale.

"Maturity definitely has its finer points," Gladys said, reading Tracy's mind. "But I think you've experienced that already."

Tracy knew she had just received Gladys's final approval. "You're coming down to see the unveiling of the mural?"

"Of course I'm coming down to see your greatest achievement, dear. I wouldn't miss it for anything."

★ ★ ★

Janya drove the two men in her life to the recreation center and parked at the back of the lot. She had tried to persuade them that there was no need to see the mural today. Instead she had promised a tour when the center was less crowded, but neither man would be persuaded. If the mural was a failure once it was unveiled, she had not wanted them to see her disgrace. But when she had hinted at this, they had only laughed at her.

Despite her worries, she was glad to have them with her. Yash was returning to India next week, so she wanted to spend as much time with her brother as she could. Once he was home, he planned to tell their parents he would not be pursuing a career in accounting. He would work for a year while he looked for the right university to study history, perhaps even here in the United States, where he could be close to Janya.

She would miss him terribly, but already Rishi was talking about a trip to India for Holi, in March. Even if no one in her family except Yash welcomed them, the remaining members of Rishi's family who had helped arrange their meeting would be happy to see them.

Janya got out and waited until they came around to join her. "You will remember the mural was painted by children? Some of the ideas they had were better than others."

Rishi put his arm around her in that American way he had absorbed. Today she was less embarrassed than grateful. "We know how it came about, Janya, and we know that without you, the wall would still be blank. So please, no more squirming."

"Squirming?"

"Yes, exactly. That's what you are doing."

"I'm worried, that's all."

"It's her big debut," Yash said. "The moment they applaud, my sister will be fine."

Janya wasn't certain she would be fine. The unveiling of the mural meant her work here was finished, and she had loved it. She had never been part of any project so large, but now her dreams had expanded. They were filled with wide walls and brilliant images to cover them. To stave off boredom she might fill the walls of the second bedroom in the cottage with a jungle scene. Tigers and elephants and foliage in a hundred shades of green. When she and Rishi had a son or a daughter to sleep there, the walls would provide endless entertainment.

As they entered the building, children enthusiastically greeted her, and Janya introduced them to Rishi and Yash. By the time they headed downstairs to the shuffleboard courts, she was resigned. Whatever the public thought, the children had loved painting the mural. For them, the project was already a success.

Outside, the atmosphere was festive. Picnic tables had been set up on the grounds beyond the pool, and a canopy sheltered the area where lunch was being sold and served. Janya was too nervous to eat, but the men went to buy sandwiches and drinks for themselves. More children flocked over to introduce her to their parents, and before long the time had arrived for the unveiling.

Janya saw Tracy conferring with several men and women in suits, including Woody. A loudspeaker system had been set up to the right of the mural, which was covered by curtains a mother had made from dark sheets. Woody began to speak, and the children pulled Janya forward. She saw Rishi and Yash approaching with their food, and she hoped the unveiling would end before they got there.

Woody did a short presentation, telling the story of how the idea for the mural had come about and crediting Tracy. Then he asked Tracy and Janya to come forward, something she hadn't known would be expected. Everyone applauded politely, and she and Tracy smiled and waved before they disappeared back into the crowd. Then the mayor was introduced. Janya hadn't known such an important person would make the final speech. Had she been able to sink into the ground, she would have.

The mayor, a middle-aged woman in a trim blue blazer, briskly greeted them. Janya thought she probably had learned many important things in her campaign, one of which was not to keep people standing in the hot sun. She ended a short speech by reciting an even shorter list of people who had supported the rec center from the beginning. Then, to polite applause, she stepped aside.

Tracy signaled two teenagers, who walked to the center of the curtains and carefully pulled them back. Janya looked straight ahead, afraid to watch the faces of those who were viewing the mural for the first time. The applause began. A full minute later she was no longer worried.

"Will every child who had any part in the mural come forward?" Tracy was up at the lectern now. "And also our star and designer, Janya Kapur."

The applause began again as the children stepped up to the front. Proud parents and families, rec center staff, local citizens there to see how their taxes were spent and, of course, the tournament attendees. Janya went to stand in front of the mural with the children for photos. Then the unveiling was over. People flocked to the front to see it up close. Rishi and Yash found her, and heaped praise on what she had done.

"I am always proud of you, but perhaps I'm allowed to be a little prouder today?" Rishi kissed her cheek.

"Amazing," Yash said. "Gorgeous. Will you ever want to work on anything small again?"

She was so happy, she didn't notice the woman who had

come up to stand behind them. She saw Tracy signaling, and she turned to find the mayor standing there.

"Mrs. Kapur?" The mayor held out her hand. Up close, she looked to be in her fifties, with a thick silver streak in her dark hair that could only be natural.

Janya shook hands, remembering to shake as Americans did, with a firm grip.

"The mural is absolutely stunning," the mayor said.

Janya had not caught the woman's name, and now she was embarrassed. She nodded her thanks. "I am so glad it pleases you. The children had so much fun with it." She introduced Rishi and Yash.

"Mrs. Kapur, the Sun County Arts Council has discussed doing a mural on the side of the main library. There's a little court-yard there, and a long wall that is simply blank space. We'd hoped to make the area a sculpture garden, but we don't have the funds. We do have enough for a lively mural. Would you be interested?"

Janya looked at Rishi, who was nodding. She turned back to the mayor. "I would be interested and honored."

"You'll be hearing from me." The mayor gave a quick smile before she headed back into the crowd.

"This is wonderful," Rishi said. "Now I am too proud. I'm bursting."

Janya thought of all the years when her talent as an artist had been at best tolerated. She would always love India, but her new country, too, had presented her with gifts. She could not be more grateful.

By the time she was on the way home Tracy was exhausted but thrilled. The day's activities had been a salute to a summer of fun for the youth campers. The Palmetto Grove Shuffle-board Team had performed brilliantly. Two of their adults—

Mr. M. being one—had won first and second in the singles division, and two teams had taken first and third in doubles. In the youth division, Bay had surprised everybody by taking a first in his age group. A rock band made up of rising seniors from the local high school had finished the afternoon with a concert, and she'd seen more than one parent tugging an unwilling camper to the car. Youth camp was officially over.

She and Marsh had taken Bay and Olivia out for pizza and ice cream to celebrate. Bay had asked Olivia to come home and watch *Harry Potter and the Order of the Phoenix,* and Alice had agreed. Marsh told Tracy he might stop by when he dropped Olivia off, and she told him to be sure he did. She had something to talk to him about.

It wasn't the job offer.

Tracy parked outside her cottage and was just about to go inside when she saw two strangers walking from the direction of Herb's. Wanda beside them made three. When they got closer, Tracy realized one of the women was Katie, who was carrying her son. The other woman looked so much like her that it could only be one person.

Tracy finally reached them and held out her hand to the older woman. "I'm Tracy Deloche. You must be Pamela."

Pamela Bishop's hair was curly like her daughter's, but the blond was heavily mixed with silver. She was slender, like Katie, and had the same warm smile.

"Wanda tells me we have you to thank for making sure we finally learned the truth about my father."

"Wanda and the others worked every bit as hard as I did. She's being modest." Tracy glanced at her friend. "I didn't know you could do that."

"Behave yourself. These ladies wanted to get inside, but you have the place locked up tight as a banjo string."

Tracy apologized. "I'm sorry I wasn't here to let you in, but I didn't know you were coming."

Katie hadn't been in touch since the women had told her the truth about her grandfather. She had accepted the news, but afterward she'd excused herself, saying she needed to call her mother, then more or less ushered them out. Tracy hadn't had time to offer details, or to explain how and why they had followed the trail. Katie had taken her phone number and directions to the cottage, and said goodbye.

Later, at the Dancing Shrimp, the women had been divided about whether they would ever hear from Herb's family again. Alice had been the only one among them who seemed certain they would.

Pamela looked tired, as if she hadn't slept the previous night. "We should have called to warn you, but I wasn't sure I could get here so fast. After Katie told me, I packed and went to the airport early the next morning and sat all day. I flew to Newark Friday night and finally got here this afternoon. Labor Day weekend's not the best time for a revelation. Of course, the best time for this one would have been about fifty years ago."

"This must be tough." Tracy didn't know what else to say.

"Do you mind going over to the house with us?"

"Let me get the key. I'll meet you there in a minute."

Inside, Tracy changed out of her youth camp shirt and brushed her hair; then she grabbed keys and took off again.

Janya had joined them by then. She was telling the women about Herb's plants. "I have most of them at my house. They needed so much attention, and I was afraid they would die. But of course, they belong to you."

"I might take some cuttings on the plane," Pamela said. "But I'd like you to have the plants if you want them. Katie?"

Katie smoothed her son's curls. "Maybe I'll take something

small and easy to remember him by, but just one. I barely have enough energy to raise Frankie here." She set the little boy on the ground and watched him toddle right for the road. "See what I mean?" She took off after him.

Pamela watched her daughter and grandson with a smile. "Katie's husband is in Iraq. Did she tell you that? We thought it made sense for her to use the house I grew up in, since she wouldn't have to pay rent. She'll stay until Richard comes home next year."

"We didn't really talk," Wanda said. "But she's welcome out here on the key any time she wants to come and visit us."

Katie joined them again. "So this is where Herb lived?"

"Let's go inside." Tracy unlocked the door. Wanda and Janya looked at each other, as if trying to figure out if they should come, too, but Tracy beckoned them inside. She didn't want to be the only one to explain what they knew.

"He lived all alone?" Pamela asked. "He wasn't...married? I mean, to somebody other than my mother?"

"No, he never married again. And he did live here by himself. But he was energetic and friendly. He was able to manage, and he seemed fine right up until the end."

"He died of a heart attack?"

"He did. Right here. Peacefully, too."

Pamela was wandering now, lifting a dish, then a magazine. "He didn't have much, did he?"

"We cleared out some old papers, but everything else is right where he left it. I hated to throw anything away. We knew he had a daughter somewhere. We were sure we would find you. Of course, we didn't know how hard it would be."

"He told you about me?"

"He told other people, and they told us."

Wanda spoke up. "It got to be a quest, if you know what I

mean. We, none of us, felt we'd given him enough time when he was living. We were all just so busy with our own lives. So I guess we felt we had to be good to him after he died."

Pamela stopped pretending she was interested in Herb's few possessions. "I don't even know how to start asking questions. I thought he was just the man I'd hired to watch out for my house. He stopped by one day when I was getting the house ready to rent, and he was willing to work for so little. I sent him Christmas presents, and always gave him a nice bonus in the summer when the yard had to be mowed. And when he got too old to manage, I hired a lawn service and repairmen, but I still paid him to stop by and just look things over from time to time." She stopped, biting her bottom lip, as if she was trying not to cry.

"I guess that's the way he wanted it," Wanda said.

Tracy knew it was time to explain how they had figured out the convoluted puzzle that was Herb's life. She launched into it, with occasional help from the other two women. Both Pamela and Katie were wide-eyed as she concluded.

"And that's everything we know."

Pamela was silent, but Katie was shaking her head. "You mean that when this Gloria Madsen left him, he could have gone home, even wanted to come home, but he didn't? He lived all those years wanting to return, but he never did? Not so anybody knew, anyway?"

"I'm afraid that's it."

"I think we learned to know Herb through this," Janya said. "I believe he was so ashamed he had left your mother, Pamela, that he felt he could never go home again."

"Do you know why we still have that house?" Pamela asked. "Why my mother wouldn't sell it when a builder wanted to buy it for good money and put up an apartment? Why *I* never sold it? Why we never changed those old-fashioned locks?"

Wanda put her hand on Pamela's shoulder. "Because you were hoping he would come home one day. He would walk up to the house and fit his key in that lock, and be welcomed home again."

Pamela wiped her eyes, because now the tears were falling. "My mother loved him until the day she died. She knew what the war had done to him, how he had changed, and she understood. I think she always hoped he was alive somewhere. She wanted him to come home to her. To us. And then we would pick up where we had been and be a real family again. I buried her in Georgia, where she was born, but even at that, I wondered if I should have buried her here, in case he tried to find her."

"He knew where she was buried," Wanda said. "We found bills for flowers from a Georgia florist. I bet he had them put on her grave."

Tracy pulled the key to the house on Pelican Way from her pocket. She had taken the time to retrieve it when she went inside to change. Now she took it to Pamela and placed it in her hand, folding her fingers over it.

"He was holding this when he died. I found it in his hand. I think he probably carried it with him always."

"The key to happiness for all of us." Pamela grasped it tight. "And he was afraid to use it."

"He wouldn't be the only one in the world who ever was," Wanda said. "But maybe it helps just a little knowing he wanted to, more than anything else in the world."

Tracy was sitting on her front steps when Marsh passed in his truck to drop off Olivia. She met him on the road, and they walked in silence down to the same stretch of beach where they had first met.

"So I guess you had some kind of day," he said when they were standing looking out over the water.

"I'll tell you about the last part another time. But here's a clue. It's all about holding the key to happiness in your hot little hand and being afraid to open the door it belongs to."

"I'll be interested to hear all about it."

She turned to him. "I finally got around to looking at that packet of papers you left me at the beginning of July."

"I knew you would eventually."

"I didn't really understand all the legal gobbledygook."

"No reason you should. I figured you'd ask for details if you wanted more information."

"Wild Florida wants my property as a conservation easement?"

"It's really not all that complicated, Tracy. You sign away your rights for certain things, like developing it down to the last inch, and we give you money."

"Marsh?" She shook her head. "Here's your chance to be the soul of honesty."

"Okay, you can't develop it at all, if you want the truth. But you can improve the houses that are already here, maintain the driveways and the yards, maybe even put up another house or two on the old foundations, but you can't build, say, a marina, or condos."

"Garages?"

"Yeah, you could do that for the houses that are standing now. You can add on some, but you can't turn them into mini-mansions. We'll be watching you."

"You'll pay me for these rights? But I keep the land?"

"Decent money, too. But your heirs have to abide by the covenants we agree to. The land can never be developed. Not ever."

"And I get tax benefits on top of that?"

"Boo-coo. The land loses value once the ability to develop it is lost. The county will evaluate it accordingly, and that's how you'll be taxed. Plus you get other tax breaks right up front.

So you can keep all this acreage, afford to live here and enjoy it, and even improve and rent out the cottages if you want. Down the road, you can sell them if you find a buyer willing to go along with the plan."

"There's a group of developers who want it. Maribel's been negotiating with them. They're tough guys and willing to fight you in the courts."

He just looked at her, tilting his head in question.

"I would be rich," she pointed out.

"You already are."

Tracy knew he wasn't talking about money.

He smiled. "You're going to let us have it, aren't you?"

"I just may." She rose up on tiptoe and kissed him.

He put his arms around her and held her there. "You decide soon, okay? Because I'm getting kind of tired of waiting for a little happiness of my own, and I don't mean Happiness Key."

"A little?" She laughed. "What makes you think it will just be a little?"

He was too busy kissing her to answer.

epilogue

Thursday night had become their night together. None of the women was sure how it happened. Nobody decreed it. The first Thursday night Janya had the neighbors to her house to practice her henna tattoos. Then the following Thursday Wanda had them over for sweet potato pie, and to show off the new marble tile Ken and Tracy were planning to install when work slowed a little at the rec center. Last week Tracy had invited them for dinner to prove that she was indeed learning to cook at the center's basic cooking class and could now make a mean macaroni and cheese—if nothing else.

Tonight was Alice's turn. She had asked them to come for dessert, and the smell of chocolate greeted Tracy when Alice let her in. She could hear voices and knew some of the other women were already there, including Katie, who was becoming one of the gang. Alice was particularly fond of Frankie, who was screeching somewhere nearby.

"Wow, look at these Halloween decorations!"

"Karen loved Halloween." In the past weeks Alice's speech had improved measurably, and she had gained much-needed weight. Without Lee hovering over every move, she had also gained confidence, which helped with everything else. She was driving again, which helped most of all with Olivia's after-school activities, although sometimes Olivia just walked to the rec center to go home with Tracy.

"Are these some of her things?" Tracy picked up a ceramic haunted house in the middle of a scary village on a side table.

"Lee stored some boxes. In the utility room. Olivia found these."

"It must be comforting for her to carry on her mom's tradition."

Alice smiled gravely. "She is so much like Karen."

Janya came out of Olivia's bedroom carrying Frankie, and Katie followed with her arm around Olivia.

"Hey, gang," Tracy said. "Do I smell brownies?"

"Cupcakes," Olivia said. "Like my mom made every single Halloween. I made them myself."

Halloween wasn't for another month, but Tracy could see that the intervening weeks would be rich in celebration. "Hey, if you're that good at cupcakes, I think you ought to have a party for your friends out here on Halloween night."

She started to suggest a haunted house over at Herb's, which was finally empty of all belongings and ready to rent again for the winter. But maybe a haunted house was too close to the truth. Herb had, in his own way, haunted each of them. Now that his ghost was finally at peace, she figured she would let it stay that way. Just in case.

Wanda arrived with a bag full of books and magazines for Alice. Janya had rooted cuttings for her, and they discussed the perfect windowsill. After they chatted for a while and watched Olivia feed the fish, Alice served coffee and tea on a lace table-cloth, along with the cupcakes, which were adorned with spiderweb frosting, and spiders made from gumdrops and licorice. The tablecloth had come from J.C. Penney's, but the last time they were together, Alice had showed them the new pineapple tablecloth she was crocheting for Olivia. She had already made headway.

"Well, I got news," Wanda said. "Kenny and I, we're taking a cruise to Puerto Rico at Christmas. I know some of you've been everywhere, but I've never been squat. So this is exciting. It's kind of like a second honeymoon."

The room buzzed with suggestions for what to bring, things to do on board. When the buzz died down, Janya made her own announcement.

"I start work on the library mural in two weeks. They like my design and found me an assistant to help with some of the work."

Again everybody talked at once. Tracy had seen the design. Janya had incorporated scenes from familiar adult and children's novels. It was fabulous.

Katie described a letter she had gotten from her soldier husband. Olivia told them she was trying out for a play at the local community theater.

Tracy had nothing new to tell. Sherrie had come for a visit and pronounced a blessing on Tracy's new life. Tracy liked her job more every day. The legal work was already in phase two with Wild Florida, and she and Marsh had moved on to a new phase of their relationship, as well, which held acres of promise—if they could figure out how two such different people could share a life. Living in Florida was a work in progress, but she had a million things to look forward to. She wasn't sure that had ever been true before.

"I have something." Alice got to her feet and disappeared down the hall.

"Your grandmother's looking good," Wanda told Olivia,

who was down on the floor setting up blocks so Frankie could knock them over.

"She's happy," Olivia said.

Tracy thought that, despite missing her father, Olivia was happier, too. She had been to see Lee once at the county jail, but she had not asked to go again. Years would pass before Olivia dealt with all the things that had happened to her family, but she had a lot of people willing to listen as she did.

Alice returned with a shopping bag. She stopped in front of Tracy and pulled out a little bundle tied in ribbon. Tracy looked up to see if Alice was really serious. "No, you've got to be kidding, Alice. You have no idea how awful I am at things like this."

Alice made tsking noises and went on to Wanda, who got the same bundle and made the same protests.

Janya took hers with a smile. "Oh, this will be fun."

Alice passed out the last bundle to Katie.

"Olivia already—" Alice took her place again "—made a scarf. She's only ten. None of you have excuses."

Tracy looked down at her crochet hook and a glittery red ball of yarn. She tried to imagine an occasion when she would wear this scarf, and she couldn't. She tried to imagine telling Alice she refused to learn to crochet.

She *really* couldn't.

Alice held up her own hook. "We start by making a chain."

Tracy thought the women had already made one, the very best kind, and every link was right in this room.

USA TODAY BESTSELLING AUTHOR

EMILIE RICHARDS

Kendra and Jamie were never storybook sisters. But after a long estrangement, Jamie has offered Kendra and her husband their ultimate dream—a child of their own.

Despite some misgivings about her once wayward younger sister, Kendra agrees, and Jamie, a promising architect and single mother, becomes a gestational surrogate for Kendra and Isaac. Jamie also designs a house for the couple on the Shenandoah River.

But when a medical crisis threatens Jamie's health and her budding relationship with Kendra's builder, the enigmatic Cash Rosslyn, Jamie learns that the most difficult choice in her life is still ahead, and its cost may be beyond calculation.

Sister's Choice

Available now, wherever books are sold!

MIRA®

MER2647TR

www.MIRABooks.com

Don't miss these touching stories
in the Shenandoah Album series
from *USA TODAY* bestselling author

EMILIE RICHARDS

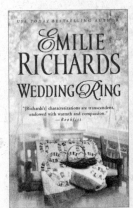

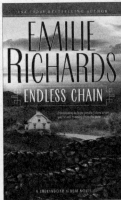

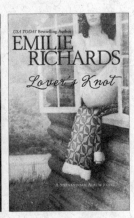

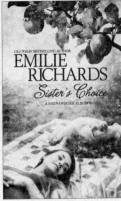

www.MIRABooks.com

MERSA08TR